Zero to Hero

In the winter of his thoughts
a teenager searches for the summer

JAMES WARD

ISBN: 978-0-6483976-0-1 (Paperback Edition)

James Ward

Publishing

Foreword

This book is the result of a conversation I had with my stepdaughter in front of the TV. We were commenting on how badly a particular movie plot was written. I said even I can do better than that. She asked me how many books I'd written – which was none. Then she challenged me to write something. An opportunity opened up to do some writing and Zero to Hero, a young-adult Sci-fi drama created. So I acknowledge without her input and encouragement this book would not exist. I also acknowledge assistance from my brother Robert with aspects of the graphics and editor Alwyn Evans for the constructive input.

To set the scene, here is a quote from John Homer Schaar, Professor Emeritus of Political Philosophy, at the University of California, Santa Cruz. [July 7, 1928 –December 26, 2011]

"The future is not a result of choices among alternative paths offered by the present, but a place that is created - created first in the mind and will, created next in activity. The future is not some place we are going to, but one we are creating. The paths are not to be found, but made; and the activity of making them changes both the maker and the destination." [1970]

With the above quote in mind, Zero to Hero is about destiny led by choice, mind and will shaping reality. The path followed depends largely upon the thoughts, decisions and willingness of the characters to step forward.

Copyright

Disclaimer

The characters and events in Zero to Hero are fictitious. Any similarity to real persons living or dead is coincidental and not intended by the author. Any Institutions, Agencies or Public Offices mentioned and related characters or activities are wholly imaginary.

Table of Contents

Chapter 1
Since when has life been fair?

$\mathbf{A}$ student at the school bus shelter cups his hands to his mouth and shouts, "hey Loser! You're wasting your time. Old- grouch-face ain't going to stop." The bus disappears rapidly into the misty rain. While a wet, forlorn teenager kicks a small rock across the road and trudges back to the bus shelter. "The name's Leo Shepherd - not Loser. I bet you Old-grouch-face saw me coming," Leo replies breathlessly.

"Boy! You sure looked like a dead-set zero chasing that bus in the rain," says the student, joining his thumb and forefinger together zero-fashioned. Leo flicks water from his forehead with his hand and shrugs his shoulders. "Whatever."
"What are you going to do now?" Leo shrugs again, "dry out and wait for the city bus I suppose Ahh-um…I don't know your name."
"Noah Shipley, but everyone calls me Arks. Anyway, how come you're so late, school finished ages ago?" Leo drops his backpack, "I got detention, didn't I."
"What for," asks Arks.
"It's all Fridge's fault. He just kept on hassling me, so I went off my face at him big-time."

"You mean Slater, that big fat bully. Phew, you're gnarly. Even the year 12's are scared of him. How come he didn't flatten you," replies Arks as he hits his fist into his palm with a whack.
"Mr Thompson, the English Master heard me and hauled my arse up to the Headmaster's office."
"Were you lucky or what! So what happened, then?"

"You'll crack up when you hear what old Thommo said to the Headmaster. He goes...*young Shepherd here was seen remonstrating with Slater and loudly uttering profanity*... then the Headmaster goes, *can you outline the nature of the profanity* - can you believe he said that?"
"Come on, what did old Thommo say?"
"This is the best part, he goes... *Shepherd made a suggestion to Slater that he do the impossible. Shove one part of his anatomy up another, where the sun doesn't shine and then, go and procreate.*" Leo and Arks both double up with laughter. "Give me some skin, man," chuckles Arks as he gives Leo a high five. "An absolute classic kiddo - can't wait to tell Dad. He's picking me up, soon. By the way, do you live around here?"
"Fielden Beach."

"Lucked out kiddo. We're cruising over to my cousin's place. Otherwise, we'd give you a lift. Anyway, been at 'FB', long?"
"Nope. We moved up to the West Coast six months ago. My folks had this farm down South until things got messed up and we had to sell."
"I thought you might be new to Fielden High. What class are you in?"
"I'm in 9-C. What about you, Arks?"
"That explains it. I'm in 11-B...hey, there's my Dad's car," yells Arks, "got to go."

Arks climb's into his Dad's silver-blue Holden Commodore. As they drive off, Leo watches until the car dissolves into the murky-grey curtain of rain. Sitting down, Leo folds his arms and settles in for a long, cold wait. The chat with Arks jogs his memory about the family farm. His mind drifts back to better times. Thinking, I wish I was back there right now. I use to be the best 'sk8er' in the district, but not up here. It was wicked when Dad built the Half-pipe. The gang would come around to show off their latest tricks and hang out, afterwards. But it's all gone now. Why did he have to sell and move to this stupid hole? It's just not fair.

A sudden downpour interrupts his thoughts, the gloomy atmosphere adding to his depressed mood. More so, when he's confronted by in-your-face type images: of an upside-down tractor, an ambulance, a coffin, an empty bed with no sheets or pillows and a sign which reads: 'Farm for Sale by Auction'.

The images bring back the feelings he had tried to forget on that terrible day. Those feelings reminding him of a similar experience - the day he had to bail off his skateboard and got slammed big-time, the tightness in the chest, the dizziness and feeling sick in the guts. "Hello, Leon. Waiting for the bus?" Leo jolts back to the present. A breathless, dumpy looking girl is smiling at him from under a bright pink umbrella.

In his current mood, her arrival doesn't impress. "Oh 'doh' Rita, what do you reckon I'm doing? And 'stop' calling me Leon." Unfazed by Leo's outburst Rita continues, "Guess what? It's my birthday tomorrow." He pulls a face and replies, "good for you." His mind wanders again, realising his birthday isn't far off, either, but doesn't want to think about it just now. Questioning, how come, in such a short time, things have turned upside down - just like the damn tractor?

Uptight and wanting to get away from Rita, Leo jumps up and walks around the back of the bus shelter. He stops mid-stride at an unexpected sight. A scruffy figure is huddled on the bench seat at the back. Leo feels uncomfortable near this feral-looking fellow. The old man has on a dirty blue suit lined with newspaper, a matching untidy grey beard and a multi-coloured beanie. "Hello, Sonny. Got two dollars for a hot coffee? If you do, I can tell you stuff about your future." Leo fumbles through his pockets. "Less my bus fare, I've only got a dollar, fifty Mister."

"Well it's going to have to do, isn't it?" The old man holds out a trembling hand. Leo stretches out and hands him his loose change, trying to keep his distance. As he does so, the old man's piercing blue eyes stare directly into Leo's eyes. Transfixed Leo can't look away and thinking, hey that's weird. Those eyes look younger than he does. "Hmmm, what's your name son?"
"It's Leo Shepherd, Mister. What's yours?"
"My name ain't important. However, yours will be on many lips. You're different. I reckon whatever you've come to do is in your blood. It's a sort of calling - which is why kids pick on you. But be warned! Some would say it's a bloody curse. You have a habit of putting girls down to jack up your ego…well then, what's going to happen when you start liking them.

One day, you're going to have to share a secret with one. I reckon you've been through a rough patch. You also might have to reach lower depths before doors open to new possibilities. Well! What are you waiting for boy? Be off with you. This is my spot!"

The old man's barking tone is unexpected. Leo complies immediately, moving quickly back to the front of the bus shelter. He blinks and shakes his head, in disbelief. It takes Leo a minute or so to gather his thoughts. "Hey Rita, did you know there's an old hobo sitting at the back?" Rita pokes her head around the corner and looks strangely back at Leo. "What old hobo?" Leo looks too. Clearly, the old man has vanished. "That's funny. Ahh-um, never mind Rita, he's gone now." Leo sits down again and reflects on the strange encounter. Thinking, maybe he's right. Since moving to this stupid place my life has been a misery. Yeah, and kids around here keep picking on me. Calling me Farmboy and making those gross animal noises while sniggering all the time. Anyway, they're all Bogans. Gee Life sucks. I hope the crazy old hobo's right. Maybe it will get better.

"Leo! Your bus is here," shouts Rita. "Errr thanks, Bogan...cough...I mean Rita." Leo looks rather sheepish and muses, boy lucky she didn't hear it. Well too bad if she did. All girls are losers anyway. Besides, you can catch Cooties from them and turn gay. That's what the guys at school reckon. Leo usually plays his Gameboy or reads a Sci-fi book on the bus. He's addicted to Sci-fi novels. It's his escape from a world he feels is against him.

Today, he stares out of the window and daydreams. Musing to himself, that jerkoff Fridge, if I had an atom blaster I could 'frag' him all over the school quadrangle. Wouldn't it be fragging cool? It is understandable for him to feel that way. Fridge's favourite pastime is hassling Leo. His bulky frame and attitude is refrigerator-sized, matching him and his name, Kelvin Slater the Kelvinator. The thing which puzzles Leo about Fridge is how he sucks up to the teachers and gets away with being a complete arsehole. Today for some reason, Leo's daydreaming makes the trip home much quicker, than usual. Leo hates the 30km trip into Fielden each day, yet going home it always seemed shorter.

4

As Leo gets off the bus, the driver grunts and closes the door. Bus drivers were always friendly in the country. Except in this place, nobody seemed to give a damn. Leo's black mood makes a comeback as he trudges home along the road as light, misty rain continues to fall. "Good day young fellow." Leo looks up. A neighbour is emptying his letterbox.
"Hi, Mr Mason."
"How are you settling in, mate?"

Leo stops and replies, "Fielden Beach is 'so' boring. Even its name is stupid - it's a long way to the beach."
"Sorry to hear that mate. But, I like the quiet life. Anyway, a young fellow like you should be out exploring. There's Mt Fielden, Henderson's quarry and Colliers Bay to explore. That's what I did when I was your age."

"I've already been up Mt Fielden - it's not a mountain, it's just a hill. My Dad doesn't want me to go to Henderson's quarry. He reckons it's got dangerous subsidence and the Bay is miles." "I dunno, you kids today, you want everything laid on for you." In no mood for lectures, Leo takes the light rain as a cue, "I'd better go before I get soaked." Opposite Henderson's quarry is a cream fibro house with a rusting tin roof, built in the fifties. Although it's neat, it needs painting. It's the only place Leo's parents, Bryan and Linda Shepherd can afford, since leaving the farm. As Leo walks to the driveway, he turns and looks across the road.

He can just make out the top of Henderson's quarry through the misty rain. From the road, the bush and the dark shadow cast by Mt Fielden hide most of the quarry. Leo has heard numerous stories about strange 'goings-on' in Henderson's quarry. Locals tell of some man committing suicide, there.

Other stories include a ghost and strange lights moving around at night. As far as Leo's concerned there are so many different stories he reckons it's all a load of bulldust. He reasons despite what Dad says, subsidence doesn't seem much of an excuse not to check the place out. Besides, it might be fun. Maybe I'll find something, who knows?

Gazing at Mt Fielden, Leo reminisces about climbing to the top with his grandad. He enjoyed the quietness and the fresh salty sea air. Yet something about the place felt familiar, something he couldn't put into words. Leo has fond memories of sharing a juicy apple, cut with granddad's old pocket-knife. Leo felt they were a long way from anywhere.

He felt King of the world as everything looked so small down below. The first time, he stood there and morphed into an eagle with arms outstretched as if circling high into the air. The last time they just sat and stared out to sea. They watched boats slip silently by and not a word said. A few days later Leo's grandad had his stroke. Leo's favourite story is the one about the strange luminous objects which regularly buzzed Gramps's fighter plane. Gramps said it was common during the war for pilots to see strange lights and objects around their aircraft. So common in fact, pilots nicknamed them, "Foo Fighters." Leo laughed the first time he heard this while thinking of Dave Grohl and the grunge rock band, Foo Fighters.

A sudden, cold blast of wind brings Leo back to reality. He dashes up the driveway, groping for his key. Putting it into the lock, he pauses for a few seconds thinking; it isn't much fun coming home to this empty dump. On the farm at least, Gramps would've been there. He had lots of interesting things to say about his life, particularly the early days on the farm and his days during the Second World War as an Australian pilot sent to England.

He had great stories and kept you on the edge of your seat. Leo like bragging to his friends, for an 'Old', Gramps was really cool. On this particular mission, Gramps had an enemy fighter in his sights, when one of the Foo Fighters got in his way. He had to dive to the left to avoid crashing into the object. When he looked around it had disappeared, yet spotted two more enemy fighters on his tail. They'd used the sun for cover.

He felt the Foo Fighters were protecting him. The warning gave him an opportunity to fly into a cloud formation and give them the slip. Leo had asked many times, about the objects. However, Gramps didn't like to say what they were, thinking the Americans might have been responsible for building them.

Each time he was buzzed, Gramps could hear a low humming sound. He described how it sounded lyrical, like an aboriginal Bullroarer. Gramps said the Aborigines use to tie a string to a piece of wood and swing it around, making the sound of their spirits. He always wondered how he could hear such a sound above the engine- noise of his fighter. This story got Leo interested in reading Sci-fi books in his spare time. As time went by the books became his obsession. He spent more time reading them than he did on his homework. Remembering all that stuff upsets Leo, for Gramps is now paralysed down his right side.

As a result, Bryan and Linda had to move him from the hospital to a nursing home. Now Leo only sees him once in a while. Also, Bryan keeps making excuses not to visit. So Leo thinks this is the reason his mother insists she go with him, each time. Leo flings his schoolbag onto the kitchen floor and immediately beelines for the refrigerator, his stomach growling. However, he doesn't open the door as there's a note from his mother stuck to it. At the bottom Linda has drawn a love heart, the note reads: *Sorry Leo, working late. We're doing the stocktake. Dad will be late too. Go over to Danicka's place until I get there. Don't forget to take your homework.*

Leo vents his feelings loudly, "Bloody hell! Just when you think the day isn't going to get any worse, they spring another surprise on me. This means I have to be nice to that Danicka Jerovich bird."

Opening the refrigerator door Leo scans the contents. "Bugger, there's nothing here I want. Now I'll have to go - only 'cos I'm hungry." Thinking, least there'll be lots of yummy food, even if she sucks. His stomach ruling his head, Leo makes his way to the Jerovich place. Fortunately, the rain has now stopped - not that he notices. His mind is totally focused on food.

Running up their driveway, Leo races up the marble stairs and knocks on the front door. Lena Jerovich answers the door in a printed house dress with a flowery apron on top. She is a short solid lady and greets Leo in her broken English, "Hello Mr Leo. Your Mama she ring. She say you come. I feed you good."

Leo recalls Gramps remarking once, that while the Slavs were funny people, they sure knew how to put on a good feed. So with mouth-watering anticipation, Leo is led into their large kitchen. "You sit, eat good young mans. Must be hungry, eh?" Leo doesn't know where to start. There are cakes, funny looking biscuits, cold meats, bread, cheeses and pickles. He tucks in straight away. Yet before he can swallow, Danicka appears at the kitchen door.

"Hello stranger, haven't seen you for a while," as she leans up against the doorframe, cross-legged and arms folded. Leo nods, gesturing towards his mouth. It's so stuffed full he can't speak. Although Danicka, who prefers we call her Dani for short, is the same age as Leo, she doesn't go to Leo's high school. She has a scholarship for guitar and goes to Molton Ladies College, a private girl's school in the city.

Dani is taller than Leo. She is slender and has black shoulder-length hair, dark brown eyes and olive skin to match. Even though they are both fourteen, Dani's definitely more sophisticated in her thinking. Leo is solidly built and not particularly tall. He has sandy-coloured hair, grey-green eyes and pale freckled skin. Lena calls out from another part of the house, "Danicka, you look after young gentlemans."

"Yes Mama," she replies with a big sigh. Despite not wanting to play hostess, Dani thinks Leo's okay for a boy. Even though she doesn't find him spunky, she feels Leo is different from most of the other boys around the district.

They always make fun of her because her parents are migrants and call her school, 'Molestown', because it's a private girls school. Leo looks like he's about to explode. He has stuffed himself with almost everything on the table, washed down with two large glasses of cordial. Dani has left the kitchen, returning with a netball tucked under her arm. "Do you want to shoot some baskets with me?"

Leo stands up from the table, holds onto his belly as if pregnant, and shakes his head, no. "But, I'll sit and watch you for a while." No sooner had he said this he lets rip: "burrrpppp!" A satisfied look is on his face. Dani reacts with a look of disgust, "you guys are really gross." Lena comes back into the kitchen to clean up. "Thanks heaps Mrs J, that Tucker was so s-w-e-e-t." She smiles and looks puzzled. Dani explains, "Mama, he means he liked everything."
"Okay. You tell your Mama, Leo come anytime. I make him big, strong young mans." The Jerovich place is a white two-story house with a double garage and lots of cement paving out the front. It has a white fence with two lion statues guarding the entrance. The basketball hoop is above the double garage doors. Leo sits down on a low retaining wall near the driveway. He watches while Dani shoots some baskets. As Dani bounces the ball around and takes shots from different angles, Leo remembers the strange encounter with the old hobo.

"Hey Dani, you know what happened today? I was like, at the bus stop and this old Hobo appears out of nowhere. He begs for two dollars for a coffee. Then he goes, if you do I'll tell you stuff about your fortune." Dani grabs the ball and turns around, "and did you?"
"I only had a dollar fifty."

"And."

"Well, he said some weird stuff like I had to be careful. Oh yes and I would share a secret, then some stuff about falling down and doors opening. Then he disappeared into thin air."

"Boy, that is really spooky. What do you think he meant?"

"I dunno…I mean, what would a crazy old man like that know anyway?"

"If you want my opinion, I think he's right. You're different than the guys around here, 'cos they all suck."

"Maybe, but a loser like him begging in a bus shelter with newspapers stuffed down his shirt…he can't be that smart." Dani can't hide her disappointment. Leo has ignored her compliment. "Suit yourself then," as she turns her back on Leo and shoots some more baskets.

After watching for a few minutes Leo is beginning to get restless. "I'm bored Dani. How about watching me do some really cool tricks on my skateboard?" Leo has brought it with him, instead of his homework. He zooms up and down the Jerovich driveway. "Hey, your driveway's radical. I can do fakies, rotations and ollies on this." Clearly impressed, Dani responds proudly, "I reckon I can skate too." Leo laughs, "As if" and hands Dani his skateboard. "Let's see how good you really are."

Dani nervously steps onto the skateboard. Down the driveway, she speeds like an out-of-control speedboat, with arms flapping like a windmill. With a scream, she disappears over the low retaining wall and into the garden bed. Leo cheers loudly. "YEEHAA! That bail was epic." Dani waves her hand from behind the wall, "Stop laughing will you and give me a hand." Leo is too busy laughing, so Dani climbs out of the garden and dusts herself off. "Okay, okay so I'm not very good. Will you teach me some really cool tricks to show my girlfriends at school? P-l-e-a-s-e."

"Well, .maybe."

Just as Leo is about to show her some basics a group of local boys approach. They shout, "Look there's Farmboy with that Jerovich chick. Hey, Farmboy you big girl. Why don't you go to Molestown too?" Leo tries to ignore them by staring at the ground. While Dani retorts, "Only brain-dead losers like you lot go to a stupid state school."

The boys make pig noises and saunter off crowing. "How come you didn't say anything, Leo?"

"Well, you jumped in first," says Leo defensively. However, the truth is Leo doesn't have any fight left in him to challenge them. He felt maybe they were right. The constant harassment makes him feel like a 'zero'.

Leo felt embarrassed and uncomfortable about it. Feeling this way, he decides to go home, "Dani, I'll see you later."

"Aren't you supposed to wait for your mum to come?"

Thinking quickly Leo responds, "Oh, I forgot my homework and I have this assignment to hand in tomorrow… Friday isn't it?"

"Yeah right," replies Dani. Thinking it rather strange, remembering how Leo never worried about homework before. "See you on the weekend maybe…you know, to show me some of those tricks."

"Maybe." yet under his breath, he mouths the words, "not if I can help it." As Leo walks down the driveway, Lena comes running with a paper bag. "Mr Leo, I make for you. You take, have for supper." Leo feels he has imposed too much already, "I couldn't really." While Lena insists, "I be very sad. Mr Leo, he no like my cooking." Well, what can he do? "Gee thanks Mrs J, you shouldn't have. Thanks heaps." On his way home, Leo opens the paper bag and finds it full of cupcakes. He wants to eat one, yet is still full and puts it back. Thinking, I'll keep these for school. Then, I'll have something to look forward to tomorrow. Wow, Mrs J is a whiz at cooking stuff. I wish my Mum had time to cook like that.

Once inside, Leo flops down on the couch to watch television, until Bryan arrives home. "Where's Mum?" He snaps, without even saying hello. "Oh, she left some note on the fridge. Guess what Dad. I went over to the Jerovich place today. Boy, what a spread Dani's Mum put…" Leo stops mid-sentence, his Dad isn't listening and rudely interrupts, "typical she is never here when I need to sort something out. Never mind. I guess we need to think about making dinner ourselves." Bryan works at the local Shell garage as a mechanic. While it's heavy work, it's the only work he can find. The owners are quite often away and leave Bryan in charge. The job along with the financial and emotional strain they are under affects his relationship with Leo. He doesn't seem to understand this.

He thinks his Dad is a 'cold fish'. The reality is, you could describe Bryan as a hard nut because this is the way he was brought up on the farm. He keeps his real thoughts to himself and never shows much emotion. Like many farming folks, when times were tough, he would just 'grin and bear whatever came along'. That's another reason why he finds it difficult to relate to Leo on an emotional level.

However, he has his own way of showing Leo he cares. Like when they moved in. He got busy making Leo a tree house with a rope ladder. He needed something to occupy his mind, while out of work. It also stopped him from thinking too much about the events on the farm. Although Leo is a bit old for tree houses, he loves it. He can read his Sci-fi novels in peace and be in a natural setting at the same time. For some reason, it gave Leo the feeling of superiority, that is, until he has to come down. Bryan reads the note, then opens the refrigerator, "Let's see what's here...hmmm, okay there's some leftover Spaghetti Bolognese." "Dad, can we make waffles?"

"Okay, that sounds good. Damn, we're out of bread! Leo you'll have to go down to the Supa Deli and get some."
"Ohhh, why do I have to go?" Bryan stares at Leo and replies, "You're the one who wants waffles." Leo grabs some loose change his Dad empties out of his pocket and quickly races down the pot-holed driveway. He turns left along the main road towards Paul's Supa Deli. Although time is getting on, the sun hasn't quite finished for the day. It struggles to stay above Mt Fielden. Leo admires the colours of the sunset. He's then distracted by a low humming sound which seems to originate from Henderson's Quarry. There's a pulsating low hum rising and falling, in a rhythmic cycle. After the stories he has heard about the quarry, it gives Leo the shivers.

He takes off as fast as he can to the Deli. Panting as he reaches the bread rack, Leo grabs the first loaf he sees and throws it and the change onto the counter. From behind the counter Paul, the Deli owner, looks at Leo. "Are you alright son?"

Not wanting to appear a wimp Leo responds, "Err yes."

"You look a little pale son. Are you sure everything's okay?"

"Well, I'm not really sure. I heard these funny noises coming from Henderson's quarry and it sure has given me the shivers."

"Yeah, yeah, I heard those stories too. Let's go outside and see what it is." Sure enough, Leo can still hear a low hum off into the distance. "Can you hear that?" Paul puts his right hand to his ear, "hear what?" Leo points down the road, "can't you hear the low humming sound?"

"No, I can't hear anything. You'd better leave right now. I had enough of smart-arses like you coming in here with jokes about that old quarry. Now nick off or you will feel the end of my boot up your bloody arse." As Leo is not making it up and stunned at the hostile reaction, Leo bolts. Strangely, as he passes the quarry again, he can't hear the humming sound at all.

Anyway, he dismisses it, because there are more important things on his mind, like making waffles. Running back up the driveway Leo trips over, forgetting about the potholes, "ahhh bugger," he shouts. The bread goes flying. He manages to save himself without doing too much damage - the same can't be said for the bread. Phew, that was close, he thought. "Bloody stinking rotten potholes," he mutters. He limps inside and puts the bread on the old kitchen table. Bryan notices Leo is back from the shop and comments, "you were quick. Mum's home and she is too tired to cook, so she'll have waffles too...Jeez son, you sure picked the worst loaf, it looks like someone's stepped on it?"

"I was in a hurry Dad and grabbed the first one," bleats Leo, defensively. "What made you do that son?"

"I heard some funny noises coming from Henderson's quarry. I just bolted into the Deli and came home as fast as I could." As Leo's mother enters the room, she defends Leo. "Bryan leave the poor kid be. Leo give your mother a big hug."

"Hi Mum, where have you been?"

"Didn't you see the note I left?"

"Oh yeah, the stocktake. Can I make the waffles now?"

"Yes okay, but go and wash your hands first." Leo is quite good at making snacks.

He has to be self-reliant as Bryan and Linda work long hours, leaving Leo on his own a lot. The Shepherds are all very tired and flop down in front of the television to eat the waffles Leo has made. While eating, Leo recounts, "the food was really wicked at the Jerovich place and Mrs J gave me a bag of cupcakes too. I'm going to take them for morning break tomorrow." Linda turns to Leo. "I hope you thanked Lena?"

"Y-e-s M-u-m," he replies in a bored tone. "And, there's another thing Leo, why didn't you wait for me at their place?"
"Oh, I ah-ah…forgot to take my homework Mum." She nods and Leo has a look of relief on his face. Not wanting to explain about the boys harassing him again. Bryan has fallen asleep on the couch and is snoring away like a hibernating bear. Linda gets up and turns the television off, "well Leo, it's off to bed for you my boy. School tomorrow, but at least it's Friday. Have a wash and brush your teeth. By the way, I just remembered on Saturday I've got to get some new medicine for Gramps." In a whining tone, Leo replies, "Mum why can't it be Saturday. Then I wouldn't have to go to school and I could see Gramps."
"Go on, off you go."

Leo yawns loudly and does all of his normal bedtime routine in automatic pilot. He makes a dive for his bed, just as Linda switches off the lights. It doesn't take him long to fall fast asleep. He's soon dreaming about riding on his skateboard. He's holding onto a car's bumper with the breeze tearing at his hair. Dani is watching from the curb as he roars by. "Be careful Leo," she warns. Leo ignores her, feeling bulletproof. "Skitching is really wicked stuff," he mumbles in his sleep.

Faster and faster he's going, until all of a sudden, the low humming sound starts up again. Leo looks over his shoulder towards Henderson's quarry. Distracted, he doesn't see the car turn the corner. Dani screams, "Watch out Leo," as he heads straight for an oncoming bus. Old-grouch-face is behind the wheel with a big sinister smile. As Leo's about to smack into the bus, he wakes with a start and sits bolt upright in bed. "Phew, that was close." Then he realises, "oh, it's only a stupid dream. That was really dumb, how come Dani was in it?

Typical she put me off while I was having a 'specky' ride. Stupid chicks in dreams it definitely means trouble." He has just started to settle down, when he hears the same low humming sound, again. This time he gets out of bed and opens his window, which faces the quarry. However, he can't see anything in the darkness. In fact, he's not sure if it's coming from the quarry. What worries him, if it's not coming from the quarry, then where is it coming from? Gawd, I hope it hasn't got anything to do with that fall from the skateboard when I wasn't wearing my stack hat. Maybe I've got some sort of brain damage or going 'troppo'. Being wide-awake now, his mind begins to tick over. Thinking, Dad will be at the garage on Sunday.

Maybe I can go and check out Henderson's quarry then and find out for myself what's going on. Who knows, there could be interesting stuff going on. He settles down and exhaustion overtakes Leo and he falls into a deep sleep.

Next morning Linda wakes him. "Leo it's time you were out up."
"No I am staying in, it's Saturday."
"No it's not," scolds Linda, impatiently. "Get up right now and have your breakfast, then make your lunch. I've got to catch the bus now. I want to make sure you are out of bed before I go."
"Where's Dad?"
"You know he opens the garage at six o'clock. Look I'm going to miss my bus if you don't get moving."

Leo drags himself out of bed. Linda follows him around like a little puppy, as she helps him get his stuff together. "Mum I can do it."
"Sure, look at you. You're hardly awake. One day you're going to forget to put your head on." Leo daydreams, hey that's really funny. Least part of me can stay home. Imagine how the teachers would react - going to school without me head. That would be really s-i-c-k. "LEO!" Shouts Linda. "Stop daydreaming and get moving. Now!"
"Yeah, yeah, okay, I'm moving already."
"I've got to go. Make sure you lock up properly before you leave and turn all the lights off."
"Yeah, yeah Mum, as if I don't do it every day." Leo hears the front door slam shut and high heel shoes going clonk, clonk, clonk, as Linda dashes down the driveway to get to the bus stop in time.

Leo is now in the kitchen burning his toast and making peanut butter sandwiches for lunch. As he stuffs his lunch box into his backpack, he remembers the bag of goodies Mrs J made for him. He opens the bag of goodies and checks them out, before stuffing them into his overloaded backpack. He sort of cleans his teeth. Well, at least he put the brush near them. Then puts on his school uniform and grabs his backpack.

He locks the front door and runs to the bus stop to get in some extra reading time. After a few pages, Leo happens to look up from his book and spots the bus approaching. As the bus pulls up, he notices much to his annoyance Old-grouch-face driving. "Hey, sonny you should have your fare ready, instead of reading that damn book. Make it snappy, I haven't got all day, you know."

As Leo climbs aboard the bus, he doesn't make eye contact with other students. Instead, he sits down and buries himself in his book. He loses track of time and is oblivious the bus has arrived outside Fielden High. One by one, as the students file off the bus, they tap Leo lightly on the head. The last one saying, "come on Farmboy this is your stop, too."

Leo feels uncomfortable hanging around the lockers like the other students. He puts the book in his pack and heads straight for the Library. It is quiet there without anybody to harass him, except Miss Marshall the crabby old Librarian. However, Leo knows she isn't as crabby as everyone makes out. She allows Leo to read his Sci-fi books, provided he has the novel inside a Library book. Miss Marshall doesn't mind what students read, so long as they're not mucking around.

Leo has read all of the science fiction books in the Library and is hoping Miss Marshall can exchange them with another school. Engrossed in his novel, Leo jumps up as the siren wails, causing the book to crash to the floor. Standing up with hands on hips, Miss Marshall gives Leo the stare. Leo picks up the book and carefully places it back onto the shelf. He whispers, "Sorry Miss Marshall" and tippy-toes out of the Library.

As Leo closes the door, he mumbles, "bloody hell! I don't know what class I've got this morning." Quickly, he fumbles through his backpack to find his diary and timetable. Then he remembers its Friday and the first class is a double period with Mr Thompson, the head of the English Department.

Looking at his timetable, the class is in room 41 in E block. Leo hurries towards E block until he glances at his diary. "Oh shit! The English assignment is due today. I forgot all about it." Leo whacks himself over the head with the diary in disgust. He arrives at the classroom thinking if I'd done some of it, I could've said I'd left it at home. Of course, old Thommo's too smart for that. You Derp! It's turned out to be black Friday, now. I wonder what old Thommo's going to say in front of everyone. If I sit right at the back maybe nobody will notice. Leo moves to a seat at the back of the class. It's his only hope. The class chatters excitedly about the weekend, while Leo sits silently, anxiously awaiting his fate.

Mr Thompson announces his arrival into the classroom by clearing his throat. "Ah-hem!" With a self-serving smile and lifting bushy eyebrows he booms out, "My, my, we are a talkative bunch today. As you would have nothing else better to talk about, I presume the discussion is about the assignment." Leo slides lower into his chair, hoping to become invisible.

"Attention everyone! We will mark the Roll as your assignments are placed in the tray. Marcus will you do the honours and collect the assignments as they're passed forward." There is a lot of paper shuffling as all of the assignments are collected for registration.

After completing the Roll, Mr Thompson announces, "Tamara Curtis, I haven't seen your assignment yet?" There is an awkward silence before a girl puts up her hand, "that's because she's got the Flu Sir." "Thank you Mary. Ah-hem, Leon Shepherd! I assume you have the 'bug' too, as I have not seen your assignment, either." Leo sinks lower into his chair to the point where he is nearly falling off it. Then one unhelpful student points, "Leo is right there Sir."

The unexpected response comes in a loud booming voice. "I can see that Woods. When I need your help, I will ask for it." He pauses and takes a deep breath, "Leon Shepherd, I will see you after class. Now get your novels out. Read chapters 5 and 6 and write a paragraph about the main theme." The class passes quietly without further incident until the siren rings. A stampede ensues as the class packs their stuff away and make for the door, including Leo, hoping to make a quick getaway in the confusion.

"Shepherd! Where do you think you're going?"

"Sorry Sir, I forgot."

"Just like the assignment, eh! You're getting rather forgetful lately, aren't you?" The room now empty, Mr Thompson sits on the edge of a desk and motions Leo to sit. The tone of his voice changes as he speaks. "I don't understand your attitude to your work, first it is detention and now this…is everything alright at home?" Not knowing what to say, Leo nods.

"You're an intelligent young fellow. You've got enough ability to 'Shoot the Moon'. Nevertheless, if you're not careful you could end up a Moonraker - it's your choice."

"Sir, I don't understand. What's a Moonraker?"

"Oh, it means someone who's brainless and tries to rake the moon's reflection from a pond. What I'm getting at is, you have the talent to make your mark on this world - just don't make it a skid mark." Mr Thompson leans forward and pats Leo on the shoulder. "I know you're fairly new here. So I expect you're finding things slightly different, eh?"

Leo nods again and feeling more relaxed replies, "I'm sorry Sir. I promise it won't happen again. I just forgot Sir." Mr Thompson gets up from the desk. He's deep in thought as he paces around the room. "I should be failing you on this assignment, Shepherd. However, I'm going to go out on a limb and give you until Wednesday. Bring it to my office."

Before Leo can thank him, Mr Thompson jabs his finger into Leo's chest. "Leon the effort you put in had better be good. Make no mistake, three strikes and you are out - get my drift." Leo nods. "Thank you Sir. Can I go now?" Mr Thompson stands aside and with his hand motions towards the door. "Off you go or you'll be late for assembly." Leo bolts before he changes his mind. Wow, thought Leo. Old Thommo seems tough; maybe he's not so bad after all. That was a close one.

During the Year's 8 and 9 assembly discussion turns to the canteen food which reminds Leo he has a date with Mrs J's bag of goodies. So he pays little attention after that, his mind focused on morning break and cupcakes. When the siren rings the students disperse like a pack of wild horses, while Leo wanders over to a shady area.

He sits down near the drinking fountain to open his bag of goodies. As he reaches in, he feels a presence behind him. "Give me a look Farmboy!" Fridge reaches over and snatches the bag. "Hey guys, look what Farmboy has brought us."

"They're mine," shouts Leo, as he tries to snatch it back.

Fridge is too quick and pulls away. Taking out a cupcake he swallows it whole and muffles, "weren't you going share these with us," as bits of cake spill out of his mouth. Laughing, he hands out most of the goodies around his 'scaly mates'. One of the gang members, CJ takes a bite out of the last remaining cupcake.

Sniggering, he puts it back into the bag and hands it back to Leo. "I left the last one for you, mate." Snatching the bag Leo hurls it back at CJ, shouting, "I'm not your mate, Dirt-brain!" The bag bounces off of CJ's shoulder as he and the rest of the gang stroll off making farmyard noises. Leo is too embarrassed to look around. Angry, he heads for the drinking fountain and sprays water on his face to cool down.

It isn't the loss of the cakes making him angry; it's the lack of power to stop them from walking all over him. Leo defends his position by thinking, what was I supposed to do. Had I chucked a mental, Fridge would have punched my lights out for sure. These guys keep on picking on me. It's useless going to the teachers because they always let Fridge get away with it. Like last time Fridge was hassling me, I got detention and he didn't. I wonder why they do that. Can't they see what's going on?

Luckily for Leo, Fielden High is hosting the Interschool Sports Carnival in the afternoon. He didn't feel like sitting in class brooding, so it's a welcome distraction. He doesn't nominate for any of the events and joins the spectators. Despite this, he gets caught up in all of the excitement and is happily cheering away for Fielden High. For a change, he has forgotten all about his situation at school and at home. He is on a high, which he carries all the way home after school.

He imagines how he has won just about every medal until he puts his key in the lock. Then reality sets in again. Yet he grins and shouts, "Yahoo! was that cool or what," throwing his cap into the air.

Once inside, he follows his usual routine of chucking his school bag on the floor and heading straight for the refrigerator. As usual, there isn't anything sweet he can get his teeth into. Instead, he takes out the bread and puts on a slice of cheese topping it with a thick layer of Vegemite. Flopping down in front of the television, he picks up the TV guide. There's a Sci-fi movie on and he punches the air, "Yes."

Leo is deeply engrossed in the movie and oblivious to everything going on around him, including Linda arriving home. "Leo!" Didn't you hear me calling? You could've helped me in with the shopping, at least?" "Sorry Mum, there's this Sci-fi movie on."
Linda has a strained look on her face as she lifts the shopping onto the table. "I might have guessed. How was school today, dear?"

"It was radical - we had a sports carnival and we won. Can't talk now, the movie's on."
"That's great dear. Phew, what a day I've had! I'm coming to watch the movie with you."
"Shoosh Mum! This bit's getting interesting." During the commercials, Linda makes a cup of tea and puts away the shopping. One bag contains novels for Leo she has exchanged at the Fielden Book Mart. "Leo, I managed to get you some more science fiction novels.

I hope you haven't read these. God knows you must have read half of the books in circulation."
"Wow, thanks Mum." Leo jumps up and grabs the bag of books during the commercial break. He quickly sorts through the titles and scans the cover summaries of each book. "Wicked! I haven't read any of these - not like last time."
"Phew, that was lucky."
"Shoosh Mum, the movie's back on." Leo's in a good mood - it's the weekend. And for a change, he has no homework, except for the assignment, which he has forgotten about.

However, his mood changes when Bryan comes home and takes Linda into the bedroom to discuss something. His Dad seems pre-occupied and Leo isn't sure what's going on. He feels hurt because he's always excluded from their serious talks.

Yet he overheard anyway; the people who own the Shell garage are thinking of selling. Then what seems contradictory, his Dad comes out and says to Leo, "The Wilsons are thinking of retiring." Leo can't see what this should mean to him personally and has a funny look on his face. Bryan realising this and adds, "I don't know what I'm going to do if I can't find another job."

Next morning Linda wakes a very grumpy Leo. "Don't bite my head off. I'm just trying to remind you to catch the bus at lunchtime and meet me at Weston's."
"What for?"
"What do you mean what for? To see Gramps of course."
"Oh Yeah." Linda shakes her head, "sometimes I worry about you."
Today Linda leaves later than usual. On Saturdays, she works in the sales area at Weston Plumbing Supplies to make some extra cash. During the week she works in the office as a bookkeeper.

Meanwhile, Leo should be working on his assignment.
However, reading his new Sci-fi novel in bed has more appeal. Leo justifying his actions, thinking, there's plenty of time. Besides, who wants to do schoolwork on weekends, anyway? He is so into the book, he nearly jumps out of his skin when the phone rings. Climbing out of bed he races for the phone to find his mother on the other end. "Leo, have you showered and dressed because you'll need to catch the bus soon."
"Yes Mum, I'm ready," replies Leo, fingers crossed. Standing there in his jocks and tee shirt he had worn to bed the night before. Glancing at his watch, he realises it is 11:15am and wonders, where did the time go?

"That's good because I want you to look your best for Gramps. I left your fare by the phone."
"Mum I've got to go. See you." He slams down the phone to stop any further inquisition. Grabs his bus fare and bolts to his bedroom, throwing on some clothes. Leo races into the bathroom and sticks his head under the tap. He gives his head a quick wipe with the towel and grabs his joggers. Trying to do two things at once, he combs his hair while jamming his feet into the joggers, without undoing the laces.

Slamming the door behind him he hobbles to the bus stop having a heal half out of one jogger. He can't stop to put it on properly because the bus is coming into view. As the bus pulls up and the door opens, Leo is still pulling the jogger on and fumbling through his pockets for his fare. He looks up, it's Old-grouch-face driving, "just my dumb luck," he mutters. "Hurry up Sonny, I haven't got all day! You saw me coming. You should have your fare ready." Leo hands over his bus fare and snatches his ticket. As he strolls towards the back, he mutters under his breath again, "I hope the wheels drop off your stupid bus and they fall on you." "What did you say, sonny?"
"Oh, nothing. "Deaf as well, thought Leo as he sits down.
As Old-grouch-face pulls out into the traffic he comments, "These kids today. I don't know what's wrong with this generation. No bloody respect at all."

Leo's oblivious to this. His mind is on Gramps. They haven't seen each other for weeks. Leo isn't the only one to cop it from Old- grouch-face. He snaps at anyone who has the misfortune to have the wrong fare. The bus is driven roughly and he curses at any vehicle which gets in his way. Leo can't wait for the journey to end. The bell rings just as the bus turns into Fielden Terrace, so Leo jumps up and slips out the back door avoiding any more conflict. The bus stop is about 200 metres from Weston's Plumbing.

Leo arrives out the front and waves to Linda through the plate-glass doors. From behind the counter, Linda gestures for Leo to come in. While Leo gestures for her to come outside. A tall, attractive girl of about twenty, in a tight revealing outfit, moves from behind the counter and breaks the standoff. She grabs Leo by the hand and drags him inside. "Hi, I'm Jemma. Come on, don't be shy!"

"Hi Mum," says Leo, surrendering with a sigh. Jemma notices that Leo's face is a fiery-red colour, she adds fuel to the fire, "So this is Leo...phew, he's pretty hot! Shaking her hand and blowing on it. "You didn't tell me your boy's, Ohhh-sooo spunky. Too bad he's not a bit older. I could quite easily have the hots for him." While Jemma flirts with Leo, Linda grabs her jumper and bag.

Putting her arm around her flush-faced Leo, Linda gives him a big squeeze. "We've got to go and meet his Grandad. If Leo's head gets any bigger, he won't fit through the door with such compliments. Jemma, can you lock up for me please?"
"No worries Linda. You and Mr Spunky there, have a good weekend."

It's a short trip on the number 128 bus out to Haywood. Leo is eagerly looking forward to visiting Gramps. His eagerness shows as he jumps off the bus and leaves Linda lagging behind. At the front door of the nursing home, he turns and waves. "Come on Mum, hurry up!" He waits for her before pushing open the double front doors. "Why does Gramps have to stay here? This place stinks - smells like the hospital." Embarrassed, Linda pinches Leo on the fleshy part of his arm. "Ouch Mum." Pulling his arm away quickly, "what did I say?" "I don't need this right now. You behave yourself." While this is going on Gramps is wheeled into the reception area to meet them. Gramps is neatly attired. He has on a beige cardigan over his brush-cotton checkered shirt, navy trousers and slippers. Leo stops squabbling with Linda and runs up to Gramps. As he does so, the old man holds out his good arm and shakes hands with Leo. "How's my boy?"

Linda joins them, putting her arm around his shoulders and kissing him on the cheek. She leaves a bright red lipstick mark. So reaches into her bag for a tissue and wipes his cheek. Gramps moves his head and grumbles, "stop fussing will you, girlie."
"Gramps, how's everything. I hope they're treating you well."
"I'm feeling better today. The nursing staff do the best they can…you know the stroke." However, what Gramps really wants is to be with Leo. However, has no option. The stroke has left him paralysed down his right side.

"It's lovely outside. Leo, why don't you take Gramps out into the garden for a chat and I'll talk to the nursing staff about the new medication." Leo wheels Gramps out into the small garden and sits down on the lawn under the shade of a Ficus tree. Leo stares at the grass, his arms hugging his legs while his chin rests on his knees. "Now young fella, how are things going?"
"Life sucks, Gramps."

"How come my boy?" Leo shifts his weight uncomfortably and looks up. Clasping his hands, he places them behind his head and swings from side to side. "I don't like it here at Fielden Beach. I wish we were back on the farm. Gramps, I don't understand why they had to sell, why Dad hardly says anything to me anymore?" Using his good hand, Gramps moves his wheelchair closer to Leo. "I think you're a bit hard on your Dad. Don't you realise Michael's accident has had a devastating effect on him, and your Mum, too?" Michael is Leo's older brother, tragically killed in a tractor accident on the farm. He was expected to take over the farm, once Bryan retired.

"Your Dad blames himself for Michael's accident, you know." The district has had patchy seasons for years. All of those things have worn your Dad down and in the end, he had no choice." Teary-eyed, Leo realises he too has put the tragic death of his older brother to the back of his mind. "Gramps I've tried talking about Michael, but they just change the subject or make some excuse. Since the accident, they never talk about him. I don't think it's right – like they pretend he doesn't exist."

Gramps thought for a long while, not saying a word. He taps Leo gently a couple of times on the shoulder. "You must realise they're not ready to deal with Michael's death. It's too painful for them. When they are ready, I'm sure they will talk it out with you. I know your Dad feels guilty about what happened. That's why he can't talk to you and for that matter, doesn't come to see me, either. He blames it all on himself. It's quite a burden he's carrying."
"But, that's not fair Gramps."

"Sure my boy, I agree. Since when has life been fair, eh?…just look at me in this chair. You know Leo young fella, life's like a game of cards. There's going to be times when you have to play the cards you're dealt. Sometimes you can't improve your hand. Yet it doesn't mean every card dealt, will be a dud. So be positive and be patient - better cards will come along. It might take time, yet if you think positively, I'm a sure everything will change for the better. This won't make much sense to you, now. I sense, if you find the Queen of Spades and the Ace of Hearts together, your life will improve. It's called 'Shooting the Moon'."

"Do you really think so Gramps?" Leo feels a little brighter. Some of the load he has been carrying is lifted from his shoulders. Linda finally makes an appearance. "There's tea being served in the dining room. I'm sure you two gents are thirsty."

"Let's go, Leo - can't keep a good cuppa waiting." Leo jumps up and grabs hold of the wheelchair and they both follow Linda into the dining room. While Leo is detailed off to get the teas and some biscuits, Linda sits close to Gramps to explain his medication.

Yet Gramps is more interested in finding out how the family is travelling financially and emotionally. "Look Gramps, you have enough on your plate, without worrying yourself about us. We're managing. You just concentrate on getting well again." Linda reaches out and puts her hand on his shoulder. Leo comes back juggling the tray. They sit quietly making small talk - the noise in the dining room makes meaningful conversation difficult. Gramps finishes his tea and declares, "I don't want to be rude. I'm feeling a bit tired. So, if you don't mind, I'll get the nurse to take me back to my room."

As Leo and Linda stand up to say their goodbyes, Gramps winks at Leo, "don't forget - shoot for the moon, my boy." Leo grins and Linda looks at them both with a questioning look. "I suppose that's secret men's business, eh?" Grabbing hold of Gramps's good hand, Leo nods. As they leave the nursing home, Leo's in a good mood because Linda takes him to McDonald's after each visit. It's her way of compensating Leo for not having Gramps around. She knows how much they love being together and she feels guilty for not having him at home.

Later in the afternoon, they catch the bus and on the way home Linda remarks, "I suppose you're a happy-chappy now you've been to McDonald's."

"Nah, I'm still hungry, Mum."

"You can't be, after what you ate today. Anyway, before you have any ideas about raiding the fridge. I want you to go down to the garage and call your Dad home. He's been there all day."

"Ohhh, why do I have to go?"

"Because you two spend so little time together."

"But, he doesn't talk to me."

"All the more reason to go, don't you think?"

"Do I have to?"

"Do you want to go to McDonald's again?"

"M-u-m that's blackmail - where's a phone, I'm calling the cops." His stomach over-ruling his head, Leo reluctantly travels on two stops further to the Shell garage.

Getting off the bus, he finds the driveway service area closed. However, he hears noises coming from the workshop. Walking around the back, he sees Bryan's legs sticking out from under a bright-red Ford pickup truck. "Hi Dad," shouts Leo. "Is that you Leo? I've just got to bleed these brakes and I'll be right with you." Leo laughs, "You sound like you got a bucket on your head."

"What did you say?"

"Nothing, Dad." While waiting, Leo browses around the workshop checking out some of the tools. Finally, Bryan shoots out from under the Ford on a trolley. "Phew! Finished for the day." Standing up he wipes his greasy hands on his overalls. "Leo, can you raise the roller door, so I can get the U-beaut-ute out?" Bryan backs out the battered old Pickup utility which passes for the garage service vehicle. As Leo jumps in, Bryan pulls down and locks all of the roller doors and stiffly climbs back into the Ford. "Dad, can I ask you something?"

"Yes, what is it?"

"Do you know what 'Shoot the Moon' is? I heard it mentioned a couple of times. What does it really mean?"

"I think it's got something to do with a card game. Never played it though. It's like aiming for something that's hard to achieve, I guess. I'm not really sure."

"Yeah, I thought it might be something like that. I suppose you know Mum and me went to see Gramps today to give him his new medicine. But, he looked really tired."

Bryan isn't in a good mood and snaps back, "We're all tired from the hours we're working. He just sits there in his wheelchair all day." The remark upsets Leo deeply. He ignores Bryan by pulling faces into the passenger-side window. As they turn into the driveway, Leo spots Linda outside in the garden picking herbs.

While Bryan goes inside for a shower, Leo sees this as his chance to talk to her about Michael - it's been on his mind most of the afternoon. "Mum how come you and Dad don't talk about Michael… like…like he's never existed?" Shocked, Linda stands bolt upright in the herb garden. "Leo, how can you say that? We both loved your brother very much." Tears welling up in her eyes as she speaks, "there's not a day that goes by I don't think about him."
"Okay, but you don't talk about him."
"It's…it's just that your Dad blames himself for Michael's accident - it's best not to talk about it when he's around." Linda puts her arm around Leo, to console him. "Let's go in and have dinner now."

During dinner, Linda looks at Leo and observes, "you're very quiet tonight dear - like you've got lots on your mind."
"Well, what'd you expect? I can't say anything about Michael in front of him. Then when I talk about Gramps he bites my head off - I'm out of here." Leo jumps and leaves the kitchen.

He goes to his room and sits down on his bed and reminisces. Thinking, I wish Michael was still here. He was my best mate, even though he was older. It was grouse on the farm with him. Yeah, like when we built a raft from old fuel drums and used it as a diving platform in the main dam.

Funny though, he was always drawing and sketching. He really liked art. Sure could draw really well. Not like me. Yeah and once he told me he wanted to be an artist one day and not to tell anyone else. He never…a knock at the bedroom door interrupts his thoughts. "Hi sweetie, are you okay?" Leo lies down and picks up his Sci-fi novel, "yeah Mum, I'm fine."

Chapter 2
What's the point of having a secret

He tries to read, yet struggles to keep his eyes open. Much later Linda realises it's too quiet in Leo's room. Getting up from the lounge she checks on him, to find Leo is fast asleep. Carefully she covers him with the doona and kisses him gently on the forehead.

Next morning Leo opens his eyes and for a change, he's wide awake. Leo isn't what you'd call a morning person. Usually, he gropes around with one eye open, his brain in neutral. Getting up he changes into his track pants and finds Linda busily cleaning. "Can't you sit down and read a book. Or, isn't there some homework you have to do?"
"Nope. I don't feel like reading."
"Well go for a walk or something. I don't want you under my feet."
Perfect idea, thinks Leo, as he grabs some pieces of fruit and dumps them into his backpack. Filling a water bottle under the kitchen tap, he tops it up with cordial, testing the flavour with a quick swig. Throwing the backpack over one shoulder, Leo slips quietly out the back door.

Running down the side of the house, he disappears across the main road. The sun is at his back as he heads towards the bush track. It's a cool, crisp winter's morning with Mt Fielden shrouded in fog. Leo notices the bush looking eerie in the morning light, with dancing, laser-like shafts of sunlight piercing the mist. Leo finds the track is overgrown, giving the impression it hasn't been used in recent years. It snakes across an old paddock, covered by grass and a few low scrubby bushes and weedy looking trees.

The track passes through an opening in a run-down fence. A rusty old gate hangs by one hinge to a gatepost. Off to the right is an area of swampy marshland. It looks boggy in parts with bull rushes as far as the eye can see. In the middle of the swamp, Leo can hear the frogs cheerfully calling, "BONG-bong." He finds this amusing, imagining a frog beating a big drum. Turning left to follow the track, Leo is apprehensive at the prospect of what he might find.

The mysterious stories about the quarry have his imagination going into overdrive. It's getting warmer now, so Leo takes off his track-top and ties it around his waist. Pausing under a gum tree, he takes a few gulps of cordial. Reaching into his backpack again, he pulls out an apple and admires its bright-red sheen. He shines it on his track pants, as the apple morphs into a cricket ball. Leo thinks he's a strike bowler playing cricket for Australia.

MAP

MAP OF FERGUSON BEACH

Putting his backpack down he walks down the track gradually picking up the pace to a gallop and delivers a fast bouncer. Jumping around quickly with his feet apart and both forefingers pointing into the air, he screams, "how's that!" Then promptly takes a large bite out of the juicy red apple. Walking back to his backpack he leaves the track and takes a shortcut through the scrub, munching as he goes.

Henderson's quarry is close to the coast. The undulating terrain of the coastal dunes is studded with Banksia trees, large rounded grass trees and outcrops of weathered limestone. Leo is fascinated by the patterns on the outcrops, with fossils pitting the surface of the ancient reef rock. He picks his way around these as he nears Henderson's quarry. Although overshadowed by Mt Fielden, it is much larger and further away than he imagined.

He remembers Gramps saying the quarry had quite a history going back to the early pioneer days. In the Fifties a guy called Merv Henderson owned it, quarrying stone for a wall to upgrade the jetty at the meat works. The quarry closed after one of Henderson's workers died in a rock fall. Standing at the top of the quarry face Leo studies the site and sees a hole in the protective fence and squeezes through. Finding a fist-sized stone, he rolls it down the steep embankment.

Thinking, this place reminds me of one of those amphitheatres. That sign says it's not safe. Looks okay to me and besides, who wants to walk around to the entrance? Let's try it the easy way. Leo drops his backpack down the slope. Putting his track-top back on for the climb down, he ignores all of the warning signs and edges his way slowly down the slope. Suddenly, a large loose rock gives way under Leo's weight and he loses his footing.

Desperately, he clings on by his fingertips, his feet clambering to find any foothold. In agony from holding on, he cries out in pain, "aaahhhhh," while his feet continue to feel for firmer ground. Unable to stand the pain any longer, Leo let's go. Crying out, "H-E-L-P," as he slides helplessly down the slope.

Call it fate, divine intervention or just dumb luck, his track-top becomes snagged on a sharp limestone outcrop. Hooked up, his scrambling feet find a secure foothold. To get free, Leo takes off his track-top, tossing it down the slope. Regaining his composure, Leo nervously inches his way down to the base. Small rocks tumble down the slope after him. Glancing up, he covers his head and dashes to safety. "Oh Boy, that was close. It's more dangerous than I thought."

Picking up his track-top he mutters, "Damn! Look at that. It's torn. What am I going to do now…Mum's going to go mental when she finds out?" Not wanting to think about the consequences, Leo thoughts switch to the quarry floor. The ground's all sandy, it's useless for skateboarding for a start, he mutters. It's a junk heap. Look at all the old tyres, beer cans and campfires. Bet they had parties here and there's broken glass everywhere. Funny though, when you move it's like millions of diamonds shining in the sunlight. Yeah, and those motorbike tracks look like some kid's finger painting.

Not impressed he shouts, "This place is boring. It's nothing more than a stupid dump. I knew all those stories were crap." The last word echoes around the quarry. Picking up a large limestone rock, he gives vent to his feelings, smashing it into pieces on the ground. "Take that! I guess I might as well trek up Mount Fielden - it's got to be better than this good-for-nothing hole." Disgusted, he leaves via the access track scuffing his runners in the sand as he goes.

Turning left off the track, Leo heads straight for Mt Fielden. The sun is now higher in the sky and in his haste to sneak out; Leo has forgotten to take a cap. Feeling hot, he wraps his track-top turban style around his head. Leo trudges along aimlessly, a sudden movement and hissing sound make Leo stop dead in his tracks.

A tiger snake is sunning itself in the morning sun. Upset at the intrusion, the snake rears up and hisses another warning. Its tongue darts menacingly in and out. As Leo slowly backs off, the snake lunges at him. In a mad panic, Leo screams, "Get away from me," crashing his way blindly into the bush. He jumps madly over small bushes and a log and only stops at the sight of an old ruin. It's hidden, cocooned in an overgrown garden. The roof has long disappeared. Only the foundations and two limestone walls remain. "Hey! This place looks really old. I wonder who it belonged to." Muttering away as he makes sure the snake hasn't followed.

Wandering around the ruin he spots an old well with a low limestone wall around it, which is guarded by a very large, shady Bluegum. Investigating closer, he notices the well is filled, almost to the top, with sand. "This place is radical," he mutters again, sitting down on the limestone wall to catch his breath. Swinging his backpack off his shoulders, Leo pulls out his water bottle. He gulps down the entire contents and thinks, bugger that didn't last long. He turns the bottle upside down in the vain hope there might be more. Continuing his thoughts, phew it's the second close call I've had today. I hope it doesn't come in threes.

Removing his 'track-top turban', Leo chuckles, "now I know why the snake got excited. He must've thought I was Swami the Snake Charmer. Come to charm its socks off. Must work - Come to think of it, I've never seen a snake with a sock on." Leo whacks himself over the head, "Don't be stupid, snakes don't have feet. "Whilst seated he takes in more of his surroundings. "Boy, this place is really well hidden. I wonder if anybody else knows it's here. With his tummy rumbling, Leo reaches into his backpack again, pulling out a banana. It's squashed at one end, the legacy of dropping his backpack down the slope. In the middle of deciding if it's worth eating or chucking, he hears a noise from behind the ruin.

Jumping to his feet, Leo moves very quietly and carefully around, yet he finds nothing unusual. Daydreaming, Leo morphs into an alien hunter from one of his Sci-fi books. He aims the banana, pretending it's a photon blaster. Crouching low, he runs to the wall of the ruin. Leaning with his back up against it, he peers around the corner. He springs out waving his 'banana-blaster' threatening to shoot. Leo turns around and makes a dash for the well, thinking it will give him cover and a 360-degree view.

Diving over the wall as if his life depends on it, Leo hits the sandy bottom with a thud. This is followed by a loud crack and a groan as the floor gives way. The banana boomerangs through the air in a slow looping motion. Leo falls helplessly, coming to a sudden stop at the bottom with a 'whump'. He can't breathe, winded by the fall. Meanwhile sand continues to pour down. In a state of shock, Leo is afraid to move a muscle. Gasping, he tries desperately to fill his collapsed lungs, scared stiff about moving in case it hurts.

As the sand stops pouring down, his next thought is, Oh shit! I've done it this time. Gingerly, Leo brushes the sand from his face. Looking up he can see the well has a false wooden floor. Part of it has broken away. As his eyes slowly adjust to the dim light, he can see he's sitting on a pile of sand, which seems to have broken his fall. Leo gently moves his other arm, then each leg, to see if he has any major fractures.

He's surprised to find he has only a few scratches, a nick on the cheek and some sore spots. Strangely, outside the well, Leo's banana has just made a touchdown. Slowly, Leo gets to his feet and shuffles around like an old man. As he becomes more mobile, he feels more confident he has escaped major damage.

Arching his back and placing both hands behind his lower back, he straightens up. As he does so, he notices tree roots dangling down into a small pool of water. "Wow, I don't believe it! This isn't a well, it's a small cave." Running his hand on the rough rocky wall, he observes it has brownish bands of colour where the water levels had been. Looking up, he sums up his situation. "Boy! Am I in b-i-g trouble with a capital T. Nobody knows where I am. Bloody hell, what am I going to do now?"

Panicking at his plight, Leo grabs hold of some tree roots and tries to climb up. They break off, causing him to fall back to the floor. As he sits up, he notices one wall of the cavern has none of the brownish watermarks with an odd looking surface jutting out of the rock face. It's greyish-blue in colour and triangular shaped with the top cut off much like a trapezium. Curious, Leo stands up and runs his hand over the surface, "Hey it's really smooth feels sort of metallic. That's weird, my fingers just tingled. I wonder what it's for." No sooner had he said it, a high-pitched sound alerts him that something is about to happen. There's movement at the centre as a rock face begins to morph. Frightened, Leo jumps back and backs off until he can go no further. "Oh Jeez, Oh Jeez, what's going on, I've got to get out of here," which echoes repeatedly throughout the cavern. A shape begins to materialise in the centre.

The movement suggests a disk is about to form. Then the outline of a large triangle appears, like a border, with the disk in the middle. Radiating from each corner of the triangle and stopping at the disk's edge, is what Leo describes as a flower petal. Three of them arranged exactly like a plane's propeller. A fine groove appears next, running down the centre of each petal shape, stopping at the disk's edge. On the centre disk, three more petal shapes appear, which are not lined up to the outer ones.

Leo is shocked, "It's some sort of door, it has to be?" Above the triangular door is a symbol with two opposing triangles with two concentric circles and a vertical line through them.
Awe-struck, Leo has overcome his earlier panic-stricken state and puts his predicament to the back of his mind. "Wow, this is 'fully sick'! This is way out there. It's the wickedest thing I have ever seen and has to be alien for sure." His excitement is interrupted by sounds coming from near the top of the well. It's a female's voice singing, "*Shine a little bit of my light on the W-o-r-l-d. Doo, doo, daa-da.*"

Leo quickly puts his discovery to the back of his mind. "Help! Is there anyone there?" The singing stops and Leo holds his breath and waits for a response. "Who-who's there," is the uncertain response. Leo shouts again, "I'm down here."
"Down where?" Given what has happened, Leo isn't in the mood for games, "down the well stupid."

"Stop mucking around and come out so I can see you." Thinking quickly, Leo picks up a broken piece of wood from the well flooring and tosses it out. After a few seconds, a girl's face appears over the hole.

"Leo! What are you doing down there?"

"Dani is that you…for a second I thought it might be Vanessa Amorosi."

"It's Bachelor Girl actually. The song is Permission to Shine, not Shine."

"Yeah okay, Miss Smartypants - you know what I meant."

"How come you're down there?"

"When I jumped over the wall, the floor busted."

In a mocking tone, Dani replies, "What sort of stupid Dumbo would even think of jumping down a well?"

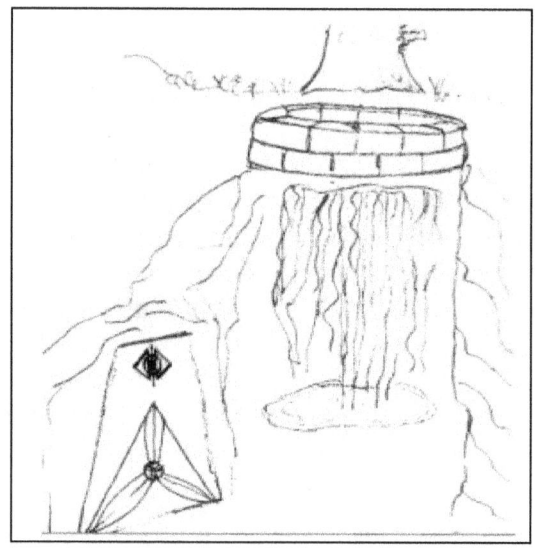

"I'm not stupid and I didn't jump, I fell. How was I supposed to know it's got a tricky floor and the boards are stuffed?" Pushing Leo for more information, Dani responds, "That's not a reason for jumping into the well."

"Believe what you want. Just get me out of here!"

"Okay, okay, I'll go and get some help."

"No! You can't," bellows Leo, not wanting his secret revealed.

"Why not?"

"You can't tell anyone. I'm not supposed to be here. If you do, I'll get belted by my Dad."

"Well then, what do you want me to do?"

Leo has to think quickly, to stop Dani from running off. Thinking, what should we do I wonder, a ladder wouldn't be long enough. A rope on its own seems pretty useless. Then a mental picture of his tree house floats through his mind. "I know; Dani remember the tree house my Dad built? There's a rope ladder on it. But, we're going to need some extra rope to tie around the tree up there. Don't let my Mum see you."

Now he's on the verge of being rescued, Leo is feeling hungry. "Dani, have you got any food up there?" Surprised, Dani responds, "how can you think about food now? All you boys think about is your stomachs. Anyway, I've only got a water bottle." Giggling she adds, "You can have it - that's if you don't mind girl germs." Parched, Leo is thankful for anything wet. His mouth is still gritty from biting the dust. Dani drops the water bottle down the well and before she goes, wants to make a point. "Oh, and by the way Leo, for keeping quiet and helping you out - you owe me big-time."
"Yeah, yeah whatever, just hurry up and don't be too long."

Leo is expecting to be down there for some time. He's surprised when after just what seems about 15 minutes he hears Dani announce, "Are you still there?"
"What a stupid question, where do you think I was going to go? Anyway, how come you're back so soon?" Dani is puzzled and replies. "What are you talking about? Did you fall on your head or something? It has taken me ages. I had to work out a way of getting the rope ladder down and get myself down. It was too heavy to carry, so I had to go and borrow my Dida's wheelbarrow. Then find more rope and bring it all the way here without anyone seeing. Phew. I'm exhausted."

Leo isn't sure what's going on. However, his main concern now is getting out of the well. "Okay Dani, are you listening, this is what we're going to do?" Dani is having none of this. "Do you want to get out of there or not?" And before Leo can open his mouth, "well you won't, if you keep going on like that." Leo doesn't like girls telling him what to do and punches the cavern wall with his fist. "Ouch," shaking his hand. "What's the problem?"
"Oh, nothing."

Dani grabs one end of the rope from the barrow and ties it to the rope ladder. Uncoiling the rope, she runs it around the trunk of the Bluegum next to the well, completing the loop by tying off the end to the rope ladder. Lifting the rope ladder from the barrow, she drags it over and begins feeding it down the well. "I'm stuffed, that rope ladder's heavy." It's just out of fingertip range for Leo. Yet close enough for him to jump up and grab the first rung.

He stiffly grabs the next rung and with a grunt, pulls his legs up wrapping them around the bottom one. He pushes up and reaches for the next rung. It isn't long before he emerges breathless and sore from the well. "Phew, thank God!" Dani points at Leo and laughs, "Yukko! You look so grotty - like you've been mucking around in some kid's sandpit." Leo's face and hands are black from the sand. He isn't amused, putting his left hand over his eyes, which look like slits, as he shields them from the sun. Having adjusted to the light, Leo brushes the sand out of his hair and pats down his soiled track pants. Still giggling, Dani makes the most of the situation, "so this is the new grunge look, eh?"

Still annoyed at being the butt of her wisecracks, Leo promptly chases Dani around the well with his hands outstretched to 'slime' her. Dani is faster. She screams and runs off behind the old ruin. Realising his ordeal has left him tired and sore, Leo calls out, "okay! I give up." "Alright then, don't you have something to say to me?" Leo has a what-is-she-on-about look, at first. "Huh". Then it dawns on him, "oh yeah. Boy, am I stoked that you came along. I thought I was a goner. Thanks for not telling anyone. Anyway, how come you were here?" "Lucky for you, I was going to sketch the old ruin. Hey, want to look at my other sketches and stuff?" Dani reaches into her black art bag, pulling out a large sketchpad. Leo looks at them closely. "Gee they're pretty good. I wish I could sketch like that. My brother Michael was good at stuff like that, too. But he died in an accident last year."

"Leo I'm really sorry. What happened?" Leo moves over to the limestone wall around the well, looking carefully this time, before sitting down. "You see we had this farm down south - Michael died when the tractor rolled over. Nobody knows for sure, what happened exactly. He would've been 23 this year."

Noticing Leo is upset talking about it, Dani quickly changes the subject. "Leo you can't go home like that. Your mum will find out and tell your Dad. Why don't you come back to my place for a wash?"

"Your right, Mum will go ballistic if she sees me like this. Actually, I do feel kind'a grotty."

"Because you owe me, for starters you can wheel the barrow back and give me a ride."

"No way! That's too far. Maybe part of the way."

"Okay, but you still owe me." It suddenly crosses Leo's mind. Hey, this bitch is blackmailing me. What can I do? She might tell someone and give away my secret. I wonder what else she wants. "Okay then, what else will I have to do?"

"Well, I like sketching people. Yet nobody will sit long enough for me to sketch them. "Hmmm, maybe I'll get you to pose for me."

"No Way! I'm not taking my clothes off for anyone." Dani can't contain herself and doubles up in laughter at Leo's outburst. Holding on to her quivering stomach she replies, "I only wanted to sketch your face, stupid." Leo feels embarrassed. "Oohh."

"Are you ready?"

"Nup, I've got to hide the rope ladder. In the ruin under these dead branches, should do the trick. "Dani points to the well. "Leo, what are you going to do about leaving the hole? Someone might fall down it?"

"We definitely can't have that happen. I dunno, I suppose this large dead branch from the gum tree might cover it. What do you reckon?"

"Yeah, that should do it…hey is this yours? It looks demented."

"That was my banana, but it got kind'a banged up." Leo grabs the banana and hurls it into the bush. Dani climbs into the wheelbarrow and gestures to Leo.

"Well! Come on then, let's go." Leo chucks his track-top and backpack into the barrow as Dani climbs onto the front. Grabbing the handles, they trundle off down the track. "Keep still will you, otherwise I'm not going to push this thing."

"Remember you still owe me." Leo is annoyed at being in debt, especially to a girl. "Yeah, yeah, so you keep on telling me."

As they trundle along, Leo's mind turns to bigger questions. Thinking, I wonder what's on the other side of the doorway and what's it doing there. How am I going to keep the whole thing secret? Leo stops and puts down the barrow. "Hey don't top", says Dani. "I was enjoying that."
"I'm just checking the time. Oh it's 1:30pm. That's funny. My watch must be busted."
"What's that supposed to mean?"
"My watch must've stopped. Look the sun is still over there, so it can't be after lunch. Dani, what do you reckon the time is?"
"My watch is about 10:30ish."
"My watch can't be busted, it's still ticking and the second hand just moved, then." Dani isn't interested and responds, "So what?"

Leo shrugs his shoulders and grabs the handles of the barrow. After a while Leo is puffing, "I can't push this thing anymore as it's too sandy, you'll have to get out."
"Ohhh all right then," agrees Dani reluctantly. They then take turns at pushing the barrow back home. Arriving at Dani's place, Leo has a quick wash in their laundry. "Dani, I'd better go before my Mum gets worried where I am. She nods and reminds Leo in a cheeky tone. "Don't forget you still owe me!"

Leo rolls his eyes. He takes off home as quickly as his tired legs will carry him, feeling guilty about his morning close shaves. Arriving at the gate, Leo's mother is in the garden, so he can't sneak in and change as he had planned. "My God! Look at you, don't tell me you have fallen off your skateboard again?" Leo thought that was lucky. I didn't think about an excuse.

"Errr-umm, yes Mum, I was going down this hill, hit a pothole, lost control and crashed into the bush." She scolds Leo. "You know damn well you're not supposed to be on the road. Why for heaven sake haven't you got your helmet on! How many times do we have to tell you...and where's the skateboard?"
"Errr-umm, I left it at Dani's place so she could try it out."
"Leo! it's not good enough. You go and take your helmet to Danicka at once. If she hurts herself, we'll never hear the end of it.

I don't want that happening. We've got enough problems to deal with - without you creating more." Leo feels like he has been well and truly roasted and scuttles off to his room. He pretends to go down to Dani's place and doubles back, hiding the helmet in bushes close to the front of the house.

Linda hasn't finished with Leo, either. "You and your clothes look disgusting. Now go and have a shower and take those dirty clothes off in the laundry. Then go to your room. Have a good think about what I said earlier. If I catch you again without your helmet, your skateboard goes... are you listening?"
"Yes, Mum." After his shower, Leo lies down on his bed thinking about all of the events of the day. He has to pinch himself to make sure he isn't dreaming. Yep. No mistake, I'm definitely awake and didn't imagine it. He has mixed feelings though. Thinking, it's really funny. It feels really cool that I'm the only one who knows about it.

But, what's the point of having a secret like that, if you can't tell someone? It reminds him also of the old man's prophecy. Thinking, how spooky is that. The old hobo might be smarter than I thought. If I'm going to share this secret, then I wonder who with?" Dani flashes through his mind. Thinking, well so far she has kept quiet about the well. I wonder if I can trust her. Trouble is you can't trust girls. They're always 'gasbagging' and full of it. Maybe I'll see what happens. Besides, I'll have to see if I can get the door open, first.

Leo doesn't seem alarmed by the prospect of what might lie beyond the doorway. As a Sci-fi nerd, he imagines all sorts of new gadgets and machines inside, thinking, maybe even meet some real- live aliens. Gee, what if it requires an electronic key or something like that. Boy, what a bummer it would be.

Leo's mind races, imagining all sorts of different possibilities, maybe it doesn't belong to aliens, maybe the Egyptians or even the Mayans. Perhaps it's even the gateway to the lost city of Atlantis. Or maybe it's some sort of secret spy base. He yawns loudly and stretches his arms. He has used up so much mental and physical energy in all of the excitement; he soon drops off to sleep.

It's fortunate for Leo he's asleep. Linda comes steaming into his room and about to go 'off her face' at him over his torn track-top. Yet seeing him there, sound asleep. She did not have the heart to wake, her dear little man. While standing there Linda recalls about how Michael always managed to stay clean and tidy - not like Leo. "Oh well," she reminisces with a sigh, "boys will be boys" and quietly closes Leo's bedroom door behind her.

It is now late afternoon and Leo wakes with a start. He stretches his tired and sore body and yawns loudly. Sitting up, his stomach rumbles reminding him he has missed lunch. As he heads for the kitchen, he can smell a lovely aroma wafting through the house. It makes his mouth water and his stomach sit up and take notice. The aroma is unmistakable.

"I must be dreaming, Mum. How come we're having a roast, I thought you said we couldn't afford it?"
"I got a bonus at work and I thought it was time for a treat. And NO, it's not ready yet." Leo's stomach goes into overdrive, he pleads, "but that smell. I'm so hungry. "Can't I have the meat off the leg bone, please, please, p-l-e-a-s-e?" Leo chuckles, remembering there was always an argument with his older brother Michael, as who got the meat off the leg bone. "Okay, you can and when you've finished, why don't you go over and ask Danicka if she wants to join us?" Leo is about to say no way, to having a girl over. Then changes his mind, "Yeah okay Mum, I'll go and ask her."

Leo has to find out if he can trust her. If she has not prattled, then he might tell her everything, after dinner. He figures Dani's sketching skills might come in handy, thinking, I haven't got a camera. Even if I did, how would I get them processed without arousing suspicion? There's a smile on his face as he imagines Lisa, the chick at the camera shop looking at the pics - Leo posing with a couple of lizard-like aliens, with big cheesy grins on all their faces. What a hoot. Imagine the look on Lisa's face. Boy wouldn't it be really sick-o. Yet he also knows, from reading his Sci-fi books he has to be careful.

Aware that government spooks do strange things around anything that suggests it might be alien. Thinking I don't want to get caught, in case they fry my brain trying to find out if I'm one of them.

As he arrives at the Jerovich place, he sees Dani's Dad, Branco sitting on the porch steps. Branco is a strong man, though what impresses Leo the most is the size of his hands. Leo hates shaking his hand as he has a vice-like grip. "Hi Mr Jerovich, my Mum wants to know if Dani can come over to dinner tonight. We're having a roast." Branco gets up and pats Leo on the head, instead of shaking hands. His hand feels like a pile driver, driving him into the ground. "Your Mama and Dida good people. Worka very hard, like our familia," trumpets Branco in broken English. Branco yells at the top of his voice, "Danicka! You come. Mister Leo here." Dani's head pops out of an up stair's window, not wanting to come down. "What do you want Dida?"
"Mister Leo come for you to have roast. You go with nice young mans for dinner. Make your Dida 'appy."

"Yes Dida," moans Dani with a big sigh. While they wait for Dani to get ready, they chat. "Mr Leo you strong young mans. Come worka for me - pick da lettuce. I pay you cash-money." Leo doesn't fancy the backbreaking work and replies, "yeah-nah...ahhh, I have heaps of homework you know and on weekends I have to help my Dad in the Petrol Servo."

Patting Leo on the head again, "you good young mans, help your Dida and worka da school books, eh." Branco calls Dani again, however there's no answer. "Womans, they always taka long time. I go see what the trouble, yes." Branco goes inside and finds his wife Lena fussing over Dani, making sure she looks her best. Lena also insists on Dani taking something with her to Leo's place. Eventually, Dani emerges just as the sun is sinking below Mt Fielden. Leo is surprised and impressed. He has only seen Dani in her college uniform or baggy track trousers and a tee shirt. They always looked too big on her slender frame. Today she has on designer jeans and a colourful jumper with a gold chain and pendant cross. Leo can smell perfume and thinks it smells like passionfruit.

As a greeting, Dani looks cheekily at Leo and sings lyrics to Summer Nights from the musical Grease: *"well-a, well-a, well-a, huh! Tell me more, tell me more, did you fall very far? Tell me more, tell me more, uh-huh, do do, uh-huh, do do, uh-huh."*

Leo claps and in a threatening tone, whispers, "very funny. You'd better not have told anyone?" She whirls around on the spot, "I was going to tell the whole world, but then I remembered you still owe me." Leo has a smug look on his face as he replies, "Yeah right," thinking, I'll tell you more alright. Just as they arrive at the letterbox, Bryan pulls into the drive, looking completely worn out from working at the garage. "Hi Dad, guess what?" Mum's cooking a roast tonight and Dani's having dinner with us."

"You beauty!" We haven't had one for ages. I'm starving. Let's not waste any time putting on the feedbag."

Inside, Leo leads Dani through to the kitchen. Dani is first with a greeting, "Hi Mrs Shepherd," placing a tin on the table. "My Mama sent these over for later."

"Hello Danicka, that's a nice thought. Give your parents our regards when you go home, won't you?" Linda opens the oven and with a tea-towel lifts out the steaming roast and vegetables, placing it on the table.

"Everyone, dinner's on the table. Danicka, you sit over here with me so we can talk." Bryan and Leo aren't interested in small talk. They seem to be racing each other to see who can finish first. The girls lag way behind, being more intent on catching up on local gossip, than eating. "How's the skateboarding lessons coming along, Danicka?" On hearing that, Leo makes a spluttering sound as he chokes on a piece of roast potato. Linda scolds him, "Leo! Slow down and eat your food properly, especially when we have a guest."

Meanwhile, Dani has a questioning look on her face. She thinks it must have something to do with Leo, making direct eye contact with him. Leo just raises his eyebrows and tilts his head to the side, in a gesture of surrender. Fortunately, Dani takes this as a cue, "Oh! I'm not doing very well. I keep falling off. But, Leo is teaching me the basics. Apparently?"

"Oh, that's nice isn't it Bryan?" Bryan's too busy eating and just nods and grunts. After dinner, they move to the lounge to watch the Simpsons on television. Linda hands out a plate each, loading with the homemade biscuits.

"Hey these are really tasty, I could get addicted to these," comments Bryan as he takes a bite out of his third biscuit. "Your Mum's a whiz in the kitchen, not like Linda here."

"That's not fair Bryan!" She gives him a dirty look and in a hurt voice retorts, "You know I work long hours, just like you."

"I just thought I'd see if you would take the bait," replies Bryan. Realising he has overstepped the mark, he adds, "I didn't mean it that way and the roast was A1." With small talk and being transfixed to the television, time races by. Linda glances at the clock on the wall and remarks, "Leo I think it's close to bedtime for you both. Be a gentleman and walk Danicka home." After saying goodbye to Leo parents, Dani is busting to know, "what was your Mama going on about at the table?"

"Going on about what?"

"Stop playing Mr innocent. You know the bit about me learning to skateboard."

"Oh, that bit…well after I left your place, Mum was in the garden and saw me. She thought I'd come off the skateboard - I had to say something."

"Ha! You were lucky she thought that." Giggling, as she puts her hand up to her mouth, "Well, well, well more 'porky pies' eh! This means I have more dirt on you than you got from falling down the well."

"That's not even funny. Also, it ain't even half the truth, because I know something about the well and it will blow your socks off. "Dani thinks she has Leo right where she wants him. "As If!"

"No. I'm serious Dani. It will really blow your mind. In fact, it's really out of this world." Dani knows Leo is up to something tricky and suspiciously replies, "Yeah right."

"Well, if I tell you, then it has to stay a secret, right. You can't tell anyone. You have to promise me - then I don't owe you anything?" Dani loves secrets, especially other people's. "Well okay. It better be good."

"It is and you have to swear you won't tell anyone and seal it with the Catholic salute."

"Why do I have to do that for?"

"Because once you make an oath sealed with the sign of the holy cross, a curse would fall on you if you tell anyone."

"Yeah, okay, whatever just tell me."

"You're not going to believe this. When I was down the well, I discovered a strange looking triangular door. It's sort of metallic and when I touched it, I got a tingling sensation in my hands." Dani mocks Leo, "you banged your head when you fell - no wonder it didn't hurt.
You hit your head and that's why you're seeing stuff and feeling all tingly."

"See, I knew you wouldn't believe me." Leo points to his watch. "Remember this morning when I asked you the time and I thought my watch was busted?" Dani screws up her face, "Yeah, so what?" "Well, it's working just fine. So when you are near it, somehow it speeds up time. But, elsewhere it's normal. I know all this sounds crazy. I hardly believe it myself."

"Let's say, what you say is true"…Leo interrupts, "It is true." Dani continues, "Then who does it belong to? Maybe it belongs to green spooky Martians…ooohhh, shouldn't we tell the police? They might be dangerous."
"Look Dani you're not taking this seriously. You can't tell anyone, anything. But, before you do anything, come and see it for yourself." As they arrive at the front of Dani's place, Leo challenges Dani, "look I will see you out the front at 4:00pm tomorrow, okay. Make sure you are here and remember we made a pact."

"Yeah, yeah I know, the holy cross etc, etc. Thanks for inviting me to dinner and for trusting me with your secret." Dani has lots of thoughts racing through her mind. She is excited because Leo trusts her with his most precious secret. She reasons Leo must like her a lot to have done that, so she quickly gives him a quick peck on the cheek.

It was so quick - like a hit and run. Leo is stunned. He can feel the blood rushing to his head, his heart skips a beat and he has a buzzing feeling in his stomach. He quickly says goodnight and races off home, holding his hand up to his cheek. He is still stunned as he arrives home.

Leo has never had such a feeling before. Thinking, it sure isn't like Mum kissing me. Leo opens the front door and trips over the mat. He makes it safely to the kitchen to get a drink of water, to cool down. He drops the glass of water onto the floor. Water goes everywhere. Leo is completely gobsmacked by the 'hit and stun', kiss.

Meanwhile, Linda decides to investigate, "Leo, what is all that racket. What 'are' you doing? Linda is standing there, hands on hips, watching as Leo bumps into the table and making an even bigger mess. "Leave it, Leo. You're only making it worse. What's the matter with you? Are you on drugs or something?" Leo isn't sure what to say, "Errr…no Mum, I'm just tired. I'd better go to bed."
"I should think so…good God, you've got water everywhere."

Chapter 3
Makes me think someone's watching us.

Leo has quite a sleepless night and no wonder, as he rewinds his mental video on the events of the day. I still can't believe from one decision, of going to Henderson's quarry that so many things have happened. None of which I could have imagined in my wildest dreams. Then to top it off a chick rescues me. Then I share my amazing secret with her and then she pashes me, too. This day has to be the best ever. How could anything else possibly top that?

After the events of yesterday, Leo finds it's very hard to go back to school. Every activity he does feels dull and utterly boring. As Leo makes his way to his Library class, he bumps into Mr Thomson. "Hello Leo, how's the assignment coming along? Remember on my office desk Wednesday morning."
"No worries Mr Thomson," he answers, as he slides open the Library door. As he sits down he mutters to himself, "No worries – OMG! I forgot all about it, after yesterday. How am I going to come up with a story and finish it by tomorrow night?"

Suddenly, he has a brainstorm. Hey, maybe I can do something on the folks who built the limestone house at the well, or on the pioneers around Fielden. Yeah, that's what I'll do. I wonder if Miss Marshall can give me some books on the early settlers.
"Miss Marshall I have to do an assignment, which has to be in on Wednesday."
"You're leaving it rather late to start your research now, aren't you?"
"No, I've got this idea to do it about local pioneers in this area, especially around Mt Fielden."

"Well, that narrows it down a bit. We've got a couple of reference books on loan from the main Library that you can read."
"That's no good Miss Marshall, I've got to do this other stuff now and I have to finish the other one tonight."
"Hmmm…what to do…Leo, I shouldn't be letting these out you know make sure they're back first thing tomorrow."

"Wow! Thanks, Miss Marshall." Leo carefully places them in his backpack and joins the rest of his class. Later on, during Society and Environment class, Leo's mind is on the events of the previous day. He's stares out the window wishing, come on siren go soon, so I can go home. Then Dani and I can check out the strange door. Then he remembers. Oh, the assignment. Just when something important happens, I have to do a stupid assignment. Then it strikes him, the well. That's right, there's a time difference when you're down there. I bet I can do the assignment, check the place out and still have tons of time left over.

How cool is that? I could make heaps of bucks by selling Timesaver tickets to other kids. They could do their homework and still have heaps of time to muck around afterwards. I could make a fortune. It's completely mad.

BANG! A book comes crashing down onto the desk. Leo almost jumps out of his skin. "Off with the space cadets are we," questions Mrs Kane the S & E teacher, standing next to Leo's desk. She picks up the book and stares at Leo, "look I know it's Monday morning, but you will have to try and concentrate a bit harder."

As she moves back to the front of the class, she adds, "and that goes for the rest of you too." Leo isn't very popular with the other students as they all give him 'the stare', for making the teacher so touchy. The rest of the day continues in much the same vein. No matter how hard Leo tries to concentrate, his mind keeps drifting back to Sunday's events.

Leo feels annoyed. Yesterday he was on such a big high - it was even better than doing drugs, he thought. Yet today, he just wanted to go home. Because of that, the day crawls at a snail's pace. The lack of concentration during classes keeps getting him into trouble and he hates the attention. To the point at lunchtime, a couple of his classmates come up to him and comment, "What's with you Sheps? You sure got a bad dose of Mondayitis."
"Yeah, something like that, I've got a couple of small things on my mind, that's all."

Nevertheless, he somehow manages to get through the day and finally the siren goes and it's not long before he's on the bus home. As the bus nears his stop, Leo is hoping Dani has remembered their pact. He also wonders how she's coping with her day and more importantly, has she kept his secret safe? He reflects on his feelings, amazing, I would've thought having a real big secret would be 'funtastico'. Gee, it's actually hard work. I wonder what's behind the door. God, I hope I can open it.

Getting off the bus he races home. He quickly changes out of his uniform and into jeans and tee shirt, over which he pulls on a blue polo top. He grabs an apple and his school bag, with the reference books he needs and locks up as he leaves. Leo decides to wait out the front of the Jerovich place for Dani. She will be on a later bus, coming from the city.

He makes himself comfortable on their front fence and takes a quick look at one of the reference books while he waits. He thumbs through a few pages looking at the old photos until he spots one of Mt Fielden. Moving to the text he reads it aloud, "Mt Fielden was originally named Clarence Fielden Hill, named after a pioneer settler... see I knew it was just a hill... Clarence a stonemason came out from England in the 1880's and married his childhood sweetheart, Mary Chambers.

Later he built the limestone farmhouse in the shadow of Mt Fielden...this is exactly what I need for the assignment. I bet the ruin was their house." Silently reading on, Leo learns they'd tried growing crops there, yet the soil was too poor. The seed sent from England did not do well in the climate. So Clarence turned his hand to quarrying the local limestone and won a lucrative contract supplying limestone blocks for government projects of the region.

As Leo closes the book, he glances up to see a bus off in the distance and hopes Dani is on board. The bus pulls up, with the brakes making a dry screeching sound. Dani gets off and waves to her school friends as the bus pulls out. He's waited for this moment all day and jumps off the fence, running to the stop to meet her. Before she has a chance to say anything, Leo gushes, "are you ready to check out the well?" Dani is frazzled, after a long difficult day at school. "Give us a break Leo. I have just got off the damn bus."

"Sounds like you had the same sort of day as me. I'll wait out the front while you get changed."

"Look, Leo. I've got music practice and heaps of homework today, so I can't come with you."

"Don't worry, I've got it all figured out. I got mine too. All you have to do is bring your homework and your sketchbook with you." Dani screws up her face, "so how's that supposed to get it all done?"

"Easy. Remember the time difference at the well I told you about. Well, you can do your homework, sketch the place and be home before you know it."

"Hey that's so cool," chuckles Dani. "Wait for me here, I won't be very long."

Dani takes her overflowing school backpack inside and runs up to her room to unpack and change into a tracksuit. Hearing her mother in the kitchen, Dani asks, "Mama I've got some sketching homework to do and going over to the bush near the quarry. Leo says he will take me. Is it okay?" This impresses Lena. "Oh, Mr Leo he's good gentlemans. She quickly makes a large salami sandwich for Leo and takes it out the front. "Dis for good boy, a gentlemans, look after my Danicka."

"Ta! Mrs J, that sambo looks wicked." Lena has a confused look. "Mama, Leo's saying the sandwich looks really good."

"Okay I sorry, no understand young peoples talk." Both are in high spirits as they make their way across the main road, backpacks swinging. "Hey, this is homemade bread," scoffs Leo. "Do you mind? Do you have to talk with your mouth full, it looks kind'a demented."

Leo just laughs and looks at Dani with bread hanging out of his mouth. Dani takes one look at Leo. She shakes her head and remarks, "you guys are gross." Arriving at the old ruin Leo takes charge, "let's make sure nobody is around before we do anything." Having decided it is safe; Leo uncovers the rope ladder and ties it off onto the shady Bluegum. He removes the large dead branch covering the hole and with Dani's help, feeds the rope ladder down the well. He expertly climbs down like a monkey. Looking up, Leo gestures in a reassuring way, "come on Dani it's safe."

"That's easy for you to say, you're not scared of heights."

Eventually, with Leo's coaxing and her curiosity overcoming her fear, Dani swings over the wall to climb down. Although very tense, she slowly begins the climb down in an un-ladylike manner. "Errrr something stinks…like rotten eggs. I'm not going any further - something's dead down there."

"Well errr, umm, to tell you the truth, ummm - it was me. I let Fluffy off his chain."

"I don't get it?"

"Ummm, you know… I sort of fluffed."

"Oh pooh, I'm getting out of here, right now." Her tense nervous state gives way to total laughter. Her body is shaking so much she can't climb out as she swings back and forth. "I get it now - let Fluffy off the chain."

"It's not 'that' funny."

"I've never heard farting called that before." I can't help it. I'll have to come down, help me I can't hang on anymore."

"I was going to say - if you knew your science, hot air rises. But you're down now."

Dani brushes her hands on the back of Leo's top, "where'd you get that saying from?"

"From my Dad," he farts all the time."

"Like father like son eh…anyway, where's this secret door you've been going on about?"

"I don't know. It was over there." He pats the wall, where the door had been and as if on cue the centre disk begins forming at the centre.

The door takes shape right in front of their astonished eyes. Dani has her mouth wide open. She's the first to speak, "that's so cool, I like the shape and this flower design thingy on it, or whatever it is. Wow! And I like the symbol thingy above the door too?"

"Dani I couldn't give a rat's arse about the 'thingys'. I'm more worried about how to open it."

"Leo, are you sure we should be messing with this?"

"Look, Dani. How many times in your life are you going to get a chance like this?" Dani takes a closer look, "maybe never, so what do we do?" Running her hand over the shiny surface, she observes, "You're right." It's kind of warm and tingly. Oh, my God! I've got goosies up and down my arm."

Leo grabs the ladder with one hand and says; "Dani, I'll go and get your sketchpad and you can sketch it before anything else happens, okay?" As Leo climbs out to get her sketchbook, Dani out of curiosity touches the centre disk. It suddenly glows a reddish colour, zapping Dani right up the arm. She screams and jumps backwards. "Shit! I'm out of here." Up top Leo enquires, "What's your problem?"

Dani jumps up and grabs the lower rung of the ladder. Yet all she can do in her panicking state is swinging wildly back and forth. "That stupid door zapped me. Stop staring and get me out of here."
"Calm down Dani. "If it was harmful it would have done more than just zap you. Anyhow, I need you to sketch the door and the symbol - stuff like that."
"Well maybe." But, I'm not going anywhere near that door again."

Leo climbs back down with her sketchpad in his teeth. Which doesn't impress Dani, "errr, you've dribbled on the cover," as she wipes it on the back of Leo's track-top.
"Did you like the teeth marks as well?"
"Ha ha. Don't be stupid or I'm going home. So, where are the pencils?"
Leo turns around, "In my back pocket, see." Dani sits down cross-legged on the floor and quickly sketches the door pattern. Leo looks over her shoulder approvingly, "jeez you're good at sketching things, looks just like it."

Placing his hand on the disk a second time, he feels a needle-like jab and pulls his hand away. "Ouch what the hell was that?" While Leo examines his hand, the disk begins to rotate. It stops rotating just as the petal shapes running from the corners of the triangular door and those on the centre disk, line up. Leo moves closer to the door and gingerly waves his hand in front of the disk at the centre. Nothing happens. Leo touches the disk and it glows a blue colour.

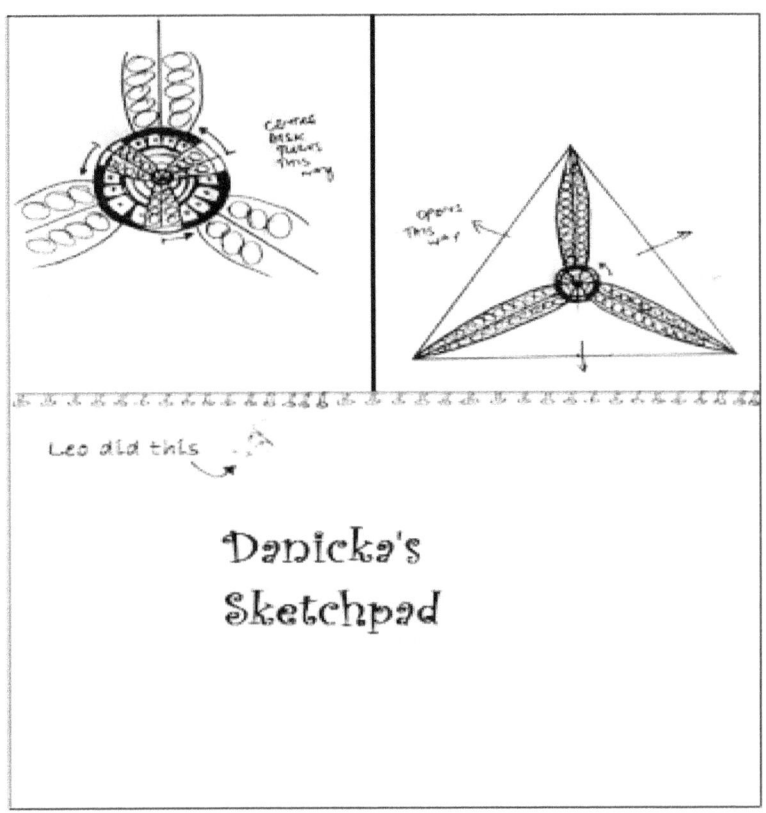

Leo did this

Danicka's
Sketchpad

"Hey, that's different to what I saw. Do it again," urges Dani, watching apprehensively. They take a deep breath, yet nothing happens. They look at each other and Leo shrugs his shoulders. "Maybe they want me to do it again?"

"Hey! Hang on a minute, what do mean 'they'. Who's 'they'? You never said anything about 'they'."

"Well, there might be someone or something waiting on the other side. That's what I want to find out."

"I'm not waiting down here in case something gross happens. I'll wait up top. If something does, I can go and get help."

"Yeah, maybe you're right. I'll give you a bunk up to the first rung." Leo reaches up to give Dani a hand. "Hey! Watch it! Watch where you're putting your hands will you."

"Want to get out or not?" Leo gives Dani a helping hand to climb out.

As she reaches the top, she comments, "God, I hate rope ladders makes me feel helpless." Meanwhile, Leo places his hand on the disk once again. There's a quick pssst sound as if pressurised and the door opens. The three panels in the door divide and slide away, revealing a passageway. Peering cautiously beyond the doorway Leo shouts excitedly, "hey Dani, there's a long passage. It goes right under Mt Fielden.

It looks the same shape as the wall out here. There's a bright glow coming from inside, hang on…there's no lights or shadows in here. You have to come down and have a look. This is amazing."
"What is it?
"No I can't explain, come and see it yourself." Dani climbs down to look. She too is amazed by the glow, "Leo, it's a pale golden colour, it's really amazing. Look you're right; there are no shadows at all. How can that be?" Both are mystified and wave their hands in and out of the entrance to the passage, trying in vain to get a shadow. "Look Leo, there's no dirt, dust or cobwebs or anything. It's like it is all brand new. Maybe we should take our shoes off if we're going in?"

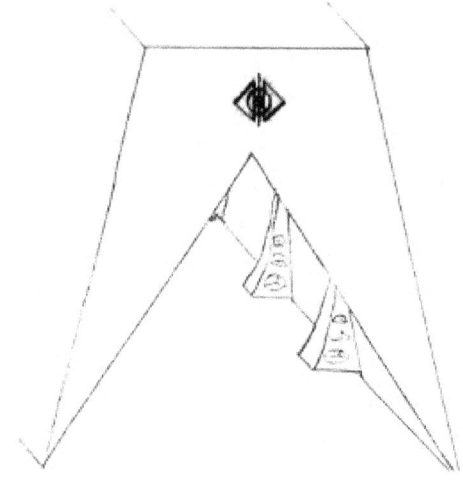

They remove their shoes and holding hands, nervously advance down the passage. "Dani, look at the end of the passage, there are steps. I wonder what's at the top."

"Shoosh Leo." Cautiously they climb to the top of the steps and peer through an archway. "Oh my God, this thing's huge." The archway opens up into a cavernous geometric structure. It too is filled with the same pale golden light. Both are stunned, unable to take it all in at once. Leo can only manage a low whisper, "Yeah, you're right, it's humungous." "Leo, do you think it's some kind of temple?" Rubbing his left forearm, "I dunno, feels kind of funny in here. Can you feel the vibes on your skin?"
"Yes, what is it?"

Trying to sound like an expert, Leo uses his Sci-fi knowledge. Yet he's having trouble thinking, speaking and taking it all in at the same time. "I'm not sure exactly, but I guess it must be some sort of plasma energy field. This place looks like one of those…three-sided pyramid thing-a-mees. You know one of those…tetra what-is-names."
"You mean a tetrahedron."
"Yeah, one of them. Look at the walls. They're sort of copper coloured." Leo's excitement grows with each discovery. "Shoosh!" Dani warns, "Not so loud. Someone might hear us."

Looking around, they notice two regular six-sided hexagons carved into the floor; one inside the other. A line radiates out along the floor from each corner of the hexagons and in between the six sections are six strange looking symbols. "I've never seen those patterns before, what do you think they're for?"
"I dunno'" shrugs Leo, scuffing his sock-covered foot on top of the first symbol closest to the archway. "Wow look up there," Leo points towards the top of the pyramid. "That's the same shape up there, and it's got a cone pointing down."

Dani looks up and pulls her shoulders together, "No way am I standing under that. Leo, I'll sketch all of this for you and then I'm doing my homework. After that, I'm out of here real fast, 'cos this place gives me the creeps." Dani has the feeling she shouldn't be there, although she didn't know why. She figures, it was Leo who opened the door. When she tried it, she got zapped. "I guess you're sort of right, Dani. I'll go and get our school bags." Dani grabs hold of Leo's arm. "Hey! You're not leaving me here."

Turning around, they retrace their steps back along the passage. As they leave the passage and step out through the door, they hear the pssst sound again. The triangular door closes behind them. Dani is getting a little anxious. "It must be getting late, my Mama will be wondering where I am."

"Look Dani can't you see, the sun hasn't even moved. So I am right about the time difference."

Climbing out of the well, Leo grabs his school bag and as he's about to drops it down the well, shouts out, "INCOMING!" Dani's not impressed. "You're not doing that to my backpack." Throwing Dani's backpack over his shoulder, Leo scales down the rope ladder. "Okay, ready. I'll open the door." Leo places his hand on the centre disk and the sections slide back, just like a three-sectioned pie. One section sinks into the floor. While the remaining two sections disappear left and right into the wall.

Dusting off their socks, they walk back up the tunnel to the main pyramid structure. "Okay Leo, I'm ready to sketch this area…but I need somewhere comfortable to sit." Just as she finishes her sentence, a table and two chairs rise silently from the floor in the centre of the pyramid. Dani shudders, jumping at the sudden movement. "That's creepy or what? It knows what I am thinking." Despite the feeling of being watched, she sits down and busily sketches the pyramid and the detail of the symbols on the floor, occasionally pausing to anxiously look around. "You know Dani looking at the floor, it's sort of like two big honeycomb cells from a beehive, one inside the other and even the colour's similar."

"Yeah, I know what you mean."

"While you're sketching, I'd better do my assignment." Leo opens one of his library reference books. Dani looks up replying, "what's your assignment about?"

"I'm going to write about the early pioneers who lived in this area, like the settlers who built the limestone house.

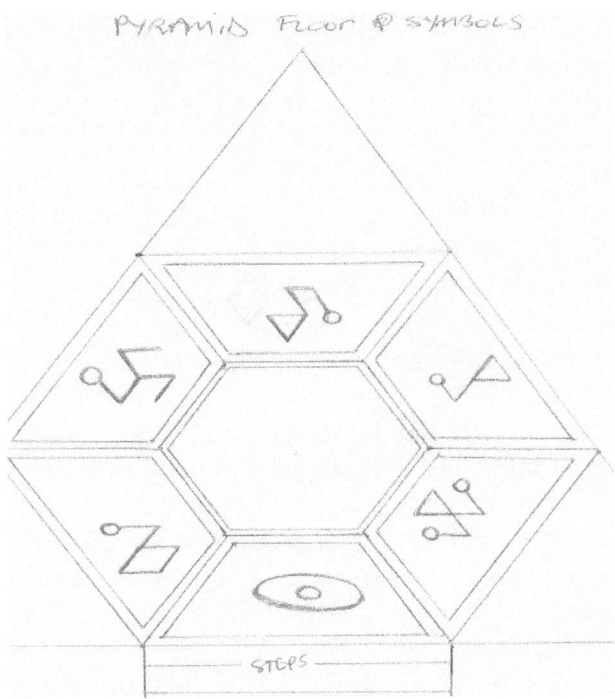

Maybe there's a connection between this place and the settlers who dug the well."

"I got some English and Maths homework. But I hate Maths."

Tell you what. You do my Maths and I'll type up your assignment on our computer."

"You got a deal. I'm good at Maths. Besides, Mr Thompson reckons my writing's like a chicken scratching. At least it will look like I have put heaps of work into it." Leo writes about what he had read earlier about Clarence Fielden. Reading on further, he finds another interesting passage. "Hey, Dani guess what? It says here old Clarry is reputed as having been a member and office bearer of a Masonic group called the Brotherhood of Light, which had connections to a little-known Order called, The Guardians. See I knew there had to be some connection. Can we check it out on the Internet and see if we can find anything which looks like these symbols?"

Dani nods, "yeah, okay." Leo finishes the first draft of his assignment.
"Okay I've finished, how about you?"
"I'm still going. I thought you said you were going to do my Math's homework?"
"Oh yeah, that's right."
"There! I finished sketching in here. Those symbols are so cool."
"Let me look. Yeah, they look pretty good."
"Dani, do I have to do these ones on page 23?"
"No, not those ones."
"Okay, then I've nearly finished, they were easy."

When Leo has finished, they both pack up their stuff. As they stand up, the table and chairs descend silently into the floor. Neat thought Leo, "I wish I had that in my bedroom."
"Leo, do you know what I reckon? Furniture appearing and disappearing makes me think someone's watching us. So can we get out of here, now?"

As they leave the passage and step out into the well cavern, the triangular door closes with a pssst sound. Leo tosses his jogging shoes out of the well. While Dani put hers on at the bottom of the shaft.
As they climb out of the well, they notice the sun has hardly moved.
"See, I told you - it does something to time when you're down there. If we come here and do our homework, we'll have more time to muck around after school."
"Isn't it like cheating?"
"No way" argues, Leo. "We still have to do the work."
"Pity it can't do that too," laughs Dani.

Leo swings his backpack off his shoulder and puts on his shoes. Untying the rope ladder, he hides it under some branches and rubbish inside the ruin. Before leaving he covers up the gap in the well floor with the large dead branch. On the way back to Dani's place, they chat about how the structure came to be there and whom it might belong to. Arriving home they go straight into the kitchen and greeted by a surprised Lena. "Danicka, Leo. You back so soon."
"Oh, ahhh…we changed our minds Mama. Can I go onto the Internet to look for some stuff? It's for Leo."

"Dani, what about your homework?"

"Don't worry Mama I did it in a free period at school. Can I go on the Internet? Leo needs help with his assignment. It's due on Wednesday."

"Okay Danicka, you look after Mister Leo if he hungry. I go upstairs to clean, yes."

Before typing up Leo's assignment, they surf the net to search for secret societies and ancient orders. They find lots of information on the Templar Knights, the Illuminati and Masonic Lodges. "Leo this stuff is so confusing. There are so many different secret groups connected to these guys. I don't think it's going to help much."

"Dani, just click on that, it's got a picture gallery."

"How's that supposed to help?"

"I dunno. I'm just sick of reading all this stuff. It's boring. Just maybe some pictures might give us a clue."

"Okay, but we're wasting time if you want me to do your assignment."

"Just this one and then we'll leave it."

Leo shouts excitedly, "Hey look there. The photo of the chateau hallway, it's got a carpet hanging on the wall. There's that symbol, the one at the far end of the pyramid away from the arch. You know the one." Dani gets out one of her sketches, "they do match. So what does it mean?" Leo thought for a little while… "hmm, all it means, as far as I can tell, is the symbol connects the pyramid thingy to some secret order called, The Guardians, whoever they are. But, I 'm not sure they had anything to do with building the pyramid as it is too advanced for them."

"Leo, let's check the link to the photo…it says here it's a really old tapestry called Tariqas and came from a monastery in Spain."

"Tari - what?"

"Let's do a word search on good ol' Google."

"This link says it means: the way of the spirit, where groups act as caretakers or guardians and…" Dani is interrupted by Branco shouting, "Dani the phone. I need da telephone to talka to Micky." "Well, that's it Leo I got to get off the Net, Dida wants the phone. He doesn't trust the Net and won't upgrade it. What do you think the symbol means?"

"I dunno," shrugs Leo. "Well, I'd better type up your assignment. If you want I can use the graphics package I have on the computer to record all this stuff we found. What do you think Leo?"

"Dani, what if someone sees this stuff?"

"Don't worry Leo, I will just tell them it's a graphic design project for school."

"I suppose so. We're the only ones to have seen it, so I guess no one will know." Dani is still typing when Lena comes into Dani's room. "You two still working, eh. Maybe Mister Leo he stay for dinner, No."

"Grouse, Mrs J."

"But you ask your Mama first, eh?" In high spirits, Leo bounds off home and for the first time ever changes his clothes for dinner. He leaves a note on the refrigerator which reads; *At Dani's place. Mrs J wants me to stay for dinner. See-you.*

"Mister Leo you back so fast."

"Mrs J, Mum's not home, so I left a note."

"It no good nobody home when Mister Leo come home from school."

"That's okay Mrs J I'm used to it now."

"Okay, you sit, yes. Danicka, you come!"

As Leo sits down at the table a thought crosses his mind. Hey, every time I have dinner with the Jerovich family, somebody always drops in. But they're never allowed to leave without eating. Tonight is no exception. At the table is the local vegetable wholesaler. Branco does the introductions, his huge hands waving. "Listen everyones, dis my friend Micky. He good mans. He buy my veges. Give me good price, no. Dis is Danicka's friend, Mister Leo from up the road." Leo and Michael stand up and shake hands politely. "Hi, good to meet you, I'm Michael." Continuing with his earlier thought, Leo muses, I wonder if anyone has ever escaped without eating anything. His vivid imagination runs rampant, thinking, maybe Mr J crushes their heads with his big hands.

As the others sit down to dinner, Branco pours the wine for everyone. "Ahhh Mister Leo you must drink some vino. I mayka myself, good. No." Leo has never tasted Grappa before and cautiously sips the homemade red wine. It's not a pleasant experience. What springs to mind is the smell - it's like cat's piss. Not that he has ever tasted cat's piss before. But figured it would taste just as disgusting. However, he knows he must drink it as any refusal of food or drink would be taken as a personal insult by Lena or Branco.

Smiling, he holds up the half-empty glass. "Ahh, good, yes. I fill your glass, yes." Leo slumps back into the chair thinking that was a dumb move. While they wait for the main meal to be prepared, Leo is curious about Dani's family. "This is such a big house for the three of you. Do you have any brothers and sisters Dani?"

"Yes, I have an older brother Marin. He's working in London and an older sister Nadia. She's married to Paulo. They have two little ones. I'm sure you're met Paulo, once." Branco interrupts, "my boy Marin's a bigshot now. He works with da-money. He read books about da-money. But I tell you. What's there to know about da-money? She come in…she go out. When the weather good, too many veges. Price no good. Weather bad, no veges. Price very good. What you say Micky?"

"Your veges always good Branco. That's why I give you the best price." Branco laughs heartily to Micky's diplomatic reply. Leo makes eye contact with Dani and shrugs his shoulders as he's not sure what Branco is on about. "Dida is saying Marin studied Economics at Uni and now works in London as an economist for Barclays Bank."

"Oh! I get it now."

After the main meal, Lena busily clears the plates away. Branco stands up and announces, "Danicka, you play guitar for our friends Micky and Mister Leo." Much to Dani's embarrassment, Branco insists she plays. This happens every time they have guests over for dinner. Including the heated discussion in Slav, this leaves Leo wondering if he has done something wrong.

Dani realising this and says, "Don't worry Leo, it's not about you. It's just that Dida gets upset because he thinks I'm not passionate about music. He doesn't talk about it. But, before he came to Australia Dida studied to be a Classical Guitarist. He has strong hands and good fingers suited to the Flamenco style. (Leo could relate to the strong hands.) But that was before the student strikes in Yugoslavia in the Seventies. Men came to his village and he got arrested. They wanted to know the names of the leaders. But, Dida didn't tell them. He told them he makes music, not war. So they broke both his hands with a hammer."

Leo is stunned. Gulping as he looks down at his own hands, but manages to say, "Can he still play?"

"He hasn't played a note since that day." Branco interrupts in a loud booming voice, "I forgive, but I no forget. They don't braka my hands, they braka my heart for my muzika."

"So Dida left and now I'm his music. I'm supposed to make up for his dreams. That's why he's always going on about it."

"I sort of understand. But, would you play for me?"

"Okay, but I'm only doing it for you." Dani returns and sets up her music stand, footrest and music. "Danicka! You play scales first, yes." Annoyed, she rolls her eyes and grits her teeth, "humph...for the hundredth time already."

Dani warms up by playing a few scales and, in an 'I-don't- want-to-be-here' manner, flicks violently through her music book. "I don't know what to play."

"I don't mind. Anything...what about something your Dad likes?" Dani flicks through the book again. "Okay, this one will do, it's called Cavatina."

Leo isn't sure what to expect and is impressed. He can see as she plays, Dani's body is moving in sync with the music. Glancing in Branco's direction, Leo can't help but notice Branco has tears in his eyes. Lena, clutching a tea towel stands at the dining room door to listen. When Dani has finished they all clap loudly. Branco wipes his tears away and shouts, "Bravo! Bravo! My Danicka she is good, No!"

"Yeah, Dani I'm really impressed. I wish I could play music."

"You can see how it affects him. I do love music, but he's obsessed. Now you know what I have to put up with."

"Come! No more sad talk, eh! We have café and special cake my Lena make. Danicka cups for café!"

After all the dishes have been cleared away, Leo excuses himself. "Look at the time, I'd better go. Thanks, heaps Mrs J for the wicked spread, everything was A1++."

"Okay then, goodbye Mister Leo."

"Oh and nice to meet you Micky, I mean Michael."

"That's okay young fellow," responds Michael as they shake hands again. Branco leads Michael to the front door. As Dani gets up from the table she gestures to Leo, "I'll see you off. Oh! That reminds me, I've got to get your assignment. See you out the front." Shortly after, Dani emerges from the house with the folder. She goes to hand it to Leo but refuses to let go. "Well." Leo is confused. He steps forward, pecking her on the cheek.

"Hey! I didn't ask for that. A thank you for doing your typing and stuff is all I had in mind." Leo's face goes a bright red colour. He grabs the folder and quickly leaves to avoid any more embarrassment. Arriving home he finds his Dad fast asleep in front of the television, as usual. His mother is in bed reading a magazine. "Hi Mum, I'm b-a-a-ck."

"Got your note. Did you have a good time, dear?" Leo sits down on the end of the bed, "yes, the food was grouse. I had a real pig out, except for the Grappa red stuff Mr J makes, it tastes like cat's piss."

"That's not very nice. I hope you were on your best manners?" Leo didn't respond and changes the subject, "see my assignment, Dani typed it on her computer. Looks real professional doesn't it?" Linda has a smile on her face and raises her painted eyebrows. "That's really nice of Dani to do that for you. You two are getting on famously, aren't you?" Leo blushes and grins sheepishly, as he jumps off the bed. "Mum, I'm off for a shower and bed. See you in the morning." Leo dives into bed, just as Bryan wakes up and turns off all the main lights. After going to the toilet, he climbs into bed and remarks. "I fell asleep in front of the idiot box again. Don't know why I bother turning it on."

Linda puts down her magazine. "Bryan, have you noticed Leo's whole attitude has changed in the last few days? He seems a lot happier in himself."
"Good for him. I'm stuffed and just want to go to sleep."

"I think our dear little Leo is growing up and has a girlfriend." "How do you know that?" As Linda reaches over and turns the bedside lamp off, she whispers in his ear. "Let's call it women's intuition."

The next morning in the Shepherd household, it's the usual routine. Leo just makes it to the bus stop. On the bus, he cooks up a plan to get back into old Thommo's good books. Arriving at Fielden High, Leo heads straight for Mr Thompson's office. Leo knocks on the office door. "Come," is the reply. "Here Sir, I've finished the assignment." "You're a day early Leo." Mr Thompson thumbs through the pages and comments, "well done. It looks very neat. I'll look forward to reading it." Leo leaves Mr Thompson's office with a satisfied look on his face. Thinking it was just like snatching success out of the jaws of defeat. School's going to be a breeze while I can use the pyramid thingy.

The timing of this statement is ironic, as he spots Fridge heading in his direction. Quickly, Leo ducks around the corner and makes for the sanctuary of the Library and returns the reference books he borrowed. For most of the day Leo manages to keep out of trouble and for some reason, can concentrate a lot easier than over the past few days.

The day passes without incident and Leo is eager to head home and explore the 'pyramid thingy' some more. He's wishing the bus would come soon, as it's later than usual. On his mind is the thought, there's more to the place than what I've found so far. I can't wait to check it out. Finally, the bus pulls in and Old-grouch-face is grouchier than usual.

"Look you kids get off my back. It's not my fault it's late. There's been some trouble on the main road during the last trip. It's thrown the whole timetable out." Leo sits down and pulls out his latest Sci-fi novel and begins reading. Leo is almost a third of the way through the book as the bus nears his stop. The bus stops suddenly in a line of traffic. Everyone stands up to see what is happening down the road. Then a passenger at the front suggests, "It must be some sort of accident, but I can't see the police or tow trucks."

Leo puts his book away and is peering between bobbing heads to see what is going on. The traffic begins to move again at a trickle. As the bus nears Leo's stop, he gets up and goes to the front, standing next to the driver. Through the windscreen, Leo can see the area opposite his home has been cordoned off. Across the track to Henderson's quarry is navy blue and white chequered plastic tape with the words, 'Caution Crime Scene', written on it.

Seeing the tape, Leo feels sick in the stomach. He jumps to all sorts of conclusions. Thinking, oh my God they're found the doorway. Maybe something has come out of the well or maybe some other kid has fallen in there. I can't believe it, just when I was going to check out the rest of the place and now this. It's not frigging fair! As Leo gets off the bus, he sees some of the neighbours standing on the side of the road. "Hey you guys, do you know what's going on?" They all talk excitedly at once.

"We dunno. The cops say a murderer is on the loose near the quarry. We reckon that's a 'BS' story. You tell us why there are army vehicles and the strange looking black van over there?" Leo has to find out if his secret has been uncovered. Handing his school bag to one of the neighbours and jumping up and down on the spot, he whispers, I'm busting for a leak. "I'll be back in a minute."

As Leo leaves the group another big black van arrives. It too has blacked out windows and strange looking aerials bristling from it. The van veers off the road and comes to a sudden stop in a cloud of dust on the quarry track. Everyone cheers, "Bloody Hoon!" A tall man in a black suit, sporting mirror sunglasses climbs out of the van. He stares at the cheering group, turns his back and walks off down the track.

While everyone is distracted, Leo makes a dash for the bush. Using his hunting skills learnt on the farm chasing rabbits. He runs crouching low through the scrub next to the road. Expertly and quietly moving through the bush, he ducks when he hears voices, dropping to his hands and knees. Crawling lizard-like, he closes in on the area where two men are standing. Leo crawls up to a tree and lies hidden behind it. He lifts his head cautiously. There are two men dressed in military uniforms, arms folded, talking in the middle of the quarry track.

In the shadow of Mt Fielden further up the track, another drama is unfolding. Special armed forces are conducting a grid search of the area. They had arrived earlier, via the coast road in military buses. Two soldiers from a special-forces group have been detailed to check the old ruin and surrounding bush. While one soldier is checking out the old ruin. The second one is patrolling the overgrown garden area, around the ruin. The soldier checking the ruin leans over a low part of the wall to check inside the ruin.

Spotting something he scrambles over the wall. Kicking the rope ladder Leo has hidden under some rubbish, he shouts. "There's nothing unusual here, just a bit of rope from some kid's rope swing." The other soldier shouts back, "there's an old limestone well over here." Both men meet up next to the well.

One of them places his foot on top of the wall, while the other complains, "what sort of mission is this? The orders say, do a recon of this area and report anything unusual. But we don't even know what we're supposed to be looking for?" The other soldier shakes his head, responding, "It's pretty pathetic if you ask me. How can you find something, when we don't know what they've lost?"

"Search me," says the soldier as he shrugs his shoulders and grins. The other one nods in agreement, "yeah I get it. Search me. Ha, ha, very funny. The way things are going, the only thing unusual to report at the debriefing, will be the bloody stupidity of this exercise." The soldier, with his foot on top of the wall, takes out his water flask and wipes his forehead on the sleeve of his combat fatigues.

Suddenly, the flask slips out of his grasp and bounces onto the wall. The cap flips off and falls into the well, under the tree branch. The soldier cries out, "what the...," as the flask drops onto the sand. Water spurts out onto the ground. Swearing as he picks up the flask, "F... it! The top's missing and now there's sand all over it." He kicks the sand around with his boot, trying to find the cap. "I didn't see it fall, can you see it?"

The second soldier points towards the well, "maybe it's fallen on that side. Why don't you move this big branch and have a look?" He starts pulling on the branch. However, it's hooked up on the inside of the limestone wall. He grunts as he strains on the branch. He stops for a moment as his radio earpiece crackles. The other soldier places his hand instinctively up to his earpiece and comments, "that's good, looks like the search has been called off. Let's get back to the bus."

The soldier holding the branch continues pulling at the dead tree branch until the other one interjects, "what a total waste of time this is. Leave it and let's get out of here!" He lets go of the branch and picks up the flask and throws it into the well, making eye contact with the other soldier for approval he shouts, "this might as well join the cap too. At least I know what's missing eh!"

Meanwhile, Leo is oblivious to how close the soldiers have come to discovering his secret. He listens intently to the men in uniform on the quarry track. Moments later they're approached by the tall man in the black suit and mirror sunglasses. He announces his arrival in a confident, broad American accent. "Afternoon gentlemen, I'm Charles Byrd. But all my friends call me Chucky." The older of the two men dressed in uniform, answers. "I didn't realise you guys had any friends." The younger man is curious, "Why. Who does he work for?" Chucky resenting the luke-warm response replies, "now, now you guys. We're supposed to be on the same side. At least do me the courtesy of introducing yourselves."

"My apologies," concedes the older man. "This is Major Brett Paull of DSD - the Australian Defence Signals Directorate and I'm Colonel Malcolm Smith of DIO - the Defence Intelligence Organisation, please call me Mal."
"Anyway, what's all the fuss about," quizzes Major Paull.
"Your Echelon, 'SIGINT' facility at Pine Gap has intercepted a signal. Our satellites have confirmed this is the location of the emanation. We have asked the local Boys-in-blue to keep things under control. They're using the narrative of an escaped felon in this area. We need to keep this thing contained."

"But what sort of emanation are we talking about," asks Col. Smith. "We ran a check on the signal through the Lab computers ...put it this way, it ain't one of yours and it certainly ain't one of ours," Chuck responds cryptically. "Then what is it?"
"The point is, we haven't been able to match the type of energy spike it produced to anything here on this planet. Our Guys managed to decode the signal, using a supercomputer. It contains six symbols.

They're nothing like anything we've seen before." Then Major Paull, without looking up, slowly raises his right index finger and points it skywards. "You don't mean what I think you mean."

"Yep," nods Chuck. "We think it might be Extra-Terrestrial in origin. So far, all we've found is a large magnetic anomaly coming from under that big hill over there, which appears natural. Whatever sent the signal must have stealth capabilities. Our satellites have not been able to detect any unusual targets or activity in this region. So it has more than likely moved on by now."

"Why six symbols?" Major Paull asks. "A good question, I'll show you using a couple of sticks." Chucky moves off the track and finds a long thin stick, which he breaks in two. Grabbing his chewing gum out of his mouth, he demonstrates. "Okay, the gum's going to be a point in space."

Crossing the two sticks, he glues them to the gum, like a cross. "There. That's four ends right. But look, it only forms a two- dimensional plane. What you need is another stick running at ninety degrees to the horizontal one. He moves off the track again and finds another twig. "See. That makes six ends or coordinates, right.

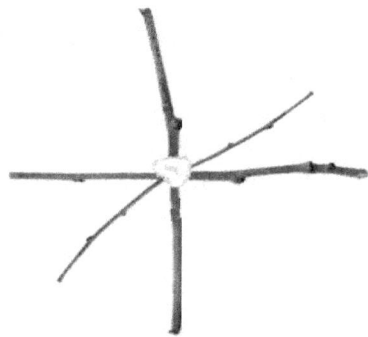

We think who or whatever sent the signal is broadcasting its location. It takes six coordinates to get a precise fix on a point in space."

"So what happens now?" asks Major Paull, moving his stance. "We're packing up. Our experts think whatever is under the hill, is nothing more than a geological phenomenon…it's too large for anything else and your special forces guys haven't found anything, either."

The men shake hands and walk off down the track towards their vehicles. Leo is relieved. His secret is safe, for now. However, it leaves Leo very concerned. Thinking, who's the American and who does he work for - he never answered that question? I bet he's with one of those secret Black Ops groups that crack's a mention in my Sci-fi books. Anyway, who'd have a name like Chucky Byrd?"

Leo is pleased with himself. Thinking, how cool is this. I get to spy on the military without them even knowing. I must be the cause of all this fuss when I opened the door. But it also leaves Leo puzzled, with so many unanswered questions. I wonder why it sent a signal. Where's it going and who's it going to? Leo rolls over and leans with his back up against the tree, contemplating all of the possible scenarios. Jolting back to reality, he mutters under his breath. "Hey, I'd better get back to the road, before someone spots me." Carefully retracing his steps and looking before crossing the road, he finds all of the vehicles have gone. Only the local residents are still standing where he had left them.

As he approaches the group and picks up his backpack, he notices Dani is with them. She immediately breaks away from the group and runs over to him. "Leo, Leo! Where have you been? I thought they must've caught you."
"Shoosh Dani you'll tell everyone! It's okay. They found nothing. I'll tell you all about it, but not here."
"Leo, do you want to come back to my place?"
"Nah, your folks might be home. We'll go back to my place. My folks won't be home for ages."

They leave the group still arguing over what the military were looking for near the quarry. The excitement just fuels the quarry's reputation for being the target for crazy and spooky stories. Little did they suspect the real truth behind the stories.

Back at Leo's place and letting themselves in, Leo heads straight for the refrigerator, as usual. He pulls out the cordial and cold water bottle. Then in an apologetic tone, "there's not much to eat. Mum hasn't come home with the shopping yet. How about we have a peanut butter 'sambo', instead?" But the true situation is the Shepherds don't have the money to keep lots of fancy food in the house.

"Oh cool, I like peanut butter. I'm not allowed to have it at home. Dida says it's rubbish food, but come on Leo tell me what's going on, will you?"

"Oh, that's right. Yeah, I snuck up on these three military guys. Well two of them were in uniform, the other one was an American from the NSA or something like that."
"Oh my God Leo, this stuff with the well and the pyramid is getting really scary. Did you find out what they were doing there?"

Leo, proud of his achievement and not thinking of the risks answers, "Well it's like this. When we opened the door it must have sent off some sort of signal. The American said a spy facility called 'Ecky-long', or something like that, picked up the signal and you know the rest."
"No, I don't. "What about the signal?"
"I guess it must be going to Extra-Terrestrials. Well, it's what the American guy reckons."

Dani is agitated, "Hey! You never said anything about aliens before, and you want me to go back in there? Don't you think we should call the police or someone about this?"
"No way! It's 'my' secret and you're not to tell anybody unless I say so. Remember we have a pact." Leo points in the direction of Henderson's quarry. "I'm not sure what the signal is for and nor are they. It must be going to whoever put it there. Isn't this getting exciting?" Dani has a horrified look on her face. "You won't be smiling if this thing goes pear-shaped. Leo, you're a 'Budala'. You have no idea what you're getting yourself into. Count me out!" Leo screws up his face. "What's a Buddha?" Frustrated with Leo's attitude, Dani shouts, "Budala - Budala, not Buddha. It means you're a stupid idiot. Stupid! My parents use that word when they think I'm not listening and being stupid."

Now Leo is annoyed. "I am not being stupid. Just because you're a scaredy cat, I'm not missing out on a once-in-a-lifetime chance to be famous, plus YOLO." Mockingly Dani replies, "famous, Huh! Try shouting 'YOLO' while getting fried by little green men." She crosses two fingers from each hand, adding: "#FriedFarmboy."
"Says who? And, don't call me that."

"Leo, you're not going to listen to me, so I'm going home. Thanks for the drink and the sandwich." Although Leo doesn't want her to go, he's determined not to back down - especially to a girl. So he holds open the door without saying another word. Dani walks past Leo and lifts her left shoulder with a 'huh' sound and flicks her long locks away from her eyes as if to say… stuff you. Leo remains motionless, with a bemused look on his face as he passively watches Dani walks down the driveway. Under his breath, he re-affirms to himself, "girls who need's them?"

Later on, Leo has had time to think somewhat more about the events of the day. Despite being peeved off with Dani's negative attitude, Leo realises her concerns make sense. Even though he doesn't want to admit it, some of the shine of his secret seems to be wearing off. Thinking, I guess it was a pretty close thing. I'd better calm down a bit. Maybe I should stay away for a few days and cool it for a while. They might be watching the place. You never know they might decide to come back. What about the signal, maybe someone or something else might turn up. Who knows?

Leo watches television until he hears his mother coming up the driveway. Jumping up, he opens the front door for her. "Hi Leo my pet, thanks for that, you're a real gentleman - how was your day dear, I hope it was better than mine was? By the way, what's all the fuss down the road? I noticed some of the neighbours talking in a group and pointing across the road to the quarry."
"They said the police were looking for someone in the quarry, but they didn't find them."
"Why, was someone reported missing?"
"How should I know Mum, I was at school. Ask the neighbours they always know everything that goes on around here."

"Leo, that's enough! I don't like your tone." I'm tired too you know, so let's just drop it."
"Sorry. Can I make you a cup of tea?"
"That would be nice dear. I'll go and change out of my work gear and have a sit-down." No sooner had Linda come back into the kitchen Leo enquires, "what's for dinner, Mum?"
"Good God. Give me a break! I only just walked in the door. Can't I even have a sit down for five 'effing' minutes?"

"S-o-r-r-y," hisses Leo. He leaves the kitchen in a huff and heads for his room. He picks up his school bag, remembering he has homework.
He can't rely on the underground complex to get it done quickly. Sitting down on his bed he decides to get stuck into the homework to take his mind off things.

Leo is engrossed in his work when his bedroom door opens and is interrupted by Bryan leaning up against the doorframe. "How's the homework coming along, son?"
"I've nearly finished, Dad."
"That's good, 'cos dinner's on the table. So go and wash up straight away, before it gets cold." Sitting down to dinner, Bryan recounts, "Guess what, customers coming into the garage were telling me something strange was going across the road at Henderson's quarry."

"Yes Bryan, I know. All the neighbours were out there pointing towards the quarry. Leo had heard someone had told the Police a missing person had fallen down the quarry. Yet the police didn't find anything."
"M-u-m, I didn't say that. All I said was the police were looking for someone in the quarry." Bryan interjects, "that's not what I heard. I was told an escaped killer was loose in the area of the quarry and the whole place was cordoned off, while they searched. But, I don't understand why the army people were there, as well?"

Leo is enjoying the moment, because he knows the real truth, while the stories are getting better all the time. So he decides to add more to the pile. "Some of the neighbours think the escaped killer story is all BS, as there were more military people there than police. They reckon the police were just directing traffic and keeping spectators out."

"You seem to know an awful lot. What do you think they were doing there?" Leo replies in a joking tone, "I reckon they must have seen a flying saucer in the quarry."
"Flying saucers! This story is getting more and more bizarre. You and your damn Sci-fi books - it's all rubbish. They only exist in your imagination. And, they're not going to help you get through life, either. I blame Gramps for putting such notions into your head and getting you caught up in this Sci-fi crap."

"It's not crap and it's nothin' to do with Gramps. You're always blaming stuff on him," shouts Leo as he jumps up from the table. He retreats to the sanctuary of his bedroom. Leo can hear Linda shouting, "that's enough Bryan! It's not fair taking your frustrations out on Leo like that. I'm tired too you know. All I want is some peace and quiet at the table."

Emotionally upset, she too storms out of the kitchen and off to the bedroom, slamming the door. Leo can hear Bryan muttering loudly. There's a loud whump as his fist hits the table, which makes Leo jump. Picking up his Sci-fi novel, Leo can't concentrate and in frustration throws it across the room.

Upset and angry, he stays in his room out of the way for the rest of the evening. With nothing else to do, he finishes off the last of his homework. Next morning, Leo is woken up by a hand shaking his arm. "Whoa, uh, wha... what's going on?"
"It's okay Leo, it's me." Bryan stiffly bends down to Leo's level. "Look I stuffed up big time last night. I was out of line with what I said and didn't really mean it about Gramps and all. You have to understand things have been pretty tough lately for Mum and me. Will you let her know I have apologised to you? She locked me out of the bedroom last night and I slept on the lounge. I'm really in the doghouse. So what can I say, I'm really sorry."

Bryan stands and groans as he straightens his back. "That lounge is uncomfortable. I've got to open the garage now, so I'll see you tonight. Don't forget will you?"
"No, I won't forget," agrees Leo, feeling a little uneasy and thinking, boy that's Karma for you. He got what he deserved, especially for the way he carried on.

Leo falls back to sleep and awoken again by the curtains being drawn back and sunlight streaming in through the window. This time it's Linda and she sits down on the end of Leo's bed, "are you awake Leo?"
"I am now." Lifting his head off the pillow, he peers through squinting eyes at the bright light. "Do I have to get up yet?"
"Not just yet Leo, I've come in a little earlier to talk to you about what Dad said last night."

Leo interrupts, "funny about that, Dad came in earlier. He said he was really sorry for the way he acted…and he's got a sore back from sleeping on the lounge. Did you lock him out of the bedroom?" Linda, with a sheepish smile on her face, "yes I did."
"Well serves him right too, for having a go at me and Gramps like that." Linda moves uncomfortably on the foot of the bed and defends Bryan, "I know it isn't right. But you have to understand he's under a lot of pressure right now and doesn't do well in the communicating department. Leo interjects, "you got that right." Linda continues, "being brought up on a farm your Dad was taught to be tough and to take whatever comes, without getting emotional about it all.

You know his mother died when he was young. Things like the death of an animal on a farm are an everyday occurrence. But not when it's personal like… especially when it's your own flesh and blood. He just doesn't know how to deal with Michael's death and I guess he blames it on Gramps. He also feels responsible for losing the farm. You know Gramps worked so hard to build up and he can't bring himself to talk to Gramps about it."

Leo sits up and adjusts the pillow, "you mean all that 'emo' stuff you girls are always going on about?"
"Yes, more or less." Linda stands up and looks at her watch. "Look I have to get ready to go to work. I'm glad you understand now, so don't be too hard on your poor Dad." Leo stretches back in his bed, his hands behind his head thinking over what his mother has said.

Like a clap of thunder, it dawns on him, that's why Dad is always blaming Gramps, cos he feels responsible. Jeez, I'm doing exactly the same sort of thing, except it's towards girls. All except Dani of course, she's different. Leo gets up and busily gets ready for school a little earlier. He wants to stand out the front of his place and see if anything is going on over the road. Leo walks out the front and wanders down to the letterbox. But it's quiet as usual. Only the birds are busily darting around, hunting for breakfast.

As nothing much is happening, he heads down to the bus stop to continue his Sci-fi novel. Sitting in the bus shelter he can feel the early morning sun on his face. Thinking spring has finally sprung and the days getting longer, so he shouts, "c-o-m-e o-n summer."

He settles down and becomes absorbed by the novel. The story is about a boy who meets an ET. How they become friends and tell him stories of the ET's home planet and all about their life. Leo begins to daydream. Thinking, it would be 'so' mad, meeting an ET and learn all about their life and stuff. Yet so far there's been no sign of anyone. I wonder if it will happen.

Maybe they use it to teleport back and forth. Sort of like; 'Beam me up Scottie' and going to all sorts of strange places. I could run a travel shop for out-of-this-world travel and call it Leo's Starsk8ing Tours. That would be wicked. Just then he hears the bus changing down gears as it nears the bus stop. Leo jumps up and grabs out his change, so as not to cross swords with Old-grouch-face.

But as the doors flop open there's a lady driver on board. She has a mop of fuzzy red hair, with a cap perched precariously on top, which Leo thinks, is good for a laugh. But is curious, "where's Old- grouch-face today?" She has a wry grin on her face as she responds, "you mean Ernest. He's got hip problems and having it checked." Leo just grunts and sits down to continue his book, thinking Old-grouch- face should have his head and attitude checked out as well.

The next few days for Leo are a real drag. He notices that he's pre-occupied with watching for any signs of activity across the road near the quarry and it's making him nervous. Impatient, he resolves to go back to the well over the weekend. Finally one morning Leo wakes and yawns loudly as he realises that, it's Saturday. Thinking, now I can check out the well and see if everything is still okay. Mum's has just gone off to work and Dad's at the garage. Still half asleep, Leo climbs out of bed. He goes into the kitchen and packs some food and cordial into his backpack. He changes into his old board shorts and a tee shirt and races down the driveway.

However, common sense overcomes his enthusiasm. Thinking, instead of ducking straight across the road, it might be safer if I walk past all of the houses and cross the road where I'm out of sight. Leaving the driveway he kicks a stone along the edge of the road soccer-fashioned until he's interrupted by his name being called. Stopping, he looks around and spots Mr Mason in his front yard. "Hi there, Mr Mason."

"Off again I see. I know it's none of my business, but I know what you've been doing." Leo is shocked at Mr Mason's bombshell.

Thinking, how could he know? I've always made sure nobody was around when I go across the road. Defensively Leo replies, "I don't know what you're talking about Mr Mason."

"Oh I think you do. I've seen you."

"Seen me doing what?"

"Look I'll say it again. I know it's none of my business, but I just wanted to warn you that sneaking over the road with that Danicka Jerovich might set folks tongues wagging. I was young once too, you know. So I reckon to go for it son. But you need to be discrete, got it."

"Leo is relieved and smartly responds, "You won't tell anyone will you?"

"Listen son, when I've got something on my mind, I will tell you face to face. I don't go round spreading stories, like some other folks around here. Anyway, I'm holding you up. You'd better not keep her waiting," chuckles Mr Mason with a wink and a nod. Leo, responds, "thanks Mr Mason." Mr Mason raises his second finger and taps his lip. "Remember, Mum's the word." Leo nods and under his breath mutters, "stupid old sticky-beak."

He continues down the road until he's out of sight of the houses. Carefully looking around to see if anyone is there, he scampers across the road. Thinking, I must be psychic. I must've known someone might be watching. For a minute there, I thought that Old sticky-beak was on to me. He had me going. Least now I've got a cover story. But I'd better not tell Dani that.

Leo takes a shortcut towards the quarry track to avoid being followed. He mops his brow with his hand, flicking off the sweat. Thinking, I'm glad I'm only wearing my board shorts, it's really overcast and muggy out here. His eyes dart everywhere as he cautiously makes his way to the old ruin. Nervously, Leo looks around the old overgrown garden, before retrieving his rope ladder. He stops suddenly, noticing a lot of large boot marks on the ground around the ruin. Checking the well he finds more boot marks, but everything seems untouched. Dragging the rope ladder from the ruin he ties the rope off to one end and walks the rope around the trunk of the Bluegum.

Chapter 4
How am I going to explain something like this?

As he bends down to pick up the other end of the rope ladder he hears a shout. Leo jumps what seems to him about 2 metres into the air. As his feet touch the ground again, he swings around to see Dani off in the distance waving to him. As she approaches, Leo has mixed emotions of fright and relief, "frigging hell! You gave me such a scare, sneaking up on me like that." Dani self-righteously retorts, "I wasn't sneaking up on you." Leo questions, "well, what are you doing here anyway?" "I saw you sneaking across the road and was worried - you know, after all that stuff on Monday." Leo throws the rope down and in disgust says, "typical! You can't keep anything to yourself around here." Dani puts her hands on her hips, "what's that supposed to mean?"

"Never mind, Dani. There's nothing to worry about. I can look after myself. But, since you're here, how about helping me with the rope ladder?" Dani shrugs her shoulders, at what seems a contradictory statement. Thinking that, in one short sentence, he's saying he doesn't need my help and then asking for help - maybe it's just a guy thing.

Leo grabs hold of the large dead tree branch, but it seems to be stuck. Tugging firmly the branch comes away unexpectedly, leaving Leo sprawling on the ground. Dani laughs, "I thought you said you didn't need any help. Looks who's got their bum pointing in the air. "Arr shut your cake hole," responds Leo.

He laughs too, as it helps to ease the tension between them. But, as he gets to his feet and dusts off the sand, his eyes catch a flash of reflected sunlight from the floor of the well. Climbing on top of the limestone wall of the well, he takes a closer look. "Dani, look what's down there." Dani moves closer, "what is it?" "It's something made of polished metal. Let's put the ladder down so I can check it out."

Leo climbs down and retrieves the object. As he climbs out he announces, "It's a water canteen." Turning the aluminium flask over he notices a stamped insignia of a sword in between two eagle wings and a banner below it, which reads - *who dares wins.* "Hey, this belongs to a soldier from the Special Air Services - you know, the SAS."

"Wow, Leo that's ever so close. They nearly found your secret door the other day."
"Nah. they weren't going to find the door anyway. I reckon it's only visible when it wants to. You come down and see for yourself."
"No way after what's happened. But now that I've seen that, I'll hang around for a while in case someone comes back, okay. Climbing down the rope ladder monkey-like, Leo drops to the floor. "Hey! What's this doing here?" Leo bends down and picks up the cap belonging to the water flask. Placing it in his board shorts, he realises that they were much closer than he's prepared to admit.

Turning his attention to the smooth silvery blue walled structure, Leo waves his hand over the area. The door begins to materialise. He still jumps back and mutters, "can't quite get used to this. It seems to appear out of 'no-wheresville'." Placing his hand on the circular disk, the door opens with a pssst sound. Respectfully, Leo removes his joggers and cautiously makes his way along the passage under Mt Fielden.

As he enters the pyramid through the archway, he again is in awe of the golden light. Walking to the right-hand side as he looks up, he stops in the centre of the second symbol. Suddenly there's a swishing sound as the floor moves. Leo gasps and jumps backwards.

The section of the floor he was standing on opens up. A ramp slowly descends to another chamber below, as if to invite inspection. Leo's hesitant, at first. Curious, he nervously edges his way down the ramp in slow deliberate steps. His eyes darting everywhere, his body ready to bolt at the first sign of movement. On reaching the bottom there's another chamber lit up like the main structure.

Leo surveys the room and his eyes nearly pop out of his head. They come to rest on a gleaming jewel encrusted urn, made of gold. It's sitting on a white pillar, at about waist height. The pillar has the same symbol as the ramp floor. Next to this is another white pillar, which has a crystal bowl and jewels of different colours embedded in it. The next pillar has two exquisite golden goblets with a large gem embedded in the middle of the stem. In all, Leo counts six white pillars, but the last one is different.

On it sits a rough looking smokey coloured crystal. Gazing at the riches he has found, his mind races with all sorts of ideas as to what he will do. Thinking, I can help my 'Olds' out and buy them a big house and go travelling around the world. I can even buy a bookshop. He picks up the jewel-encrusted urn and examines it closely. Thinking, boy I bet this is worth heaps. It's got polished and cut gemstones of different colours and shapes under the rim too.

He hears a voice and quickly puts the urn back in place. The voice calls out in a nervous tone, "Leo are… are you there? "Moving to the bottom of the ramp Leo looks up. Dani is at the top of the ramp. She is bent over, with hands resting on her knees peering down through the floor. "Dani, I thought you didn't want to come down?"
"This place still gives me the creeps. You know like that low humming sound. But, I just had to find out what was happening."
"Come and look at all this stuff. It's got to be worth a mint!"

Picking up the urn, Leo's about to explain how he can help his mother and father out, by buying them a new business, when he realises one fact he has completely overlooked. "Ooohhh typical," he complains, putting the urn back down. "How am I going to explain something like this? Nobody will believe I found this. And even if I could sell it, they'd want to know where it came from. So there goes that idea - what an absolute bummer."

Dani admires all of the artefacts. "Don't you think this is strange? This stuff is just sitting here. "I dunno, I guess it's a bit weird." Dani turns to the right and points to the last of the white pillars, "what about that one over there?"
"You mean that oval rock."

"Yeah, you know what Leo? I think this is some kind of test to see what you take out of here."

"Jeez, I didn't even think of that. I was so gobsmacked by all this stuff." Leo is beginning to realise that this is no game. Nor is it a fantasy he's acting out in one of his books. "You know Dani, that's the most important thing you have said to me so far. You're right; I have to choose very carefully. Just like Indiana Jones in that movie The Last Crusade. "What do you reckon, this rock thing?"

Picking up the oval-shaped crystal he examines it and juggles it up and down in his hand, before shoving it into his pocket. As they both climb up the ramp and back to the centre of the pyramid. The ramp slides shut. "What do we do now, Leo?" Leo points, "Dani just go over there to the right and stand on that symbol next to this one."

"So what's that supposed to do?"

"You'll see." Dani half skips over to the third symbol and looks at Leo as she jumps onto the symbol.

After a pause, there's a swishing sound followed by a scream as she jumps backwards. Leo chuckles as she grabs hold of Leo's arm tightly and makes excited panting sounds. The ramp slowly descends to the chamber below. Dani protests, "you knew that you arsehole," elbowing Leo in the ribs." Leo grimaces, "ouch, careful." They both bend down trying to peer into the chamber below. Dani pushes Leo towards the ramp, "you go first, 'cos I'm scared."

"I'm not. It's been here waiting to be discovered - that's what I reckon."

As Leo enters the chamber, he observes that the walls and floor are the same coppery gold colour as the main structure. However, this time there's a series of eight white square tiles lined up in a chequered pattern on the floor. "Come on Dani, it's safe," assures Leo. Dani wanders down and points, "I wonder what those white tiles are for?" Leo raises his arms, "I dunno, but they all got these oval grooves in them and see how the tiles have a gap between them.

You know what it reminds me of something. I wonder what it... oh, that's it, the eight spades in a pack of cards." Dani points at the first tile. "That first one has one groove, that next one has two." Bending over, she moves down the outer line of tiles and points at each tile counting, "that one's four, this one's eight."

Leo does the same down on the other side, "five in this one, seven here, and the ones in the centre are three and six." Leo makes eye contact with Dani, "so they're all numbered, but it doesn't mean..." Leo stops mid-sentence. Three white pillars rise silently out of the floor at the back of the room. "Hey, they're got coloured crystals in them. Let's check them out," shouts Dani eagerly.

Turning around Dani skips over to the first bowl and picks up a red coloured crystal and examines it. "I like the red colour and the oval shape is really cool." Leo picks up a crystal from the second bowl, "Dani these ones are light green. But this third bowl has smokey-grey ones. But there's not as many as the first two bowls. That means they somehow fit on the tiles, I bet you." Taking the crystal they are holding, both kneel down to place the crystal into the tile with two grooves. "I was right they fit alright," boasts Leo. Dani's looks at Leo, "well then smarty, what goes where?"

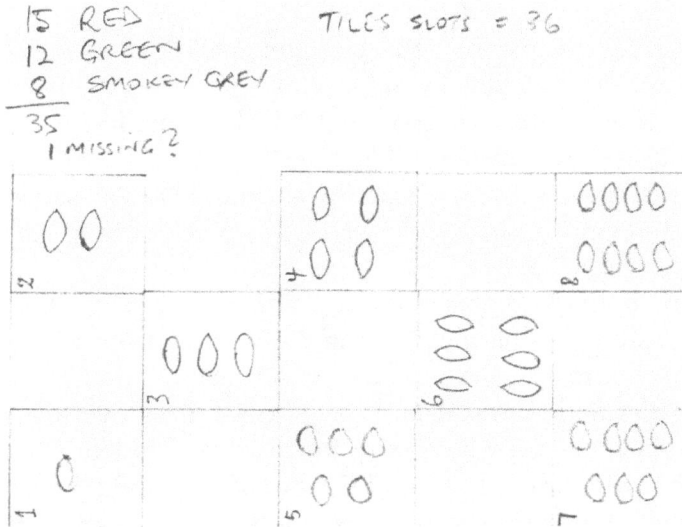

"I love puzzles. This is going to be wicked - breaking the code. Do us a favour will you and get your sketchpad so we can work it out? While Dani goes back up to the main chamber to get her sketchpad, Leo busily counts the coloured crystals. "Oh good, you're back. Can you write this down," commands Leo.

"How about please," reminds Dani. "Okay, please write down 14 red ones, 13 green ones and 8 smokey-grey ones. That is 35 in all. While you sketch the tile layout...p-l-e-a-s-e, I'll place these around and see what happens." As Dani is just finishing the last line of the tile layout, Leo shouts, "Hey! There's one missing?"
"Are you sure? Let me count them."

As Dani counts them using her fingers, she too agrees, "You're right. Maybe the first tile doesn't have one."
"This makes it harder than I thought. I don't understand why it's one short, let's check the bowls again." Leo moves back over to the bowls. "Nope, there's none left."

"Leo, I know we've got plenty of time down here to solve this, but I'm scared someone might find us here. Don't you think we should work it out somewhere else and come back later?"
"You're right Kiddo. Up there for thinking and down there for dancing."
"Leo you're weird. Where do you get those sayings?"
"I'm not weird. I was paying you a compliment."
"That's a funny way of showing it."
"Suit yourself. Why don't we go up to Mt Fielden and have a look around up there and see if we can crack this thing."
"Yeah, I think I need some fresh air. I'm starting to feel closed in down here."

They both walk back up the ramp and leave the chamber. Dani cautiously pokes her head out of the well, pausing to listen for any sound. Looking around, she announces, "It's all quiet up here." They hide the rope ladder and place the large tree branch back over the gap in the well floor. As they make their way towards Mt Fielden, Leo tosses the shiny cap he found into the air and decides to stop and try it out. "Yep, it fits," placing the flask back into his backpack to keep as a trophy.

As they walk up the track Leo's right hand accidentally bumps Dani's hand. They look at each other and nervously reach out and hold each other's hand. Walking along the quarry track to Mt Fielden they're in a world of their own, swinging each other's hand like an elephant's trunk.

It's the first time that Leo feels he belongs and no longer a nobody. He sums things in his mind; yep I'm so lucky to have such a friend I can rely on. For him, this is a new experience, given that in the past he has been let down by both family and so-called friends when things had got really tough.

Having reached the turnoff to the quarry, Dani asks, "Leo, let's go check out the quarry, I haven't been there yet." Leo shakes his head no and explains, "believe me. It's not worth it, Dani. There's nothing there except junk. It's just another place for idiots to dump stuff." "Some people are real jerks messing up the environment, aren't they Leo? I bet if we dumped our rubbish on their doorstep they would really spew."

Leo just nods, preferring to concentrate on the moment with Dani, rather than worry about things he can't do anything about. Shortly after this, Leo motions for them to leave the track. They start picking their way through thick bush, the flat ground giving away to a steeper climb.

Both are huffing and puffing as they reach the summit of Mt Fielden. "Wow, this place is really wicked. Those shade-sails look really cool. You can see everything from here," says Dani breathlessly. Leo takes a deep breath and replies, "yeah the seating looks cool, but trees would be more natural than shade sails. By the way, how come you haven't been here before?"

85

"I'm not allowed to come here on my own as Dida and Mama are always working. Of my God Leo, the view's breathtaking. Everything looks so small from up here even that ship. Look at our place. It's tiny. Yours is over there," points Dani. Spotting an eagle overhead, she has the urge to hold out her arms eagle-like. Closing her eyes, she imagines she is soaring over the coastline. She opens her eyes again as if they belong to an eagle.

Looking out over the ocean, she can see the white caps of the waves and can feel the rush of the wind pushing against her body and tearing at her hair. She smells the salty air and takes a deep breath and sighs, "aaahhh." Wheeling around as she looks up the coast, then across to the bushland area and back to the market gardens. "The paddocks look like a patchwork quilt, don't you think Leo…Wow, it's really cool up here." Whirling around again, Leo has to duck underneath one of Dani's wings, "Hey watch it, Babe!" She laughs and stumbles as she whirls around again, falling into Leo's arms.

They both fall awkwardly to the ground. "Oops, OMG I feel dizzy now. I wouldn't make a very good eagle, would I?" They both sit there making the most of an intimate moment with Leo admitting, "Yeah, I've done the eagle bit too. You just can't help it up here. It's eagle territory, that's for sure."

Untangled themselves, they choose a shady spot under the shade sails and pull out their water bottles, to quench their thirst. That is until Leo starts squirting Dani with his water bottle. Shrieking, Dani dashes off and hides behind a navigation pylon and squirts Leo as he sneaks past. As Leo tries to grab her water bottle, the top comes off in Leo's hand and spills all over him.

Dani puts her hand over her mouth and laughs in loud shrieks. "Ha, ha you asked for that." Leo is in a playful mood and decides to play the fool by tipping the contents of his bottle over his head. Thinking it is now safe, she moves closer to Leo. However, Leo shakes his head like a wet shaggy dog. Beads of water fly off in all directions, catching Dani by surprise. "Aaahhh, you scumbag you got me, wait till I get you." Dani takes off after Leo, as they run around the top of the hill.

The chase is short lived as they both collapse panting behind the shaded seating. Once they regain their composure and get their breath back, Dani is the first to speak, "hey that was fun, haven't laughed so much in ages." Leo too puffed to say much replies, "Yeah fully sick!"

They recline on the ground and stare at the blue sky. Leo's thoughts turn to the 'puzzle' room and the sketch Dani has made of the tile layout. It gets him thinking, how come it's one crystal short. I wonder how hard it's going to be to work out. Maybe it's another test or maybe it has some other purpose?

While Leo is lying there, Dani gets up and brings over her backpack. Taking out her sketchbook, she makes a copy for Leo. Writing down the number of crystals and using symbols R, G and S for the three colours. "Here Leo I made you a copy." Leo sits up, "thanks, Dani. Let's see if we can figure it out." They sit there studying the diagrams together, but neither of them has any idea as to how the crystals fit. "Leo I'm getting bored and my brain hurts - you know Maths turns me off. Besides, it's getting late and I have to do guitar practice. I've got to play in our school concert tonight."
"Why don't we use the pyramid, then we can muck around more."
"I don't think that's a good idea, Leo. I'm scared that the more we hang around someone's going to find out. Anyway, if I keep going there people will get suspicious."
Leo replies, "I hear you five-by-five," and mutters under his breath, "yeah, if you only knew."
"Sorry, I didn't get that, Leo?"

"Oh, it's a military term for loud and clear. But I..I wanted to...you know, to spend more time with you." It's a confusing moment for Leo. He's experiencing feelings he has not felt before. He's really calm inside and for a change is at peace and not angry at the world. The problem is that he doesn't want it to end, not just yet. "Sorry, Leo. I've had the best-est time today, but I have to practise for tonight, you know what Dida's like." After seeing Dani safely home, all of the old thoughts and feelings come flooding back again. Leo goes straight to his room and drops his backpack on his bed and decides to change into his tracksuit.

As he dumps his board shorts onto the floor, there's a loud clunk. As Leo glances at the floor, the oval smokey-grey crystal rolls out of his pocket. Leo has a flash. "Of course that's the extra crystal that is missing from the puzzle. Aren't they sneaky buggers? It's the one from that first room. I forgot all about it."

He grabs the diagram out of his backpack and mutters, "this is going to be wicked, there are now 9 smokey-grey ones." Tossing the crystal up and down in his hand, he looks at the numbered square tiles. "Jeez, this ain't going to be easy, they can fit into squares 1 and 8, 3 and 6, 4 and 5 or 2 and 7. But, which two tiles do they belong to?" Leo continues tossing the crystal up and down in his hand. Frustrated he gripes, "Oh, I don't know where these fit. They're all opposite to each other so it could be any of these." Leo is miles away when he hears the phone ring. Racing out of his room, he picks it up, "hello?" It's Dani quite excited about the puzzle. "Leo guess what? While I was doing my practice, I had this thought that maybe the puzzle has a musical connection.

Because there are eight tiles and a scale contains eight notes.
See when I sing, "Doh, Ray, Me, Fah, Soh, Lah, Ti, Doh."
"I don't get any connection. I reckon you're in Lah-Lah land."
"Are you going to listen or what? Because I think it could have something to do with music octaves. You know the 'Doh' at the end is an octave higher than the 'Doh' at the beginning."
"You've lost me. The only 'Doh' I know about makes bread."
Dani is getting frustrated. "Look, Leo. It's the same as taking a piece of string and putting your finger in the middle and halving it. If you twang the half-a-string, the sound of one half is double the original sound. It's the same with numbers, by doubling the original number, like 1+1 = 2 and 2+2 = 4 etc."

"Hang on while I get the diagram." When Leo examines the tiles he can see down one side, numbers 2, 4 and 8. Picking up the phone again, "Dani, you're an Einstein. I'm sure you're on to something. Thanks heaps, I'll check it out and come over later."
"What a bummer. You can't. I've got that dumb concert tonight. Can I ring you after - to see if works?"

"No worries. Good luck with the concert and all that. Break a leg, a finger - whatever it is they say for music concerts." Leo goes back to his room and sitting on his bed, counts out aloud the octave tiles. "That's 2, 4 and 8 down this side. That comes to 14 and matches the number of red ones. That means that these 9 smokey-grey ones must be for tiles 3 and 6. Hot stuff! That's one of those octaves too, 3 + 3 = 6. Cool! I've nearly cracked this thing already. That means that the 13 green ones belong to the ones that are left. Let's see tiles 1, 5 and 7.

I've cracked it. I can't wait to see what's in the next chamber, with only three symbols left. Excited, Leo wonders if Dani will mind if I go and check - have to make sure it's right. Quickly grabbing his backpack Leo drops the crystal into the front zip pocket and dashes enthusiastically out of the house. However, instead of going past Mr Mason's place, Leo decides it might be safer to go the long way around. Thinking, I don't want that old sticky-beak Mr Mason poking his nose in my business. It's probably better if go left along the road and cross further down away from 'Old-eagle-eyes'. I'll have to change my movements otherwise what Dani said might come true.

After trekking back through the bush and across the quarry track, Leo finally makes it to the ruin. He mutters, "Phew, finally got here. Jeez, I'm stuffed from all this walking and running around. I think I'll have a sit down for a breather before I do anything." He sits quietly getting his breath back and listens to the birds chirping and chasing each other in the afternoon sun. Having had a drink and recharged his batteries, Leo hauls out the rope ladder and climbs down the well, after making sure nobody is snooping around.

As usual, the pyramid door materialises on cue. He takes off his runners and grabs his backpack as the door opens. Entering through the archway to the main chamber, Leo is immediately aware of the low humming sound vibrating his skin. He rubs his arm in response to feeling Goosebumps. Standing on the symbol, as Dani had done earlier, Leo is keen to get on with the placement of crystals. A swishing sound alerts Leo that the ramp is about to descend. Leo jumps onto the ramp and rides it to the bottom. Moving around the tiles he removes all of the crystals that they had placed earlier.

Unzipping the front pocket of his backpack he takes out the smokey grey crystal and puts it in his pocket. Gathering up a few red ones, he places those on the tiles with oval slots of 2, 4 and 8. Then he moves some of the green ones onto the 7- slot tile. He finishes off placing the red ones, followed by the rest of the green ones. Leo then places all of the smokey grey ones onto the 3 and 6 slots. Taking the final one out of his pocket, he tosses it into the air.

However pauses before placing it, wondering how come only tiles 2, 4 and 8 and the 3 and 6 tiles are all octave numbers. Yet the 1, 5 and 7 don't match up the same way. Then it comes to him in a flash. Of course, the difference between 2 and 4 and 8 is (2) and (4), a ratio of 1:2. That's the same with 1 and 5 and 7, except it's opposite (4) and (2), a ratio of 2:1. It's all about octaves. As he investigates the numbers further he finds that the adjacent numbers in the tile pattern are either (1) or (2) apart, noticing that 3 for instance, relates to 1, 2, 4 and 5 in a diagonal direction.

He mutters to himself, "wow, this whole thing is amazing and I've cracked it." As he places the last smokey grey crystal he hears a high pitched whistling sound and the light in the room becomes very bright. Leo feels very light-headed and dizzy, at first. His whole body feels as if it's vibrating. Disconcertingly, he begins to feel almost weightless. It reminds him of being in a fast lift.

His heart is racing as if revved up by the sensations. Frightened by the discomfort, he hastily retreats out of the chamber and up the ramp. On reaching the upper level the noises and sensations stop. Even the Goosebumps on his skin have gone altogether. In fact, he feels calm and peaceful, a feeling he rather enjoyed and shouts, "Karumba! That was an adrenalin rush and a half. That was better than doing a couple of Red Bulls," he muses with a grin.

Rubbing his hands he remarks, "okay, let's see what's in the next room and skips quickly to the next symbol. Leo playfully jumps onto the symbol, but there's no reaction. Turning around to face the archway, he decides to try the one on his right. However, that one fails to react too. So he moves along to the next symbol and the ramp slides down to the chamber below. "Ah ha, this must be number four."

Leo skids down the ramp in his socks, in a mixture of excitement and nervous anticipation. However, as he enters the chamber he stops and exclaims, "No, this can't be! There are still two more rooms to go." To his horror the chamber is empty. He throws his backpack back up the ramp in disgust, "Now I'll never find out what's in them." After being in such high spirits from cracking the last puzzle, he's on an emotional roller-coaster ride that's descending rapidly.

Disappointed and disheartened, with nothing but an empty feeling, Leo leaves. As he steps out of the doorway and into the well cavern, he turns and angrily kicks sand into the passage. He mutters under his breath, "Bloody stupid pyramid." Climbing up the rope ladder he doesn't bother to check if anyone is around, before climbing out. However, he thought better of leaving everything, just in case.

He hauls out the rope ladder, dragging it back to the ruin and places the dead branch over the hole in the well floor. That night after dinner, the Shepherds are sitting watching television and all half- asleep from the mesmerising movement of the screen.

That's until a young girl in the movie is having a birthday party. Linda suddenly shouts out, "Hey Leo darling, it's your birthday next Saturday! With all that's been going on, I almost forgot about it." Bryan, slumped in his chair stirs and sits up. "Hells-bells you're absolutely right Linda. What are we going to do for Leo this year?"
"Hey, Mum your right, with everything going on, I had forgotten about it too." Bryan moves uncomfortably in his chair, "I'm really sorry Leo. Money's really tight you know, so a party's out of the question." Leo is so caught up in his secret. Not even a birthday party mattered to him. Commenting, "I don't need a party this year. All I want is a present and get to go and see Gramps."

Linda is about to speak and is interrupted by the phone ringing. Getting up she answers it and waves the phone, "Leo it's for you. It's Dani." Linda put the phone down and looks at Bryan, mouthing the words, "Leo's in love." As Leo picks up the phone he looks over to see his parents whispering away and tickling each other in a playful way. "Hi Dani, can't really talk much. You know, the folks are here. Yes, I managed to crack it. Look I'll tell you more tomorrow.

No, I can't say much…yeah, they're staring at me and doing stupid stuff. No, they're just stirring. By the way, guess what…it's my birthday next Saturday…no my parents can't afford one. But it doesn't matter, so long as I can go and see Grandad and get a few prezzies, I'll be happy…how did the concert go. Were you nervous?"

"Okay. See you tomorrow maybe…what's that, blow you a kiss over the phone? No Way! The folks are looking." Leo turns around with his back to his parents and blows a kiss down the phone and quickly hangs up. To avoid an interrogation, he slips out of the room and heads for his bedroom. He flops down onto his bed and picks up his Sci-fi novel. He reads for a while until he can't keep his eyes open much longer. The following Sunday morning, after breakfast, Leo wanders over to Dani's place. "I'm bored, what do you want to do? Let's go over to the pyramid thingy." Dani screws up her face, "Nah can't be bothered today and I hate that stupid rope ladder. Let's get an ice cream or a Chocy. How's about we go down to your Dad's garage?"
"Well, I guess so. I don't really want to go there. But, it's better than doing nothing." Arriving at the garage, they find Bryan busy in the workshop.

Bryan doesn't seem to want company, so Leo and Dani go off into the shop and pick out a chocolate-coated ice cream and decide to eat it on the way back home. "Leo Shepherd, what a Guts. You nearly finished it in one gulp," observes Dani, as they wander back up the road. Leo leans towards Dani, "can I try your flavour?" Dani pulls her hand away from Leo's shark-like mouth. "No way! You're not getting your bugs all over my ice cream." She then gives him the elbow for good measure. Leo grabs his side, "ouch, what was that for?"
"That's for being a greedy-guts and having unnatural desires for my ice cream. Anyway, changing the subject, what do you want for your birthday?"

"I really would like the new Gameboy, but my folks can't afford one. They're too expensive, with the games included."
"That's too bad. I'm sure your folks will come up with something spesh. By the way, I forgot to ask about the puzzle."
"Yeah, I managed to crack the thing and went back and re-arranged all of the crystals."

Dani stops and has a hurt look on her face. "Hey, that's not fair! I helped you work that thing out and you go off and do it behind my back. That's the thanks I get for helping you."

"But…but you were at the concert. I know I couldn't have figured it out without you. I'm sorry, I had to be sure it would work?"

"Well then, what happened? Not that I really care now."

"I'm not really sure, I think it did something to my body, as I don't get those goosies on my arms any more. But the ramp to the next room opened and there was nothing in there."

"What do you mean nothing there?"

"Yeah, what a complete fizzer and just when things were getting interesting they pull the plug."

"That doesn't make any sense, Leo."

"Come and have a gander yourself, if you don't believe me."

"Well after the way you've carried on, I don't want to go back there, now."

"Suit yourself then," retorts Leo.

"I am! I'm going home to do my music practice. You're the weakest link - Goodbye!" Dani pokes her tongue out and shakes her head as she storms off. While Leo shouts after her, "same to you too, with bells on and stinky dog poo as well."

The following few days for Leo are forgettable. After his tiff with Dani, his secret is no longer keeping his spirits up. It had made his life bearable - now there is only an empty feeling. While Leo's having withdrawal symptoms, he clashes with everyone and seems to draw angry people to himself, without being consciously aware of it.

Like Fridge, who he has successfully avoided in the recent weeks, unfortunately not today. Leo has just come out of the Library as a piece of paper blows past. At the same time Fridge and some of his cronies, just happen to be passing. Fridge jumps in front of Leo blocking his way. "Hey Farmboy pick up that paper you just dropped!" Leo raises himself up to his full height and responds, "It's not mine." Fridge half turns to his mates for support, "hey you guys.

Didn't we just see him drop it?" One of them adds, "Yeah Fridge's right. Sheps you're a frigging litterbug." Fridge glares back at Leo, "see they saw you. Now pick it up F-Boy!"

"No! I didn't drop it." Fridge places his hands on his hips and forcefully states, "you've got two choices Bozo, the easy way or the hard way. Pick it up or I'll make you." Leo's face begins to turn red as anger rises up. Thinking what do I do now? He's having none of this and refuses to back down any longer. However, a little voice inside his head whispers, "don't get angry just pick it up and walk away." Surprised by the voice, Leo picks up the piece of paper. He walks over to the bin and drops it in. He walks away to the shout of, "Farmboy you're gutless," accompanied by noises of a cowering dog.

As Leo leaves the group behind, he hides a 'one-figured salute' in front of himself. But quickly brushes his shirt when Mr Thompson calls out. "Well done Leo. You're not gutless to walk away from the likes of that crew. But even smarter to back off when you're outnumbered like that But, don't worry, they won't get away with it. I've got just the job for that lot." Mr Thompson pats Leo on the shoulder as he turns his attention to Fridge and his mates. This is a rare moment for Leo, like finding an island in an ocean of despair. Despite the difficult week he's having, things change on Saturday as he gets out of bed.

"HAPPY BIRTHDAY TO YOU......."
"Hey, thanks Mum and Dad. You're out of key, though."
They kiss and hug Leo, which makes him feel uncomfortable. They weren't in the habit of doing that since leaving the farm.

Linda points to the kitchen table, "They're yours, go and open them." Leo tears at the paper hoping for the new Gameboy, but one present is a grey Nike Beanie and the other a set of new psychedelic coloured super wheels for his skateboard. Putting on the beanie Leo responds, "Thanks, Mum. Thanks, Dad. I'm a real cool dude, with this on."
"As it's your birthday, I'm going to take you into town to have breakfast at McDonald's and then see Gramps."
"But, don't you have to work today, Mum?"

"No. I've asked for the day off so I can spend time with you and get my hair cut while you're with Gramps." This surprises Leo. Thinking, that's unusual for Mum to take time off. She only ever has her hair done if something special is happening. Anyway, ain't my problem. I just want to go and eat and see Gramps.

They get dressed just as Bryan leaves for the garage, a little later than usual. Leo is really hungry and hoping that the bus is on time. Luckily today, it is. As the Fielden bus nears the stop, Leo notices whose driving and warns, "watch it! It's Old-grouch-face." Linda pays the fare and Old-grouch-face grunts as he closes the door and waits while they find a seat. Sitting down Linda whispers, "Leo that's not nice. You should have more respect." As the bus negotiates its journey into town, Leo's thoughts are on how many McValue meals he can fit in. The bus stops near the restaurant and Leo jumps off first and is almost through the front door, but Linda grabs Leo by the arm. "Leo, it's not very polite to leave a lady behind when you're taking her to a restaurant."
"But it's only McDonald's," he retorts.
"I don't care. You should know better, what's Dani going think, if you act like this – where are your manners?"
"Aw, get off my back will you Mum, it's my birthday."

They go inside and order. Later, Leo finishes by being an absolute pig, much to Linda's disgust. But, because it's his treat she says nothing. Leo waddles out of the restaurant as if he's going to burst. Luckily for him, they have a long walk to the nursing home and can walk off some of the food.

Arriving at the nursing home, Leo waits in the reception area. There's an earnest discussion between Linda and the nursing staff. Leo is expecting them to wheel Gramps out. But the nurse comes back out to say, "Mr Shepherd is bedridden today. He's not really supposed to have visitors today. But he's asked that you wait while we tidy him up for your visit."

A little later the nurse calls out, "okay you can go in now, but he's very tired, so don't stay too long." On entering the ward, Leo can see Gramps propped up by two big pillows.

His old face lights up when he sees them. Raising his good arm, Gramps points in a jerky motion and says weakly, "look everyone, my best mate has come to visit me. It's Leo's birthday today, you know! My body might be tired, but my memory's still sharp."

There are grunts from two of the other residents sharing the room, in acknowledgement. One of the other residents beckons Leo over and shakes Leo's hand. "Happy Birthday, young fella," and reaching into his side drawer, he gives Leo a bag of sweets. Leo is embarrassed, thinking I'm too old for this stuff. He tries to hand them back, but the old guy insists. Gramps waves to Leo. "Come and give your old Gramps a big hug."

Leo has to stand up on a steel rung of the hospital type bed to reach Gramps. Leo can feel how frail he is and careful not to squeeze too hard. Gramps hugs Linda and motions for her to reach into his bedside drawer. As she opens the drawer, the top of a paper bag pops up. "That's it girlie, pull it out for me." Shakely, Gramps opens the paper bag and with difficulty pulls out a number of shiny objects. They make a clinking sound. "Here Leo, I want you to have these. I think you're old enough now to look after them. I wanted to get you something special for your birthday, but I am too old and tired now to get around. So I thought of these they're the most precious thing I have. And you my boy are precious to me. So I want you to keep these medals safe for me."

Leo carefully takes the war medals and holds them up to show Linda. He admires the images stamped on the medals, the multi-coloured fabric on the bar and the line of gold silver and brass medals attached to striped ribbons. With tears welling up in his eyes Leo responds, "I can't take these, they're special. What if I lost them?"

"Leo, I'm not long for this world, so it's important that they go to someone who will value them as much as I do. And that's you, son." Linda, is quietly standing in the background, has watery eyes and blowing her nose with a tissue. It's too emotional for her, so she moves away. "I've got to go. I got a hair appointment. I'll be back soon and then we can have a chat." Gramps pats the bed, for Leo to jump up and sit next to him. "Leo, I'm going to tell what each medal is for and which campaigns they represent."

"Wow, it must be really grouse Gramps, to be a heroic pilot. Maybe one day I can be like you." Gramps raises himself up higher in the bed. "Listen, my boy, if there's one thing I've learnt about war, is that killing someone you don't even know and who's probably got family too, isn't very heroic. Just remember wars are started out of fear and ignorance. Sometimes through the actions of morally bankrupt politicians and those self- serving bastards, who profit from it."

Gramps and Leo have been chatting for quite a while when Linda comes back into the room with a nurse, discussing how elegant her hairdo looks. The nurse serves them some tea and biscuits. "How are we, Mr Shepherd? I hope it's not too much for you?"
"Nonsense girlie, having my best mate here is all the medicine I need." It surprises Linda, as Leo usually eats everything in sight and remarks, "Leo, you haven't touched a biscuit, are you feeling okay?"
"Come on boy have a biscuit," urges Gramps. "Sorry, Gramps no can do. I'm still full from stuffing myself at McD's. Gramps raises his good hand and points to Linda, "how's Bryan getting on these days?"
"Oh, he's working very hard, you know - at the garage. The Wilsons, who own it, are away again. So he's kept pretty busy looking after things."
"And what about you, how are things with you?"
"I'm still at Westons. I've got a really good boss and the staff there, very friendly. Gramps, enough about us, is there anything you need?"
"No, I'm just glad to see you both, particularly seein' how it's Leo's birthday."

They chat for a little longer until the nurse interrupts, "I'm sorry folks, but Mr Shepherd needs to rest now. Gramps looks at Leo. "They're giving us the wind-up sign, so come over here young fellow." Gramps reaches out to shake hands with Leo, "you look after those medals and watch over your Mum, she's special too you know."
"You bet," affirms Leo enthusiastically.

Arriving home, Leo eagerly goes to his room to check out the medals. He pulls out an old singlet and begins polishing the medals until they glint from the afternoon sun streaming through his window. Leo stands to attention and holds the medals over the left side of his chest, and looks into the dresser mirror. He imagines he's an ace fighter pilot like Gramps. He salutes, then carefully places the medals in a small box and hides them in his secret spot.

He flops down onto his bed for a while and then rolls over and picks up his Sci-fi novel, deciding to finish it. He's completely absorbed by the book and it isn't until a pale golden ray of sunlight catches his eye that he realises that it's late in the afternoon. On hearing voices, he gets up to investigate and finds Bryan is home early. Thinking, that's unusual. Dad's not normally home before six on the Saturday shift. Feeling hungry Leo wanders into the kitchen expecting dinner to be underway.

However, the kitchen is empty. So he wanders down to the main bedroom and finds Linda going through her dresses. He leans up against the doorframe and asks, "What's going on Mum?"
"Oh, Leo you've finally surfaced from your room. I thought I'd keep it as a surprise. We've been invited over to the Jerovich place for a party to celebrate their 25th Wedding anniversary."
"Oh," frowns Leo, thinking that maybe it was a surprise party for him.
"Well, I suppose you want me to have a shower and get dressed, then?"
"Yes, but get your clothes ready first, while Dad has his shower. Make sure you put on clean undies and I want to see a tie and jacket."
"Oh Mum, do I have to. Can't I go casual?" Linda points a threatening finger at Leo and replies, "no, because I want you to look your best. There will be lots of people there tonight."

Just as the sun is dropping below the horizon they are all ready to go. Although it's fine, the air has a crisp feel to it as they walk down the road to the Jerovich place. Out the front, there are cars everywhere and the house lit up like a Christmas tree. From the backyard, they can hear voices and a piano accordion playing lively. What strikes Leo the most is the aroma of cooking meat. As they come around the corner, Leo's eyes home in on two enormous sides of beef on spits, roasting over hot coals.

The back garden is filled with lots of fold-up tables and plastic chairs, in long rows. There are people excitedly chatting over the top of the accordion music. It seems as the music gets louder so does the chatter. The tables are lined with white sheets and covered with platters of different foods. It's the biggest feast Leo has ever seen. A big booming voice shouts over the top of the music. "Ahhh-haaaa! Here are my friends from up the road," welcomes Branco. "You come, that mayka me so 'appy. You come, drink vino with me," his big hands raised in the air.

They're each given a glass of Branco's infamous Grappa red wine, while he introduces them to some of their relatives and friends. He pats Leo on the shoulder, "Mister Leo, you want find Danicka - she inside, okay."

Before Leo ventures inside, he has something on his mind. Thinking, now where can I ditch this Grappa stuff? Oh, I know, in that large palm pot over there. He quickly glances around and stealthily pours out the glass while nobody's looking. He's feeling pleased with himself until a pair of ladies shoes appear at the base of the pot. He jumps, glancing up quickly to see Dani standing there. His face goes bright red. She giggles and puts her hand to mouth, "Hello there. I see you like Dida's homemade wine. Would you like some more?"
"Shit, excuse the French, thank God it was you. Jeez you gave me a scare and a half."

"Aren't we the guilty one," responds Dani with a big smile. "You've got it written all over your face." She grabs Leo's hand and leads him inside to their large kitchen. It's a hive of activity and noise as more food is being prepared. Leo feels very self-conscious as he's out-numbered by all of the women and girls in the kitchen and is reluctant to go in. Dani tugs on his arm, "yoo-hoo, everyone this is my friend Leo." They all shout, "Dobar Dan Leo!" Giggling when they realise the greeting's in unison. Self-conscious, Leo replies weakly, "hello."
"Leo do you want a cool drink?"
"Anything will do, but not that…" Leo stops mid-sentence as Branco appears and ushers everyone outside.

The music has stopped and everyone is surprisingly quiet. Branco puts his arm around Leo's shoulder and leads him into the centre of the gathering. The weight of Branco's arm on Leo's shoulder reminds Leo of the side of beef roasting on the spit. "Listen everybodys, is good you come - this our 25th Wedding party, Yes. Lena and me very 'appy you come and make big party. But, I have some-ting else to be 'appy. Mister Leo here, this nice young mans, his birthday too-day. So, we make even bigger party now, eh!" Just at that moment the accordion springs into life with Happy Birthday. This is followed by three hearty cheers. Then Branco shouts, "now we eat, we drink and we dance - make big party. Yes!"

Leo is overwhelmed by all of the attention and has people he doesn't even know coming up shaking his hand or giving him a hug. It's something he's not used to. But thinking, hey, one could quite easily get used to this. "Okay, everybodys roast is ready, you come, eat." After the meal, Dani wanders back over to talk to Leo, carrying a gift. "I couldn't give this to you earlier, because I had to help out."

"It's okay. I wasn't expecting anything. Can I open this somewhere quieter, I can hardly hear what you're saying," shouts Leo. They move away from the crowd and Leo rips open the paper on the parcel. "It's a picture frame, I think," comments Leo, a little puzzled and not sure what else to say. Waving his hand through the middle of the frame, he looks at Dani as if to say, isn't there supposed to be something, here?

"See, I was going to sketch your face and have it framed for you. But with everything going on, I haven't gotten around to doing it. So I thought I would give you the frame and do it tomorrow. Oh, and I got you this too." Dani hands Leo a small matchbox-sized gift. He excitedly tears at the paper to open the box. In the box is a pendant. Leo admires it and has a questioning look on his face. Dani realising this adds, "It's Saint Christopher. He's our Patron Saint for travellers you know. He will protect you. It was given to me by Baba, but I want you to have it."

"Who's Baba?"

"Oh, that's what we call our grandma."

"Gee-wiz that's really wicked. I will carry it all the time, to remind me of you."

"Ohhh, that's really sweet." Dani gives Leo a passionate kiss. His face turns a bright red. "Dani, I…errr…umm think we should go back to the party." Joining the rest of the partygoers, Leo tucks into more food. However, Dani interrupts his favourite pastime, to dance a traditional Slavic dance. Although Leo has no idea what he's doing, he doesn't care. Everyone is clapping and singing along with the music.

Finally, the piano accordion stops playing. A breathless Leo breaks away from Dani, "hey I puffed. I need to sit down for a bit." Looking around, it crosses his mind that this is the best birthday ever. Thinking, Gramps gave me his war medals and this party is totally sick. Look even Mum and Dad are getting stuck into that Grappa stuff, dancing and laughing. Hey, here comes Mum and she looks like she's got the staggers. I've never seen her like this before. She sidles up to him, "come on Leo dance with me?"

They join the group dancing on the lawn, yet Leo spends most of the time holding Linda upright. Her speech is slurred as she asks, "how's my birthday boy?" Leo has a serious look on his face, "Mum you're embarrassing me." Linda laughs, "ha-ha, that's ironic. Usually, it's the other way round."

A lull in the music is the cue Leo is looking for and leads Linda to a chair. "Mum, I'll be back shortly." He quickly disappears to look for Dani and goes off into the house. He meets Dani as she is about to come outside. "Enjoying yourself?" She asks. "Man, your 'Olds' sure know how to put on a wicked party."
"Yeah, we Slavs sure know how to party. So do your Mama and Dida, they seem to be having a good time."
"Sure are. I reckon Mum's pissed."
"Well, at least somebody likes Dida's vino," chuckles Dani. "Anyway changing the subject, I want to know what happened when you went into that chamber...you know the one with the tiles."

"It was really strange. When I put that last crystal down, the room lit up like a Christmas tree and it felt like I was in a lift. It was just weird. Then I went and checked out the next chamber and nothing. If you have time tomorrow, I'll show you that it's empty."
"I don't know if I can. I have to see what's happening here first." As the night wears on guests start to disappear and the noise dies down to a few people chatting. Bryan wanders over, "well birthday boy, your Mum's a bit tiddly so we better get her home. Don't forget to thank our hosts before you go."
"Aw, Dad. As if."

Leo stands up and says goodbye to Dani and gives her a big hug. He marches over to Branco and Lena to thank them. "Dad said we have to take Mum home, 'cos she liked your vino too much. Thanks heaps for inviting us, we've had the best-est time." As they leave, Leo is on one side of Linda and Bryan on the other. "Dad I thought you said Mum was just a bit tiddly. She's really pissed. She can hardly stand up?"

"Okay Leo," objects Bryan in a stern tone, "I don't think you should use that kind of talk." Then Linda pipes up in a slurred tone, "talking about piss, I could do with one right now." Leo chuckles, as Bryan interrupts, "we're nearly home, so just hang on.

Leo, here's the key and don't take too long about it." Unlocking the front door, Leo holds it open as Bryan plants his broad hands on the back of Linda's shoulders and steers her inside. "Right I will take care of things from here. You can go off to bed now." Leo yawns loudly and stretches his arms out as he heads to his room. It's been a big day for him and it doesn't take him long to be in sleep mode. After a short while, Leo's in a dream-state imagining he's a Roman General called 'Leonaddidas'. His toga covered in war medals and wearing white basketball runners. He's celebrating a big victory with a huge banquet. There are dancing girls, covered in veils, whirling around in time to the accordion music. Suddenly the dream shifts to Leonaddidas swimming or rather drowning in a Roman bath filled with Grappa wine. Leo wakes up gasping. He mumbles, "Even in my dreams I hate that stuff," and then slowly drifts back off to sleep again.

It's about nine o'clock the next morning when Leo wakes and despite the late night, he is still pumped up from the previous day's events and can't sleep in. As he gets up and wanders into the kitchen, he meets Bryan coming up the hallway. "Shhhh Leo, don't make too much noise, Mum's still sleeping off a whopper hangover."
"Yeah, it was a real mad night out. Wasn't it Dad?"
"Yeah, the Jerovich family sure knows how to throw a good party and what about that food. What are you going to do today Leo?"

"Errr, I have to go over to Dani's place, she's going to do a portrait of me. That's what the picture frame is for."
"Oh, I wondered about that?" I've got a couple of cars to work on. I'll be at the garage if you want to drop by later. "Okay Dad, see-ya." Leo decides not to have breakfast, in case it wakes Linda. So he wanders down to Dani's place. It's a hive of activity, with Dani and her cousins cleaning up. Branco is shovelling the coals from the fires into a barrow and stops to wipe the sweat from his brow, "Hey Mister birthday boy. You no can sleep in today, eh?"

"Hi Mr J, hi everyone, I thought I'd come down and help out."
"Oh, you good young mans to come." Please, you stack chairs, yes." Leo busily stacks the white plastic chairs.

He helps Vlad, one of Dani's cousins, to fold up the trestle tables. One thing that intrigues Leo is there seem to be cousins coming out of the woodwork. He hasn't met anyone before with so many cousins as Dani. As they finish clearing up, one table is left with a white sheet over it. Leo isn't left wondering for long, as Dani emerges carrying a tray with leftovers from the previous night, "Hey Leo. I didn't expect to see you this early." Leo is in food heaven, again. "Wow, lucky I didn't have breakfast this morning."

After breakfast, Dani excuses herself and Leo so that they can start sketching Leo's Portrait. Dani loves sketching faces, but no one else, not even Branco or Lena will sit to have theirs done. Leo isn't that crazy about the idea either and enquires, "how long is the sketch going to take?"
"I don't know, as long as it takes, an hour or two, maybe?"
"An hour or two! You've got to be kidding me."
"Do you want me to do it properly or not?
"Okay, I'll pose for you. But only if you do it you know where. Then we can check out that empty room. That way we won't waste the day away."
"Hmmm, I don't really like the idea. But seeing how it's for your
birthday, well okay - this time. I'll tell my folks we are going to your place, okay. "Thanks, Dani. I'll see you out the front."

Dani tells her parents that they are going over to Leo's place as it is quieter and no distractions. Instead, they both head off in the direction of Mt Fielden. Arriving at the old ruin, Leo carries out his usual ritual of checking the place out before venturing down the well and making sure they aren't seen. As they enter through the doorway Dani notices sand and dust in the tunnel entrance and stops in her tracks. "Hey! Someone has been here." Leo replies with a guilty look on his face. "No, it was me. "Okay, so I chucked a 'Sad'. You know, when I found that room was empty."

Dani shakes her head and they move off down the passageway. Dani rubs her arm and comments, "I still don't like that humming noise and that funny feeling on my skin. Look at the goosies I've got." Leo looks at his right arm and realises that he no longer has goosebumps and can't hear the humming sound, either.

Actually, he feels lighter and brighter than when he got up that morning. He now realises that physically, something has changed and keeps that to himself. Thinking, something's going on. But what? I haven't a clue, so how can I say something to her? When they reach the main chamber area within the Pyramid complex, only one section of the floor area is open. Leo points, "see it's still open and I'll show you its empty." As they climb down via the ramp from the level above, they both become excited. "Look Dani, there's a white stand it definitely wasn't there yesterday."

"Leo, there's a silver box on it. Quick! Go and grab it. I want to know what's in it."
"Well let's find out." Leo quickly lifts the lid off the box. "Hey, this reminds me of one the space fighters in one of my Sci-fi books. Those silver wings look like a boomerang. Maybe it's a game controller because of the screen." Leo lifts it carefully out of the box and examines the object. "There's a crystal display, but where are the buttons? There's no buttons or joy-pad on this thing?"

Dani walks over to the silver box and peers in. "Leo didn't you see this, there's a white card at the bottom."
"What does it say?"
"I dunno. There's no writing on the front or the back."
"Well open it - see what's inside." Annoyed at Leo's tone, Dani says, "you open it' and hands him the card. Leo opens the card. It triggers an electronic voice that seems to come out of nowhere. Leo jumps and promptly drops it and the silver object. "That was well done Leo," quips Dani. "Get off my back, will you. I didn't know it was going to do that. If you keep going on like that, I won't pose for you." Dani folds her arms, "look who's talking." Leo picks them both up and opens the card, again. The electronic voice announces, "congratulations on being integrated into the collective soul of the Guardians of Knowledge. As your gift, we have provided for your amusement and growth, a game console.

Only your mind's power and focus can operate it. Concentration and willpower is the key." With mouths wide open, they look at each in astonishment. "Leo, what was that all about?"

"Don't look at me like that," shrugs Leo. "I suppose I'm part of some sort of secret group. Apart from that, I haven't got the foggiest." "Well, I guess that's why all of this stuff's here - to find out," gestures Dani. Taking a wing of the game console in each hand, Leo stares into the screen display.

"Hey, the screen just lit up. Look it's playing a funky tune too. It's just like a Gameboy. It's even got a menu of games. See it's got levels 1 to 6." Dani moves closer to Leo's side to look at the display screen. "Hey, that's cool. It's a coloured maze and that funny looking thing, bouncing up and down at the gates. It reminds me of…you know, ohhh, umm, what's-his-name. Oh yeah, Sonic the Hedgehog."

As soon as Leo focuses his attention on the character at the maze gates, it starts to move. It isn't long before Leo has the little character bounding up and down the pathways. "Oopps that's a dead end." Dani grabs Leo's arm. "I can't see it properly." Distracted, Leo loses focus and the screen goes blank. "Sod off! See what you made me do." "Oh, s-o-r-r-y," snaps Dani, equally annoyed that Leo isn't giving her a proper look. Leo peers at the display, once again. On cue, it lights up and the game begins again. It isn't long before Leo has the little character, bouncing up and down at the centre of the maze. "Boy this is so easy," boasts Leo. Acting like he has mastered the whole thing.

The display flashes with coloured patterns. Another tune plays, with the words scrolling through, "CONGRATULATIONS. YOU HAVE COMPLETED STAGE 1.1." Dani jumps up and down on the spot impatiently pleading. "It's my turn. I want to have a go."

Leo hands the console to Dani. Excited she grabs each wing and concentrates on the display. Nothing appears on the screen. She suddenly feels weak and buckles at the knees. Feeling faint, she hands back the console, "Oh my God, you can have it back as it nearly fried my brain just then." Leo looks anxiously at Dani, "are you alright?"
"I am now. It's definitely made that clear – obviously not meant for anyone else."
"Gee, I'm really sorry. I didn't know it was going to do that."
"You weren't to know. Anyway, let's go back up top. So I can get on with your portrait. You can play with your new toy, so long as you don't move."

As they leave the chamber, the ramp slides back closing it off. As this is taking place the panel to the next chamber Lowers. "Dani, don't you think that's weird? This one's opened, yet I haven't finished." "Who cares, let's see what's down there." Before Leo has taken a step, Dani charges down the ramp. "Hey," shouts Leo as he's caught off guard. He too sprints down the ramp. However, Dani stops suddenly at the bottom causing Leo to crash into her. She teases Leo, "watch it, Buster. What do you think this is some kind of race?" Leo has Dani in a bear hug. She doesn't protest very much about the contact. In fact, she wanted it to happen. Both of them can feel the stirring of emotions surging through their stomachs and hearts pumping. However, they quickly regain their composure, when a white pillar rises majestically out of the floor.

Dani is first to respond, "look Leo, there's a case on top of that white stand. I bet it's another test."
"Okay, let's take a closer look." They both stand on either side of the case. Leo runs his hand across the top, "I don't think its glass, it feels like some sort of plastic stuff."
"Look Leo, there's a clear glass ball at that end. It looks like a soap bubble and there's a hole at the other end. "This puzzle will be a pushover.

Obviously, the ball goes into the hole. How easy is that?" "Leo, I wouldn't be so sure. My feeling is that it may be a lot harder than you think."

Showing off, Leo picks up the glass case, "look it's easy, all you do is tilt the case and guide the ball... Hey! The ball's not moving." Dani pokes her tongue out, "see I told you." What Leo has also failed to notice, is that the transparent ball's outer membrane reacts to conscious thought. The membrane distorts as Leo thinks about it or looks at it. "Well, I'll smash the case and then we will see what happens." Turning the case over, Leo dumps it on the floor. The noise echoes loudly throughout the chamber and up into the main structure. Dani quickly places her hands over her ears and she closes her eyes.

When she opens them to her amazement, the case just bounces with not a scratch on it. "Leo the bubble didn't even move." Picking up the case Leo shakes it. "There's got to be a trick to this." He places it back onto the pillar, "I'll come back another time with water and pour it through the hole and see if it floats."
"I'm bored with this, come on Leo let's go back up top." Dani grabs Leo's arm and they march back up the ramp and to the centre of the main chamber. As if on command the table and the two chairs rise silently out of the floor. Dani sits down and makes an observation, "this place is really weird." Reaching into her backpack she pulls out a range of pencils and charcoal sticks. Then some sheets of cartridge paper, which she unrolls. Meanwhile, Leo is busily playing with his new toy. "Move your head this way."
"Damn it! I missed it," hisses Leo, losing his concentration. "Boy, this is not as easy as I thought."
"Stop talking and don't move so much."

Leo is totally into the new gadget and oblivious to Dani sketching away. He doesn't even notice she has finished, until she stands up and stiffly stretches out her arms, letting out a series of yawns. "I've finished!" She announces triumphantly.
"Already?"
"What do you mean already? I've been doing it for ages."
"Let me see," says Leo impatiently.
"Is that me? Do you reckon that it looks like 'Moi'?"

"Of course it does stupid," snaps Dani. She's annoyed that Leo is iffy about the likeness and hasn't thanked her. "Sorry. I've never had a portrait done before. It's really good. I can't wait to show the folks." Leo gives Dani a hug and quickly kissing her on the cheek. "Well let's go back to your place and I will help you put it into the frame."

They pack up and leave the underground complex in high spirits. Leo is holding Dani's hand and swinging it as they walk back along the track. Arriving back at Leo's place they let themselves in. Leo heads straight for the refrigerator and opens the door and asks, "Dani do you want to drink?" Dani is jumping up and down on the spot. "After. Right now I'm busting. Where's your toilet?" Leo points, "through there and turn left before the back door." While Dani is gone, Leo pours out a drink of cordial each and disappears to his room. Dani wanders back into the kitchen finding only the two glasses of cordial standing there.

Meanwhile, Leo is stashing the game console in his secret hiding place. Dani grabs one of the glasses and heads for Leo's room. "There you are." Leo stands bolt upright. "Jeez, you made me jump.

You like sneaking up on people, don't you?" protests Leo, trying to kick the floor rug back in place with his foot. Dani leans up against the doorframe, "how come you're so jumpy - got something to hide, eh?" Leo flops onto his bed, "Well the truth is I was putting the console back in my secret hiding place." Dani's face lights up, "can I see it?"
"No way! It wouldn't be a secret hiding place, would it?"
"Well, I guess not," she pouts.

"I can see you're disappointed, so I'll tell you what. If you turn your back I will show you the war medal collection Gramps gave me for my birthday." Dani turns around, while Leo lifts the floor mat and removes a short piece of the floorboard. Removing the war medals, he puts the game console in its place. "Let's go back to the kitchen and I'll explain the various medals and campaign ribbons. And..and I'll tell you the story Gramps told me about the Foo Fighters too."

Dani is thirsty and skulls what's left of the cordial. Leo recounts everything Gramps had told him. Dani is hanging on every word. "Wow your Gramps is a real hero and you're really lucky he trusts you to keep his medals safe. Can I hold them?"
"Yeah, okay. Gramps is very special alright. But I'm really worried about him. He seems to have gone downhill ever since going to that dumb nursing home and not his old self. I wish I could take him away from there, but there's nobody to look after him." Seeing that Leo is upset, Dani changes the subject, "Leo why don't you get the picture frame, so I can put you in the frame - get it."
"Ha, Ha Miss Smarty-pants." Leo leaves the kitchen and is soon back with the picture frame, putting it in front of his face, "I reckon this is a pretty good likeness, what do you think?"
"Well, it would be, except for the snot hanging from your nose."
"Where?" Leo wipes his nose with the sleeve of his shirt."

Dani is overcome. She puts her hand to her mouth and chuckles, "I got you big-time." Leo wipes his nose on his sleeve again, except this time he makes a sickening snorting noise.

He pounces towards Dani and tries to wipe it on her. Dani screams, "Errrrr gross," as she bolts out of the kitchen and into the laundry. She half-closes the door on Leo, so he can't 'slime' her.

"Want to boogie with me?" Laughs Leo, as he pushes hard on the door. "Errrrr, you're a random, responds Dani, desperately trying to hold the door closed and laughing at the same time. "Yeah I'm one sick random and I'm going to slime you as soon as I open this door."
"You got no chance, Booger Boy."
"Okay, truce then. "Cos I've got to go to the Loo."
"I'm not falling for that one," shouts Dani. "You'll have to go outside."
"No lie. I am really busting."
"Too bad, I'm not opening the door." Leo lets go of the door and races outside behind the back shed. Dani realising Leo has gone. She has a quick look and goes back to the kitchen.

She sits down and unrolls Leo portrait and centres it on to the picture frame to trim the edge. Meanwhile, Leo sneaks back in through the back door of the laundry hoping to catch Dani out. To his surprise, she isn't there and wanders into the kitchen as if nothing has happened. "Oh, Leo there you are. Have you got some sharp scissors so I can trim your portrait?"
"Sure."

While Leo is looking through the utensil drawer, Dani removes the glass and the backing, marking where the portrait is to go into the frame. "Here's the scissors."
"There how does that look," comments Dani, holding the portrait up, proudly. "Gee, that looks wicked. Here, can I hold it?" Leo holds up his portrait and smiles, "I've been framed, I've been framed. It wasn't me your Honour." Just at that moment, Linda comes in through the back door. "You two are having fun. I could hear you from the end of the driveway. They both look sheepish. Dani puts her hand over her mouth and laughs, "Hi Mrs Shepherd."

Chapter 5
Splosh was the sound my boots made in wet cow dung.

Leo quickly changes the subject, "look what Dani did. She sketched my portrait. What do you think? Pretty good, huh?"
"Wow, that's a really good likeness of my Leo. He's even got that cheeky look about him," laughs Linda playfully.
"Aw M-u-m."
"Dani, you've done a wonderful job, but there's one detail missing."
"What's that Mrs Shepherd?"
"You didn't sign your name and date it."
"Oh, I don't think it's that good," responds Dani.

Leo chips in, "yes, Mum's right. I want you to." Dani unhooks the backing board and signs the portrait, putting a little love heart next to her signature, and the date. "I'll get Bryan to hang it in Leo's bedroom, so it reminds Leo of you. How romantic," sighs Linda. Her mind drifts back to better times in her younger days, as she sways her hips from side to side.

"Mum, we're hungry, let's have some afternoon tea."
Apologetically, Linda replies, "Oh yes, I'm not a very good hostess, am I? I'm still getting over the wonderful party your parents put on last night."
"Yeah and Mum still has the hangover to prove it."
"Alright Leo, that's enough from you."
"Oh look at the time. I got to go. I've got guitar practice. If I don't do it, Mama will give me extra jobs to do."
"Are you sure you can't stay," pleads Leo.
"No. I'd better be going." With a disappointed look, Leo responds, "I'll walk you to the road." Dani waves as she says, "Bye, Mrs Shepherd."
Linda waves back, "Love the portrait you did, Dani. See you later."

As they make their way down the drive, Leo tentatively puts his arm around Dani's waist and gives her a squeeze, "thanks for doing that portrait, I'll treasure it always."
"That's okay, I enjoyed doing it. Besides, it's fun being around you, even without all that spooky secret stuff. Although, I have to say that's been pretty amazing too. Actually, I have to be honest; I can't wait to see what's in that last room. I reckon it's going to be awesome."

On the way back up the driveway, Leo stares at the ground pondering. I wonder what it's going to take to crack that case with the ball in it. Maybe that game console has something to do with it? I can't wait to find out what's in that room down the end. It's got to be something 'spesh' otherwise, why would the whole place be there?

The afternoon passes quickly and during dinner that night Leo is restless. All he can think about is the underground complex and spending time with Dani. Linda interrupts Leo thoughts, "Leo, its school tomorrow. You need to get your bag ready." Leo picks up his novel. "I'll do it tomorrow morning. Anyway, I've got better things to do." Linda stands up and puts her hands on her hips, "you're not reading that book until you bag's packed and any homework finished."

After dinner, Leo helps Linda do the dishes and decides to go to his room rather than watch TV. This invokes a comment from Bryan, "that's unusual. Normally we can't drag that boy away from that idiot box. I wonder what he is up to."
"Oh give him a break will you Bryan. You must admit he is a changed boy since Dani came on the scene - he's really growing up."

In his room, Leo's sitting on his bed fiddling with the console and talking to himself, "damn, this one's hard, I give up. I'm too tired to concentrate. Maybe I'll take it to school. Then I can finish it quicker, in case there's heaps of homework. I'd better put it back in my secret spot in case the folks come in."

*****

The morning at school passes agonisingly slow. Leo thinks, after the mad weekend with the game console thingy, the party at the Jerovich's and having my portrait done everything seems so boring. At recess, Leo searches for a quiet, comfortable spot to concentrate on the game console. He finds an empty bench under a tree, near the quadrangle. Sitting down and leaning forward over the display screen, Leo is a picture of total concentration. So preoccupied, he fails to notice Fridge sauntered up to him. "Hey, Farmboy! Gimme a look at what you have there?" Sitting up straight, Leo reacts by pulling the console close to his chest and responds, "no way."

Fridge sticks out his hand and gestures as if it belongs to him. "Where did you get that? Give-us-it!" Thinking quickly, Leo answers, "I got it for my birthday, it's the new Gameboy."

"Bullshit," is the quick reply. "Your folks can't afford one. They're not even in the shops yet. I bet you stole it." Leo stands up. "Crap off," hiding behind it behind his back.

"If you don't give-us-it, I'll take it off you." Fridge grabs Leo by the shirt and puts him in a headlock. A struggle ensues. Fridge grabs the console and pushes Leo to the ground. "Well looky what we have here." Examining what he thinks is the latest Gameboy. Grabbing the wings of the console, Fridge is puzzled.

"Hey, where are the buttons and joypad?" No sooner had he got those words out, his face goes pale. "WTF, what was that? He drops the console on the ground. Fridge's head feels like it's about to explode as the console zaps him. While Fridge is still in shock, Leo sees this as his chance, swooping in and grabbing the console. He heads for the sanctuary of the Library, with Fridge shouting after him, "it's a God-damned dummy. It doesn't have buttons or anything. I bet you pinched it from a display."

Later in the day, Leo notices that Fridge seems to be avoiding him since the morning's incident. This is not lost on Leo, remarking to himself, "that's ironic usually it's me doing the avoiding." He sure must've got a boot-and-a-half from that game console. Maybe the power's getting stronger, 'cos Dani didn't get it that bad. Leo punches the air, "Ahhh, sweet justice."

*****

For Leo, the week passes quickly, as he's totally pre-occupied with mastering the games and passing levels on the game console. He also notices that he's doing better in class as well. Seemingly able to focus more and pick the essence of any subject very quickly. He has come a long way since the first time he picked up the console at stage 1.1. Now he's on the final stage at 6.1 with five sub-levels to go.

It's Friday afternoon and instead of catching the 3:45pm bus home. Leo and Dani have arranged that Leo waits until the 4:30pm city bus. Leo doesn't mind waiting, as it gives him an excuse to complete more of the last remaining games. Leo's completely engrossed in one game when he hears a grinding gear change and the screeching of dry brakes. He looks up to see Dani waving vigorously on the bus. Racing up the steps, he's greeted by the lady driver with bushy red hair and a cap perched on top. Leo fumbles for his change.

The lady driver smiles as she says. "Don't worry love grab a seat, your girlfriend's paid." Leo looks down the aisle. Suddenly he's self-conscious as all the passengers eyeball him to see which girl he sits with. He smartly charges down the aisle as the bus pulls out of the stop and swings into the seat, all in one motion. "Hey, go easy will you Leo. I know you're pleased to see me, but do you have to crush me as well?" Retorts Dani as Leo bumps into her. Leo in a hushed tone replies, "Everyone's staring."
"Yeah right. What do you expect them to do? They're all facing the front," jokes Dani pushing Leo's shoulder with her hand playfully.
"Yeah, yeah okay, I get the message. Guess what? I've nearly finished all of the levels of the 'you-know-what'."
"Wow, you've done really well. I think you should get a reward. Let's go to the movies on Saturday?"
"I'd like too, but we can't afford it. Besides, I have to go and see Gramps."
"Ohhh, p-l-e-a-s-e come with me. I'll pay for you. We can also visit your Djeda too."
"Are you sure? That would be really wicked. Can we see that new Sci-fi flick, Zero Point II - please, please, please?"
"You and your Sci-fi stuff! I suppose so. Otherwise, I'll never hear the end of it."

Leo raises his fist into the air and pulls an imaginary chain, "Yessss." Looking at Dani, he plants a giant grin on his face and declares, "I'm in heaven. One, it's the weekend. Two, haven't been to the movies in ages. Three, I'm going with you and four, it's a Sci-fi flick. Is that mad or what?" Dani turns and stares at Leo. "My God Leo, get a life. It's just a dumb movie." Leo looks down his nose at Dani and forms a cross with his fingers, "that's sacrilege." The jousting between them eventually stops as both are mentally exhausted from their day.

Leo stares down the aisle of the bus as his mind drifts. Thinking, Jeez, I'm going on my first date. Man, if someone had told me that month's ago. I'd say you're one of Old Thommo's Moonrakers and lock 'em up. Gramps was spot on about the cards bit. Man, I feel like I'm already 'Shooting the Moon'. An elbow jolts Leo back to the present. "Hey dreamer, it's our stop." Leo rubs his upper arm, "hey, watch it will you - that elbow's lethal."

Leo jumps up and is off the bus in a flash, leaving Dani to untangle her backpack from under the seat. The lady driver looks in the mirror and then at Leo, "typical, where are all the gentleman these days. She turns and looks at Dani as she comes down the aisle. "Listen Love, he'll do the same at the altar - leave you standing there. I know his type." Dani climbs off the bus in fits of laughter. Leo stands there stunned.

He stares at the driver as the bus pulls away. "Is that woman off her trolley or what?" Dani pouts, and in a playful-hurt tone, "that'll teach you to leave me, you bastard." Leo plays along too. "Love 'em and leave 'em. That's what I always say." Their playfulness is interrupted by someone calling. Dani is first to respond, "Leo, I think your Mum wants you." Leo turns around. "Yeah, you're right - what's she doing home, this early?"

"Leo, you'd better go. I hope everything's alright." Leo meets an anxious Linda at the letterbox. "Leo! Where have you been? I was worried sick about you?" Leo stops and looks around. "Where's the problem? I waited for Dani and caught the 4:30 city bus," replies Leo, defensively. Linda ushers Leo up the driveway and in an annoyed tone scolds Leo, "Next time you decide to do that, please tell me first. There I am thinking something has happened to you." Leo snaps back, "As if." Linda looks Leo straight in the eyes. "Well, you just never know. I don't need to know what you're doing, but just to know that you're safe. Is that too much to ask?" Leo sighs, "No Mum."

He quickly changes the subject, "guess what Mum? Dani's taking me to the movies on Saturday. Then we're going to see Gramps, after." Linda shakes her head as she puts her hand on Leo's shoulder. "Sorry Leo, we can't afford the movies right now."
"No, you didn't hear me right - Dani's paying for me."
"Hmmm, I'm not sure that's right - Dani paying for you?"

"M-u-m, this is the new millennium. Not the Nineteenth century you were born in."

"Things might have changed, but at least get your facts right. I was born in the twentieth century, the same as you." Both see the funny side and begin to laugh as they walk up the driveway. "That's what I like about you, Leo. You're so funny at times - the things you come out with.

I guess I was brought up with different ideas and attitudes about life and the way things should be. But, the way things should be and the way things are today, in these changing times, is questionable."

"Mum, can we drop the philosophy lesson, I'm hungry."

After dinner, Leo decides to go to bed early. He figures, if I go to bed early, the sooner I'll wake up and it'll be tomorrow. "Goodnight Mum, night Dad."

"Hey it's early for you isn't it," comments Bryan looking at his watch, then at Linda. "Well our son has got to get his beauty sleep. He's got a big date at the movies tomorrow."

"Woo Hoo. Leo that's my boy," crows Bryan proudly. "Go get em!"

"Aw, you're embarrassing," says Leo, retreating to his room.

"You know that takes me back to when we were first dating."

"Yes, it sure does. Those days at the midnight Drive-ins," sighs Linda.

"Yep, I remember alright. One night I got lost in the dark and got into the wrong car and bailed up by a big panting Rottweiler dog, with drool hanging from its mouth."

"Hey, you never told me about that?"

"I was embarrassed, wasn't I? Wanted to impress you- it was only our second date."

"You sneaky so-and-so, you kept that from me all this time. Now I want to know the full story."

"There's not much to tell, except I counted the rows wrongly and this car looked like mine. It was really dark and I jumped in and there was this dog sitting in the other bucket seat. I think the only reason he, well I think it was a he, didn't have a piece of me is that he was as shocked as I was. So I jumped out as quickly as a flash and that's basically it, I suppose."

Linda is laughing loudly, trying to get out the words, "what a classic." "I can see the funny side now. But I tell you what, ever since that time, I made absolutely sure where I parked and always check the number plate." Bryan and Linda cuddle together on the couch in front of the television and watch a movie. Re-living the good times when they were younger. "Yep, those were the days - things were fancy-free, weren't they Linda? What I would give to have those days back again."

Meanwhile, Leo is reading his book. However, he's struggling to keep his eyes open. He puts the book down, turns off the lamp and shouts, "Hurr-a-y for Satur-da-y!" Next morning Leo's alarm goes off. This is a first for him, as he usually sleeps in most Saturdays. He wants to get up early to shower and be dressed in time. This sudden strange behaviour also extends to him fussing over his looks and what to wear.

Looking in the mirror he mutters, "mongrel thing, I got a zit right there." Bryan suddenly appears at the bathroom door. "Sorry, I thought you'd still be in bed. Do you two want to be alone?"
"Ha-ha Dad, says Leo, clearly not impressed. "By the way, you can use my aftershave. The girls go wild over that stuff. It's on the second shelf," remarks Bryan playfully. "Wow, thanks Dad." Leo takes the top off and sniffs. Throwing his head back, "phew that's strong, you're sure this stuff is okay?"
"My solemn oath son, you wait and see." Leo waves his hand in front of his face at the wafting smell of the aftershave. He retreats from the bathroom and goes to his room to dress. Leo puts on his jeans, yet the shirt he wants to wear is crumpled. "M-u-m!"

"What is it Leo? Can't you see I'm getting ready for work?"
"Yeah I know, but this shirt's creased and I can't find the hairdryer."
"Since when have you been using a hair dryer? And, why for heaven's sake didn't you ask me last night?"
"'Cos last night I didn't know I was going to wear it today," pouts Leo logically. "Look give it here," snaps Linda in an annoyed tone as she snatches it from Leo's hand. "I'd better not be late for the bus, otherwise you'll cop it when I get home."

The Shepherd household is a hive of activity. "Okay Leo, I'm off to the garage. Good luck with your date and all that. Don't forget to whack on the smellies, chuckles Bryan as he leaves. "Oh you mean the aftershave," acknowledges Leo.

"Leo, your shirt's hanging on the chair in the kitchen. I've got to go now. Have a good time, won't you?" Linda dashes off to catch the bus. Meanwhile, Leo is busy looking at himself in the mirror. After lots of adjusting and re-adjusting, Leo is ready. He slams the front door, jogs down the driveway and makes his way over to Dani's place. He finds her standing out the front, staring at the ground and 'virtual writing' on the concrete with her foot. "Hi Dani, good you're ready, we've got heaps of time for the bus."
"We're not catching the bus, because Dida is going to take us." Leo whispers, "how come. I thought we're supposed to go on our own." Dani whispers back, "I can't help it, you know what Dida's like." Leo has a disappointed look on his face and questions, "he's not coming with us to the movies, is he?"

Dani looks strangely at Leo, "don't even go there. No, Dida's got business in town."
"Phew." Reversing the bright yellow Ford station wagon out of the garage, Branco shouts, "Okay we go now, yes!" For Leo things were to go from bad to worse as they climb in. Dani jumps in the front with Branco, while a face-pulling, arms-folding Leo, is relegated to the back seat.

However, things change when Dani and Leo arrive at the Capital Movie Theatre. Both are excited. They're out and about being seen as an 'item' and line up with other Sci-fi nerds for their tickets. "Let's go in early so we get the best seats," urges Leo. Dani has other ideas, "but I want to get popcorn and a drink, first."

"Yeah you can, there's plenty of time, responds Leo. But I don't want anything, I didn't bring any cash."

"I'll pay for you, remember it's my treat," replies Dani. Okay, I'll have a choc ice cream and a big coke."

Having bought their 'supplies', they find plenty of empty seats and although undecided where to sit, eventually settle for the back row. No sooner had they got comfortable, Dani spots a girl from a rival college. "Oh no there's that bitch from St Joseph's, She calls herself 'Posh', but her name's Portia Harland. Her folks are loaded and she's an absolute drama queen. She thinks she's a walking advert for what's hot - but she's not - always strutting around like she's got a carrot up her backside."

Leo is bemused, "like - don't hold back or anything, will you?" Dani screws her face up. "Everyone, hate-hate-hates her." Posh is with a group of giggling school friends and wearing the latest label and always gets what she wants. Dani is hoping that Posh doesn't see them, as she slides lower in her seat and tries to hide behind the box of popcorn. Just as the group realise they're in the wrong movie, Posh notices Dani out of the corner of her eye. She elbows one of her friends. "There's that Jerovich chick from MLC. You know the one." Posh's friend replies, "Yeah. Why don't you go over and find out who is the 'Loser' with her."

Posh flicks back her long blonde curly hair, "Yeah. This should be good for a laugh. I'll put on my posh accent."

"Oh no! Here she comes, Leo. Watch out she's a real bitch." Dani is trying to shrink down further into her seat, while Leo isn't sure what is happening, "Who's what?"

"Oh don't worry Leo. Just don't say anything, that's all." Posh's friends are all within earshot, so she turns to make sure they are watching her performance. "Well, h-e-l-l-o Danicka, haven't seen you in these parts for a while. My, my we are an item I see. Aren't you going to introduce us? Well, obviously not judging by that stupid look on your d-r-e-a-r-y face." Ignoring Dani, she turns her attention to Leo. "Hi, I'm Posh and what's your name, Loser?"

"My name's Leo. But what sort of name is Splosh. I used to live on a farm and splosh was the sound my boots used to make when I stepped in wet cow dung." Dani bursts out laughing. Posh's stuck-up look turns to horror. Her mouth now wide open, the bottom lip quivering. Posh is frozen to the spot and lost for words. Then with a flick of her head, she walks straight out of the theatre. Her so-called school friends all laugh and giggle making sploshing sounds as they leave.

Leo surprises himself, thinking, what just came out of my mouth. Usually, I'd be lost for words. Or think of a clever answer two hours later. Dani has laughing-tears rolling down her cheeks, "that's the funniest thing I have heard in ages. It's the first time I have seen that bitch completely speechless." It takes a while for them all to settle down, even with people going, "shoosh will you." But as soon as the movie starts, Leo is glued to the screen right to the end. Later, as the credits roll and the lights come on, Leo is the first to comment.

"That movie was really cool. Zero Point II was better than the first one. What do you reckon?" Dani responds with a big yawn. She stretches out in the seat and arches her back. On her mind is the look on Posh's face. "I can't wait for college on Monday to tell everyone about Posh and spread around: #Poshthe Splosh."

After the movie, Leo is hungry. However, Dani has other ideas. "Leo, I don't want to go to McDonald's. Let's go over to KFC as I'm hot for some spicy chicken." After ordering and finding a place to sit, they both review the day. "Boy. You should've seen that look on Posh's face. I wish I had a movie camera."
"I can't understand why you didn't like the movie. The special-FX blew me away. You would never know that those robots weren't real."
"And those so-called girlfriends of Posh, they soon turned on her, didn't they?"
"And I liked that bit, where that robot's severed arm grabs the girl by the leg." Leo looks at the clock on the wall and stands up with the tray and asks, "Dani are you about done. We have to catch the 507 bus. It goes past where Gramps is staying." Arriving at the nursing home, Dani is a little nervous. She pushes Leo to the front, "you go in first as I've never been inside a nursing home, before."

"Don't panic. It's like a hospital, except it's full of old people." They push open the double doors and go up to the main counter. "Hi, we've come to see Mr Shepherd he's in room 23. The lady clerk behind the counter asks, "Is Mr Shepherd expecting you?"
"Well, no. But, we came all the way from Fielden Beach to see him."
"Okay then. Please wait over there and I'll let him know you're here." A nurse comes out into the foyer and in a cheery voice announces, "Hi, I'm Amanda. Now, if you both like to wait out in the garden - seeing how it's such a lovely day. I'll go and check on Mr Shepherd." The nurse goes into Gramps's ward, "Mr Shepherd. I have two young people out in the garden waiting to see you. But I don't think it's a good idea for you to…" Gramps interrupts in an assertive voice, "listen here girlie. I don't want my best mate seeing me laid up in bed like this. So don't make this any harder for me, do you hear."
"Okay Mr Shepherd, I'll help you to dress and get you into your wheelchair."

Meanwhile, Leo and Dani are sprawled out on the manicured lawn under the shade of the large Ficus tree. Leo's in a reclining position with his legs stretched out and resting on his elbows. While Dani sits upright with her long legs crossed, yoga fashion. After some difficulty, Amanda finally wheels Gramps out into the garden. He shields his eyes with his good arm, as it's very bright. "Where's my mate," asks Gramps impatiently. He spots them on the lawn. "Don't get up on my account. This is such a nice surprise. I wasn't expecting you to come in today, my boy. And who's this very attractive young lady you have with you?"
"Hi Gramps, it's really great to see you up and about again," responds Leo enthusiastically, as he gets up and about to give Gramps a hug. But the old man holds out his good arm and shakes Leo's hand vigorously. Leo turns and gestures, "this is my friend Danicka, but she likes to be called Dani."

"Hello Dani, so I finally get to meet the Queen of Spades." Dani looks at Leo suspiciously. As if to say, what have you been saying? Leo looks away at first and then shrugs his shoulders, "ask him what it means." A shy Dani leans over to Leo and whispers, "you ask him." "Dani wants to know what you mean by Queen of Spades." Gramps looks at them both and smiles, "oh, that's because she has dark hair.

Remember I told you that to 'Shoot the Moon' you would need the Queen of spades - I was right wasn't I? Anyway, I thought I was Leo's special friend. Looks like I have some unfair competition."

Both feel uneasy. Gramps realises this and adds, "It's okay. Leo and I have a special bond that goes beyond words." Leo quickly changes the subject. "Gramps, Dani and I went to the movies this morning and saw a Sci-fi movie, called Zero Point II."

"Ah Dani, you can blame his passion for Sci-fi on me. I assume it's not your passion?"

"Music and drawing are my passions, Mr Shepherd."

"Ah, the Arts. Yes…without them our society would have no imagination, no imagination at all."

"And, you my boy, what have you been up to lately?"

"Not much," is Leo's reply and rolling his eyes in Dani's direction. "A young fellow like you with lots of energy and so much to learn about the world, I find that hard to believe."

"Well, I have been doing a few things…like I am working on a puzzle at the moment."

"What kind of puzzle, Leo?"

"It's a glass box with a ball at one end and a hole at the other and you have to find a way to roll the ball through the hole. But you can't lift the box or move it or anything like that."

"Well, maybe you can smash the glass, eh?"

"Oh we tried…I mean…no, you can't smash it either, babbles Leo.

Glancing at Dani as she has that, 'you've-put-your-foot-in-mouth', look on her face. "Well, my boy that is a hard one. It's beyond this tired old mind. That's for sure. You'll have to use your head on this one…just use your head, son. And before I forget, did you have a good day for your birthday. You must have gone out because Linda had her hair all done up?"

"Did we ever. It was really wicked. We went to a party at Dani's place. The food there was really s-i-c-k and Dani sketched my portrait and it's in a frame and everything."

"I glad you all had a good time. You all deserve it since things have been so tough, lately."

"Gramps, I've been doing some thinking. You know the story about those Foo Fighters; I don't believe they belong to the 'Good-old-USA' or the Germans. I believe they're from out there," affirms Leo, pointing to the sky.

"Come closer. I've never told you this, but I have spoken to American pilots and they thought the Foo Fighters were German and I have spoken to some 'Kraut' pilots after the war and they thought that they belonged to the 'Yanks'. So that only leaves one possible explanation. Governments have hidden the truth for years. It's too late for me. But in your lifetime, the truth of these things will be revealed to you." "Yes Gramps, you're usually right about most things," agrees Leo with a wink. Leo reaches out and clasps Gramps's good hand and with the other hand, grabs hold of Dani's hand too.

"You know Gramps you talked about the cards we are dealt and Shooting the Moon and stuff. Well, I have been dealt some good cards lately. You're absolutely right, Dani is the Queen of Spades, even her Dad owns a market garden - you know digging? Anyway, I understand now about the Ace of hearts bit too."

"That's great my boy because I remember weeks ago you were really down in the dumps. See our little talk has changed things for you. Now don't go getting upset by what I say to you now. But I know my time is near - this old body has done its job over the years and is ready to be put out to pasture. There are a lot of things I don't know. But, one thing I feel sure about - one day you're going to make me proud. Remember I will be watching you every step of the way. I feel certain that someone will come after me to help you along the way, so don't you fret. Okay, we're going to shake on it…you too Dani."

Leo still has hold of Gramps's hand as Gramps gives it a hard squeeze. Dani moves out of her sitting position and shuffles on her knees over to the wheelchair. She reaches up and shakes Gramps's hand. However, decides to stand up to give him a hug and a kiss. Both Dani and Leo are now misty-eyed. Gramps's sensing this and is annoyed, "Now see you didn't listen to what I said. You're both young, so you won't fully understand this until you are old like me. But I have had a full life and I am too tired now to be in this game anymore.

It's time to put the cards away. And you know the best thing is; I can toss in my hand when I'm good and ready."

"Now it's getting late and time for my afternoon nap, so go and have fun together…life's so short and I don't want you to be wasting it on an old fossil like me." Leo wipes his watery eyes on his sleeve,

"Gramps you couldn't be 'so' wrong. Not one minute of the times we spent together has ever been wasted. You've taught me so much. How can I ever repay you?"

"Leo you can repay the faith I have in you, just by simply paying close attention to what is going on around you. Really listen to what people say. Now you grab hold and wheel me inside, please." Back inside, they both wave good-bye. Dani is wiping away tears from her eyes and blowing her nose.

Leo has a sinking feeling. Thinking, I can't help but feel that it might be one of the last times we will have together. I don't know what I'm going to do when he goes. Leo and Dani leave the nursing home hand in hand. Dani squeezes Leo's hand tightly remarking, "Wow your Djeda is really cool. His mind is still sharp for someone that old. I can see why you two are so close. I wish I had someone like that who's that smart." "Yeah Gramps is one in a million, that's for sure." Just outside the nursing home is the bus stop. However, they have some time to wait for the next bus to Fielden Beach. "Leo, let's sit over there on the lawn in the shade."

Leo lies down staring up at the sky, with hands behind his head. While Dani sits cross-legged, with her shoulder bag in her lap. They're both quietly thinking about Gramps, which triggers off thoughts about their own futures and what they might like to do. "Dani, what do you want to do when you leave school?"

"I'm hoping to go to Uni, that's if my grades are good enough."

"Doing what?"

"Dida wants me to study music."

"No. What do you want to do?"

"If I get to choose, I want to do fashion design or maybe marketing. What about you Leo?"

"I dunno, yet. Everything changes so quickly. The world's all over the place.

For instance, 12 months ago I was going to go to Agricultural College and I end up here. Then I fall down that well and find, probably the discovery of the century…don't even know where that's going, either."

"Yeah, I know what you mean. The environment's all wonky and terrorists doing bad stuff around the place. It sure makes you wonder where things are heading." The bus arrives and both sit quietly. Their energy sapped, they choose to be lost in their own thoughts. Having arrived at their stop and get off, Dani announces, "Leo I'm stuffed. I think I'm going to be horizontal for a while, what are you going to do?"

"Maybe I'll do that too. See-you. Thanks for taking me to the movies and all that. I've had a really grouse time."
"Me too…can I have a hug?" They give each other a bear hug and lean on each other for a minute and separate. Leo happily marches up the drive and around the back, but finds the back door locked. He mumbles, "Oh, there's nobody home. "That's good. I need some space from the Olds."

Letting himself in, Leo heads straight to his room. His thoughts are of his big day out and Gramps as he removes the medals from the secret hiding place. Lying down on his bed Leo holds them up. At the same time, he's mulling over what Gramps had said and what lay ahead once he has completed the final puzzle. Leo rests the medals on his chest and stares at the ceiling. He battles to keep his eyelids open before sleep overcomes him.

*****

For the next couple of days, Leo feels his life is dull, colourless and boring. Thinking, after another really wicked weekend, school's a real drag. I'm even over that game console too. However, that's about to change. One night after dinner, Leo is supposed to be doing his homework, but can't be bothered. He's mucking around with the console and not taking it seriously. He finds a shortcut and all of a sudden text scrolls across the display, "Congratulations. Well Done. You have passed the final stage."

Shocked Leo remarks; "is that it," expecting something more. He flops back on his bed holding the console and adds, "what a waste of time and energy that..." Suddenly, a high pitched whine is emitted from the console. Leo feels a spiral burst of energy, that starts from the base of his feet and whirls up through his body and out through the top of his head. Leo sits up with a start, "What the hell was that?" The game console display flickers and holographic blue orbs appear.

They hover above the console as Leo places the console on the bed and gazes at the orbs in amazement. The orbs begin to take on the appearance of universes and galaxies studded with shining stars.

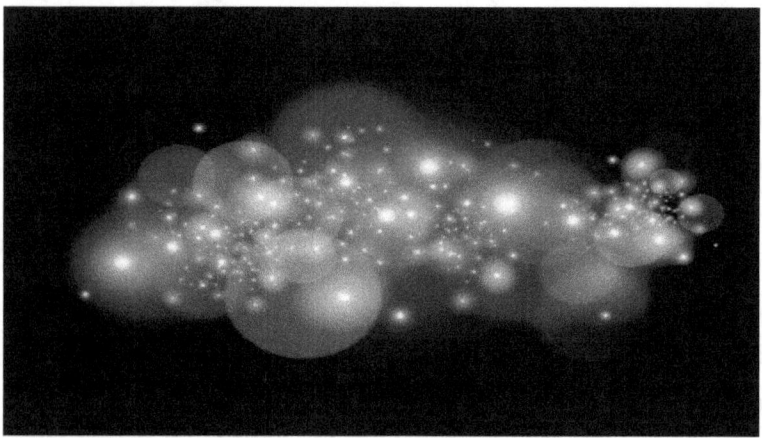

Then a God-like voice with an electronic tone, speaks. Leo isn't sure if the voice is male or female. "Our dear friend, we urge you to take down this message we are about to convey to you." Leo madly jumps up and grabs a pen out of his school bag and a scrappy torn piece of paper, which seems inappropriate in the circumstances. Leo looks stunned, but focused, as he jots down the message. A blue/violet colour lights up his room and is reflecting off his face, creating a surreal atmosphere as he writes down the message, which reads:

We are the chosen ones. We came to Earth many aeons ago to help transform planet Earth to the next evolutionary stage. This task is still to be completed.
At the end of each major evolutionary cycle, time accelerates. We call it, the quickening. You must awaken out of your slumber and prepare yourself for the quickening so that your task will be completed.

This is a great time. An event humanity has long awaited. Time is of the essence, you have been called. Begin your work. We celebrate for that time is near. We have waited a long time. You, and we will not be disappointed. May the truth that you are called, resonate upon your very being and the love and joy that a new cycle brings forth, unite us all as one. May the truth you carry, herald a rebirth of this planet into a new golden age. Your destiny has been foretold, now live the truth. May we all join together as one, loved forever."

The blue orbs fade away. "Hey, don't go yet. I need to know what you want me to do. What's this great event you're going on about? How do I fit into it? Bloody hell! I've got so many questions to ask, don't brush me off like this!" Angry at being cut off, Leo grumbles to himself, "I don't understand this stuff. And, how come I was chosen? What am I supposed to do? Why me? The responsibility he feels at this moment is humongous. It's just too much for him to bear alone. Leo sneaks out of his room and quietly rings Dani to talk to her. However, nobody answers. He slams down the phone and goes straight back to his bedroom. Leo goes to close the door, but Linda holds it open. "Leo what's with the phone and all that commotion coming from your room, I could hear it outside." "What commotion Mum?"

"You know. Don't play dumb with me. I heard the noise of someone talking in your room. Have you and Dani had a fight or something?"
"No Mum. I was just, errr-um…just practising for a school play." Yeah, that's right, just doing some lines in various voices to see what they're like."
"How come you didn't say anything earlier about it?"
"Oh, I forgot. Then I realised we're having a rehearsal tomorrow." Leo tries to close his door, so Linda barges her way into his room. "Maybe I could get some time off work and come and watch you perform. Leo, wouldn't that be good?"
"Well, ahhh… no, you can't! "It's for the education people and parents aren't invited."
"That's not very fair. I think I'll have a talk with your drama teacher about that."
"No Mum you mustn't. I will get really embarrassed and muff my lines if parents are there. If you come along, I won't turn up."

"That's not a nice thing to say to me when I'm interested in what you're doing." Meanwhile, Leo is thinking, you Dumbo. You've really done it this time. How am I going to get out of this porky pie? I'm digging such a deep hole, I wonder if I'm going to be able to climb out. "Well if you like Mum, I will talk to Mrs Hill and see if parents can come."
"Well alright then. I am so looking forward to seeing you doing some acting. How about doing some for me now?"

"No, Mum I'm really tired. I need to put some 'zeds' together."
"I guess you're right. I need my beauty sleep too, as it's been a long day. Good night Leo and don't forget to brush your teeth."
"Y-e-s M-u-m." Leo bolts out of his room and into the bathroom to stop digging a deeper hole from himself.

He looks into the mirror as he cleans his teeth thinking, OMG I'd like, be 'so' in trouble if they find out about any of this stuff. How could I possibly explain it to them? If Dad finds out that'll be the end of it. The next day it's pretty much routine for Leo at school, except he's feeling a little strange and queasy in his stomach. He doesn't feel sick. But thinks, jeez I feel a bit Crusty. Maybe it was that spicy chicken we had at KFC's. Perhaps it could have something to do with that console and that whizzy energy thing. I wish I could go home. I've had this feeling all day that I shouldn't be here. Added to the feeling of being off colour, the afternoon seems to drag on endlessly. Finally the siren rings.

Leo is relieved and chucks his books into his backpack and dashes off to catch the earliest bus home. After an uneventful journey, he gets off the bus and walking home, he can't explain a dreaded feeling. This feeling is reinforced, when he sees the old battered garage Pickup in the driveway. Thinking, how come Dad's home now? Maybe it's nothing. He must've had needed something. As Leo dashes onto the porch and goes to put his key in the door, it opens. Linda is standing there with tears in her eyes and running eyeshadow.

"Mum, what's the matter?" Linda put her arm around Leo's shoulders and leads him into the lounge, where Bryan is sitting silently in an armchair, his head bowed. "What's happened, Dad?" Bryan looks up. He has a grim look on his grease-splattered face and in a choking voice replies, "I'm sorry son…it's Gramps…he's gone."

"Gone where?" Is Leo's response, not wanting to believe something serious has happened. Bryan struggles to get the words out, "He, umm, he passed away this afternoon, peacefully in his sleep." All Leo can get out is, "Nooo," which bounces around inside his head, as if in an echo chamber. Then all of the unexpressed emotions that he had suppressed about Michael's death and all of the events after that, suddenly flood back to the surface.

Leo can't cope with all these feelings at once. His response to this volcano of emotions is to bolt. With tears streaming down his face he turns and runs out of the house and down the driveway, falling over in one of the large potholes. Scrabbling to his feet, he feels no pain from the fall. His left hand and right knee are grazed and bleeding. He doesn't even hear his Mum calling him, nor his Dad chasing after him.

He just runs as fast as his legs will carry him. He sprints across the main road, without looking and runs straight into the bush. He cannot see where he's going due to the salty, stinging tears and what's more, he didn't care. He crashes his way through the thick bush, which lashes at him without mercy. All of his feelings and emotions blocked off, he doesn't feel the sting of the prickly leaves as he brushes past them. Out of breath and overcome by exhaustion, he stops. Gathering his thoughts Leo finds himself at the base of Mt Fielden. Not able to walk another step he sinks down to the ground on his knees and wipes tears from his eyes with the sleeve of his school jumper. Leo stays that way for some time, trying to catch his breath. His lungs feel like they're about to burst. His head dizzy and heart pumping loudly from the sudden exertion and emotional trauma.

After a while, Leo's breathing settles down and as his feelings return, he has to stand up, his right knee very sore. His hand is also throbbing and he realises now, that it's bleeding. Self-preservation kicks in as he thinks, how did I do that? I need something to cover it. I know I'll use my snot-rag. Taking it out, he binds it around the grazed area on the palm of his hand. Now that his emotions have calmed a little, he casts his mind back to the times he and Gramps trekked up Mt Fielden.

Despite the exhaustion, he decides to make his way to the summit to think things through. Slowly he trudges his way up the slope, in stumbling painful steps. Sniffling as he goes and using the damp sleeve of his jumper. Now covered in what looks like snail trails. Exhausted, Leo makes it to the top and immediately sees the sun low in the sky partially hidden by cotton-wool clouds. The light is subdued, matching Leo's state. He notices that from behind the clouds a strong shaft of light shines through the haze, lighthouse fashion. It traces a sharp geometric path across the sky, from west to east. Leo imagines Gramps riding that beam of light on his way to heaven.

While the scene is a peaceful one, it's of no comfort to Leo. He has a sense of great loss and feels angry. Thinking, I've just got my life together and things were looking up. So why did Gramps have to go now? Who else can I talk to about stuff? I use to be able to talk to him about things I couldn't talk to anyone else about. I've got so much I want to share with him. Now, he's gone, forever. Standing there he ponders how things should be. He vents his anger by picking up a rock and hurls it, with all the energy he has left, in the direction of the well. The bouncing rock shatters the stillness. Suddenly out of the well spirals a shiny silver sphere followed by three coloured orbs of a blue, yellow and red colour. They spiral after each other following in the wake of the silver sphere.

They rise into the air and circle around Mt Fielden. Then head slowly towards Leo, hovering a short distance away at head height. Not even this event in any way reduces Leo's anger or his grief. In fact, it only inflames it. Leo picks up a fist-sized piece of limestone and hurls it at the objects with the last of his strength he has left. For someone so angry, Leo's aim is spot on, causing the silver sphere to move to one side as the missile flies by. The three coloured orbs do the same in unison and continue their spiral dance near the sphere. Having spent all of his energy, Leo slumps to the ground on his knees again and stares at the sphere. It moves in a circle around Leo. In his grief, Leo screams out, "Leave me alone!" The sphere moves off and circles back and moves off again with the three coloured balls spiraling behind.

The silver sphere acts as if it were a puppy dog wanting to play or wanting him to follow. The sphere and the coloured orbs suddenly fly off vertically into the air and disappear out of sight, leaving Leo feeling very much alone. His anger turns to disappointment that they chose not to stay. However, a roaring sound like strong winds rushing through trees, make Leo look up. The orbs have returned diving at high speed. They stop in front of Leo creating the rhythmic low humming sound and dancing up and down as they do so.

This goes on for a couple of minutes. Leo is glued to the spot where he has slumped to his knees. For Leo, it's a revelation. He shouts, "Hey! I know who you are. You're the Foo Fighters. That's the same sound Gramps heard and I've heard that sound too." This gets Leo thinking. They must be here for a reason. They helped Gramps. Maybe they're here to help me. Leo shouts at them, "What do you want from me? Are you guys going to just hang around or are you going to help me?"

As Leo stands up the sphere and the coloured orbs quickly spiral off in the direction of the well and disappear down the shaft. In the last of the fading light, Leo slowly wends his way down Mt Fielden. He makes his way through the scrub to the ruin. However, he's still angry at life as he pulls the rope ladder out roughly and attaches it to the gum tree. He finds that the big branch he usually struggles with comes free easily.

Dropping the ladder down the well, he didn't care if anyone sees him or not. He finds the climb down harder than usual, as he's now stiff and sore. Grunting as he makes it to the bottom, he notices that the door is already open and the orbs are hovering just inside the tunnel. He doesn't bother to take off his shoes and as he steps in, the sphere and the coloured orbs float off up the tunnel. They wait until Leo is in the main pyramid chamber.

As Leo arrives, the orbs and the sphere disappear down into the open chamber below. Leo's body is feeling the strain as he makes his way slowly down the ramp and into the chamber. The sphere and the orbs are now circling over the case sitting on the white pillar in the centre. Leo is still angry and yells out, "Hey you guys. Give me a break! My best friend in the world has just died." The orbs float out of the chamber, leaving Leo to ponder what is going on. He sits on the side of the ramp with his head in his hands, quietly sobbing for a few minutes.

Chapter 6
Your name sounds like a brand of Spanish coffee.

Then he hears what sounds like Gramps's voice in his head urging, "use your head son, use your head." Leo jumps up, thinking that Gramps is in the chamber. Yet there's no one there. Tears flow down Leo's cheeks as he ventures over to the case and with his emotions running rampant; he summons all of his focus. Using his mind he glares at the ball and with an angry cry of, "aaahhhhh, the ball begins to move. This time Leo sees that it reacts to his presence. Leo decides to picture the transparent ball rolling out through the hole.

Slowly the ball wobbles down to the hole and drops through it. The transparent ball re-appears and is now glowing brightly, like a star. It dances around like a Dragonfly and darts out of the room. Punching his fist into the air with a loud, "Yessss,"

Leo promptly leaves the chamber. Knowing at that moment, he has released a lot of held-down emotions and now more nervous than anything else, approaches the sixth symbol at the far end. The bright star-like orb is now hovering over the last ramp as it descends slowly to the level below.

Leo follows and annoyed about what he finds. "Hey, this room's empty...wait a minute, that glowing light's going down another ramp. I wonder where that goes." Continuing down to a third level, observing that the orb has disappeared and he whispers, "there's another passage, it must go right back to the centre, maybe?" Anticipating something special, he quickly walks along the passage, "what's this... there's one, two, three...it's a six-sided room. Wow and what's this for...oh, it's only that spacey looking table and those chairs that kept popping up out of the floor." Sitting down, Leo surveys the room. Leo is right, it's hexagonal in shape and there is a symbol on each wall that matches the symbols on the floor above.

Five represent each room he has entered, plus the symbol on the archway. Leo is just starting to relax until he's alarmed by a 'pssst' sound. As he jumps up the sliding panel door closes. Feeling isolated and nervous Leo comforts himself by talking as if someone is with him, "Jeez this looks serious. I hope everything's okay. Hello you guys, go easy on me, please." Sitting down again, he stares at the table, "what's this... it's moving."

The top of the table slides open. "There's gloves in...Oh My God! They've got six fingers on each hand. Whoa! Hang on! What am I supposed to do with this panel?" Examining the gloves, Leo finds they look like a black gauntlet worn by a knight with raised tubes and markings across the top and the fingers. Each raised section has what appears to be a crystal embedded. He tries on one glove, but has a problem, "bloody hell, what do I do with the sixth finger? Oh well here goes."

He slides on the left glove and reaches over and fits on the other, worming his fingers in until it fits comfortably. Pensively, he examines the panel display and declares, "Well there's one way to find out what happens next. YOLO! Let's bring it on!" Taking a deep, deep breath and exhaling, Leo waves his hands over the panel display. As he does so the gloves begin to heat up.

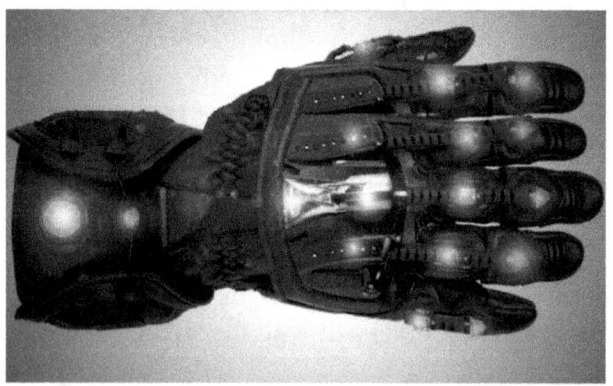

Leo looks down at the gloves with a shocked look. They suddenly tighten around his hands, like a vacuum seal. Before he can recover from this, the ceiling above him draws up in six sections.

Like a sliced up pie, it exposes him to the pyramid main chamber. "Wow. Here I go. Or, maybe it's…here they come," he shouts bravely. "Whoa! What's going on, the floor's rising?" The floor section under Leo's feet begins to rise gently. It moves up until its level with the floor of the main chamber. The crystals embedded in the gloves begin to glow like LED lights. They're of different colours and around one centimetre above the gloves. They emit a high pitched zinging sound, which makes Leo feel uneasy.

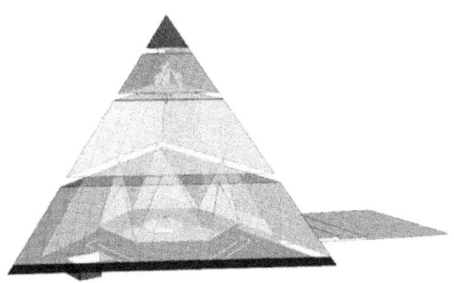

Suddenly and without warning, a see-through holographic head-up display appears in front of him. Leo's body jumps at the unexpected sight. The blue coloured display looks like a 3D cube. It has symbols and writing Leo has never seen before floating around inside the cube. Including small pastel coloured oval buttons. "Okay, I've got your gloves on - they're making funny noises and lit up. What do you want me to do now?" The answer came in the form of a messenger. The silver sphere descends into the main chamber with the red coloured orb, dancing around the sphere.

"I got it. You want me to do something with that red button. But, which hand do I use? This is weird. I feel like a loony-tune talking to a ball of light." As he checks each hand the laser lights on the left-hand glow red. Holding his breath Leo waves his hand through the red button, but nothing happens. He let's go of the breath, "phewwww, what now?" Leo looks up, to see the yellow orb spiralling into view. He takes this as a cue to activate the yellow button, with the right-hand glove as that is now emitting yellow laser light. "Hey, Mr Foo fighter, this is really cool stuff.

Is this a highly advanced craft? …okay, then you're not talking, eh - what do I do now?" A blue button appears inside the display and begins to glow. At the same time, the blue orb spirals into the main chamber and dances around the sphere with the other two orbs.

Leo activates the blue button and immediately two glowing green boxes appear each blinking on and off. "Well, he goes nothing!" Leo plunges the two gloves into the green buttons. The apex of the pyramid begins to pulsate with flashing rainbow-coloured lights and a hexagonal disk is rotating at high speed above him.

From this flows a gentle golden liquid-looking light, which to Leo, looks like a clear plastic shower curtain. The light pulsates like a jellyfish until it forms a three-sided tetrahedron pyramid. It's apex pointing menacingly at Leo.

It descends until the tip of the tetrahedron touches the floor, enveloping Leo completely. Meanwhile, Leo's mouth is wide open in amazement. His heart is pounding and his breathing rapid, with short shallow breaths. His body is reacting to the acceleration as if spiraling upwards in a Roller Coaster. The helpless out-of-control state turns to shock, as he hears a voice. "Don't be afraid my dear friend. I am here to help you. Please relax and take some deep slow breaths." Leo is confused, "wait a minute. That voice came from inside my head. What's going on?"

"Please don't be afraid as we are not going to hurt you. I'm speaking to you via thought transference." Leo looks around bewildered, "I'm not scared. But who are you?"

"My name is L-CRO, it sounds like E-l-c-a-r-o. And in a sense, we are one family. The only difference is I exist in your future, while you are in my past."
"El-Caro, El-Caro. Hmmm… your name sounds like a brand of Spanish coffee."

"That's what I like to hear, a sense of humour. To understand my name and our connection - when you go home, look in the mirror and you will have your answer. I'll give you a hint. Look where the beginning ends and where the end begins. Also, do you know that you don't need to speak out loud to communicate with me? I am tuning into your thoughts via the geometric structure around you. So, if you're comfortable that way, then talk on."

"You're lucky I found you and came here to help, I think."
"Correction my young friend - you didn't find me. I found you. But I agree we can help each other."
"Well El-Caro, I have so many questions - I don't know where to start. I'm still finding this funny; that you're talking inside my head."
"Then I will begin. Firstly, I am what you would say, the 'Head Cohuna' of the Guardians. We all send our support to you at the transition of your beloved Grandfather. You know he's also of our family too."

Leo nods, "I knew it, I knew it. He's so wise, I mean he 'was' wise and now miss him so much."
"It is necessary that we must keep this communication short. Your father is frantically looking for you - he needs your support too, right now."
"But, I haven't even asked any questions, yet."
"Well, I will allow just one, for the moment."
"What do you call this thing I'm sitting on?"
"It's called a Sentinel Pod."
"I can feel you have another question. Dimensional emissary is the best way to describe my role. There will be plenty of time for more questions. So don't worry. I think it is best you find your father." As Leo emerges from the well it is nearly dark. He's disappointed about the short contact, particularly after all the effort he has put in.

Meanwhile, Bryan has been searching for some time and frantically calling out, "Leo! Leo! Where are you?" Leo puts his disappointment to one side, "Dad…Dad. I'm over here."

"Thank God, son, I was really worried. Where have you been?"

"Ohh…ummm, well it was like this. I went up Mt Fielden and sat for a while and thought about Gramps."

"Leo, your hand it's wrapped up. What have you done to it? "Oh, I fell over - it's nothing much, really."

Bryan puts his arm around Leo's shoulders, "okay my boy, let's go home now. Mum will clean it up for you." They arrive home to find Linda standing by the letterbox, anxiously clutching hold of Leo's old teddy bear for comfort. "Thank God you're safe Leo. You gave us such a fright when you raced off like that. Look at you, you're a mess. Let's get you inside and get you cleaned up."

Later that evening there is a knock at the door and Dani is standing there with a bunch of flowers. "I heard the news about Gramps and came over to see if Leo is alright and oh, these are for you Mrs Shepherd, from my Mum."

"How thoughtful, they're lovely. Don't forget to thank Lena when you go home, won't you?" Dani nods as she hands Linda the flowers. "Here Danicka, you sit here, while I get out a vase.

But if you like, Leo's in his room. Knock on his door first, because he gets really grumpy if you don't." Dani knocks on Leo's door. "It's me, are you okay?" Leo has tears in his eyes, but doesn't want Dani to see him this way and pulls himself together. "Yeah, I'm okay I suppose," he pauses before he lets Dani in. "I'm sorry to hear about Gramps, I know you were really close. I just don't know what to say." Dani reaches out to give Leo a big hug. "Here Dani, sit on my bed. I'll just move this stuff." "Leo! What happened to your hand?

"Oh, it's nothin'. I tripped in the driveway and took some bark off and some off me knee." Leo changes the subject quickly, "guess what! I have some other news for you too. I've made a breakthrough, you know in the underground thingy."

"Wow," you mean you moved that ball?"

"Dani, this is hard. But it took Gramps's death for me to get angry enough to move it with my mind."

"You mean you actually moved it - just by looking at it?"

"Well, there's more to it than that. I imagined it rolling down to the other end and falling out of the hole."

"What happened, then?"

"The ball thing lit up like a star and flew out into the main area. Then the last floor panel opened and it flew down there."

"That's amazing. I wish I'd been there to see it. What's in the last room?"

"Well, when I went down the ramp, the room looked the same as the others. But there was another ramp down to a lower level."

"There's another level to that place?"

"Sort of, the lower level had this doorway leading to a completely different area." Dani wriggles with delight on Leo's bed, "This is getting exciting. Then what happened?"

"There was this table thing and it's called a Sentinel Pod. It's like a control panel and there were gloves you put on. And guess what? They had six fingers."

"Six fingers, that's unbelievable. Go on, I want to know more."

"I sat down to put my hands into the screen that popped up - it looked like a blue cube. I waved the gloves over some coloured buttons. Then this liquid light stuff came down and a man's voice came through loud and clear inside my head. It was as if he was standing next to me. And, and, get this. His name is L-CRO which sounds like El-Caro."

"That name sounds like an Italian brand of coffee."

"Yeah, that's what I said too, except mine was Spanish. And he goes, "Don't be afraid. I'm here to help you.""

"Wow! Who is he and what did he say?"

"He said he has something to do with the Guardians or something like that."

"Where is he from and why is he contacting you?"

"Well, we didn't get much of a chance to say anything, because Dad was looking for me. El-Caro thought that I should find Dad first as he had been looking for me all over the place."

"Why was he doing that?"

"Errrr, well, put it this way, when they told me about Gramps I got really upset and chucked a mental and sort of bolted.
I went up Mt Fielden to think for a while. Yeah, and when I was up there I got buzzed by four of those Foo Fighters." Leo demonstrates with his hand, "yeah they zoomed around like this and went out of sight and came zooming back."
"Amazing, so they do exist?"
"Yeah, and what's more I can go back and talk to El-Caro.
Because Dad said I don't have to go to school tomorrow if I don't feel like it."

Dani places her index finger across her lips and her thumb under her chin as if pondering on something, "you know Leo, I'm doing Italian at the school and Caro in Italian means "beloved" or "dear." So El-Caro might mean he's "The beloved or special one."

Sitting down on the bed, Leo moves up and down trampoline fashion with excitement. "Oh and that's right, I remember now. When I said about the coffee bit, he goes..."look in the mirror and you'll have your answer. Oh! He also gave a hint, but it's really weird. He said look where the beginning ends and the end begins."
"And did you?"
"Yes, but I couldn't see anything but me."
"Maybe he's you, but from the future?" Leo shakes his head, "Nah," I doubt it."
"Go on Leo write his name down and see what it looks like."
"Okay." Leo grabs a piece of paper and scrawls El-Caro in big letters. So what do I do now?" Dani shrugs her shoulders, "I don't know. Maybe look at it in the mirror or something. How should I know?" Leo jumps off his bed and goes over to the dresser and looks into the mirror.

Mucking around he licks the paper and sticks it to his forehead. "You mean like Celebrity Heads?" Leo looks at the piece of paper and then at Dani's reflection in the mirror. "See this! When I spell it out.....O-R-A-C-L-E, it spells the word oracle as the letters are all back to front. Dani, what's an oracle?"

"I don't know. Do you have a dictionary handy?" Leo leaves his bedroom and calls out, "M-u-m!"
"Is everything alright dear?"
"Yes Mum, do you know where the dictionary is?"
"It's over on the fridge. While you're there, shouldn't you offer Dani a drink?"
"Oh yeah, I forgot." Leo grabs two glasses from the cupboard and takes out a bottle of cool drink and tucks the dictionary under his arm and goes back to his room. While Leo pours out the cool drink, Dani thumbs through the dictionary.

"Here it is...it says an oracle is a person who with divine guidance, speaks of a revelation, vision or prophecy."
"What do you think Leo?"
"Yeah, maybe that's it. I'll ask him tomorrow. I can't wait."
"What about the other bit you said?"
"Oh yeah, it was about looking at the beginning and the end."
"Maybe it also has something to do with his name."

Leo picks up the notepaper with El-Caro on it. "Maybe if I take the first and last letter...all it says is 'eo'."
Dani moves closer to Leo holding the note. "That's nearly your name. Why don't you write down Oracle and try to match the ends?"

"Okay." Leo sticks his tongue out subconsciously, as he loops the ends. "OMG! Look at this Dani. When I wrap it around like this, the end and the beginning meet. If I flatten it - it spells Leo. How clever is that?"

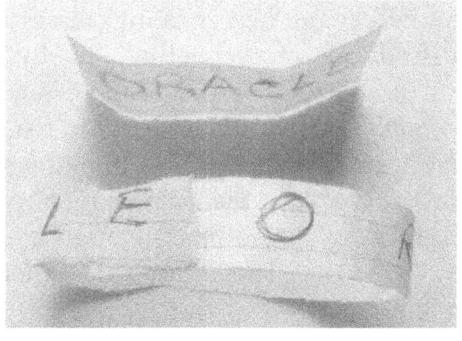

"Yeah, that's so cool, huh. Leo, can I try it, too?" Dani checks it and then jumps up from Leo's bed and hands the piece of paper back to him. "Well on that note, I'd better go. Unlike one lucky person I know, I have to go to school tomorrow."

"I wouldn't exactly call it lucky, after what's happened."
I'm sorry. I didn't mean it that way."
"Yeah, I know. Can I walk you home?" Leo escorts Dani back to her place. As she opens the front door, she looks at Leo and speculates, "Wow things are really getting exciting. I wonder what that dude wants."

"Yeah, I was wondering about that too. I'll see you later." They give each other a little hand wave goodbye as Leo turns and walks down the porch steps. Walking home, Leo has mixed feelings. Thinking, I feel so mixed up at the moment. I really miss Gramps, but I can't help being excited about what this El-Caro dude wants to tell me.

Right now I feel like a stuffed maggot. My brain feels like mush right now - I'm going straight to bed. Arriving home Leo heads for his pillow. After a couple of loud yawns, he falls asleep. However, it is not a restful slumber as he begins to toss and turn. Soon he's awoken with cold shivers, his teeth chattering. Leo gets out of bed and puts on a sweater and adds another blanket to his bed. He climbs back into bed and curls up into a ball. However, this doesn't stop the shivers, either. Soon he finds that he's sweating profusely and yet he still has the cold shivers. He mumbles to himself, "what's going on. One minute I've got cold goosies and then I'm sweating. I've never felt like this before. Maybe I'm getting the flu or could it be something emotional?"

Getting out of bed again, Leo goes into the kitchen to get a drink and cool down. He finds his mother sitting quietly at the table, head bowed, fiddling with a lock of her hair. Linda looks up with a start. "Phew! You gave me such a fright, then. I couldn't sleep either. I got up for a drink and have been just sitting here thinking. What about you?" "I couldn't sleep either. I've got the cold shivers, yet I'm sweating." "I know you're still upset over Gramps. Let's go and sit in the lounge together, with just the lamp on." They both sit together on the couch. Leo cuddled up to his mother.

Drifting off, Leo isn't sure if he's half-awake or half-asleep, as he feels a presence in the room. Linda is aware of this too, but is too scared to speak and doesn't want to disturb Leo. In the dimness of the light, they both see a shape suggesting the outline of a person over in the far corner. The light around the figure is much brighter than the dim light from the lamp.

Although they both feel edgy, a warm friendly, loving feeling sweeps over them. The bright light and the presence fade away. Neither Leo nor Linda say anything to each other. Words are not required. Both understood Gramps had come to say goodbye. However, they both jump when they hear the back door open. Bryan has just come in from the garden. "Sorry I startled you both. I couldn't sleep either and I've been pacing up and down the garden. I'm not sure if I imagined this, but I thought I saw someone out there by the lounge window and when I went over, there wasn't anyone there."

Linda and Leo look at each other and smile, but say nothing. Linda moves her arm. "God you're a dead weight, now. Leo, are you alright to go back to bed as I feeling really tired now."
"Yes, mum."
"What about you Bryan?"
"I'm getting a torch and just going to check around the place."
"Okay, suit yourself." Leo and Linda disappear off to their beds. Finally, both sleep soundly in the knowledge that Gramps had been there for Leo.

Meanwhile, Bryan can't sleep and is out prowling around the garden with a large torch. The next morning Leo wakes early, before realising that he's allowed to stay home from school. Earlier, Bryan and Linda had gone into town to pay a visit to the nursing home. They're sorting out Gramps's affairs and arranging his funeral.

Leo is exhausted and promptly falls back to sleep. Around lunchtime, Leo surfaces from his bed. His stomach is grumbling in protest - about missing two meals. Getting up and stretching, he quickly gets dressed and heads for the kitchen. Scratching his foggy head, he mutters, "What was I going to do?

Oh, yeah, make some food and take some cordial with me. Can't wait to get over there and talk to that El-Caro dude." Leo cooks some toast, topped with vegemite and munching away remarks, "El-Caro, El-Caro, where for art thou, El-Caro." He puts some fruit and cordial into his backpack for the trip. Setting off he is greeted by a fine spring day, but complains, "Jeez it's bright out here," shielding his eyes as they adjust to the light. As he ducks across the road, Leo acknowledges to himself, I can't wait to get down there and have more time with that dude.

I wonder where he's from and all that kind of stuff? Leo makes sure that he isn't being followed and carefully surveys the site around the well, before venturing back down into the complex. Leo opens the triangular door and runs up the passage, in his eagerness to find out more.

He makes his way down to the third level and onto the Sentinel Pod. Settling down in the seat at the console, he acts like an old hand. "Okay, here goes nothing," as he places his hands into the gloves. The head-up display lights up on cue, as Leo places his hand over the red, then yellow and blue buttons. Then, holding his breath plunges both gloves into the flashing green boxes.

Again the liquid curtain of light descended on Leo, bathing him in a champagne-coloured light. Again, his body feels like it's on a roller coaster ride. However, this time he's ready for it. Holding his breath, Leo waits for L-CRO voice to come through. "Welcome back, my dear brother. You don't need to hold your breath." Leo speaks hesitantly - not use to telepathic conversations, "Errr… ahhh, I didn't know we were brothers - is that right?"
"We are 'Brothers of Light' are we not?"
"Well I dunno, you're telling the story."
"I can feel that you want to know everything about me, so I will tell you my story. So that way what we discuss will make some sense to you."
"Yeah, I'm all ears. No, I mean - I'm all head…oh, I'm not sure what I mean."
"I know what you mean. It would make it easier if you could see my world, but your mind is not yet fully developed to handle such information. You understand that we have to accelerate your cellular structure to achieve this connection; hence that funny feeling."

"Yeah, I was wondering about that. Still, it was a cheap thrilling ride."
"Okay. I can give you a quick glimpse of what I look like, so don't be afraid if you feel a power surge in the Pineal Gland in the centre of your head. Some call it the Third Eye and it's shaped like a pine cone. The surge will soon pass." A tight band forms around the top of Leo's head and he feels a warm surge around his face and cheeks. Closing his eyes, he is shocked to see a meta-face forming with radiating shafts of light from behind the face, as if projected out of space or a wormhole. Slowly a figure emerges and Leo can't decide if it's male or female. Leo is surprised to see L-CRO standing in front of him with a raised six-fingered hand. L-CRO is bluish in colour and wrapped in a blue robe and a brown cape with a silver edge. Leo feels it's male and looks closest to an ancient Egyptian.

He is tall and hairless except for a platted goatee beard. Leo is fixated on the white light emanating from a broach or crystal over his heart area. Behind L-CRO is a colourful city of lights with buildings of all sorts of geometric shapes and sizes. What astounds Leo is that he assumed L-CRO would be a wise old man and yet he has a young fresh looking face with a blue tinge. After Leo recovers from the energy overload in his head, L-CRO brags, "Well do I measure up to your expectations?"

"Well, errr, I don't know. I thought you'd be older."

"I am old, I'm 231 cycles old. A cycle is the time it takes our two suns to circulate around our great central sun in what you would call our galaxy. Genetically I am similar to you, except my hands have six fingers and a different level of vibration in my energy field. That's why you noticed that I have a bluish tinge to my skin."

"How tall, are you?"

"We measure our height in terms of our energy column. My energy column reaches 2.5 metres or 8 feet in your Earth measurements.

"You have two suns. It must get really hot?"

"Yes two suns and in our language, as we have no vowels, phonetically for you we say NeCTR and RoNCN. However, they're not in the same colour spectrum as your sun. They are Blue/Violet in colour and produce rays of high energy. My home planet is called, 'KMN-JL' and it is located in a galaxy cluster called, 'L-TRN 3', in the 7th Universe."

"Man, that just blows me away. I've read heaps of Sci-fi books, but I just can't get the grey-matter around the idea of other universes actually existing. I thought it was just science hocus pocus."

"Yes, I can understand the difficulty in comprehending this. It's quite simple, really. If you understand something about music, then you vibrate at one particular beat and we vibrate at a different beat and hence a time-phase difference. That's the reason you can't directly perceive an alternate existence at a higher frequency - certainly not with your level of technology and mind capacity."

"Then how come we can talk, if what you say is true?"
"A-r-e! That's what I like, an inquiring mind. Our technology is highly advanced and the complex you're in is what you could call a 'Sentinel'. It acts as a gateway between your world and ours. Our frequency is higher so we can detect your presence, but you cannot detect ours, yet."

"I was wondering what to call this place, so 'Sentinel' sounds pretty wicked, so what's a Sentinel?"
"In your language, a Sentinel is someone or something that observes. It actually does more than that. We use it to passively gather knowledge from other worlds."

"There are other Sentinels across different galaxies within our own universe and other universes that have a different frequency, expression and density to ours."
"Why are you doing that for?"
"We gather knowledge to preserve it and to exchange it."

"El-Caro, isn't that like spying on other people?"
"Not quite, Leo. We are seekers of truth and understanding. However, spying is a war-like activity where truth and lies are two sides of the same coin. "I don't understand what you mean by frequency, expression and density?"
"It's important that you understand that each universe, galaxy and planet has its own consciousness and a collective or group consciousness. That this is not restricted to just humans, plants and animals.

What this means at a spiritual level, is that for consciousness to exist, it must have an expressed purpose."
"El-Caro what do you mean when you say collective consciousness. I don't understand that bit."

"Put it this way, when you look in the mirror each morning you recognise yourself as existing independently from the mirror, Yes. That means you have a separate awareness or consciousness. When I look at you via the Sentinel, I can see the energy fields around you. I can see them because my energy fields vibrate higher than yours. You have a number of energetic layers around you, which get thinner as your energy field spreads out. Eventually, your energy field overlaps with the fields of everyone on your planet."

"We call these overlapping fields, a collective or group consciousness. There is also a separate planetary consciousness too. It has its own frequency, expression and density. You might have heard in your science studies about The Hundredth Monkey Syndrome."
"Oh, oh, I know that's the one where enough monkeys can do a new trick and other monkeys can pick it up from other islands, somehow?"
"Well yes. Those monkeys on different islands are part of a group mind. They can do new things without being aware of where it came from."

"Can you please explain the words, frequency, expression and density so that I've got it right."
"Frequency is the level of spiritual awareness of a person, place or thing. The closer it is to a creator-like action, the higher the frequency.

The expression means how we act it out, how we think or feel about different situations presented to us for our learning. Really, the expression is about how you go about it in your own life. The density is just the dimensional level. For instance, on Earth, you exist on the third-dimensional level, but there is also a fourth and fifth-dimensional aspect to your realm."

"Okay El-Caro, I sort of understand that from my Sci-fi books. So then what's your purpose?"
"Our planetary expression is Knowledge in Action and my individual one is to express it through communication."
"Then what's Earth's expression?"

"Don't you know what the expressed purpose is?"
"Well no. Nobody has ever spoken to me about it before."
"Hmmm, I guess it's an issue of the Freewill Charter."
"What's free will got to do with it?"

"Connected Awareness is your planetary purpose. This is meant to be expressed through a separation of consciousness, or free will. With each person deciding on how and when they will contribute to the purpose - making choices which take them closer to that purpose. I can feel that you are not getting this, so I will give you an example. All people of the Earth have free will to express their life in any way they wish, without the presence of other existences, whether past, present or future. This is a collective agreement as a way of giving full and complete expression to the purpose of connected awareness. To demonstrate this, your people are attempting to achieve this purpose, firstly through a World Order and then Globalisation. I am sure you have heard of those."
"Yes, we've covered stuff like that at school."

"In addition, your people are trying to express this purpose through the Internet, use of mobile phones, SMS messages and e-mails - to get connected, so to speak."
"So even though we're not aware of it, we're doing it. Aren't we?"
"There you have hit the nail on the head, I think is the phrase."
"My Dad says, "You've swallowed the canary.""
"An interesting turn of phrase, I think your Dad's one sick puppy."
"Hey! You pinched my line." Both L-CRO and Leo laugh. Leo needs the light relief after such heavy insights. But he's hungry for more. "Go on El-Caro."

"The point I made earlier before we got side-tracked, your people are trying to connect with each other. However, it's not with full inner awareness. But through external technological means. You already have the power to communicate from within. You don't need the technology. All it requires is for your people to be more tolerant and loving to each other and the full expression will occur. But it requires a significant change of awareness from a small percentage of people to achieve this."
"It requires a full appreciation of your natural world. You all have telepathic abilities and have forgotten how to use them. There is little awareness of how powerful thoughts really are.

Little attention is paid to how your people feel on the inside, is mirrored in their outer world. Inner conflict is being expressed externally all over the world at this time. You've seen the dramas in the news and on your television, have you not?"

"Yeah, the World's been going ballistic."

"Well, if there's an inner conflict through anger, hate, intolerance and fear in a person's mind, then that's what they attract in their outer world. If you are an angry person you will attract angry people, even when you are not aware that you're angry. An angry country of people will attract disasters even though they are not conscious of it."

"The most important thing is that you might not know what's happening on the inside. But if you are aware, or conscious of what's happening to you on the outside in your daily life. Then, you can change it should you not like what's happening."

"Well, I must be doing something right then because I feel my life's really cool at the moment."

"Sorry to spoil your party, but who was the angry ant that came into the Sentinel not more than 24 hours ago. And, who threw a rock at my Polymath Sphere?"

"You mean the Foo Fighter. Give me a break! My Gramps had just died and it was just one rock."

"Fortunately you were able to release your anger, but many people simmer away without realising the damage they are doing to themselves and to others on all levels of existence."

"Do you know that your negative thoughts, particularly about girls, led you here? By putting girls 'down' the way you did, to boost your own self-esteem, you fell 'down' too - right into the Mount Fielden well. What's more the very gender you were putting down happens to come along and rescues you. I'm sure you can see the irony in that."

"Yeah I get the message El-Caro, I feel pretty stupid now. I can see that I ended up being lower than them in the end - at the bottom of the well."

"That is true. But the message is that from the depths of a well you can see the stars shining in daylight - something you can't do from mountaintops. I can feel that you don't understand my analogy."

"You got that right."

"What I am saying is that it can take a fall or a feeling of being really low emotionally before you understand that this is not what you want from your life. There's something better out there to be enjoyed. The really tough moments are those you really learn from."

"Oh, I get it now. You mean no pain no gain."

"Ah, now I feel we are getting somewhere. It's a duality - you cannot know and experience what love is unless you also understand what hate is. I hope you can see the importance of your thoughts creating your reality and how that can have an impact on your daily life. If you have lots of angry thoughts, they will soon spill over into your outer life. You then attract angry people and situations to you. These events tend to escalate. Left unchecked the anger can gain momentum and at a certain point spill over on a planetary scale and then onto higher planes of existence."

"So you and everyone else have a clear responsibility to monitor their behaviour and feelings."

"El-Caro, you mean that if enough people became really angry, then we will have an angry planet and angry ants everywhere going ballistic?"

"That would depend upon how many happy, well-balanced people there are to counteract such a situation."

"El-Caro, what do you mean when you say, higher planes of existence?"

"They're an extension of your energy fields and just because you can't see or hear other realities it doesn't mean they don't exist. And, it doesn't mean that you are not connected to them. That's the reason people on the planet have cut themselves off from other realities, because you can learn about making choices via free will without affecting everything else. That's why thoughts carry such power and it comes with great responsibility. However, that is soon going to change and that's why you were given that message after you finished the game console."

"I was going to get to that, as I don't understand why you picked on me? I mean what you're telling me is humongous and how is, little- ol'-me supposed to fix it. I don't even know where to start."

"That's easy. Every journey starts with one step. So take one step at a time and make it a 'baby' step."

"How do I do that?"

"Well Leo, it's time now to walk the talk, as your people say. You can make a difference and in doing so can become a future leader of your people. But you can only do this if you decide not to be a victim of circumstances and take responsibility for your actions, your thoughts and your emotions."

"Okay, but how do I do that?"

"It's quite simple. All you have to do is treat every living thing, as you would like to be treated. If you want respect, then respect all living things. If you want love - then love all things. Let's take a look at your life - what's working and what's not?"

"Well let's see. "I feel happy. I've got a girlfriend and I met you. What else…hmm. Oh yeah, I just lost my best friend in the world and my Dad doesn't relate to me very well since Michael died."

"Okay, now you're starting to see where things might not be right. What about your school?"

"Actually, there's this kid at school who bullies me. Oh yes and a bus driver that gives me grief. They're both absolute arseholes."

"Okay, let's call this homework. It won't be as hard as you think and no, it won't be painful. In fact, you will gain more from the experience than you give. The insights will amaze you. Things are not always as they seem. Try and see it from someone else's perspective.

You might see a totally different picture. So in a sense, there are many realities, all of them true from the perspective of the observer. It is called the 'Parallax Perspective'."

"The Para-what?"

"It's when an object appears to change because of a change in the position of the observer."

"I'm sorry I asked."

"Never mind, you'll get it when you put it into action. Why don't we pick an easy one, like the bus driver?"

"You mean Old-grouch-face? He hates everyone. Why should I go out of my way to do the 'touchy-feely' stuff with that loser?" Leo pouts and raises his hand to his head, making a capital L shape with his thumb and finger.

"There's an angry thought. However, with an attitude like that, you'll be the 'L' for loser. When you work on him, you work on yourself. You will gain inner self-confidence and that act of kindness will rub off onto others that Old-grouch-face contacts. That one act of unconditional love, because that's what it is, will multiply a hundredfold."

"You mean the monkeys again."

"At least, that monkey will be off your back. Isn't that reward enough?"

"What do you mean by unconditional love? I haven't heard that before."

"Let's say that the opposite of unconditional love is; I will love you if you do as I say. Or, if you give me things and keep giving, then I will love you. That's placing conditions on your expression of love. Love properly expressed it is giving without the expectation of receiving."

"Okay I get it, sort of. So what's the homework, then?"

"I'll leave it to you to decide what to do, as I can't interfere with your right of choice. Maybe if you talk to him, you might gain a better insight into why he is, the way he is. I think it's time to stop. Your brain's going into overload. You've got lots to mull over. We shall continue our chat some other time."

"Okay El-Caro, I'll calc-u-later." Leo has a big smile and he takes a big outward breath.

"We have a saying too, Leo. But it's a hand gesture and not in words. Imagine that we are parting and as we do, I hold my hand open above my head, then touch my forehead with the tips of my fingers and hold my hand over the heart. That is followed by a slight bow of the head. Roughly translated, because it has far more meaning than words can convey - I acknowledge the Great One. Together with my thoughts and my heart, they are connected as one."

With that, Leo waves his gloved right hand through the holographic cube and touches the red button. The curtain of light lifts and fades away towards the apex of the Sentinel. Removing the gloves,

Leo places them on the desk panel and sits quietly for a moment or two, his head still spinning. He's trying to take it all in and make some sense of what has been revealed to him.

As he leaves the Sentinel and climbs out of the well, he again has mixed feelings. Thinking, I don't understand why this dude picked on me. I don't understand what's going on. What's more this stuff makes me feel like I'm at the deep end of the pool, without the water wings. Maybe they've got the wrong person. I feel so small when you think about the scale of what El-Caro's talking about. He's so wise and I'm such a Derp.

Walking back home on the track, Gramps comes to mind, as Leo recalls vividly their last conversation. Yeah, that's right he said I was to listen to people and really observe what's going on around me. Leo arrives home and lets himself in. He finds himself alone, as Bryan and Linda are not back yet from their trip into town. He feels mentally deadbeat and decides to head to this room and take a nap.

However, the nap doesn't last long. He stirs on hearing Bryan and Linda arrive home with a small pile of things belonging to Gramps. Bryan dumps the belongings onto the kitchen table. "Bryan, don't put them there! I got to make dinner," snaps Linda. Bryan snaps back, "Where am I going to put this stuff, then? It was your idea to bring this junk home." It's obvious to Leo that putting Gramps's affairs in order has brought up lots of issues and they're taking it out on each other.

On hearing this Leo mutters under his breath, "I think I'll exit, stage-left. I don't need them going on like that just now. Where's my skateboard? I think I'll duck out the front and do some ordinary kid stuff for a change." After doing a couple of runs, up and down the driveway, he can't be bothered with skateboarding either and decides to head off to the shop. "Mum, can I have some change to go down the Supa Deli?" "That's a good idea. We need some milk and bread." "Do I have to," bleats Leo, not wanting to be responsible for anything, right now. "Do you want to go to the shop or not?"

"I suppose so." Despite his protests, the walk does him some good, feeling more grounded after being in the Sentinel. On the way home, he mulls over what he might say when he confronts Old-grouch-face. He imagines getting onto the bus and rehearses different lines, to hear how they feel.

*****

The next morning Leo gets to the bus stop earlier than usual to rehearse what he's going to say to Old-grouch-face. After rehearsing his lines many times, to get it right, he's still nervous as the bus pulls into the bus bay. The door opens and Leo takes a deep breath as he climbs up the steps and hands over a $5 note. Old-grouch-face snatches it and snaps at Leo, "why can't you kids use a bus pass, like everyone else." Leo has built up so much tension thinking it through, that he drops one coin. It rolls under the driver's seat. "Leave it sonny. Here take this," he snaps again. "I haven't got all day, you know." Leo takes this as a cue. Breathing in, he takes a deep breath and responds, "Why are you always grumpy to everyone?"

Old-grouch-face stares straight back at Leo, "nobody has said that to me before." He turns around in the driver's seat to the other passengers and what about the rest of you?" A man in blue overalls shouts, "Yeah, the boy's right."
"YAH," cheer the passengers. Further support is added as an old man in a suit at the back of the bus shouts, "good on you mate. You tell the old bastard what you think of him."

"I'm...I'm really sorry. I didn't know I was that bad. Since my Betsy died - she's my wife of forty years - things haven't been the same. "He places his hand down on his left leg and pats it. "I've got this bad hip, it makes driving a real chore. But, you wouldn't know what it's like to lose someone you love - you're only a youngster."

"You're so wrong. I do know what it's like to lose someone close. My grandfather died two days ago and my older brother Michael was killed in a farm accident. So, don't tell me I don't know what it's like. If you don't like driving buses, why don't you chuck it in?"

"I've been driving for 35 years - it's the only thing that keeps me from thinking too much about Betsy." A shout comes from further down the bus. "Okay, enough of your life story. Let's get moving. I'll be late for work," grumbles the man in the overalls.

Old-grouch-face shifts in his seat and closes the door, swinging the bus into the traffic. Leo sits down with his brain ticking over. I feel like an absolute goose, now. That lot went down like a lead balloon. What happened to all that stuff I was going to say? I stuffed it up and now nothing's changed.

Leo sits there brooding about how it should have been until the bus pulls into the school bus bay. Leo decides to get off via the back door. As Leo stands up and turns, he notices Old-grouch-face looking intently at him in the mirror.

Leo bounds out the back door. As he does so, he can see in the corner of his eye, Old-grouch-face looking at him in the side mirror. The bus is standing motionless as Leo walks away. Leo looks back as the bus pulls out. Old-grouch-face waves goodbye out of the side window. Leo instinctively waves back, but pulls his hand down self- consciously and looks around. Thinking, I hope no one saw. You dummy, that wasn't cool.

Leo makes his usual trek to the Library before school starts, yet can't set his mind to reading. He sits pondering, taking stock of where he's at. A million thoughts go through his mind, but nothing seems to make sense. The siren rings, jolting him out of his contemplative state.

Leaving the library he wanders off to his first class. Looking at his timetable he mutters, "b-o-r-ing, not Community Awareness with that loopy Miss Arnold, again." As Leo finds an empty seat, nearby students are discussing something about a special assignment. They all go quiet as Miss Arnold enters the room. "Hello, girls and boys. Are we happy 'Petals' today?" The class groans in unison. "That's good. I'm sure you all remember what I was going to reveal today? Yes, that's right the subject of your assignment. I think you'll find this will be lots of fun. What I want you Possums to do is interview another student and craft a story about them."

There are further groans from the class with Miss Arnold raising her voice, "Quiet please! To make this more interesting, you can't pick someone you know. In fact, we are going to have a secret lottery. In this tin are names from the other class. How does that sound?" Jason pipes up, "Pretty gross Miss. What if I get some Nerd?"

"My heart bleeds for you, Jason. I'll read out the Roll and you can each come forward and choose a name."

As Miss Arnold reads out the Roll, the first student reluctantly comes up and takes a name from the tin. This proves to be a noisy affair as each student nervously reaches into the tin. There are numerous reactions that include, phew, "errr gross" and questions like; "can I double dip?"

It takes a while before Leo's name is called out. He fishes into the tin and silently reads out the name, "Fridge". Oh, No. You gotta be kidding me. What did I do wrong? Did I step on a black cat or what?" The class in unison asks, "Come on Sheps read out who you got." "No way," he responds, "it's supposed to be secret." Walking back to his desk, he scrunches up the paper in his fist. A bright spark shouts, "I bet you got Kelvin Slater." The class responds with the chant of, "Fridge, Fridge, Fridge, HOO, HOO, HOO!" Battling to keep the peace, Miss Arnold admonishes the students, "okay, okay everyone. You've had your fun, now all pipe down."

The room goes suddenly silent as the school Headmaster Mr Sharpe, appears at the door, "what in the devil is going on in this class, Miss Arnold?" Miss Arnold, now red-faced explains, "I'm sorry Mr Sharpe. They're selecting a student from another class to interview for their assignment - I'm afraid they got a bit boisterous." He acknowledges Miss Arnold's apology with a quick nod. Clasping his hands behind his back and moving to the front of the class, he clears his throat, "Ahem!"

"I would like to point out to you, that while education is meant to be fun, there's a serious side too. The topic for this assignment was chosen so that each of you gets to know other students from this school. Hands up those who know the names of every student in the other Year 9 classes?"

"I see only a few hands, just as I thought. Your assignment is to get to know at least one student. To find out what their attitudes to life are, what their likes and dislikes are, and most importantly, to listen to what they have to say and respect their point of view. It's about tolerance and acceptance. You'll probably find you have more in common than you imagine." He then nods to Miss Arnold and quickly marches out of the room with his hands still clasped behind his back.

"Okay everyone you heard the Headmaster. Now I want you to quietly, work out an assignment framework on your own and prepare your interview questions for homework tonight." More groans, "Do we have to do this for homework?"
"No my little Butterflies, you can stay after school and finish it here, if that's what you want." Leo doesn't hear Miss Arnold. He's still caught up in Mr Sharpe's message. A number of things are flashing through his mind. If I'd closed my eyes, I could swear it was El-Caro talking. There's a message in this for me, I'm sure. I reckon getting Fridge was no accident. Or, maybe was it just dumb luck. If I can survive Fridge without him punching my lights out, maybe I can meet El-Caro's challenge. Given what's going on, how ironic is that - getting Fridge?

I think I'd like to talk to El-Caro first. But I got to finish the assignment questions, 'cos I've got Gramps's funeral tomorrow. His mind wanders again. Daydreaming, he imagines being at the Zoo. He has a microphone in his hand, to interview an animal. Instead of drawing out something furry and cuddly in the lottery, he draws a ferocious lion to interview. It crosses his mind that the lion's going to be like Fridge. No matter what I do, I'm going to get mauled in the process. He pictures the lion eating the top off the microphone.

I bet I'm not the only one - not looking forward to this assignment. In those other classes are some real nerds. Anyway, why am I worrying about a stupid assignment, when I have to front up to the funeral tomorrow? Aw jeez, now I feel all yucky, it's brought back all that stuff that was going on at Michael's funeral. I don't know if I can handle that all over again. Now I feel depressed, just when I was starting to feel good.

*****

The next morning Leo wakes with a start, as if in danger. He immediately climbs out of bed remembering he had the same feeling on the morning of Michael's funeral. Leo stretches and arches his stiff body as he shuffles over to the window. He parts the curtains and looks out and is greeted by a dull and cloudy day. It matches the solemn air in the Shepherd household. Breakfast is a quiet affair, as they prepare themselves for the day ahead. While Leo and Bryan are tight-lipped, Linda suggests to Leo, "Why don't you wear the medals Gramps gave you. I'm sure he would be really proud if you wore them today."

Having finished breakfast Leo immediately goes back to his room and kicks back the rug to reveal his secret hiding place. He takes out Gramps's war medals and sits on his bed and begins polishing them with an old singlet. Getting up from his bed he reaches into an old wardrobe and lifts out his jacket and puts it on. He turns around and stands in front of the mirror and pins Gramps's medals onto his jacket. Back in the kitchen he asks, "Mum, how does that look?"
"Come here, I'll straighten them for you."
"When do we have to go?"

"We're just waiting for the people from Ashton & Co Funerals to pick us up." While Linda is adjusting her outfit, Bryan is pacing up and down the hallway and Leo is admiring the medals in the mirror. A knock at the door reveals a polite, tall man in a dark suit. "Hello, I'm Callum Ashton. I'm here to escort you all to the Funeral Parlour. Please call me Cal. I hope I haven't kept you waiting long?"

As they leave the house and climb into the black limousine, Cal remarks, "it's a solemn day for a solemn occasion - looks like it might rain." They all nod, not saying a word, as they psych themselves up for the viewing and paying of last respects. Leo whispers to Linda, "Mum, I don't want to see Gramps in a coffin. I'd rather remember him as he was, the last time I saw him."
"That's okay. You can pay your last respects in any way you want. I'm sure Gramps wouldn't mind."

After Bryan and Linda pay their respects privately and say goodbye. Gramps's coffin is loaded into the black Hearse and draped in the Australian Flag, topped with a blue RAF peaked cap.

The journey seems to take forever as they arrive at the Crematorium, in convoy. They're met by three WWII pilots that Gramps knew during his war service and are introduced to members of the RSL. Stepping out of the car they're also greeted by relatives and old friends from down South. Leo's heart jumps when he sees Dani and her parents standing to one side. Dani gives Leo a little wave and he wanders over to them and speaks briefly before being herded off to act as a pallbearer. Both Bryan and Leo join the RSL reps as they accompany the coffin down the drive and into the Crematorium.

An ex-service pilot in a uniform with a walking stick presides over a eulogy celebrating Gramps's life. It is poignant and laced with humour, befitting Gramps attitude to life, perfectly. The ex-service pilot recites the Ode of Remembrance which finishes with "Lest we forget."

As the coffin is lowered out of sight, a Piper plays the Last Post which moves many to shed a tear or two. Leo looks around to see that Bryan is stony-faced, reminding Leo that he had done the same at Michael's funeral. After the service, Leo notices that Bryan is missing. He searches around the reception centre and outside in the garden. The dull grey morning begins to give way to sunshine. The sun makes an appearance from behind rolling clouds, sending out a strong shaft of light across the sky, just as Leo had seen from the top of Mt Fielden. Wandering around the gardens, he stops when he hears a loud cry.

Turning around, he spots Bryan way off in the distance amongst a clump of trees, a picture of a very lonely figure sobbing loudly. Leo's in two minds as to what to do - to go over or to give him space, deciding space might be the best thing to do. Leo feels he's come to terms with his grandfather's death because they had already talked. Also, he had done his emotional releasing a few days earlier when he bolted up Mt Fielden. For Bryan it's a lifetime of emotional stuff with his Dad, he never dealt with, including Michael's death. He blames himself for the accident. Thinking of all things he could have - should have done.

After pleasantries and condolences are exchanged with those gathered in the reception centre, they decide to meet up for afternoon tea. Particularly as there are friends and relatives from down South they haven't seen since leaving the farm. However, Leo has other ideas.

"Mum, I don't want to hang around. It's boring. They're all old people. Can't I go home with Dani's folks?"

"I don't know, Leo. It wouldn't be right. They'll want to see you, too."

"Aw Mum, It's going to be boring. P-l-e-a-s-e."

"Well, I guess it will be okay. So long as it's okay with Dani's parents."

"Cool Mum. See-you."

Arriving back at the Jerovich place, Leo is the centre of attention as Lena and Dani take good care of him. Making doubly sure he's eaten and drunk plenty. Finally, Lena goes off outside, which gives Leo the opportunity to tell Dani all about L-CRO. They move off to the lounge room. Leo decides to lie down on the plush pile carpet. He stretches out on his side, his hand holding up his head. Dani also decides to sit on the floor, cross-legged opposite Leo. "Okay, Leo tell me all about this El-Caro dude."

Leo recites what happened in the Sentinel and all that he and L-CRO had discussed. "Well, what you reckon is that wicked or what?"

"That's too much info for me. I can't get excited about that kind'a stuff. You're the Sci-fi nut, not me."

"Okay, so it's not your bag."

"What else happened?"

"Oh, yeah, I got an image of El-Caro, which nearly blew my brain circuits."

"Cool, why didn't you mention that before. What does he look like?"

"I just thought of it, then. He looks like us, even has a young face.

He doesn't have any hair like us. He's sort of Egyptian looking. His skin has a blue tinge though, on account of their sun being different from ours. Oh yes, and he has this platted goatee hanging off his chin."

"He sounds really cute. I wish I could meet him."

"Here comes your Mum - better change the subject. Ahem! Oh yeah, guess what? I got somebody from the school for an assignment. You know, to find out stuff about what they like and dislike."

"So what's so special about that?"

"We had a lottery and I drew Kelvin Slater. Can you believe that?" Dani laughs, "Wow, did you draw the short straw or what. Will he survive?"
"That's not even funny. What if you got Posh for this assignment?" Dani puts her hands over her eyes. "Errrr, I don't even want to go there."
"See."
"Anyway Leo, what do you have to do?"
"Just ask heaps of questions."
"I want to do it."
"Okay, it's pretty simple. I know your family stuff."

"What's your favourite food:"
"Anything chocolate."
"I thought it was peanut butter?"
"No way."

"What's your favourite movie or video:"
"Sweet November."
"Errr, a chick flick with all that mushy stuff."
"It's better than complicated Sci-fi."

"What music do you like:"
"Madonna, Joni Mitchell and Killing Heidi."
"Who's Joni Mitchell?"
"The best singer-songwriter around, before you were born."
"You got that right."

"What was the name of your first pet and the name of the road you first lived in?"
"I don't get it."
"You will. Just say the names straight out."
"Hmmm…ummm, I think they were Fluffy Fogerthorpe. Oh, ha, ha." Leo points and laughs. "See I told you."
Alright then, what about your first pet's name and the street you first lived in?"
"My first pet's was a lamb called Rowdy. Dani laughs as she asks, "why would you call a lamb Rowdy?"
"He used to keep on going 'Ma-a-a' all the time."
"How did it go, again?"
"Ma-a-a…hey! You heard me the first time. You having a lend of me, you rotten bitch. Dani rolls over onto the floor laughing, got you that time."

She sits up again and asks, "what about the street you lived in?"
"You'll crack up when I say this…it's comes out as Rowdy Donuts."
"You're bullshitting me, Leo. No street would be called Donuts."
"Hundo-P, it's true.
There's this rock formation called 'The Donuts', it's named after them."
Dani gives Leo that I-don't-trust-you look, "Well maybe. What about more questions."

"Where would you like to go on holidays:"
"Anywhere away from here."
"And here comes the 'Biggy'.

"If you could change the world what would you do:"
"Hmm, wow, errr, umm…I wish, I wish… there would be more love and less hatred. And, and free chocolate for everyone."

"You're not taking this thing seriously."
"So! Do you want a drink, Leo?"
Leo holds his throat. "Yeah, I'm dying here. My mouth's like a desert."

"After that, come and I'll show you the graphics I did from the sketches. Then if you give me a rough sketch of the rest of what you've seen, I'll do that too, if you want? Let's go to the kitchen." Dani opens the fridge door and pulls out a can of cool drink. "Do you want the whole can?"

"Nah, let's share one?"
"I thought you were dying for a drink?"
"Just wanted to make you feel lousy about being a hopeless hostie," says Leo with a wide smirk on his face.

Dani shakes the can in Leo's direction, "Instead of sharing. Do you want to wear it?" Leo covers his face, "I was only joking." Dani grabs two glasses from the cabinet and pours. She bends down and looks at the glasses. "Okay, does that look like its level?"
"Whatever, I don't care. Let's go and look at the stuff you've done on the computer." They leave the kitchen glass in hand and head for her room."
Leo, while I start the computer up, can you bring a chair over?"
"No worries."
"There, I got the first one up and guessed what it may look like."

"Wow, that's really good. Gee, thanks a million. Looks almost real and exactly as I imagined it would look like. Must've taken ages."
"No, not really. I'm pretty good at this stuff, you know."

"Look who's got tickets on themselves."
"What's wrong with being proud of your work?"
"Yeah, I suppose so; I mean these are really detailed, almost like you're there."
"Thanks Leo."

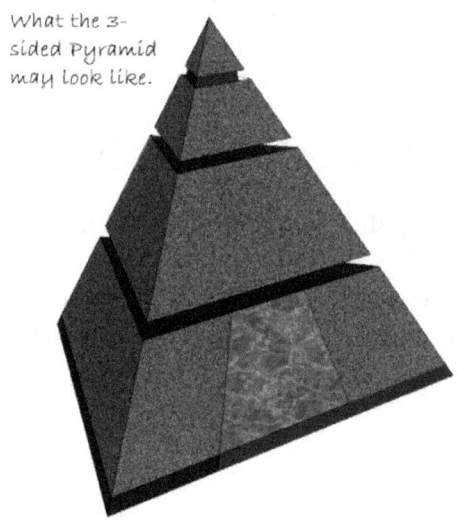

What the 3-sided Pyramid may look like.

"Dani, I'm starting to feel really stuffed, you know after the funeral and all that. I think I'd better go. I hope you don't mind?"
"No Leo I understand. I know you were really close to your Djeda." Dani sees Leo to the door and before leaving gives Leo a big hug and a quick peck on the cheek. "Thanks for everything Dani, I'll catch you later."

*****

The next day Leo can hardly drag himself out of bed. He feels emotionally drained and finds that his folks are the same as he drags his tired body into the kitchen. Bryan is hunched over a half-empty cup of cold coffee and Linda is still in her dressing gown staring out the window.

"Leo, what are you doing up? You know you don't have to go to school today if you don't want to. Bryan and I have decided to have the day off too."

"Mum. I think I'd rather go to school, 'cos if I stay home I'll only mope around. Is that okay with you?"

"It's up to you. I'll help you get your stuff ready. What do you want in your lunch?" Bryan looks up, "don't worry Linda. Here Leo, I've got some change, so you can buy your lunch from the canteen today."

"Wicked, thanks Dad."

After breakfast, Leo is dressed and off to the bus stop, a little earlier than usual. He sits down and stares at the concrete paving. Thinking, it makes you wonder about life and stuff. I wonder where Gramps is and what he's doing right now. I wonder if you just leave your body behind and fly off somewhere else. I wonder if there's really a soul. Or maybe when you die, that's the end of it.

Meeting El-Caro makes me feel like there's so much more out there than we know. If what he says is true and there are other realities, maybe Gramps is still around. I reckon that it was Gramps the other night. Mum felt it and even Dad thought something was going on too. Oh well, might as well do some reading. This book, I dunno. I can't get into it. But it's better than thinking too much. 'Cos that could make you go bonkers.

Leo reads for only a few minutes, because to his surprise the bus comes into view, earlier than he expected. He tosses the novel into his backpack and makes sure he has his fare ready this time. As the bus draws near, Leo can see that it's Old-grouch-face behind the wheel. As the bus pulls up, Leo hesitates and stays close to the bus shelter. He's trying to sum up the courage to jump onto the bus, after his last effort.

Thinking, that's all I need right now is him going off his face." As the door opens Leo is greeted with a smile. As he hands over his fare, he's thinking, can't be the same guy. It must be a clone. Maybe it's his twin brother. "Don't worry about that matey, the fare's on me. I'm retiring today and this is my last shift. But before you sit down, I've got something for you." Old-grouch-face reaches behind the driver's seat and picks up a large plastic carry bag, handing it to Leo.

"I've seen you reading Sci-fi novels and I like them too. These are my favourite reads. I want you to have them for helping me see the light. They're the hardcover 'Questor Trilogy'. They're hard-to-get first editions and signed by the author."

"I can't take these, ummm - sorry, but I don't know your name."

"It's Ernest, but you can call me Ern or Ernie. I want you to have them, as you'll appreciate them as much as I have."

"Gee thanks Mr Ernie, I don't know what to say."

"It's me that should be thanking you. As you were the only one interested enough, of all my passengers, to ask me what was wrong.

I've been thinking about retiring for some time, but didn't have the courage to make the change, when Betsy died. Now I can begin a new chapter of my life, thanks to you." Ernie closes the door and waves a car through, before pulling onto the road. Ernie starts whistling a little tune as he drives. Leo sits down and keenly opens each book. He reads the author's message to Ernie on the inside cover and the book summary on the back.

Leo is gob-smacked. Thinking, wow, this is the most amazing thing. I've always wanted to read these. But the folks couldn't afford them, 'cos they're rare hardcovers and never released in paperback. I wonder why they never did that. And, here they are in my hand signed by the author. Yeah, and what's more amazing is Old-grouch...I mean Ernie listened to me and he's a completely different person now. As the bus pulls in at the school bus stops, Leo stands waiting for the other students to get off. As the last student makes a noisy exit, Leo gets up and moves to the front. "Ernie, I still don't know what to say."

"Look son, don't worry about it. I'll give you my phone number and when you've read them, perhaps you and I can get together and talk about them and other Sci-fi books we've both read." Ernie winds off a blank ticket from the ticket machine and writes his phone number on the back. "Here, make sure you keep in touch, won't you?" They shake hands as Leo steps off the bus.

He turns to watch the bus pull out. Ernie toots the horn and holds his hand out of the window as a wave. Leo stands motionless until it disappears out of view. Leo's mind is jolted back to the present.

Thinking, better not go to the library. I should put these safely in my locker. Don't want to get them pinched or wrecked.

As he arrives at his locker and places the bag inside, a student sidles up to him. "I heard you drew the short straw and got Fridge for the assignment. What did you do wrong, break a mirror, walk under a ladder or see a black cat? Or, did you do all three?" Leo is annoyed by the attention and angrily replies, "He's no different to anybody else."

"Let's see you say that when he's sitting on you, squeezing the last bit of life out of you." He had only just gotten those words out, when he spots Fridge sauntering down the corridor, "I'm off. Exit stage left," and disappears into a classroom leaving Leo to his fate. "Hey, Farmboy! I heard you and me have got this dumb assignment to do. What did I do to get a loser like you?"

"That's funny," retorts Leo, drawing himself up to his full height. "I was thinking the same thing." This rocks Fridge, as he isn't expecting such a response. Most students run away or become a feeble, dribbling mess to his obvious size and reputation. He chuckles as he speaks, "Farmboy! Are you brave, got a death wish, or just plain stupid?"

"My name's Leo, not Farmboy. And, the only thing stupid is the direction of this conversation."

"Well for the record my name's not Fridge, either. It's Kelvin Slater and my Dad calls me Vinny. So you'd better write that down for this dumb assignment, 'cos I ain't going to repeat it."

"You want to do it now?"

"Let's get this show on the road, Farmboy. I've got better things to do than muck around with you."

Leo sits down on a bench in the corridor and takes out his folder with his interview questions. While Fridge stands there, hands on hips, impatiently kicking the steel leg of the bench with his boot.

Unfortunately, the interview gets off to a bad start as Leo asks his first question. "What are your parent's names and what sort of work do they do?"

"Nope, not answering that question."

"Why not?"

"Because I decided to do my questions first, that's why." Fridge drags out his question sheet, his notepad and snatches Leo's pen. He listens and taps the pen on the pad as Leo explains, "my Dad's name is Bryan and my Mum's name is Linda and we had a farm down south at Coreydale. But we lost the farm after my older brother Michael was killed in a tractor accident. After that Dad wasn't making good decisions and because of the drought, we had to sell up and leave.

My grandfather used to live with us on the farm, but I think losing the farm caused his stroke and he had to go to a nursing home. But he died a few days ago and I went to his funeral yesterday." Fridge sits down. His attitude changes and in a quiet voice responds, "About your brother and your grandad...I don't know what to say - must be really hard talking about it. "Thanks," sniffles Leo, wiping a tear from his eyes. Fridge shifts his weight uncomfortably on the bench, dragging his left boot back and forth on the concrete floor. He puts down Leo's pen and his folder on the seat and begins rubbing up and down on the tops of his legs. He goes to say something, but hesitates and takes a deep breath and bites his lip.

"I know how you feel Leo. My mum died a year ago from cancer." Leo has his head bowed thinking, that's incredible. Fridge is human after all. That tough stuff he puts out is bluff. He's got problems like the rest of us. I can't believe this. We've both lost people we were really close to. It makes me almost feel like we're Bros. Man, is that's weird or what? The siren interrupts the awkward silence. Fridge, feeling decidedly uncomfortable, jumps up. "Can we do this after school? You can come back to my place. I've got PlayStation and all the games." Leo is surprised by the invitation and hesitates, "well, I don't know if I can." Fridge is impatient. "Can't you make your own decisions?" Leo stands up, "okay then. I'll meet you at the bus stops after school."

Leo's first class is on the other side of the school, so he has to hurry to get there on time. Lots of thoughts are going through his mind. Jeez, you could knock me down with a feather. How different was that? It's nothin' like I expected. The guy's almost normal, can you believe that. And, I'm going over to his place. Leo chuckles to himself and makes an observation. Now I know why Fridge can suck up to the teachers and get away with being such an arsehole. I bet they know about his Mum.

Just the same I can't imagine what it would be like without my Mum. As Leo arrives at his class, he shakes his body and mutters, "I don't even want to go there." Sitting down, he takes out his books and stares at the cover of the book. Thinking, in a blink of an eye, I've gone from hating this guy to actually feeling sorry for him. But, I still don't understand why he's such a big bully. Leo's mind is elsewhere, until he hears,

"Hello, girls and boys. How are my precious 'Petals' today." The class groan in unison, as Leo muses, oh I forgot it's that loopy Miss Arnold again. "How are the fantastic assignments coming along, I'm sure you're all having fun." The class groans in unison, again. "I want you all to work on your interview questions. If you've done them and sorted out your notes, then start preparing your story."

As Leo reviews his list of questions, his mind wanders. Musing, I can't get over how the two people, who have given me grief lately, are almost mates. I mean it's only been a couple of days and everything has changed. I can't wait to tell El-Caro. I wonder if he's had something to do with this, maybe through mind control or something. I wish it was lunchtime, and then I could start with that first novel Old-grouch...I mean Ernie gave me. For Leo the day just drags.

Except at lunchtime, reading the new novel's opening chapter. He feels cheated. Thinking afterwards, why can't the day go fast and lunch drag out so I can read more. It's not fair. Finally, the home-time siren lets out a wail. This followed immediately by a "Yahoo" as students race out of the classrooms to get to more exciting activities.

While Leo makes his way to the bus stops to wait for Fridge. As he gets to the bus stop he hears a loud voice calling. "Hey, Farmboy...I mean Leo. I'm over here, this is our bus." Leo looks up the queue, as Fridge brushes two students aside with one arm and beckons Leo with the other, "hey you! Get out of the way for my friend or I'll drop you."

Leo marvels at the aura of power Fridge has over the other students. Thinking, man, you got to see this. The threat's enough; he doesn't have to do anything.

Fridge lives on the other side of Fielden Beach from Leo. Closer to the ocean in a small pocket of expensive looking houses up on a rise. As they get off the bus Fridge jokes, "See where that line is - see where the ocean meets the sky. I told you we've got ocean views." Leo jokes back, "Hey man, I want my money back. I've been had."

Fridge opens the front door and as they go inside the house is deafly silent. "My Dad's at work too, so we have the place to ourselves."
"What does your Dad do?"
"He owns Slaters Smash Repairs."
"Hey, my Dad's a mechanic too. But he works for the Wilsons who own the Shell Garage, near Mt Fielden."
"I thought you said your Dad's a farmer."
"He was, but we had to leave the farm to come here."
"Oh, that's right. I forgot."

Fridge tosses his backpack down and heads straight for the refrigerator. He grabs out a bottle of cool drink and a pile of ham to make a sandwich. Leo looks around and notices that they appear to be well off. His eyes dart everywhere, from the expensive furniture to a big flat-screen television. However, the house is untidy and it's obvious to Leo that it lacks a women's touch.

Fridge, meanwhile takes a big bite out of his sandwich and in a muffled tone asks, "Do you want one, Leo?
"Okay."
"Well help yourself. I ain't your servant, you know." Leo moves over to the table and comments, "you're really lucky. You've got lots of neat stuff."
"That's only 'cos my Dad is trying to make up for me Mum not being here." Fridge clears some room on the kitchen table so they can sit down while they eat. Leo takes this opportunity to ask Fridge some basic personal questions for the assignment. "Fridge are you ready to answer some questions?"
"Yep, fire away."

"What's your favourite food:"
"Burgers and chips."
"But that's two foods?"

"No it ain't. The burger always comes with chips."
"What's your favourite movie or video:"

"Terminator II. You know, 'I'll be back', 'no problemo'."
"That Arnie Schwarzenegger voice isn't bad."

"What music do you like:"
"Anything by Guns N' Roses."
"I like the Foo Fighters."

"Where would you like to go on holidays:"
"Queensland, maybe?"

"What's your favourite sport:"
"WWF."
Leo screws up his face and asks, "But, the World Wildlife Fund isn't to do with sport?"
"World Wrestling Federation, Dumbo."
"Oh yeah. Then who's your favourite star?"
"Hulk Hogan, obviously."

"What's your first pet's name and the first road you lived:"
"That's a weird question if you ask me?"
"No, it's just a fun game to do. Mine's Rowdy Donuts." Fridge screws his face up, "That's stupid. But my first pet was a rat called Ben and we lived in Burns Place. Oh, I get it now. Listen to this…Ben Burns rubber, while Rowdy does Donuts. Get it, eh, eh, eh." At the same time, Fridge elbows Leo in the arm. Leo responds by licking his finger and marking a 'one' in the air, "I'll give you that one Fridge," as they give each other a fist-bump. Now here's the big question. If you could do what you liked, how would you change the world?"

Fridge is deep in thought for a while and jokingly replies, "free PlayStation for all the kids around the world. Seriously, if I had the power, I would want people to get to know each other better. So there would be less ignorance and misery in the world. And, and cure cancer to bring my Mum back, of course. That's enough boring assignments. Ready to get your arse whipped on Playstation?" Leo finishes the last of his sandwich and swallows, then responds, "I don't know. I've never had one of those to play before. But I'll give it my best shot."

They go into the family room, where the games system is set up. Leo sits down and comments, "You've got your own TV too." Fridge switches on Playstation and responds, "yeah and I've got a smaller one in my room too." Fridge hands Leo the controller, "here, do some practice, seeing how you haven't played it before. You're going to need all the help you can get."

It doesn't take long for Leo to master the controls. "This is a bit like Gameboy. I reckon I'm ready to play."
"You'll regret you said that," boasts Fridge. As they move through a couple of games Fridge is finding out he's no match for Leo's quick mind, reflexes and concentration. "Hey arsehole, you just beat me again! You're a lying rat; I don't believe you've never played this before."
"Honest. My folks can't afford one. I don't know who's got one."
"Well nobody else has been able to beat me. So you're either a natural or it's got something to do with that thing you gave me. You know that Gameboy thing that gave me a boot."
"I didn't give it to you...you took it off me." Leo glances at his watch and changes the subject quickly, "wow look at the time, I've got to catch the bus shortly, or I'll cop it."
"You don't have to go just yet. I want you to meet my Dad. He'll drop you off."

Fridge doesn't have any real friends and is enjoying Leo's company, even if it means getting thrashed on Playstation and adds, "let's have a break from the games. Do you want another drink?"
"Yeah, that would be cool," as Leo gestures with his tongue out. Fridge goes off into the kitchen and quickly returns with a can each. Leo has something on his mind that has been bothering him for a while. He asks, "Fridge, what did I ever do? How come you and the other guys at school call me 'Farmboy' and make those dumb animal noises?"

Fridge has a guilty look on his face, "I dunno. I guess you were new to the school, 'cos everyone else is from around here and for some reason you're different, I suppose. Anyway, how come you're so touchy about it? Everyone calls me Fridge. It doesn't bother me, so why should a nickname bother you?"

"Yeah, but they call you that out of respect. You don't get that with 'Farmboy', followed by squealing pig noises, do you? Fridge, has a cheeky smirk on his face as he responds, "can't argue with that."

The noise of a car pulling into the drive catches their attention. Fridge jumps up, "that's my Dad's car. He's got a new Monaro Utility." Leo strains his neck and peers out of the lounge window. He sees a tall solid-looking man getting out of a black, Holden Monaro Pickup utility. Leo glances back at Fridge. Thinking, that's where he gets it from. He's almost as big as him. Fridge seems strangely jumpy when he greets his Dad at the door. They start to spar at each other, pretending to be boxers without actually hitting each other. "Come on Vinny. You can do better than that." Ignoring Leo, they spar their way into the lounge. Then embrace and wrestle each other to the ground, trying to pin each other's shoulders to the carpet.

Meanwhile, Leo is standing there with his mouth open. Thinking, that's different. I've never seen that before. Even me and Michael didn't do that stuff. I suppose that was because Michael hated anyone fighting. I can't imagine my Dad doing that stuff either. He's not what you'd call the touchy-feely type. Maybe it's some sort of bonding ritual or something. Hey! I just had a flash. I bet this is his Dad's way of showing that he loves him. No wonder Fridge's that way. The guy just wants attention.

Both stop after a few minutes of wrestling, realising Leo is standing there somewhat bemused by it all. Fridge's Dad gets up puffing, "g'day who's this Vinny?"

"Oh. I forgot to introduce you."

"Dad, his is my school buddy, Leo."

"It's nice to meet you Leo." They shake hands, leaving Leo with a greasy feeling. Instinctively he wipes his hand on his school shorts and responds, "How-ya going Mr Slater?"

"Ken's the name. I don't go for this Mister stuff. It makes me feel like an Old-timer."

Fridge also scrambles to his feet. "Dad, Leo came over 'cos we got this assignment we have to do on each other. You know, find out about each other's life and present it in class."

"That's great Vinny. We never did stuff like that in our day, because everyone knew each other. But it's different today.

It amazes me that we can travel to the bloody moon and back, but we can't walk across the road and talk to our bloody neighbours." Leo joins in the conversation, "Yeah Mr Slater…I mean Ken, I know what you mean. I use to live on a farm and we knew everybody."

"Dad, can Leo stay for dinner?"

"Well Vinny that's up to Leo, what do you say, mate?"

"Oh, I would like to stay. But my Mum will go ballistic if I'm not home soon."

"Well, just leave a message on your answering machine," pleads Fridge, hoping that he can stay. Leo shakes his head. "We don't have one."

"That's okay Leo, perhaps some other time. Where do you live? I'll give you a lift home?"

"Gee! Thanks Mister…I mean Ken. Fielden Beach near the old Henderson's quarry."

"Yep, know it well. Use to muck around there when I was your age." As they leave the house and walk down the driveway towards the Monaro, Ken turns and hands Leo the keys. "Do you want to try out the driver's seat?" Enthusiastically Leo responds, "Could I what?"

Ken explains all of the dials and knobs and asks Leo to start it up. Leo presses the start button and pushes down on the accelerator. "VRHOOMM…VRHOOMM"

"Wow! It's got some serious grunt," yells Leo over the throb of the engine. He hops out and gets into the passenger side. There's a loud squeal as Ken backs out of the driveway and more squealing of tyres as they drive off.

As they approach Leo's place, a bus has just pulled up at the Leo bus stop. Ken is about to indicate and pass, when Leo shouts, "there's my Mum getting off the bus. Can you stop here?" They pull over and Leo jumps out and waves to Linda. He turns and salutes, "thanks heaps for the lift Ken… Man, that car's got some guts. And, thanks for inviting me Fridge, sorry about whipping your arse on PlayStation."

"Wait 'til next time. Watch out 'cos I'll be practising. We'll see who's got the balls, then." Leo watches the revving black Monaro turn around, its rear tyres spinning. It roars off tyres squealing and disappears into the lengthening shadows.

He turns around to acknowledge Linda, but doesn't get a word in. "Leo! Who was that maniac you were with? I told you, never get a lift from strangers, even if you miss the bus."

"M-u-m! Stop going on will you? It's just one of the guys from school and that's his Dad's car. We had to do an assignment on each other, so he invited me to his place. That's all. Okay!"

"Alright Leo, I'm sorry I snapped at you. I've had a busy day and you know I worry about you." Linda puts her arm around Leo's shoulders and hugs him. "So tell me more about this assignment?"

"We had to draw someone's name out of a tin and make up some questions to do an interview on them."

"That sounds like fun."

"You will never guess in a million years who I got."

"I'm too tired to think. So how about you tell me."

"It was Fridge."

"Who's Fridge?"

"You know, they just dropped me off - Kelvin Slater he's a big kid at school."

"You mean the one that bullies everyone at school?"

"Yeah, that's him, well it's amazing he invited me to his place because of the assignment and I met his Dad too."

"What about his Mum?"

"Oh it's really sad. His Mum died about a year ago from…I think it was cancer - yeah, and when Fridge's Dad comes home they both have a fight."

"What a real fight?"

"No Mum. Just mucking around…anyway, what's for dinner?"

"I knew it wouldn't be long before you'd get around to that subject." Because it's Friday, Dad's going to get fish and chips for a change."

"Yum-mie, my favourite. Can I invite Dani too? Please, M-u-m."

"Everything's your favourite. Okay. But you change out of that scruffy old uniform first," orders Linda as she opens the front door and lets Leo lead the way. Leo quickly changes and races for the phone…"Oh Mrs J. Hi is Dani there? Oh, she's not. Yeah, I'm good. Yeah, my folks are good too. Yeah, school's good too. Can Dani come over later? 'Cos we're having fish and chips. Hang on I'll ask mum.
M-u-m what time?"

"Six thirty, Leo."

"Mum says about six-thirty, thanks. See ya."

Bryan arrives home just before 6:30pm with the fish and chips. He loves his fish and chips. But today he's clearly in a bad mood, dumping them on the kitchen table. He walks out of the kitchen and flops down on the couch in the lounge, without saying a word.

Linda goes into the lounge and sits down. "Bryan, what's the matter?" Bryan has his head bowed and is running his hands through his hair nervously. He mumbles, "The Wilsons have decided to retire and are putting the garage up for sale. That means I'll be out of a job, soon."
"What makes you think that? Won't the new people want someone to run the servicing and repairs?"
"It'll be snapped up by the Shell Oil Company for sure. They've made offers to buy it, before. Shell has their own people. They'll want to bring them in."

Linda places a supportive hand on Bryan's shoulder, "I'm sure it will all work out for us, so don't worry dear." Standing up suddenly, Bryan shouts in an angry voice, "Jesus! It's one bloody thing after another. Just when things are looking up and now this. I'm going for a shower." Bryan's outburst surprises Leo and he asks, "Dad aren't you going to have fish and chips with us?"
"Sorry Leo. I've just lost my bloody appetite."

Linda tries to smooth things over, "don't worry Leo we'll save some and warm them up in the oven later. You know, once he has had a chance to calm down." Leo wanders back into the kitchen. He pauses in front of the wrapped up fish and chips, taking in the unmistakable smell. Thinking, I can't win in this place. I was having such a good day and everything was going good and he comes home and stuffs it all up. I was looking forward to fish and chips. Now I don't feel hungry, either. Leo's depressed thoughts are interrupted by knocking at the door, "I'll get it, Mum." Leo answers the door with a sour look on his face, "Hi Dani, come in, I think." Dani senses the tension in the air and responds, "you're sure it's okay?"

Linda sensing the air of uneasiness calls out, "Dani, don't you worry, please come in. Bryan's upset because the Wilsons, who own the garage, have just told him they are selling. It means he might have to look for another job. Anyway, it isn't your worry.

You sit at the table and I'll get the fish and chips ready. Leo, can you get some cups and that bottle out of the fridge and pour Dani a drink." Linda shares out the fish and chips and places a platter of salad on the table.

Silently they sit concentrating solely on eating the fish and chips. Dani feels very uncomfortable. However, to break the icy state of affairs, Linda asks Leo, "why don't you tell Dani about that boy at school." "Oh yeah, Kelvin Slater. But before I do, I got to tell you about the bus driver. You know the one I use to call Old-grouch-face.

Well, his real name is Ernest and he likes to be called Ernie. Anyway, I asked him why he goes off his face at everyone all the time. He said he didn't even know he was doing it. So I then asked him why he was still a bus driver if it was giving him the shits." Linda interrupts, "Leo! You didn't say that to him?"

Dani throws her head back and covers her mouth as she giggles with delight at Leo's turn of phrase. "No mum. Course not... you know what I meant. Anyway, where was I? Oh yeah, and he's like, nobody had taken any interest in him, before. Then later he tells me he's retiring. So, the best bit is that he gives me first edition novels to the Questor Trilogy on his last day and they're signed by the author and all."
"Why would he do that?" Replies Linda, suspiciously. "Because he knows I read Sci-fi books on the bus and he's a Sci-fi fan too. He even gave me his phone number so we can talk, once I've finished them."
"Leo, you will have to give them back when you finished. They sound like they're expensive."
"Yeah Mum, course I was. Even though he said I could keep them."

Dani sits passively, as the two spar at each other. However, she decides a change of conversation is needed, "Leo, what about that Slater dude at your school?"
"Dani, there's not much to tell really. We had to do this assignment together and I went back to his place. At the bus stop, he pushed all the kids in the line out of the way and let me in. Everyone's scared of him. Dani flicks her hair back, "How come you're not?"

"Because we're sort of friends now, I think. He's got a neat pad and has PlayStation and I beat him on all the games."

Linda scolds Leo, "that's not nice. Couldn't you let him win, at least once?"

"No way, Mum. After all the crap he's done to me and others."

"Why didn't you tell me stuff was going on at school?"

"Nothing's going on, not anymore."

Dani decides to change the subject, again. "Guess what Leo. I told some of the chicks at school about Portia Harland at the movies.

Dani chuckles as she remarks, "they reckon you're hot stuff." She licks the tip of her index finger, which she points at Leo, making a "Tsszzz" sound. This is news to Linda, as Leo hasn't said much about going to the movies. She pushes for more information, "a legend eh! How come you didn't tell me about that?"

"There's nothing to it, Mum. This chick at the movie thinks she's pretty cool and calls herself 'Posh.' She came over to stir up Dani and intro'd herself. I thought she said her name was 'Splosh' and her so-called school buddies gave her a hard time about it."

"I think there's more to it than that. Is that right Danicka?"

Leo jumps up in protest, "M-u-m! That's too much information. Phew, it's getting too hot in here. Come on Dani let's go down to the Supa Deli for an ice cream." Linda looks disappointed at missing out on the gossip. But realises, Leo is not going to give anything away. She ushers them out of the kitchen, "okay, off you go then," and starts cleaning up.

On the way to the Supa Deli, Leo defends his actions. "It was getting hot under the spotlight. Mum's finding out stuff I haven't even told her about."

"Least she doesn't know about that other stuff."

"Yeah, that reminds me I need to go back and talk to El-Caro again."

"Did you ask him about his name?"

"I forgot. But, I might get a chance to ask him tomorrow."

They buy their ice creams and sit outside on a low wall for a while watching people come and go, until Dani announces, "Leo I'm feeling a bit tired. Can you walk with me back to my place?"

"But I haven't finished mine yet."

"Can't you eat it on the way?"

"Yeah okay…oh look it's starting to dribble everywhere."
"Man, you're a messy eater. Here have my tissue."
"Thanks."

As they arrive out the front of the Jerovich place, Leo tries to give Dani a kiss. She steps back and whispers, "Leo! You can't pash me here, Dida's watering the garden, over there." Leo whispers back, "jeez, I didn't see him in the shadows."

"Maybe I'll see you tomorrow, you know after you catch up with that El-Caro guy. I want to know everything."
"Okay, Dani see-you...Hello Mr J."
"Mister Leo, how are you? Good young gentlemans. Walka my Danicka home, safe."
"No worries Mr J, See-you."

Chapter 7
It's like a shark when it circles its prey.

Arriving home, Leo goes into the kitchen for a drink. Bryan is now sitting at the table and eating the leftover fish and chips. He puts down his fork and gestures, "Leo, here's some drink left, if you want it. Sorry about earlier on. I got a bit carried away."

Leo reaches for the bottle, "thanks Dad. Don't worry about it, that's ancient history now." Linda stops at the kitchen door and leans up against the doorframe, arms folded. She reminds Leo, "before you go anywhere tomorrow, you clean up your room. I just went in there and it's disgusting. You've been warned. If it's not cleaned up, you won't be seeing Dani or doing anything else is that clear!"
"Yeah mum, whatever."

Next morning Leo wakes early and is too lazy to get up. Thinking, cool I can go over and talk to El-Caro again. Oh, bugger, no I can't. Mum's warned me off about cleaning my room up. What an absolute bummer. Leo drags himself out of bed and dresses, mumbling to himself, "If I skip breakfast and clean up this mess, I might be able to sneak off over the road, early." He busily starts to clean his room. In the process of taking his floor mat out to give it a shake, he decides to check out his secret hiding place.

Lifting the loose floorboard, he takes out Gramps's war medals and the game console. He admires the medals and gives them a quick polish on his shirt, before putting them carefully back. Holding the game console, it crosses his mind he no longer needs it and decides to take it back to the Sentinel.

Leo finishes what he thinks is a tidy room and shouts, "Mum! I've done my room. Can I go now?" Linda comes in and with hands on hips exclaims, "You call this clean. What about those clothes over there? Look there, your bed's not made properly. Why is the draw sticking out, like that?" Finally, after some negotiation with his mother over quality control and an argument about the definition of a clean room, she relents. "Leo I don't have time for this. I have to go to work, now. But you won't get away with it next time."

Leo waits until Linda has caught the bus before he ventures across the road and down the track towards Henderson's quarry. Arriving at the limestone ruin, Leo follows his usual routine. However, this time as he enters the main chamber of the Sentinel, he steps on the symbol to the lower chamber where he had received the Game console. The ramp descends on command.

Leo quickly makes his way below and places the console back in the box on top of the pillar. He dashes back up the ramp so he can talk to El-Caro about his news. Leo moves over to the far end of the complex and stands on the symbol to the Sentinel Pod and makes his way to the pod room. It doesn't take long for him to be in a curtain of liquid light with a shimmering tetrahedron descending upon him.

"Welcome my dear friend. I have read your thoughts already.
I can tell you're the smiling cat who's just discovered baths are banned."
"Hi-ya, El-Caro, well this cat is grateful for setting up all of those events for me."
"Whoa, hold your paws! Let's get something straight, right now. I didn't do anything. I don't have power or control over you or any of the people you've contacted. For me to do so is a breach of your free will. And, even if I could influence them, they have the freedom to choose what to think, believe and feel. Leo, it was you who set up those events."

"Your thoughts attracted the right people to you and they responded appropriately because you wanted to help them."
"You mean I did all that?"
"Yes. All I did was point you in the general direction, nothing more. You're not powerless to influence events. To understand how powerful you are; the energy that binds your atoms together has the same power as all the atom bombs on Earth, set off at the same time. That's the extent of your true power."

"But El-Caro, what am I supposed to do to make stuff happen?"
"Leo to appreciate the importance of what I am about to tell you. I shall use an analogy. I know you find my methods to explain things somewhat weird just bear with me."

"Yeah, you can say that again. It's like a shark when it circles its prey."
"Now look who's using analogies, but nonetheless a good one Leo. Better to be patient and know your prey, than to rush in not knowing all the true facts. These concepts are vital, so you experience them in your own way and can judge for yourself if what I am saying is true. Put it this way, what do you think is the most important element of a music piece?"
"I don't know. I suppose the beat or maybe the rhythm."

"Very close guess. But it's not the answer - it's the silence between the notes that punctuate the count or the rhythm; it's the most important element. It's the same with your Earth physics. The silence is the most important component. Otherwise, your world would be frozen in a solid state. Each energy particle contains the silence or it wouldn't vibrate. It could not play its tune, nor could it be in a constant state of change."

"But how does that apply to me? I don't get it."
"The point I'm making is you must embrace the silence as your friend. Begin to listen to your breathing. Listen to your body's feelings and its moods. But this can only be done in the silence - by sitting quietly on a regular basis. Then, and only then, will you find your true self."
"El-Caro how will I know when it starts working?"

"In the dead of the night and you are awake, alone. And, there is nothing to distract you from your thoughts and feelings. Do you feel comfortable in that space?"
"I'm not sure. Ahhh, maybe sometimes I'm scared. Sometimes I'm not comfortable I suppose, a bit restless I guess."
"Leo, your world is an expert at distracting you from their true selves."
"In the silence, there is no judgement, no hatred, no Gameboy, no Sci-fi books to read and no television. No doing - only being."
"But El-Caro, just sitting there is for monks and old folks - that's boring!"

"Your statement just then, means you're not comfortable being 'with' yourself. Better to become a good friend, than a stranger in your own house, I'd say. You can't exactly up and move, can you?

Better to build a castle within and make it comfortable, than to banish your soul to the cold dark night of winter. It's your choice…I know what I'd choose. Your material world will keep you from knowing who you truly are. That's the strategy; that's the ploy and only one of many realities open to you. Change the strategy and change the reality. So you will find out who you truly are…come home. Be welcome in your own house. Only in the silence will you truly come to this understanding."

"But my Dad says meditation is 'mumbo-jumbo' for monks, hippies and ferals."

"I am not talking about meditation. I'm talking about communicating with your body - not your mind. That way, you can feel the tiredness, to feel the pain, to feel the sensations within the body and acknowledge them all. Talk to your muscles and your precious organs and feel what it's like being in a house built by the Great Creator - do you want to live in a palace or in a jail? You must decide."

"Wow. When you put it like that, there's not much choice."

"There are plenty of choices. You have to decide what's worth having. And decide; am I worthy of having it?"

"Do you think I am worthy, El-Caro?"

"I don't live in your house. So it's your body, your choice. So make your choice wisely."

"Ok, I sort of understand that bit."

"Well Leo, we shall see if you do. To know who you are requires a measure. So how do you measure who you are?"

"I don't know El-Caro, I've never thought about it before."

"Do you measure yourself by what you look like? From the clothes you wear or the labels on them. The friends you have or the lack of them or even the number of Likes on Facebook. What you have or don't have. By the way you feel on the inside. By how well people treat you. Or the goals you reach or don't reach?"

"Which one should I choose?"

"It's for you to feel what your measure shall be and determine if it feels right for you."

"El-Caro, I feel at the moment it should be feeling calm inside and not so angry."

"Leo that's excellent. Not only did you choose something worthy and I like the words you chose…'at the moment'. Because all things are temporary and as you change, so will the measure you choose to use."
"El-Caro. My head is spinning with all this new stuff. Can we change the subject?"

"Of course, tell me what else you would like to know."
My friend Dani and I were talking about your name, and I found out your name can be read 'Oracle' backwards and Dani's doing Italian at school. In Italian, your name means 'beloved' or 'dear', or 'expensive', something like that. Oh and I found out my name is part of the word oracle too"

"Excellent. I like lateral thinkers. Understand that I am as much a part of you, as you are a part of me. That's the message. Many things are multi-layered in meaning, so sometimes you have to dig below the surface to reach the true meaning. For instance, your friend Danicka's name means the morning star Sirius in Slavic languages. In your case, Leon spelt backwards is Noel. In Latin it means Christmas. So what does Christmas mean to you?"
"What it means to me? …ahhh, lots of fun things, lots of yummy stuff, presents and catching up with friends."
"Your name backwards holds the essence of abundance - giving and receiving. But, you need to get the essence of your name going forwards in your life. I might add you're already starting to do this when you undertake good deeds. You already have the example of the bus driver and you will find Kelvin Slater might surprise you too."

"El-Caro, I want to know more about you. I am getting bored with just me all the time."
"That's a fair comment, Leo. Why should you hog all of the attention?"
"Oh. Thanks a lot. You've hurt my feelings now," jokes Leo playfully.
"Hmmm, where shall I start? Firstly, we have evolved to a level in our group consciousness that if I want to travel to a place I can experience it through someone who's there with the same level of awareness. You would call it mental telepathy, except I get to see, feel and sense exactly what it's like without actually being there. I can travel there physically if I need to, but there's generally no need."

"You can do that? You know exactly what they are thinking, feeling and seeing?"

"Yes, there are no secrets within our group. We are beyond passing judgement on our people."

"But what happens when you're…ahhh you know, doing something…umm, and personal like."

"Leo I'm reading your mind, but I'm confused as there are so many thoughts running through your mind on this one. I'm not sure how to respond." Leo shifts in the chair awkwardly and his face is slightly flushed, "well I was thinking like someone going to the toilet or someone doing horizontal dancing with their missus."

"Ahh I see, bodily functions - releasing waste and coupling. We know when to respect someone's privacy. We can block a telepathic intrusion if we need to. Yet mostly, our people treat each other as they would like to be treated, so it's not an issue for us. This is how we've reached our level of spirituality. "But, I can see the funny side of it too Leo, as you do. I could not think of anything as gross as connecting to someone's mind just as they are about to...and I am choosing your words here - about to drop a 'chocolate log' down the toilet. Yet I might like to experience their delight at the relief."

Leo's embarrassment turns to laughter. However, he finds it confusing, as El-Caro is laughing inside his head too. But it helps to lighten the heavy conversation somewhat. "Wow, imagine being able to do that telepathic stuff. I could go anywhere in the world and save on the airfare. When will we be able to do that, do you think?"

"Leo, it's possible now, but your people have forgotten how."

"Tell me more stuff about your world."

"We're very protective of our world. We mine only asteroids for essential minerals and metals we need. We leave the oil in the ground as we have other sources of energy. "The oil is important as it lubricates the tectonic plates and acts a shock absorber. We do not start a project unless we have properly considered the impact and can demonstrate a zero waste factor. We have harnessed hidden energy fields from our suns what you would call anti-matter. However, we also use bio-energy accumulators generated by genetically modified microbes."

"Yeah, I know about that stuff from my books, but what about money?"
"Luckily for us with our level of advancement, we have no need to store wealth. Though, each person is required to make a contribution to the community group they belong to. The contribution is based on age, level of awareness and skills."
"What do you manufacture on your planet?"

"Our planet is the home to the "Keepers of Knowledge. We are the guardians of this knowledge. Our wealth is knowledge and wisdom. We exchange it for the things we need."
"El-Caro, where do you keep all of the knowledge?"
"This might surprise you Leo, but we do not have a hall of records or a Library, as such. Our people are the record keepers. All knowledge is stored within our DNA structure."
"We are not carbon-based life forms like you. We are a silicon-based crystalline organic form."
"You mean a walking, talking bio-computer."
"If you want to put it that way. However, that's an oversimplification. Our planet is also a record keeper. It is also crystalline in structure. It holds the knowledge of the whole history of our universe."

"But El-Caro, you told me our DNA is similar. It can't be so if what you are telling me is true."
"It is so. Ask your scientists about your DNA structure. They will tell you there are thousands of so-called junk sequences of DNA and inactive sections. But they carry the knowledge of your past in the DNA. How do you account for the fact a person born on Earth can read a music score, but has never been taught and never played an instrument before? How do you account for a person who at a young age is a 'whiz' at Mathematics, but has not been taught Algebra? Ask your scientists about the brain. You are currently only using part of its capacity. That's because you have forgotten your true nature, you have forgotten who you really are."

"OMG, El-Caro. If I am related to you and have similar DNA, then do I hold all of the same records inside of me, as you do?"
"No. Not quite the same. You're carbon-based and have not reached the liquid crystalline state in your development. But your body does contain many crystalline forms and your planet contains silicon and quartz, which holds a record of the history of your universe."
"It's ironic don't you think, that your scientists are busily looking up at the stars back into the past with their telescopes. When all the information is not out there, it is contained within the planet's crystalline structure and within your DNA."

"What better message can I give you Leo; all your answers are within. You can spend a lifetime looking through books, asking other people and travelling the world to find your answers. Eventually, all of those pathways will lead you back home. So how do you feel at the moment, Leo?"
"Overwhelmed."
"My apologies, I should have made myself clear. I meant in your body, not mentally."
"I'm not sure I feel anything."
"Just sit quietly for a moment, take some deep slow breaths and when you're ready, let me know."

Leo shrugs his shoulders, thinking, what's he on about? However, he relaxes his whole body for a few minutes. L-CRO asks Leo to scan through his whole body feeling what is happening inside. "I can feel my heart beating. I can feel my lungs filling. Oh, there's a twinge on my right elbow. I've got an itchy leg and they feel like they want to walk somewhere. There's tingling in the tips of his fingers. Yeah, that's familiar, my stomach's rumbling. I knew I should've had breakfast."

As the minutes tick by, Leo notices the constant chatter in his head has calmed down. Despite being relaxed he feels anger rising up inside. Thinking, Hey! What's the story? What's this all about? I've got no reason to be angry, right now. "Leo I'm feeling what you're feeling too. I know you think such a feeling is out of context with what we have said so far. But I want you to go back into the feeling again and tell me what comes to mind without analysing it."
"I don't have to tell you, you already know."

"No Leo it's important you go into that feeling again and bring it to the surface, out aloud." Leo relaxes again and scans through his body from his toes up to the top of his head. It takes a few minutes before the angry feeling returns. Leo feels tightness in his chest and a constriction in his throat. He swallows, trying to keep the feeling down as it's uncomfortable. He hears a whispering voice, "don't hold it down. Let it out and go with the feeling." All of a sudden images come flooding in. The same images and feelings he had at the bus stop many months earlier. This time the postage stamp-sized images are off into the distance and rush up at him as theatre-screen sized images. "El-Caro, I now understand what they mean. This angry feeling is about Michael and Michael's accident." L-CRO whispers, "That's excellent, but keep going with the feelings and images, don't stop it now."

The images stop rushing up to Leo and give way to a vista of Michael standing in a golden field of wheat, smiling. A gentle breeze creates ocean-like ripples through the heads of wheat. Michael has a white dove in his left hand and a three-sided black pyramid in his right hand. But, Michael's image fades away. Leo's anger gives way to sadness. "El-Caro, I know you saw what I saw. I don't know what I should feel about it. Can you explain it to me?"

"You subconsciously blamed Michael for the situation you found yourself in six months ago. You loved the farm and country life. Deep down, you think Michael took it away from you. That he's responsible for the way your life has panned out. But then, how do you defend the guilt, the thoughts, the feelings, when Michael's not here to speak for himself? You believed you have no right to feel that way. So this anger has been bottled up with nowhere to go. You couldn't express it to Michael. You couldn't express it to your Mother and certainly not to your Father. Believing it was a selfish thing to feel."
"But El-Caro, if Michael had not died the way he did, then you and I might not have met."

"Well Leo, if that's so, then explain to me why the angry feeling is still there?" There's silence as Leo's not sure how to respond to this question. "Then you need to understand more about the power of thoughts and feelings Leo and you need to understand more about Michael.

I'm afraid you didn't really get to know your brother - that is not your fault. Michael did not allow you to get to know him. He was a sensitive person and very creative. Did you know that he wanted to be an artist and not a farmer?

Because of the expectations of the district that all farmers' sons take over the farm, he felt trapped and was living a lie."
"El-Caro, I knew he was very artistic and better at drawing stuff than me. He never said nothing about leaving the farm."
"He couldn't talk about his feelings, because the expectations are that as a farmer, that's how things are and you just get on with it. The land is in your blood.

Did you know that he was also what your people would call 'Gay'? But never let on. Michael had an inner conflict, which in the end he could not resolve. He thought that to die was his only choice. Your Dad is not to blame for the events that occurred. Nor are you, It was Michael's thinking that led to the tragedy." Just at that moment, Michael's image comes back into Leo's view. Michael smiles, as he hurls the white dove into the air. The pyramid he holds changes colour.

It turns from black to a metallic gold colour. The three sides open up like the petals on a beautiful flower, revealing a stunning orb of white light, with rainbow colours arcing out of it. The orb shoots up into the sky and disappears into a glowing silvery moon. Michael holds his hand above his head, then touches the tips of his fingers onto his forehead and places his hand on his heart and bows his head, just as had L-CRO described it and fades away as he does so.

L-CRO comforts Leo as all of the hurt he feels inside is suddenly released and a wave of peace and calmness comes over Leo. "Leo, I am proud of the way you have worked with me. Your level of understanding for someone so young is really commendable. Michael was our great hope to make your world a better place. But the baton has been passed to you, now. This is a good time for us to stop. You need some time to yourself and take in what has been revealed to you."

L-CRO's image appears in Leo's mind's eye, "Go with lightness and joy my young friend." He waves Leo goodbye with the same salute as Michael. Leo leaves the Sentinel in a surprisingly upbeat mood as he and Michael had come to an understanding. Of which he wasn't sure. But he trusted his own feelings that everything between them had been resolved. Thinking, it's almost like what I was carrying was weighing me down. Now it's dropped off my shoulders.

I wish that could happen for Mum and especially Dad, 'cos he feels it the most. Leo arrives home to find the front door open and his mother in the kitchen, having finished her Saturday shift at work.
"Hi Mum, the front door was open."
"Yes, I was just airing the place out." Leo makes for the refrigerator, "what's there for lunch?"
"I thought you would've had lunch already. You were going to be with Dani this morning. But she just called to see if you were around."
"Oh. I was…umm, I went for a walk up Mt Fielden to think for a while."
"That's nice dear. So what were you thinking about?" Leo closes the refrigerator door and sits down at the kitchen table, while Linda presses the button on the kettle. She also sits down and gets comfortable to listen to what Leo has to say.

"Well, I was thinking about Michael again and had this…ahhh…sort of dream. In this dream, Michael came to me and we had this…ahhh…talk and resolved a few things."
"Leo dear, that's really wonderful."
"Mum, did you know Michael batted for the other side?"
"I didn't know he liked to play cricket. He wasn't exactly the sporting type."
"No mum. I meant he's different."
"Yes, I know that too, you're the sporting type, while Mike was the sensitive artistic type. You were always a scruff, while Mike kept himself clean, even on the farm."

"Well doesn't that tell you something about Michael, Mum?"
"Oh…Oh, I know what you're getting at. Yes, I knew Mike was gay if that's what you mean." Leo has a shocked look on his face. "How did you know?"
"Leo you should know by now a mother's intuition is always right. I knew a long time ago."

191

"Does Dad know? Does he know that you know?"

"No. I have never told him. I couldn't tell you either, because Mike wanted it kept a secret. That I've kept until today."

"Mum did you know that he wanted to be an artist and not a farmer."

"No, he never confided that to me. I always thought that he would take on the farm when we retired. But that's never going to happen now."

Linda is visibly upset by her last statement and pulls out a tissue from the cuff of her sweater and wipes the tears from her eyes, "Leo, I don't want to talk, so please tell me more about your dream."

"Sure Mum. I saw Michael standing in a field of golden wheat and he had this white dove in one hand and this black pyramid in the other. The pyramid changed colour to gold and he was smiling. Then he chucked the dove into the air and this pyramid thing opened up like a flower and all this bright coloured stuff flew out up into the sky and disappeared into the moon."

"That's just so beautiful Leo. I just wish your Dad could have such a dream. It would make such a difference to know Mike's okay - wherever he is now." While Leo is still seated, Linda gets up from the table and hugs Leo, resting her chin on his head. "I'll make you some lunch since you were so kind to share your dream with me."

After lunch, Leo decides to go over to Dani's place. As he sets off on a tropical afternoon, he's in a buoyant mood. It's spring, and he has a spring in his step. As he walks along the edge of the road he soccers at small rocks as he goes. Arriving at Dani's place, Leo spots Branco out the front on the porch sitting in a patio chair slicing up a big red apple.

"G'day Mr Leo. Come you sit and we talk. Yes."

"Hello Mr J. How ya going?" Branco with a puzzled look on his face, points at his chest with the knife, "me, no go anywheres."

"No. what I meant was how are you feeling today." Branco raises the knife into the air, "Ah Mr Leo. Me I'm very, very well on such a beaudifall day," but my English she not so good...we sit. Yes?" Branco gestures to the patio chair for Leo to sit down.

It crosses Leo's mind, while Mr J might be missing stuff in the language department, but he sure makes it up with sign language. I guess those huge hands are hard to miss. "Mr Leo, this beaudifall apple, you want?" Branco swiftly slices the apple and promptly jabs it with the point and passes it to Leo. Leo observes, "My Grandad use to do that too."

"Ah yes, very sad your Djeda he gone, No. But such is Life, eh!" Just then Dani appears at the front door, "Hi Leo, come in. We'll go into the lounge, Mama's in the kitchen. Leo is ushered into the lounge, while Dani goes off to get him a drink. "Here Leo, are you thirsty, or do you want to share?"
"I reckon I can go the whole can."
"Okay, I want to know all the 'goss'." Dani nods her head to the right, "you know…over the road?"

Leo pops the ring-pull off the can and replies, "It was mind-blowing stuff. He talked about his world, how they don't use money and protect their environment and stuff like that. Then he goes on about our body as being a house built by the Great Creator."
"Oh how cute. I wish I could have met him. He sounds really spunky."
"Not only that, he told me about how they can go places, telepathically. They can see it and feel it too, without going there via someone who's actually there."

"Wow. That would be neat-o. That would be so mad. Come on, what else did he say?"
"Oh and he mentioned stuff about music. I think it was…oh yes, how the most important bit is the silence between the notes and the beat." Dani shakes her head, "I don't get it."
"I think he means that without the silence spaces in between, we would have no music. In fact, without the silence, there would be no Earth and no Universe."
"You sound like him talking."
"Get out of here! Do I?"

"Yes you do, too. But seriously, I never ever thought of silence standing for anything. I guess it's really something. How come if it's that important, why we have never been told about it at school or in science?"
"Yeah, Dani, 'Hundo-P' I don't know the answer to that one, either."
"Why don't you ask him next time…go on, what else did he say."

"El-Caro said that it was only in the silence that you can find yourself or something like that. He goes, when you wake up late at night, you can tell how you doing by how you feel. Like sad, scared or uncomfortable - stuff like that. That all the things we do on the outside distract us from finding out who we really are.

He also talked about our DNA and that we only use 10% of our brain and forgotten about our natural selves. I think he means the wild nature in us." Leo gets up and drops to the floor and crawls over to Dani. She is sitting cross-legged on the lounge floor. Leo roars loudly in her ear. Dani holds up her hands and pretends to fend off Leo as they collapse in a heap on the floor. "Looks like you're re-discovered the animal in you," chuckles Dani, loudly. The afternoon moves on swiftly as Leo chats on about his adventures. He becomes a virtual prisoner in the Jerovich household. That is, he has to stay for Sunday night dinner - as if he had any choice in the matter.

*****

The next morning, the first thing Leo hears is, "come on Mr Sleepy Head it's time you were up."
"Aw, mum. Can't I stay in for just five more minutes?"
"No, you can't. Your idea of five minutes is different to everyone else's."
Leo reluctantly drags his sleepy body out from under the doona, yawns loudly and stretches his stiff body. "Look at the time, I've got to go. Are you sure you can manage to get yourself organised?"

Leo pushes Linda out of his room. "M-u-m! Drop off, I'm fifteen years old." Leo grabs Linda's bag and jumper, "here Mum you'll be late for your bus."
"Leo, are you trying to hurry me off?" Leo smiles, "do one legged- ducks swim around in circles?"
"I'll take that as a yes. See you tonight, Leo"
"See-you Mum."

Later on, Leo makes it to the bus stop, hoping to get in a few minutes of reading. However, he gets in more time than he expects as the bus is late. As it pulls up and the door opens Leo half expects to see Ernie, forgetting for a moment that he has now retired. However, Leo is greeted by the lady driver, the one with the flaming mop of red hair and a cap perched on top, "Hello Love."

As Leo climbs the steps he's thinking, that's the 'man-eater' from the other day. She has to be off her trolley. Leo glances around and finds an empty seat. He settles down with one of the Questor Trilogy books. Leo's totally into the book and only looks up when the bus slows and pulls into the school bus bays. As Leo jumps off the bus, he's in two minds. Thinking, if I go to the Library, I can't keep the book safe, 'cos I'll have to go straight to class. Maybe I'd better whack it in the locker. I want to read it, but better not risk getting it pinched.

Approaching his locker one of Fridge's gang, CJ steps in front of Leo, pushing Leo in the chest. "Hey Farmboy, what are you doing here. Looking for trouble, are you?" Leo tries to step around. But CJ blocks Leo's path, again. Leo takes a step backwards, but before he utters another word a hand reaches in from behind Leo and grabs CJ by the shirt. "What's up Fridge? Is the startled response from CJ Fridge pulls CJ in close and eyeballs him. "Listen, dirt-brain. You call my buddy Leo that name again and I'll squeeze the life out of you. Got it. CJ has a confused look. "But, but, he's not one of us and we hassled him the other day."

"Leo's off limits, so spread the word. If anyone hassles Leo, I will come looking for them. You got it turkey-breath."
"Yeah, yeah I got it Fridge, let go will you?" Fridge releases CJ. He quickly retreats which leaves Leo bemused by the turn of events. Thinking, this stuff with Fridge is looking better all the time. "See Leo, I always look after me mates."
"Thanks, Fridge. But do you really have to be that aggressive?" Fridge scratches his head as he answers. "I don't know what happens. I just get this real angry feeling."
"I know. I've been on the receiving end. Remember the paper thing outside the library?"

"Yeah. But I didn't know you, then. Anyway, we really copped it from old Thommo and got stuck with yard duty. Listen, after school, why don't you come over to my place for a while?"

"Okay, I'll see you at the bus stops."

Most of the school day is uneventful for Leo, except, for one thing. He couldn't help but notice that in his travels around the school, others students are whispering and pointing in his direction. At first, Leo wondered what was going down. Then it dawned on him. Thinking, of course, the word's gone around. I'm covered by 'Fridge Protection'. After the final siren, Leo meets Fridge and they catch the bus to Fridge's place. On arriving, Leo asks out of curiosity, "Are any of your friends better than me on PlayStation II?" Fridge, doesn't answer straight away.

His focus is the contents of the refrigerator. He grabs a pile of snack type foods and dumps them on the kitchen table. Leo sits down and waits patiently for an answer. However, Fridge seems pre-occupied. He doesn't sit down, but fidgets with the end of the tablecloth. As if he has something weighty on his mind. "We're friends, right."

"Yeah, I guess we are."

"Well, to be honest, I don't have any real friends - only you." Hoons you hang around with at school. Aren't they your friends?"

"No way! They only hang around me, 'cos they want to act tough.

Truth is they're a bunch of dead-set losers. They'd run away at the first sign of a rumble."

"Then why hang around with them?"

"They're the only ones that will hang out with me."

"Why do you think you can't be friends with somebody else?"

"I think because they're scared of me. But you're not."

"Why do you think they're scared of you?" Fridge shrugs his shoulders, "I don't know."

"I reckon it's because you get angry a lot, without meaning to." Fridge picks up a knife and jabs it a few times into a chopping board. "Well, I can't help it."

"Do you know why you get angry?"

"Well, sort of. I've always been a bit of an angry ant. My Dad says so. But after mum died, it got worse."

"You mean you're angry with her."

Fridge has a shocked look on his face. "Who told you that?"

"Nobody, I know the feeling. When Michael died and we lost the farm, I thought it was his fault. How was I going to tell him that? I got real angry because there was no saying goodbye, there was just nothin'."

Fridge sits down and fidgets with the knife, "didn't you go to his funeral and all that stuff? You know, say goodbye and all that."

"Stuff like that hadn't happened to me before. I didn't know how I was supposed to act. I didn't even know what to say. How did I know things would end up the way they did." Fridge puts down the knife and with both arms leans with his full weight on the end of the table, in a nervous-uneasy fashion. His lip quivers as he struggles to control his emotions, biting down on his bottom lip to stop his feelings showing.

"Hey Leo, you should be one of those 'Shrinks'. How come you understand all this head stuff?"

"Only because that's what happened to me."

"Yeah, but how did you know how to work it all out."

Leo, eyes look up to the right searching for an answer, "Just lucky I guess. I sort of fell into it, you might say."

"There I am, thinking I'm angry at God and the rest of the frigging world for taking my Mum away. And you know you're right, I guess I was angry at her too. You're the Shrink what do you reckon I should do?"

"What I did was sit quietly and talked to Michael, just as if he was here. I told him how I was feeling."

"And that helped?"

"Yep, the angry feeling went away."

Fridge grabs the knife again, "I'm hungry, let's eat. Then, Doctor Shepherd I going to ask you how I can get more friends." Leo feels embarrassed and replies, "Aw Fridge. Get out of here, with all that doctor stuff." As they make a snack each, Leo feels good inside.

Thinking, it feels good to help someone like Fridge with such a tricky problem. But at the same time, he's thinking, the guy's got the personality of a 'Bronta-bloody-sore-arse'. How in the hell do I help him attract more friends? I'm no expert and I don't have heaps of friends, either.

"Okay Leo! Ready to get your arse kicked on Playstation? I've been practising."
"No way, I'll whip your arse. Just wait and see. But before we do that Fridge, I was thinking. What if you started watching out for anyone being picked on at school? You could step in and stop it. I bet they'd think differently, then. What do you reckon?"
"You mean like Robin the Hood of Fielden High?"
"That's not exactly what I had in mind, Fridge."

Chapter 8
I know who you are. You're the last.

That night, after spending time with Fridge, Leo settles down to do his homework on the kitchen table. Just before dinnertime, Bryan comes home and into the kitchen. He fills the jug, "boy do I need a cup of tea. It's been a lousy day at the garage. The Wilsons want the place tidied up for the sale and at the moment I couldn't give a rat's arse about the place. Seeing how I'm not getting a cracker out of it."

Leo stops writing and put his pen down, "Dad. Why don't you buy the garage?" Bryan responds in a sarcastic tone, "Oh that's a great idea, Leo. So what great ideas do you have for raising the money?" "What about that man from the Bank? After the auction he said if you needed help, to contact him."
"With our credit rating, you must be joking. He was only feeling sorry for us. Don't you understand that son? Even if I could get a loan, I don't have a deposit to put down on it. Anyway Leo, this whole discussion is a complete waste of time as one of the big oil companies will snap it up for sure."

"But Dad, you won't know that unless you try. You have to think positive like you really want it. You do want it don't you?" "Well err-umm yes, I bloody do. But I just can't see how that's possible?" Linda is going past the kitchen with the laundry basket and stops to ask, "what's going on between you two?" Bryan folds his arms defensively, "Leo's trying to help me, but he doesn't understand about what it takes to run a business.

Leo interrupts, "I might not know much about business, but the Wilsons are loaded. Maybe they'll let you buy the garage, somehow? They said you have helped build up the customers. Couldn't they lend you some money for the deposit? Surely that counts for something." "Wake up Leo! This is the real world. And you Leo are just a dreamer. Go back to your science fiction books, because what you are talking about is exactly that, a bloody fiction." Linda raises her voice, "Bryan! I can't believe what I am hearing. Here's your chance to do something positive and all you can do is sit there and criticise. I think Leo's right."

Bryan throws up his hands in the air, "okay, okay have it your way. I'll talk to Grant Smith from the Bank in the morning and to the Wilsons, just to keep you guys happy. But remember I told you so."

Next morning Leo wakes early with an uneasy feeling. Exactly why, he doesn't know. However, he's restless and can't get back to sleep. He sits up and reads for a while until the alarm goes off. Thinking, I'm going to hate that clock. Maybe I should've gone off the deep end at Mum about being older. She's getting back at me by making me responsible. I still have this weird funny feeling. But everything's been going well and with El-Caro's help, everything's bullet-proof. So what's there to worry about? The journey to school proves to be uneventful for Leo.

However, as he jumps off the bus he notices an unusual looking black car with rear wings. The only reason he takes any notice is that some of the students are admiring it. One shouts; "hey dudes! Get your optics on that cool American car. It's a Sixties Cadillac, El Dorado. Man, is that retro or what?" Leo's attention shifts to the man standing next to the car, staring in his direction. Leo feels a cold shiver going up his spine and looks away thinking; under those dark sunglasses, that guy's eyeballing me. It's warm and he's wearing a black suit and an overcoat and looks as retro as that car. What a weirdo. Man, this feels creepy. I'm getting out of here and going to the Library.

In the Library, Leo is looking forward to finishing the second book in the Questor series, but can't get the mysterious retro man out of his mind. However, as the day progresses Leo becomes absorbed into his work and has forgotten all about the mysterious man and his black American car. Leo's first-afternoon class is a double period of Art Classes. Leo's not that interested in art, but like all the other boys, interested in the dark-haired Cathy, the young attractive Arts Teacher.

Today they're studying model making, using different media. During the second period, a student comes in and hands Cathy a note. She announces, "Leon Shepherd please report to the Headmaster's office immediately."

Leo is shocked and points at his chest. Cathy nods, "yes he wants to speak to you." Leo quickly stands up to leave the room. The class erupts, "Oohhh-Wahhh."
"Come on you lot that's enough, unless you want to join him," demands Cathy, regaining control of the class. On the way to Mr Sharpe's office, Leo's mind is racing. I wonder what he wants. I haven't done anything wrong, today. In fact, I haven't done anything this week. I'm not worried. Oh God! I hope nothing's happened at home. Jeez, that must be it. I'd better get there quick smart.

Arriving at the Headmaster's office, a breathless Leo announces his presence, "Hi Mrs Watts I'm Leo Shepherd and I got this note to come and see the Headmaster." Mrs Watts points to a row of seats, "take a seat Leo and I will let him know you're here." She disappears into the Headmaster's office, leaving Leo nervously pacing up and down the reception area.

The phone rings and an already edgy Leo jumps. She returns to answer it and ignores Leo. Finally, after what seems an eternity, Mr Sharpe is ready to see Leo and calls out, "Come." As Leo opens the door Mr Sharpe ushered him in and gestures for Leo to sit. While Mr Sharpe paces up and down with his hands behind his back. As he reaches the window he peers out and without turning around says sternly, "I don't know what you have been up to Shepherd. But I have just had what I can only describe as a most bizarre visit from a very strange gentleman asking questions about you."

"What does he look like Sir?" Mr Sharpe turns and faces Leo. "The reason I found it bizarre, is that he was wearing a suit and overcoat, with leather gloves and you know how hot it is today. But he looked as cool as a cucumber."
"Did the guy have a black hat, Sir?"
"Yes, and carrying a black leather satchel. You seem to know an awful lot about him Shepherd, which surprises me because he had a most threatening manner."

"No Sir I don't. I just saw that guy this morning over the road from the bus stops. He was standing next to his car. That's all I know."
"Shepherd, I think there's more to it than that?"
"Sir, did he say who he was or what he wanted?"
"He introduced himself as Charles E. Byrd. He wanted to confirm if you were a student here. But I told him unless he was prepared to reveal more about why he wanted that information, I would have to ask him to leave the premises. The more I think about this, I think it would be wise to contact the police. How do you feel about that? Do you want me to do that or discuss it with your parents, first?"

"I don't know anything about that guy. I haven't done anything. So can't we just drop it?"
"Well, I guess he hasn't done anything wrong. Mark my words, you stay well clear of him and let me know if he comes near you again." Mr Sharpe walks over and half opens the door. "Make sure when you go home to tell your parents. They can contact me if they feel it necessary."
"Yes, Sir." Leo leaves the Headmaster's office quite shaken and anxious. There are lots of questions dashing through his mind. Thinking, I'm sure it was the same guy I saw near the Sentinel with those military guys.

He's got the same name. It must be him. How come he knows it was me? But how could he know? How come El-Caro didn't say anything? What am I supposed to do about it? I had a feeling that guy wasn't from the NSA and a government spook. I wonder what he wants from me.

Arriving back at class, everyone is anxious to know if Leo's in trouble, but Cathy is having none of this, "Shoosh everyone! Concentrate on your work." After a while, one student whispers quietly, "did you get detention?" Leo whispers back, "no you Derp. They got me mixed up with someone else." The Arts teacher interrupts, "I can hear talking again at the back. I won't tell you to quieten down again.

If there's any more of this, then the culprits will be sent to the Headmaster's office, mark my words." Leo is unsettled and can't concentrate on his work. All he can think about is going back to speak to L-CRO. I'm sure he'll be able to sort this out. Leo looks at his watch and realises the home time siren is about to go. Quietly he begins packing up. The shriek of the siren sees Leo stuffing his work into his bag and bolting out of the room to avoid any more awkward questions. He's on high alert for the mysterious retro man as he makes his way towards the bus stops.

However, Leo decides not to cross the road to his own bus stop. He feels much safer with other students around him, while he waits for his bus. Standing with his backpack between his legs, Leo feels a presence behind him. He turns around. His worst fears are confirmed. The man in the black suit and overcoat confronts Leo and barks threateningly, "are you Leon Shepherd?" Leo looks at the man without answering. He has the darkest penetrating eyes of anyone Leo has come across. They look very menacing, sending shivers down Leo's spine.

Leo is thinking, it can't be the same Charles Byrd I overheard, he had an American accent. Whoever that guy is I'm not answering nothin'. The man moves closer. "I know who you are. You're the last. I know about that signal too. Your galactic friend has been very careless." Just as Leo goes to open his mouth to deny everything, a figure moves between them.

"Listen Mister. I don't know what your game is...but you'd better get on your bike, otherwise you're going to see stars." Leo recognises the voice. It's Fridge. He and the dark-suited retro man are so close they almost touch noses. The man backs off and points at Leo in a jabbing motion. "You've not heard the last of this." Clearly shaken by the encounter, Leo takes a deep breath and exhales.

"Phew, thanks mate. I have no idea who that guy is. I reckon he's a bit of a nut-case." Fridge just shrugs his shoulders, "I'm just doing what you said. You know Robin the Hood of Fielden High." Leo is in no mood for jokes, "I've got to go. There's my bus." Leo races across the road. He leaves Fridge bemused, scratching his head and wondering what is going on.

As Leo clambers onto the bus, he decides to sit down the back to see if he's being followed. As the bus pulls out, Leo glances over his shoulder. As expected the black American car pulls out behind the bus. Leo realises he can't go home and has to think of a plan. Hell, what am I going to do? Maybe I'll just stay on the bus. Nahhh that's no good, what will I do after that? It's too risky to get off somewhere and hide in the bush. Bloody-hell! I've got to calm down, I can't think straight. I just keep thinking what does that guy want? What does he mean about me being the last one - the last one of what? That's what I need to do - be around lots of people.

I know, maybe I get off at the garage, where Dad works. There's bound to be heaps of people coming and going. Then I can think of something, there. Maybe get Dad to help me. Least that's better than nothing. Leo looks out of the side window as the bus passes his house. Two stops later, Leo rings the bell and quickly gets off at the Stop. He dashes into the garage not wanting to look if the black American car is still following. He quickly disappears into the office. Bryan looks up and is surprised, "Leo what are you doing here? I thought you didn't like hanging around here because it's boring?"
"Ahhh, Dad, um… Bryan interrupts, "quickly, will you, I've got to finish this paperwork."
"Dad, I need some pocket money. So, umm, I thought you might give me some jobs."

"You betcha, there's heaps to do. You can do some cleaning up or help the customers by cleaning their windscreens and pumping petrol." For Leo, the work helps to keep him around people. It temporarily takes his mind off his predicament.

That is, until Bryan grabs the closing sign, "okay Leo. It's time to shut up shop. Can you get the leftover pies and pasties from the pie warmer and turn it off. We will have those for dinner tonight." Leo has to think very quickly, without letting on that he has a problem. He asks, "Dad can I hop in the back of the Pickup utility for the ride home, instead of upfront with you?"
"What for son?"
"I don't know. Ahh-umm, just want to do something different."
"Well it's not far, so I guess it is okay."
"Wow, thanks Dad."

Leo hops into the back of the Pickup utility parked inside the workshop. Clutching onto the bag of pies, Leo pulls the cover over himself, thinking, I hope this works. If it doesn't I've got an awful lot of explaining to do. Trouble is, Dad probably won't believe me anyway. I hardly believe it myself.

Bryan starts up the Pickup utility and shouts, "Okay, are you ready Leo. Hang on!" Meanwhile, the mysterious retro man is slumped in the large black car across the road from the garage. He sits up immediately and looks carefully at the Pickup utility as it drives past. As he only sees Bryan, the man jumps out and strides across the road to the garage. He checks the front door and looks through all of the windows. Finding nothing, he then searches around the back before going back to his car. Arriving home, Leo is careful to make sure no one is watching.

He quickly jumps out of the Pickup utility and dashes inside. Leo goes straight to the lounge room and peers out of the front for any sign of the big black car. His heart misses a beat and begins to race as he spots a black car pulling up out the front. A man wearing black jeans and a black t-shirt gets out and goes to the car's boot. He pulls out a bag and climbs back into the car.

Relieved, Leo takes a deep breath. He lets out a big sigh, "phew" and folds his arms and continues his vigil, pacing up and down until Bryan calls him. "Leo where's those pies, I'm starving."

"Dad here they are.

I feel a bit crusty at the moment. I'm going to my room. Save me one will you." With a pie half demolished, Bryan mutters with his mouth half full, "are you sure you don't want a pie before they get cold? This one's steak and mushroom?"

"No, I need to be horizontal, Dad."

"See! Now you know what it's like. The work's a lot harder than you thought, eh?"

"Yeah, you could say that," replies Leo as he goes to his room. He needs space to think things through. However, he doesn't get much time to think as Linda comes into Leo's room, having just gotten home, too. "Hi Leo darling, are you okay. Dad said something about you feeling a bit peaky."

"Nah, I was just a bit tired. Is there any pies left?" They both go into the kitchen. "Bryan I hope you left something for Leo."

"Yeah, course I did. There's a Potato Topper here and a Pasty too. Do you want go halves in the Pasty?"

"Only, if I can have that potato one."

"Sounds like you've got your appetite back, son."

That night his parents retire to bed early as they're both worn out. Leo however, is planning to go across the road in the dead of night and have an urgent talk with El-Caro. He opens his bedroom window and throws out his torch. Climbing out, Leo quickly adjusts to the light. He stands still and listens for any unusual sounds. It's much brighter than he expects, as there is a three-quarter moon. Picking up his torch, Leo sneaks across the road and into the bush.

Leo is very apprehensive and edgy, expecting the mystery retro man to be close by. He's on high alert. Any noise or movement in the shadows makes Leo jump. Thinking, I'm not sure this is a good idea. I feel really scared right now. Maybe I should've left a note. I could disappear and nobody would ever know what happened…what was that? A startled bird makes an escape as Leo nears the ruin. Using his torch he locates the rope ladder and drags it to the well.

As he runs the rope around the tree, he stops for a moment to listen for any sounds. It is deadly quiet, except for a Mopoke calling. Leo's mind is doing overtime. Thinking, I've never been here at night, it's really eerie. I've got to get moving. I've got to get El-Caro to sort everything out. Oh hell. How am I going to climb down this thing in the dark? Maybe I'll use my hanky and tie the torch to the ladder.

Talking to himself as he climbs down, Leo remarks, "jeez these are hard enough to climb down, during the day. At least I don't have to worry about a torch in the Sentinel." Leo's relieved when he finally makes it into the Sentinel room and settles in for contact. After the curtain of light descends, Leo anxiously waits for L-CRO to come through. "Leo my young friend, I can feel that you're distressed."
"Distressed," yells Leo. "I'm frigging scared I can tell you - Who is he and what does he want from me?"

"I was hoping you would be spared having to deal with that entity. But I have to tell you, there is also another."
"You mean there are two of them?"
"Unfortunately, yes. This is not one of the predicted outcomes we were expecting. It seems they have somehow bridged the space-time gap."
"El-Caro, I wasn't expecting this either. Now you really got me scared. I don't know what's going down, here. That retro looking guy whoever he is, said you gave me away and said something like I'm the last one - the last of what?"

"Please calm down Leo and I will explain it all to you. In our universe and yours, there are dark forces at work. They're against any change of a spiritual nature. There have been many battles over Millennia for control of your planet's resources and destiny. Those two entities are part of the dark forces. It seems they have picked up our signal and decoded it when you opened the door at the Sentinel entrance."

"But El-Caro you still haven't told me, who they are and what they want from me?"
"Let's just say for your own safety, that it's better you do not know who they are or what they are capable of...I know my response is puzzling to you, but you must trust me. Be aware that you have information they desperately want."

"But I don't have anything they'd want."

"Unfortunately, I have to tell you my friend that is not the case."

"Well whatever it is, can't I just give it to them and make them go away?"

"Leo it's not quite as simple as that. Because the information they want is stored at a cellular level, in your DNA. The information is so critical and sacred to the evolution of your planet. It was hidden in the DNA of our lineage so that it would not be lost or stolen away and would be preserved for a very long time. I was hoping it would not be necessary to reveal this to you, but your life is in danger now and possibly our futures as well."

"Then why can't I let them have the DNA from some of my hair or something. I don't want to be part of this thing anymore." Tears flow down Leo's cheeks as he realises he is part of a game, which he doesn't understand, over which he has neither defence nor control.

"Leo they don't want the information you have, they want to destroy it completely. Because, when Michael and your grandfather died, you're the last in the line and these dark forces know this."

"El-Caro how do they know this and what about my Dad, isn't he in danger too?"

"The dark forces have psychic abilities and they can tell that your Dad has the DNA sequence embedded. However, it's either dormant or defective, while yours has been activated; you recall the low-frequency rhythmic humming sounds." Choking back tears Leo sobs, "El-Caro you have to stop them. They're going to kill me aren't they?"

"Leo you must pull yourself together and be clear about one thing. I cannot interfere. To do so breaks planetary laws and may do more damage to both our futures. As it is, I am taking a risk now, just with the current communication with you. My location has been compromised."

"But that's no good to me. I'm as good as dead... just like that. I wish I had never come here in the first place. I wish everything to go back as it was."

"Leo, you are not without your own powers. You're not powerless. Remember they cannot interfere with your free will, either. Your thoughts are more powerful than you know. You can use them to harness your defences. You will get through this period.

Please believe me. When you're in any trouble, just remember what Gramps said to you and remain totally focused on what you want to happen. Under no circumstances must you think about negative outcomes. Because fear and anger are the Dark entities source of energy and power. That way, you will come to no harm."

"So what's so important about the information I have?"
"The information is the key to unlocking the records of human history, the true history of your people. In you, is the key to that knowledge. The timeline for access is not yet precisely calculated, because of Earth's Freewill Charter.

That means until the majority of your people are ready, the truth will not be revealed. However, there are forces who hope that it is never found and they can continue to manipulate the collective consciousness of Earth…Leo, you must gather your resources."
"I don't have any…like who for instance?"
"I've scanned your mind and you have the phone number of Ernest the bus driver." Leo in a sarcastic tone replies, "oh yeah, right - like as if a retired bus driver with a dodgy hip is going to be able to fix this problem - like Superman. Seeing how you like analogies El-Caro, I feel like I'm one those Christians being fed to the frigging lions."

"Leo, get one thing straight, whether you like it or not, you are here on this planet to help its progress. Now you have a job to do and I have given you clues and techniques to help you through this difficult time. At some risk, I might add, that you couldn't possibly understand."

"It's not my fault. All this stuff is a real shock and I need all the help I can get. Maybe I can go to the police?"
"They can't help you. That would only play into the manipulator's hands. Ernest has friends, so use them. If you hold that thought in your mind that help is at hand, and be willing to ask for and accept any help that comes your way. You'll be surprised what is out there for you. I want you to take comfort from an old saying; *as the sun's light grows, the shadows darken, until they give way to the light.* Darkness to light my friend. I think it's time to end our talk. It has to be this way.

Understand that everything will work out for you, but it's in your hands now. I must say goodbye to you my dear friend and remember the Great Creator has given you all the skills you will ever need. Remember the pledge you made to your grandfather."

Leo calls out in a panicked tone, "El-Caro don't go. I need you. Please don't go. You can't just leave me like this. El-Caro!" The curtain of liquid light disappears in a flash. Leo is alone, his anxious thoughts make for poor company - not knowing what to do and overcome by impending disaster. He leaves the Sentinel weighed down by the burden he now carries. This makes the climb up the rope ladder out of the well more difficult than usual. Clearly exhausted, he grunts and puffs as he removes the rope ladder. However, Leo makes sure it's hidden properly and begins to wend his way home.

On the way, Leo has many unanswered questions stampeding through his head. Thinking, if I'd known what I know now, I would not have come here. El-Caro is supposed to know everything. Then how come all this 'doggie-doo' has happened? I didn't ask for it. I don't even want it. If I don't do something I'm going to be a dead duck, for sure. I can't go to the cops. They won't believe me, anyway. I don't understand what's going on... so how do I explain it? Seems to me like, I have no choice. I'll have to ask Ernie to help me. But what can he do? I wonder who his friends are. I'll ring him in the morning after the Olds go to work. Leo stops before crossing the main road. He stands still, listening for cars or any movement near his house. But all he hears is his heart beating loudly and a dog barking in response to two cats fighting.

After carefully checking that nobody is around, Leo climbs back through his window. Back in bed he tosses and turns and can't get comfortable. He drifts in and out of sleep, but periodically wakes with a start each time the tin roof creaks.

As the morning light falls on his window, he finds that it has been an exhausting night. It's not long before his mum is ushering him out of bed. "Leo, you look awful this morning didn't you sleep properly last night."

"Yeah Mum, I had a crappy night. I feel really crusty."
Is there something bothering you at school?"
"No mum, school's alright." But under his breath he mouths, "but I wish the rest of it was."

"Leo, I have to go now. I hope you have a better day - today."
"Me too, see ya Mum." Leo gives Linda a big hug. "That's unusual for you? But nice just the same," comments Linda, as she squeezes Leo back.
"Look at the time I really must go. Sure you'll be okay?"
"Yeah, of course Mum…get out of here." Leo turns Linda around and points her towards the front door.

As soon as Leo hears Linda high heels going clonk, clonk, clonk down the drive, he immediately turns his attention to the phone and ringing Ernie. Leo begins dialing, but hesitates and puts the phone down. He taps on the hand-piece thinking, what do I tell him? How am I going to explain everything? But if I don't ring him now, he might go out and then I'm stuffed. Maybe if I talk about the books. Yeah, that's what I'll do.

As Leo dials he has his other fingers crossed that Ernie is at home.
"Hello is that Ernie. Oh cool. I'm ringing because you gave the Questor Trilogy books."
"Oh Yes, Leo isn't it?"
"Yeah."
"Don't tell me you have read those books already?"
"No, I'm only up to the second book, but there's something I need to talk to you about, urgently."
"Okay, but you don't know where I live. I'll tell you what. I will come over to your place this afternoon. Is that alright?"
"Well, I was hoping this morning."
"Don't you have school today?"
"Yeah, I do. But I'm not feeling well enough to go."
"Well, perhaps we can make it another day if you're not well?"
"No Ernie you have to come. I can't talk over the phone. It's really, really important."

"Well if you say so. But I can't see why it can't wait and why all the cloak and dagger stuff?"
"Thanks Ernie, I really need your help." Leo decides not to risk going to school.

Convinced the mysterious retro man will be out looking for him at school. Leo impatiently paces up and down the lounge room anxiously waiting for Ernie. He hears a car approaching and is excited. But the car drives straight past, leaving Leo with an empty feeling. After what seems an eternity, Ernie pulls into the driveway. Leo rushes out to greet him and has a quick look around before they go inside.

Ernie notices that Leo is edgy, "It's good to see you again, but you're acting rather oddly, with the phone call and all. What's going on that's so urgent?"

"Well it's like…there's this strange man in a black suit and overcoat and he's like been following me and there's supposed to be two of them and they think I have stuff they want, but I'm like…I don't have it or know what it is."

"Whoa! Wait a minute Leo. I'm not following you at all. Slow down and start from the beginning." Leo retraces his steps of the previous day, leaving out the bit about the Sentinel and L-CRO. "Why didn't you go to the police?"

"With what?" replies Leo. "Besides, they will get to me first."

"You mean a Men-in-Black scenario."

"No, it's not quite the same. They're not government spooks."

"Then what have you been up to that warrants their attention?"

"Ernie, I think it's a case of mistaken identity. But this friend told me that these guys are psychic and do stuff like that."

"If that's the case, then you're not over-reacting. You're dealing with some very serious people. You must know something or have something they want, even if you don't know what it is?"

"Can you help me or not?"

"Look, I belong to a small group that's kind of into alternative knowledge, like. We discuss UFOs, Sci-fi stuff, psychic information, prophecies, conspiracy theories and stuff like that. I can ring the guys and you can come along and we can see what we can do for you. One of them is a psychic and another is our resident clown and remote viewer. We'll see what they come up with."

"Thanks Ernie. I'm really scared at the moment."

"Okay, I will pick you up at six o'clock. It will be at my place at seven. Make sure your folks are okay with this too…I mean what do they think of what's going on?"

"They don't know and my Dad thinks this stuff is mumbo-jumbo, so I can't tell them anything…Can't we meet the guys any earlier, because my folks might not let me come?"

"Leo you're making this difficult. Can I use your phone? I'll have to ring around and see if the group can meet at 4:00pm after school.

You're lucky these guys have mobiles, so it shouldn't be difficult to contact them. But I don't know if they'll make it any earlier. Anyway, we'll see." After a number of phone calls, Ernie announces, "Okay Leo you're in luck, it's all arranged. You need to go to school now. So I will take you and pick you up straight after school. That way if you're being followed, I can see who it is for myself."

"Thanks Ernie, I don't know what else to say."

"That's okay, at least I can return the favour you did me. Well go and get your school bag and stuff ready?"

Leo's eyes are everywhere as Ernie drives him to school. The sight of any black car gives Leo heart failure. However, much to Leo's relief there's no sign of the retro man. "There you see Leo, nothing happened. Take my advice, get stuck into your schoolwork and don't worry. That way your day will go quicker. I'll pick you up afterwards, so there's absolutely no need to worry."

"Thanks Ernie, you're really cool for helping me. I'll see you at 3:30pm okay." Leo climbs out and races inside the school gate as if his life depends on it and makes his way to his first class. While in class Leo feels safe. However, between classes, he still feels nervous and uncomfortable. At lunchtime, Leo seeks the sanctuary of the Library. He tries to read but can't concentrate. Anxiously looking up each time the Library door slides open. Sitting there he stares at the book and wishes that it's all a dream and that it will all go away.

Back in class Leo does as Ernie suggests and gets stuck into his schoolwork, temporarily putting his problems to the back of his mind. However, it all comes flooding back when the siren rings. Leo crams his books and homework into his bag. "Damn! It won't all fit in. Now I'll have to go to my locker.

I was hoping to stay away from there. There's no way I'm taking all this stuff to Ernie's. I'll have to stuff these books away," he mutters as he leaves the classroom.

Arriving at the lockers, Leo meets up with Fridge. They fist- bump each other. "Hi-ya Fridge, how's it going, Dude."

"Yo there Bro. How-ya doing?"

"Yeah alright I suppose. Look I can't talk much. I've got someone waiting for me"

"I hope it's not that clown I nearly creamed yesterday."

"Nah. But thanks for yesterday. No, it's not anybody like that. Fridge, I'll catch you later."

"Yeah, see you later." Leo heads for the school bus bays and nervously looks around. He becomes concerned, as he can't see Ernie's green old Holden as they'd arranged. Then to Leo's relief, he hears an adult voice call out, "Leon Shepherd!"

As he turns and walks towards the line of parked cars, he expects to see Ernie. Suddenly from behind him, a man grabs Leo by the arm. "Ouch! Let go, your hurting me." There's no response from the man in the black suit. He forcefully bundles Leo into the back seat of the big black American Cadillac, flicking the child-safety latch, before slamming the door. He opens the boot and removes a pair of handcuffs, while Leo tries desperately to open the door. Leo panics, thinking, what's wrong with this door? He's done something to it. Oh God! I got to get out of here or I'm history.

The mysterious retro man jumps into the driver's seat and reaches for the ignition key. His head rocks back with surprise. The keys aren't in the ignition. He glances out of the open car window and spots Fridge standing there dangling the key in a taunting fashion. "Lost something Arsehole?" The man half reaches out of the window and snarls, "give them to me or you will be in more trouble than you can possibly handle."

Fridge moves backwards, "not until you let my buddy out." The man quickly throws open the car door. He jumps out and angrily rushes at him. Fridge sidesteps, but leaves a well-placed foot behind, that trips the retro man up. He sprawls to the ground as Fridge promptly throws the keys onto the roof of the science block.

214

There's a clattering sound as they keys slide down the metal roof and into the gutter. "Now look who's in trouble. You'll have fun finding those, you A-hole." Meanwhile, Leo jumps over to the front seat and scrabbles out through the driver's door. He joins Fridge as he watches the man get to his feet and goes off searching for his car keys. "My God Fridge, I think you just saved my life."

"That's the same guy for the other day. Leo, what the hell's going on?"

"Look Fridge I don't want to hang around here. I'm supposed to be picked up by my friend Ernie. Can we talk about it later… thank God! There's Ernie now. I think you'd better come with us. Ernie will drop you off, so that guy can't hassle us."

"You still haven't told me what this is all about. Didn't that A-hole just try to kidnap you?"

"Fridge, the truth is I don't know who he is or what he wants."

"Man, we should go to the cops. This is the second time I've had to save your butt."

"Yes, I know Fridge. I really appreciate it... it's that I…I don't know what to say."

"Try saying thanks and say… let's go to the cops."

"But, thank you is so little for what you've done."

"We're friends, aren't we? That's what friends do."

"Okay, I'll get Ernie to take me to the police after we drop you off. But, keep this to yourself. Won't you?"

"That depends on what that guy does." Ernie waves to Leo and they all pile into his car. "Hi Ernie, this is my friend Frid…I'm mean Kelvin, do you mind if we drop him off, first. He lives in…what's the name of your street. Fridge adds, "Ocean Drive, number 22."

"That's okay fellas. I know that street it's around the corner from my place." As Ernie indicates and moves off, they pass the empty black American car. Leo keeps his eyes fixed on the car until they turn the corner. There's an awkward air of silence in the car. None of the trio are sure of what to say to each other, without saying too much.

Arriving at 22 Ocean Drive, Fridge grabs his backpack and jumps out. "Bro, I hope you know what you're doing. I'm not going to be there every time, to save your butt." Leo closes the door and winds down the window. "Thanks again Fridge, we got to go."
As Ernie drives off, they leave Fridge standing in the driveway. He scratches his head and has a puzzled look on his face as the old green Holden disappears out of sight. Ernie takes the precaution of going around the block, before going back to the house. But there's no sign of the black American car.

Ernie parks in the driveway and lets them both in. "Okay Leo, while I set up the afternoon tea for the guys, you can make yourself a snack. Just help yourself to whatever's in the refrigerator."
"Thanks, Ernie, how'd you know I was hungry?"
"I was your age once too, you know."

While making a snack, Leo tosses up ideas in his head. I wonder if I should tell Ernie about today. But, if I do, he'll want to go to the cops. El-Caro said that if the cops get involved I'd be a sitting duck. I think I'll wait and see what happens. Anyway, I don't even know if I can trust him. Oh my God! I never thought of that. Hang on Leo you Derp; he must be all right 'cos El-Caro said to contact him. God, he'd better be right.

An antique clock on the mantle-piece chimes the quarter hour. It has just gone 3:45 pm. The chimes jolt Leo's attention back to the present and his half-eaten sandwich. A knock at the front door soon after, reveals two of Ernie's friends. "G'day Ernest, how are you doing? I know we're early. But we're keen to find out what the fuss is all about?"

"Thanks for coming. This is Leo Shepherd, the boy I told you about. Leo, this is Arjan and he's the psychic in our group. This is Graham he's our computer expert and does searches over the Internet for us - stuff like that." Leo shakes hands with the two men. Arjan is in his fifties. He has an alternative look about him. His grey receding long hair is tied back in a ponytail with a white beard. He has on a black tee shirt and sporting a beaded necklace with a Ying and Yang pendant. His baggy linen pants and sandals complete the picture.

In contrast, Graham is younger. He's in his early twenties. Has spiky dark hair with matching black-rimmed glasses and a dark coloured suit. However, the white shirt with green collar and cuffs and socks, with a lime pink tie seem out of place for the conservative look. "Why don't you all take a seat? I'm sure the other two will be here soon." To fill in time Arjan decides to give Leo a reading, "Leo, have you had your palms read before?"

"Nup. Does it hurt," remarks Leo, trying to make light of his situation.

"No haven't lost a client yet," laughs Arjan as he shifts his chair to face Leo. Sitting down and making himself comfortable, Arjan reaches forward and holds onto Leo's hands, palms up and adds, "of course the hole in the wallet after a reading might hurt a bit." Arjan looks intently at Leo's palms.

"Hmmm... this kid is really special! He's got important work to do." Arjan takes a closer look at Leo's right hand. "Hmmm your right Ernie, there is negative forces around this kid, no wonder he's scared. I'm getting the impression there's been contact or a visit with someone or something very unusual, but I can't pick up what it is..." Ernie interrupts, "I knew it. It had to be something like that. Why would that bloke be interested in him? Leo, what do you know about this?" Leo's still unsure about trusting them and replies, "I don't know what you mean by contact?"

Arjan lets Leo's right hand go and comments, "Okay, we won't push this now." He stands up and moves his chair back. "Maybe when Derek gets here, he might be able to find something. He's our remote viewer you know. He's like a bloodhound, except he uses his mind rather than his nose to find things. You will like him - he's a real character." Graham also attempts to re-assure Leo, "the other member of this 'motley crew' of ours might be very helpful too - Desmond Clarke. Des is an ex-cop with good contacts. He seems to get stuff from God-knows-where."

Leo's fascinated by the different characters and is inquisitive, "so Ernie, what do you do as a group?"
"We originally formed a discussion group to talk about Sci-fi books and swap them.

But now we cover metaphysical topics that come up in alternative-type, underground magazines and on the Net. Covering science fiction books, UFO's, hidden agendas and that sort of stuff. You know stuff the media don't talk about and governments don't want you to know about.

Also what big companies across the world get up to. We like to sort-of monitor what's happening below the surface. We want things to change for the better. So as a group, we...well let's put it this way, we send out positive vibes to counter the garbage that's going on."

A loud knock at the door makes everyone jump. Ernie gets up and goes to the front door. "I bet that's Des." As Ernie answers the door, Leo can see an imposing figure. His big frame fills the doorway. Desmond is tall, with a big potbelly. His shiny balding head looks like it has been for a wax and polish. He has a big red nose and huge shoulders.

Although retired from the Police force, he acts like he's still there and is always secretive about what he's doing. Including what his role was while in the Force. "G'day Des, come in." Ernie leaves the door open having spotted Derek pulling up on the verge. "Afternoon gents, sorry I'm late. I had to run a last-minute errand for the Missus. Ahh, you must be the young lad Ernie was talking about. Good to meet you son." Leo shakes hands with Desmond and immediately feels uneasy about him. Thinking, something's not right about him. Can't understand why maybe it's because he was a cop or maybe I'm a bit suspicious of everyone at the moment. Yeah, that's probably it. As Desmond sits down, Derek announces his arrival.

"Am I the last one to arrive? That means I have to pour the bloody teas again! Jeez I'm a slow learner, aren't I?" Derek is tall and in his late twenties. Has an ear stud in his left ear and brown hair with stubble to match. His jeans are new and a white tee shirt, which has; 'I'm with Stupid', printed on the front. Derek bounds over to the table and introduces himself to Leo. "I'm the clown of this outfit, as you can guess. Give me a High Five." Derek holds his hand in the air and Leo slaps Derek's hand lightly.

"Give me a Low Five and make it like you mean it." Derek turns around and put's his hand down behind his back. Leo slaps it again with a whack. "Ouch! That's more like it. Right, that's the formalities out of the way. Now, who wants tea and who wants coffee? By the way Leo, I make shit-house coffee."

"Okay then I'll have tea," replies Leo as he warms to Derek's child-like manner. Ernie gestures for everyone to sit at the table. "Okay, let's bring this meeting to order while Derek's doing the honours. By the way, whose turn is it to chair the meeting?"
"Ernie, you called the meeting, so why don't you chair it."

"Okay then. I called this extraordinary meeting because my friend Leo here needs our help. Leo, can you explain what's has happened."
"Thanks Ernie. Yesterday morning when I got to Fielden High and the guys were checking out this car - it's one of those 1960's black Caddy's. I think they said it was an El Dorado. Anyway next to it, this guy was standing there and he was decked out in this black suit, had a black hat and wearing an overcoat. He was weird looking because his gear was totally retro. I didn't think much of it until I got hauled up to the Headmaster's office. The same guy had asked the Headmaster about me. Even Mr Sharpe, the Headmaster, thinks he's a weirdo."

Desmond interrupts, "did he give his name, at all?"
"Yeah, the Headmaster said he called himself, Charles E. Byrd."
Desmond comments as he writes the name down in a notebook, "I'll get one of my mates to run a check on that name - see what we get. "Derek mate, why don't you do some of that remote viewing stuff on this Byrd fellow? See what you can pick up."
"Why not, can't do any harm. Might not get much, but we'll see." Derek sits down on the floor in a yoga position for a few minutes with his eyes closed and his hands resting on his knees.

He begins to do some deep breathing exercises and then goes quiet again. Leo hasn't seen anything like this before and is intrigued to the point where he mimics Derek's breathing. The deafly-silence is broken as Derek speaks, which makes Leo jump. "That's strange I'm not getting any information about this Byrd fellow.

I can only imagine that he's aware that I am targeting his presence and blocking my contact. "Or, he's not part of our group Consciousness. If I'm right, then he's dangerous and has advanced capabilities.

Hang on! I'm getting something else though - the words, 'The Called One' and 'Golden Age'. And it has something to do with a saying or maybe some sort of prophecy. It doesn't make much sense, but that's what I got."

Derek emerges out of his yoga pose and breathes in deeply and stretches his neck and arms. Standing up, Ernie hands Derek a large glass of water to drink. Derek skulls the water, almost in one go. "Ahhh I needed that. This stuff is thirsty work you know. Leo, do you know what 'group consciousness' means?"
"Yes, I think so. It means you and me and every human being is a part of the same energy field."

"You're a smart kid. I didn't know about this stuff when I was your age. You know what Leo; this remote viewing stuff isn't new, either. The American and Russian military have been dabbling in it for years. I believe the Yanks had a project called Stargate back in the Seventies. But it's not so hot at predicting the future accurately and you can't turn it on like a tap. That's because events can change in an instant, when someone decides to act in a different way, straight after you think you've nailed it."

Ernie stands up and limps into the lounge. "Bloody hip, I'll just boot up the computer and log onto the Internet. Then Graham can conduct a search using those words Derek mentioned. Seeing how he's the expert at this stuff." After Ernie has finished setting up the computer, Graham sits down and taps away at the keyboard. "I'll type in: Prophecy+Golden+Age+The+Called+One and see what comes up." Waiting for a return list of web pages he laughs. "Look the first link here is to a web page dedicated to the Goose that laid the *Golden Egg* and is *called one* of the most popular children's fables.
Funny, the only Goose around here is me. I typed in E-g-e instead of A-g-e, no wonder I'm getting such a strange response. Let's try it again… there."

Graham is surprised as the search returns two references. He clicks the mouse onto the link. "Hey, this is one of those websites dedicated to the works of Nostradamus. It lists and cross-references all of his Quatrains in English.

There are only two results for 'The Called One' and 'Golden Age'. Shall I read them out? Here we go then:

"Nostradamus Prophecy - Century #21 Quatrain 54

When the two evil brothers of Anger and Fear join forces to defy God's holy order.

A boy shall be called to do a man's bidding, but the Called One shall not knoweth of the man.

However, his body shall bear witness to the truth. His name shall stand for the Lion and with the lamb.

But when the oracle has spoken, the cards shall be revealed. The evil ones shall taketh the Queen of spades and the Ace of Hearts shall weigh heavy with anguish.

Nostradamus Prophecy - Century #21 Quatrain 55

The evil ones shall measure the Called One lightly as a boy. His calling shall be to taketh upon him the strength of the evil ones and will tremble before them.

The evil ones will not pity the boy. But the man within him shall vanquish them, one by one.

The evil one of Anger weighed heavy from the evil shall fall from grace. While his brother of Fear, shall turn from grace and be struck down by the Iron Serpent.

Peace shall return to the land and God will rejoice. For the sun shall rise on the first day of the Golden Age."

Desmond leans his big frame back in his chair, "Gawd! What was all that about." Graham presses the printer's on button and replies, "I don't know. But I'll print a copy out for each of us." Each of the group takes a copy and look at each other, unsure of what to say. Leo senses the unease and pipes up, "I've heard of Nostra-what-is-name before, but Graham what is a Quatrain is?"

"It's a rhyming four lined verse in Spanish." Arjan interjects, "I told you this kid's real special. I reckon he might be 'the called one'. But I don't know what the rest of this means, what about you guys?"

Derek nods in agreement adding, "Leo must have some information that these dark forces want and I'm concerned that they will stop at nothing to get it. So we have to be very careful from now on."

"I reckon," confirms Ernie. "Let's finish this meeting for now, as I have to get Leo home. I will ring you guys to meet when we have more information. Des might find something out about this Charles Byrd fellow and let's see what the rest of you come up with."

The group files out of Ernie's house, while Leo waits for Ernie in the car, as he locks up after everyone. Leo reads his copy of the prophecy again. Thinking, this is all funny language. I can't even follow what it's going on about. How could it refer to me? Who knows even if this Nostra-what-is-name is real. As Ernie climbs back into the car, he makes grunting noises as he settles in behind the wheel, muttering, "bloody hip."

"Ernie this is an EH isn't it?"
"Yeah, you know your cars, don't you?"
"Yep, sure do and I know this one's in mint condition - like brand new."
"Thanks Leo. I love this old car. You know it's been round the clock three times. But, everything is original. Yep, they don't make cars like this anymore.

Anyway enough on cars, I was wondering if that prophecy thing has rung any bells with you."

"Nope, it's all too flowery for me. I mean, 'The Called One' could be anybody. Same with *his body shall bear witness to the truth.* It's like a code. Why didn't he just come out and say what he meant."

"Well, as far as I know, he had to do it that way, as in those days it was considered witchcraft. But getting back to your problem, you do realise we can't help you much if you aren't telling us the full story. The only reason I say that, is that when there are reports of contacts with ET's. Both government people and these other blokes in black suits seem to turn up. But you're telling you've had no contact. It doesn't figure?"

Leo desperately wants to tell Ernie everything, but is conflicted. "Ernie, if I knew anything else that would help, I would tell you. I think they have got the wrong person." Leo also knows that it would mean exposing his contact with L-CRO and the existence of the Sentinel. It's something he strongly feels he must keep secret, for now. It's now six o'clock as they round the last bend before Leo's place. Suddenly, Leo sits bolt upright in the seat and points through the windscreen and shouts, "Ernie! Pull over, you have to stop."

"Whoa! What's happened?" Ernie brakes hard and pulls off the road. They're about 500 metres from Leo's house. "I don't know Ernie. But there are two cop cars at my friend Dani's place. I've got a real bad feeling. Can we get closer?" Ernie slowly edges his vehicle along the verge until they are in front of the Jerovich house. "I have to go in and find out. Ernie, can you wait for me here?"
"Sure. I hope everything's okay."

Leo jumps out. But hesitates at first, finding it hard to walk up their driveway. In his heart, he knows something bad has happened. Thinking, something's definitely not right. I don't even want to think about what it could be. Or, maybe it's just a break-in. It seems to take an eternity for him to reach the front door. As he does so, he hears Lena Jerovich wailing and talking in her native tongue. Leo's heart sinks. He hesitates before ringing the doorbell.

Branco answers the door with teary red eyes. "Ohh Mr Leo, me and Mama very, very sad. Our Danicka she missing. Bad mans take her. What we do?" Leo is stunned. The realisation is like being hit by a demolition ball. His chest tightens and tears well up in his eyes. He feels it's his fault and has trouble getting the words out, "what do you mean missing?" Choking on tears, Branco explains, "policemans say two men in black suits make my Danicka get into big black car." A uniformed policewoman joins them at the front door. "Excuse me, are you Leon Shepherd?"

"Yes, Miss, ahhh…Officer."

We have been told by students from Danicka Jerovich's school that two men in dark suits drove up in a big black American type car and spoke to her. She didn't get into the car until one of them said that they were friends of yours. Do you know who they are?" "No Officer, I don't. But someone like that has been following me. They went to my high school asking the Headmaster about me." "Why didn't you or the school report this to us?" "Because he hadn't done anything and was just asking questions." "Now why do you think that he would be asking questions?" "I don't know. I think that they are picking on the wrong person because I don't know who they are or what they want."

As the uniformed policewoman jots down some notes, a man in a dark brown suit appears. The crumpled suit has that slept-in look. "I'm Detective Sergeant Maclean of the Fielden CIB. We think your friend has been kidnapped. We're waiting for the phone call. I want to make it perfectly clear, Leon. If you know something you'd better tell us. Because we will find out and you'll be in more trouble than Ned Kelly."

"I don't know any more than you do," sobs Leo. "Okay son, you can go home now, but I need your address and phone number. Are your folks at home, as I need to talk to them too?"
"No my folks are at work. They won't be home yet."
"Okay then. I will contact them tomorrow. In the meantime, we'll see if we can trace that car. Leon here's my card if you think of anything… anything at all that might help, you can ring that number."

Detective Sergeant Maclean points to the phone number and hands Leo his card. Feeling numb, Leo walks back down the driveway. As he gets back into Ernie's car, the numbness turns to anger. "Those rotten frigging bastards have nabbed Dani. They're going to use her to get at me. What are we going to do now?"

"Leo, you do realise that this might fit one of the lines in that prophecy. You know the bit…the evil ones taking the Queen of spades."
"Look Ernie, I couldn't give a rat's about this Nostradamus stuff. It's Dani I'm worried about. I mean she's got nothing to do with this. She doesn't know anything." The guilty feeling returns as it crosses Leo mind, maybe if I had gone to the police earlier, none of this would've happened. But that's because El-Caro said not to go there. He never said anything like this was going to happen. What are we going to do now? Leo looks despairingly across at Ernie, "what are we going to do?"
"Hmmm, what to do…what to do. Leo, maybe we can talk to Des and see what he says?"
"I don't want cops or ex-cops even, in this thing. Can we go to my place and maybe tell my folks I'm going to a Sci-fi talk with you? Then, can we get the guys back together tonight and see if we can do something?"

"Aren't you going to tell your folks what's happened? They're going to find out, you know."
"If we tell them, they won't let me go with you."
"True, but I don't like where this is heading. It's not right." Leo arrives home to find that his parents aren't home and calls out, "Ernie, they're not home. What do we do now?" Ernie pops his head out of the car window shouting, "ring your Mum at work. You just can't go off without them knowing where you are."

Leo goes back inside and rings Westons, but Linda has already left. He tries the garage, but the phone rings out. Ernie gets out of his car and walks up to the front door to see what is happening. "Did you speak to your Mum?"
"No she must've just left and I tried the garage, but there's no answer there, either."

"Well, I guess we'll have to wait for them."

"Ernie, we can't wait. Dani is in great danger. You got to help. Can't I leave a note, please?"

"Well I guess, that's better than nothing. I still have a bad feeling about doing this." Leo quickly scribbles a note explaining, *Mum/Dad. I'm with Ernie the bus driver who gave me the books. We're going to this talk about Sci-fi stuff. Back soon. Ernie's number is 87512246.*

Leo leaves the note on the kitchen table and dashes out of the house. Ernie backs out the car to go back to his place. They stop off at a Mister Chicken outlet for a dinner pack. Leo's hungry despite what has happened and asks, "Ernie, do you mind if I eat this in the car, I'm starving?"

"No, it's okay. But, make sure you don't spill any on the upholstery." When they arrive back at Ernie's place he makes calls to each of the group. Explaining the situation and asking them to come over as soon as possible. They all turn up about half an hour later, except Desmond who isn't home. Ernie addresses the group in a serious tone. "I called you all back because events have turned from threatening to downright nasty. I was taking Leo home and when we passing Leo friend's place, the police were there. She's been grabbed by two of those mysterious blokes claiming to be Leo's friends. You know what that means." Derek responds by making a winding-in-a-fish gesture. "Bet they're using her as sucker bait to get at Leo, obviously." "In some sort trade, maybe? I guess we won't know until they contact someone," adds Graham.

"We can't wait for that," responds Leo in an alarmed tone. "Who knows what they might do to her. We got to do something now." Arjan shifts uncomfortably in the chair. "Leo what about the cops, what are they doing?"

"They're only looking for the car. It's that black American Cadillac with rear wings."

Ernie takes the floor, "okay guys, let's try and see if Derek can do some remote viewing to locate the girl using the roadmap. He's done it before." Derek interjects, "Yep, once I narrow down the possible locations we can check them out for that car. It's our best hope."

Everyone is keen to help out and Graham chips in with, "but before we do that, let's look at the Quatrains again. Part of it has already come true. Let's see if anything else is related."

"It's related alright," states Arjan, firmly. "I feel he is 'The Called One', I told you he's got something special about him. There are now two of those shadowy figures, which could be the evil ones. They've kidnapped the Queen of Spades - maybe his friend. Leo, the Queen of Spades is a black card. Does Dani have dark hair?"
"Yes, she does."
"Do you know if there is something else about her that matches that card?"
"Not really. The only thing I can think of is that she plays the guitar. Her folks own a market garden and that card keeps coming up for me. You know the Hearts card game; you have to win the Queen of Spades and all of the hearts to 'Shoot the Moon'."

"There are a lot of possibilities, there. So let's look at each section, then?" Arjan continues, "Well what I think the first section is saying, is that the boy is being called to do a man's job and a boy can't know a man until he becomes one."
"Well it fits," agrees Graham, waving the printout around. "But what about the lion and the lamb bit?"
"Okay let's think about a name related to a Lion…of course Leo the Lion and what stands with a lamb? You think about it."
Derek, pipes up, "its Mum?"
"And what else?"
"Other sheep maybe?"
"What about the Shepherd. See we cracked it. It might be Leo Shepherd."
"That's great," comments Ernie, but he's not convinced. "You missed out the section about his body bearing witness to the truth. Tell me what that's all about?"

The group sits staring at the verses in silence as none can offer an explanation. However, Leo's mind is ticking over. Thinking, yeah I know what it means. El-Caro said it…it's whatever's in my DNA. I want to tell them what I know. But for some reason, I get this funny feeling about trusting these guys. Even if I tell them it won't find Dani.

So maybe, I'll wait and see what goes. "Okay let's leave that bit. The Queen of Spades we might already have. What about the oracle bit?"

"Maybe that was one of us, because the girl disappeared after we said Leo was special and all."
"Fancy yourself as an oracle do you Arjan?" Jokes Derek. "Oh I don't know about that, it's not for me to say."
"Okay, let's move on guys," reminds Ernie impatiently. "What about the next Quatrain?" Derek points at Arjan with a cheeky grin. "You're the oracle and seem to be doing well at this, what are you getting?" Leo meanwhile, is deep in thought, yeah I know about the oracle bit, that's El-Caro's name spelt backwards.

Arjan strokes his beard and comments, "well the way I would read it, is that those guys think because he's a kid and scared stiff, he hasn't a chance. And because of that, it will be their weak point, I guess. "The rest of it I don't follow…except I can tell you this, Leo. My gut feeling says you will have to use all the skills you have. You will come out of it okay if this thing is correct. But you will have to stand as if you are a man and be very brave. You must not under any circumstances be in fear of them and you must not get angry at them otherwise they'll get the upper hand. "Now it's over to you Derek, let's see what you get."

"Leo, do you have something personal-like, belonging to Dani?"
Leo reaches into his pocket. "Yes, I have. Dani gave me this Saint Christopher Medal for my birthday. It belonged to her Grandma." Leo reaches over and hands it to Derek. "Great, that might just help me tune in on her vibes when I'm remote viewing. It can make all the difference getting close to her. Ernie, have you got the roadmap handy?"
"Look I'll have to go out to the car."
"Okay, I get myself psyched up, while you're doing that."
"Leo, do you understand what we're doing?"
"Not really," responds Leo, sitting down on the floor next to Derek.

"With concentration, I can pick up details and feelings about a place, a person, an object - anywhere. Provided I am totally focused, stay clear and don't let my mind chatter away. You know the chatter, like what I'm having for dinner, gee my leg hurts, what Ernie is doing now, etc.

228

Basically, my mind goes blank for a while, then pictures or impressions just drift in. Okay, I'd better calm myself down and concentrate. Graham you ready to act as scribe. Ernie, can I have the roadmap now? Ta."

Leo watches intently, as Derek is going through his breathing exercises and relaxing his body. Time seems to stretch out. Leo is impatient, wanting desperately to find Dani as quickly as possible. At the same time, he's having strong doubts that they will get anything. Derek flicks through the pages of the road directory quickly, until. "Ah-ha! I'm getting a reaction to the map on page 27. Can you write that down?" He continues flicking the pages and gets reactions on two other pages, numbered 37 and 136.

"Okay, what was the first-page number?" In unison, they all shout out, "27." Holding the Saint Christopher medal and studying the map, Derek responds, "I'm getting an impression of a railway track and there's one on this map. Also, I see a derelict building, possibly an old factory. There's a picture or sign with a giant Eagle on a big bag...not sure if that's right?" Ernie looks over Derek's shoulder, "well what's the location covered by the map of page 27...Oh, I know that area. It's the industrial part of Waterloo and the railway line is on this side. Your right there's an Eagle on a big bag. It's the Flourmill and it's a flour bag, I've passed it many times. It's quite a landmark.

Graham also moves over and looks at the map, "what about the other sites?" Derek concentrates on the other two sites. "I'm getting the impression of a school building. This page covers Bexley. On this other page, I'm getting a run-down old cottage standing on its own. It's weird though. It's surrounded by what looks like stacks of metal boxes. But the map's for Bakersfield. Oh, hang on that's not far from the docks."

Ernie looks at his watch and comments, " we'll have to check all the sites tonight and see if we can 'suss' anything out, like that black American car. I'll ring Des again and then we can split into groups of two and cover all of the sites." Ernie picks up the phone and quick dials. "Des, thank God you are there. Listen we think we are on to something and need your help. Can you come over straight away? Okay, we'll see you in thirty minutes."

"Des will be over shortly. He's an expert at surveillance. If we find anything we can call the police in straight away. By the way, have you guys got torches? I've only got two in the house."

"I got one in my car," responds Arjan. "We'll need our mobiles too. We'll need to keep in touch and call the police."

The noise in Ernie's lounge room increases as the excitement for action grows. However, Leo is quiet. He's more worried about Dani. Desperately hoping that they can find her and the police can arrest the mysterious retro men before anybody gets hurt. Ernie calls everyone to order. "Listen up guys. I think Arjan and I will go to the derelict building, while Desmond and Graham can check out the school. I think it's best if Derek and Leo check out the old house in Bakersfield.

Now, all we have to do is wait for…" Ernie is interrupted by a knock at the door. "Des, thanks for coming back, we're just about to check out three sites that Derek has targeted. I've paired everyone.
You're with Graham and going over to the old school." This does not suit an agitated and upset Desmond, "that's not the way to do it. Couldn't you blokes have waited? I'm the bloody expert, not you Ernest."
"Okay, okay Des, settle down. We're only trying to help Leo, here."
"Look fellows I'm sorry. But the Missus is on my back about spending too much time with you guys, that's all."
"Okay Des, then what would you do?"
"I think that Leo should come with me, so I can protect him. We'll go to the factory. You guys pair up so that Arjan and Derek aren't together. That way you guys can use your special talents - Everyone agreed."

As they file out the front door, Desmond calls out, "remember if you see anything, ring the police first. Don't go trying to be a hero. Oh, and don't have your mobiles on because you might give yourself away."
Graham looks at his mobile and calls out to Des, "what do we do if we need to talk to each other?"
"Use your message bank and check it regularly, okay." Keen to get moving Derek and Graham jump into Graham's dark red Peugeot convertible. The revving of the engine and a squeal of tyres see them disappear quickly down the street.

Meanwhile, Ernie and Arjan are still deciding whose car to take. "Arjan, I'm not getting into that thing." Arjan holds out both arms and pleads, "What's wrong with taking the Combi van, Ernie? Anyway, you know you don't like driving at night."

"It's those bloody signs plastered everywhere - 'peace is love' and 'grass is good for the soul', you got to be kidding me!"

"Are we here to help Leo or not. It's dark enough, isn't it? Nobody's going to notice."

"Alright Arjan, let's stop arguing and get moving." Arjan revs up the lime green Combi van, which sounds like a lawnmower engine and chugs off down the street.

Desmond starts his car as Leo climbs in. He reaches into his glove box and hands Leo his mobile. "Do you know how to work one of these? "Leo examines the mobile closely and shakes his head, "No not really." "See that button on the left it says 'Menu'. Click on it and the top one says 'Messages'. You click the same button again. Listen to the voice. Then follow the voice prompts. You will know when we get a message. There'll be an envelope symbol next to the phone icon. Can you see the phone icon?"

Leo nods and feels uneasy. Thinking, I don't know Desmond very well, but he's isn't saying much. Not like the others. I feel he has something else more important on his mind. But what could be more important than finding Dani? As Desmond pulls up to turn right he hands Leo the roadmap. "Can you find the Flour mill? I know where Waterloo is. I'm just not sure about the mill."

While further away, Derek and Graham have located the old cottage. They quietly pull up down the road. "So this is Bakersfield. I can see why I've never been here before," observes Graham.

"This place gives me the creeps – should've bought my crucifix and hung it around my neck."

"No. We should've brought a bloody great big dog and hung the crucifix around its neck," quips Derek, as he nervously runs his hands through his spiky hair. "What do you think Derek, does this look like the place?"

"Could be it. There's only that house and all those shipping containers beside it. Sort of stands out, doesn't it? It's dark and there's plenty of hiding places."

"I wonder if anyone lives there. Let's get out and take a closer look. Better check the mobile and see if there's any message yet." Graham checks his mobile before climbing out of the car. "Nope," he says. "So let's go. Got the torch Derek?"

Derek nods as they cautiously creep towards the cottage, keeping to the shadows. "I don't think anybody lives here. Look the power's been cut off and there's an old garage around the side. Let's see if that black car's in there," whispers Derek. They creep up to the garage, brush away the cobwebs from the window sill and shine the torch through the dirty windowpane. "No, the car's not here. There are just old boxes and junk. Let's check out the house."

As they turn around and creep towards the front of the cottage, it looks dark and silent with an unpleasant vibe about it. There are no obvious signs of life. However, before going any further they stand still, quietly listening for any sounds coming from the cottage. "Can't hear anything, let's get a bit closer."

They creep around the front and onto the verandah. As they do so, Derek stands on a squeaky floorboard. They both pause, holding their breath momentarily, as Graham attempts to look through a window on the porch. An old drawn blind blocks his view.

Then Derek notices that the front door isn't shut properly and slightly ajar. He whispers to Graham, "Look, the door is open, let's look inside. Shine the torch in first and be ready to run like hell, if something moves, okay?"
"Okay". Nervously Graham pushes at the door and steps back. The door groans loudly, as Derek nervously shines his torch inside. There's a sudden movement and a loud 'clunk' as something hits the floor. Derek turns and runs, "Shit, I'm out of here." But crashes into Graham - who hasn't had a chance to move. They both sprawl to the ground, the wind knocked out of them." The door creaks as it opens wider and a dark shape emerges.

Graham looks up and hisses, "Bloody stinkin' rotten cat." A ginger Tabby looks at them with eyes reflecting in the light and strolls off, tail sticking straight up in the air. Derek picks up his torch and hurls it at the cat, "Take that you bloody mongrel." The torch misses and the cat bounds away into the darkness. "Are you alright Graham?"
"I think so, jeez you bolted so fast, I didn't even get out of the blocks."

"I told you if anything moved I was out of here."
"Yeah, okay. Well, they won't be now. We've made such a racket. Let's go and see what we can find out. They cautiously go inside. "Someone's been here alright. Look, camping equipment and a candle on the table. Hey! This candle I touched is still warm. So someone's definitely been here not long ago."
"What do you reckon Derek?"

"See, I'm getting better at this remote viewing stuff. But on the other hand, this stuff could belong to squatters. Let's send a message to Arjan and Des and tell them that those black-suit guys might be at their sites." On the way back to the car, Graham leaves a message for Arjan and Desmond.

Meanwhile, Leo is staring blankly out of the car window. Thinking, Dani has to be all right. I wonder how her folks are going. It's got to be a real shock to them. They've got no idea what's going on. Hell look at the time, it's 8:00 o'clock. I wonder what my folks are thinking. I wonder if they know that Dani's missing. They might be in a panic too.

Hey, there are spots on the window - just what we need now, rain. However, what Leo doesn't know is that Linda has rung Ernie's house just after they left. His parents are frantic. They know that Dani has been kidnapped and that the police want to talk to Leo, again.

Chapter 9
I'm so sorry. There was no other way.

The mobile Leo is holding beeps, which makes him jump. Desmond glances over, "bit jumpy aren't we son. Who's the message from?" Leo notices the envelope icon flashing and presses the menu button, hoping for good news. When he selects messages a voice responds. "If you want to listen to your messages, press 1."

Leo obliges and listens to the message and looks at Desmond. "That was Graham, there's nothing at the old house in Bakersfield so they must be at the old school or the Flour Mill."
"That's if Derek's got this targets right. Leo, it's not an exact science. You do realise we might be just groping in the dark."
"I know, I know, but we just have to hope that he's right. It's the only chance Dani has."
"I wouldn't say that. As long as you're okay, she'll be okay."

Meanwhile, Arjan and Ernie have just arrived near the old school and are sitting in the peppermint-green Combi van carefully surveying the site. "Hang on my phone's vibrating, there must be a message. Arjan hits the keypad and puts the earplug into his ear. Graham reckons that it's not the old house. That means it's either here or the Flourmill. We'd better be really careful from now on."

"This school does look derelict, there's graffiti all over it.
Let's check the school grounds - see if we can spot that American car."
"Yeah, that's a good idea. You know I've got a funny feeling about this place. I feel they're here or at least been here."
"Oh, thanks Arjan. That's very reassuring," grumbles Ernie, his old bones feeling the pressure.

They carefully look around the school grounds for any sign of the American car. "Funny, I was sure they'd be here. We'll have to check out the main building. Got the torch?" Cautiously they creep up to the main building and shine the torch inside various windows. "Look's empty. We'll have to do the classrooms, too." They move along the block of classrooms until they get to the end of the building. "Well it looks like they're not here either," whispers Arjan.

Ernie, shrugs his shoulders and points around the back. On their way back to the Combi van they pass a toilet block, with Arjan remarking, "funny, my gut feelings are usually…" He stops and listens, intently. "That sounds like someone crying. It's coming from inside the toilets, what do you reckon Ernie?"
"It might be that girl."

"I'll go and have a look. Ernie you'd better wait over there with my mobile. If anything happens, punch the SOS button and call the police." Arjan carefully opens the door of the toilet block. The door makes an eerie grinding sound. Arjan calls out, "Danicka are you in there!" The sobbing sound stops, but there is no answer. Arjan turns on his torch. As the torchlight penetrates the darkness, it reveals a woman and two children gagged and tied together on the cold concrete floor.

"Don't be frightened. I'm not going to hurt you," re-assures Arjan. "Is anyone else here?" The woman has a terrified look on her face and manages to shake her head no. Tears are streaming down her face. Arjan goes to the doorway and shouts, "Ernie, it not the girl. There's a woman and two kids in here and they're tied up. Ernie emerges out of the shadows and looks through the door with an astonished look on his face. "That's definitely not Leo's friend. What the hell's going on?"
"I don't know Ernie… didn't expect anything like this."

Arjan and Ernie set about untying the woman and the two children. Helping them remove the masking tape over her mouths. They're traumatised and huddle together without speaking. Arjan squats down and speaks softly to the terror-stricken woman. "We're not going to hurt you or the kids. We need to know who you are and what happened to you."

In a trembling weak voice, she replies, "two men in dark suits came to our house. The men said my father wanted them to pick us up. They said if we didn't go with them he would be in serious trouble." "Who's your father?"
"Desmond Clarke."
"Oh my God," yells Arjan, standing bolt upright. "Leo's in terrible danger. Those mongrels must have got to Des somehow. Who knows what Des will do?" Arjan grabs the mobile phone from Ernie and rings Graham's mobile to leave a message, "Graham, Derek, you guys go straight to the Flour mill ASAP. Leo's in trouble. Des is somehow involved. Meet you there."
"What are we going to do here, Arjan?"

"I'll call the police and you wait here with them. Can't leave them alone, they're terrified."
"Hello, I need the police straight away. Can you put me through?"
"Come on, what's taking so long…hello, hello is that the police. Oh thank God, my name's Arjan Sumara. It's about that Danicka Jerovich kid that's missing. No, but we've found three people tied up at the old abandoned school in Bexley. It's the old Clayford High School. They're related to Des Clarke. Yes, he was in the force. It's a long story, but you have to send a car here and someone to the Eagle Flour mill. Why, because that's where Des Clarke is heading to where the Jerovich girl might be. What…oh my friend Ernest is going to wait for you. He'll explain everything." Arjan throws the mobile to Ernie and jumps into the Combi van and chugs off into the darkness.

Meanwhile, Desmond and Leo have just arrived at the Eagle flour mill site, after crossing over the railway line. As they get out of the car next to the mill, Desmond takes the mobile phone back from Leo. He turns it off as Ernie is sending a message to say that his daughter and grandchildren are safe.

"Right Leo, we'll check around these buildings first…see if we can spot that black Cadillac." It's still raining lightly and Leo feels a cool easterly breeze coming off the land, sending a chill up his spine. Leo carefully surveys the Mill site before running over to the wall of one of the derelict buildings, behind the Mill. He checks inside, but it's completely empty except for some building rubble. Desmond checks the building next to it and signals that it's empty too. There's only one building left, a four-story brick building. It has a large roller door along one side of the building.

However, it too appears derelict. All of the windows on the lower floors have been smashed and a hole punched in the wall next to the roller door. The windows of the upper floor are painted out.

Des gestures for them both to head for the roller door. As they run across the car park, the rain clears and the clouds roll back to reveal a full moon. It shines proudly in the night sky. They reach the roller door and as Desmond shines his torch through the hole in the wall, the torchlight falls onto the shiny black paintwork of the Cadillac.

Just as they're about to lift the roller door, Leo is thinking I wonder what we do now? He hears a strange whispering voice.

"Remember who you are. Remember what you have been taught. Remember your thoughts control your destiny." The voice is coming from inside his head. They quietly lift the roller door, revealing a large open floor area.

On the opposite side is a heavy, wire-meshed cage. It has wooden cladding on the walls inside the mesh and an open steel gate covered with wooden planks. Behind and to the left of the cage is a stairway. Desmond flashes the torch around in all directions. The ground floor is concrete, covered in dust and littered with broken glass, scraps of metal and broken wooden planks. Pointing the torch upwards, they both can see that the next level has a wooden floor.

All of Leo's senses are on high alert. There's a musty, damp smell. It's so quiet he can hear his heart beating loudly. Leo tries to breathe normally. But the short, quick breaths he's taking make him feel out of breath. Seeing the black American car, Leo is having trouble controlling his feelings.

He feels angry because the mystery men have picked on Dani and not him. However, he's also scared of what lies ahead. Leo tries to pull himself together. Reminding himself, come on Leo breathe properly. Everything is going to be okay. Have to stay positive and remember that everything will be okay. God, I hope so. I wish El-Caro was here.

I must remember not to get hooked up in the anger and fear stuff. Desmond puts his right index finger to his lips as if to say quietly. He then motions with his hand and the torchlight for Leo to go around the car and look inside the wire cage near the stairs. Desmond points at himself. Then with two fingers pointing downwards, he moves them walking fashion and points upwards. When he turns off the torch everything goes pitch black. Slowly, Leo's eyes adjust to the light. It looks eerie. Some areas are brightly lit up by shafts of moonlight, while other places are clothed in total darkness. Leo carefully glides past the car and picks his way through the maze of junk. He reaches the cage and cautiously peers around the gate. The cage is empty.

Suddenly without warning, a hand is shoved forcefully into his back, between the shoulder blades. His neck snaps back as he sprawls to the floor. Stunned, Leo is slow to react. He hears a grinding metal sound as the gate to the caged area swings shut. Then a clunk sound, as the bolt slides home. Leo is still trying to gather his thoughts together as Desmond cries out, "I'm so sorry Leo. There was no other way. They've got my daughter and my grand-kiddies. I love them so much. I can't let anything happen to them. Those guys are deadly serious. If they don't get the information they want, I'll never see them again. They said if we co-operate with them, no one will get hurt."

Leo panics like a trapped feral animal. He jumps up onto the mesh gate, shaking it violently. He shouts, "Des you got it all wrong. Des you can't do this, those guys will kill us all. They'll kill you too. Don't believe a word. Des don't leave me here to die," pleads Leo. "I'm sorry Leo. I have no choice, you've got something they want and I want my family back. That's all there is to it."

Leo feels doomed. He slumps to the floor sobbing at the realisation that everything is slipping away from him. That he might never see Dani or his family again. A thought runs through his head, I wish someone was here to help me. He stops sobbing as he hears the voice inside his head again.

It whispers, "Remember the rolling ball. Remember the prophecy. Remember your thoughts control your destiny." Leo stands up and calls out, "Des are you there? Des, answer me." But there's no response. Talking to himself, Leo tries to talk up his chances, "I've got to get out of here. There has to be some way of getting out of this mess. God, it's dark in here. If I feel around there might be a way out." Leo feels around the cage for any loose boards. Where there are gaps he finds the wire mesh blocking any escape. However, the sound of the metal bolt sliding home comes back into his mind. He knows it's his last hope. Leo takes deep breaths and tries to calm himself down. He mimics Derek's breathing, which he remembers while watching him during the remote viewing sessions.

He also remembers the angry feeling he had when he moved the ball in the glass case, back in the Sentinel. Focusing his attention on the bolt, Leo gathers all of his anger he feels at the thought of the mysterious men taking Dani and screams out, "M-o-v-e." At the same time picturing in his mind, the bolt sliding out and the gate swinging free.

The bolt starts to vibrate. Leo can hear it rattling against the metal loop that's holding the gate shut. This spurs Leo on more. The vibration loosens the bolt and it slowly vibrates back until the wire gate springs open. Leo slips out of the cage and dashes around the gate. As he does so, he kicks a piece of metal pipe. It makes a hollow clunking sound that echoes through the building.

Leo picks up the pipe and charges up the first flight of stairs. He can hear Desmond climbing up the next flight, as there's a gap between the staircases. Leo hurls the pipe upwards and runs back down the stairs to avoid the falling pipe. He hopes it will attract Desmond's attention. The echo of the pipe bouncing down the stairs subsides and Leo holds his breath. He listens intently for any sign of Desmond coming back down. The creaking of the staircase gives Leo the sign he's hoping for. Quietly, he finds a place to hide in the shadows.

Leo can see the torchlight waving around laser-like as Desmond gets closer. He cautiously moves around the wire gate and shines the torch into the caged area. To his surprise it's empty. He moves forward to take a closer look. Leo jumps onto the gate and rides it shut, quickly pushing the bolt home. "Leo what are you doing? Leo! Answer me. Leo," cries Des in a desperate voice. Leo doesn't respond, thinking only of Dani and of them both running away from the place. Leo picks his way slowly and deliberately up the darkened staircase, lit only by the moonlight. He peers carefully around the corner of the stairwell into the first-floor area. The area is empty, except for some old cardboard boxes. The only thing Leo can hear is Desmond calling out and shaking the wire gate. Leo decides to look around the first-floor area, before moving on.

It's lit up brightly by the moon, framed by a big window with broken panes of glass. As Leo ventures into the centre of the area, the wooden floor groans under his weight. Realising that it's dangerous, he cautiously backs out of the room, thinking what do I do next? Again he hears the whispering voice. "Remember, go lightly and feel your feet as you go. Remember do not feel any fear or harbour any anger towards them. Remember your thoughts control your destiny."

Leo continues up the steps to the next level and notices an eerie light flickering through a doorway as he approaches the third floor. He hears a man's deep eerie voice. "He's here. I feel his presence." A chill goes up Leo's spine when he hears Dani sobbing as she cries out. "Leo! Don't come in here. They've got guns." The dark-suited man grabs hold of Dani and shakes her. "Shut up you little bitch, otherwise, your dear boyfriend is dead meat." Leo nervously peers around the corner of the stairwell and sees a lit doorway on the left at the end of the corridor. Leo quietly creeps up and peers through the door. In the centre of the room is a flickering portable gas lamp, shining brightly. The windows still have glass in them, but painted out, so no light can enter.

His heart jumps as he spots the silhouette of one of the men holding Dani by the arm at the far end of the room. The other man is standing with his arms folded and feet apart just in front of the lamp. Then a whispering voice reminds Leo again, "remember tread lightly and go to the right side of the room. Remember the prophecy. Remember your thoughts control your destiny." His heart pounding harder and harder, Leo decides that the best form of defence is to attack. He deliberately marches into the room and stares directly at the man with folded arms. "I got the information you're after. Let Dani go and I will take you to the information."

The man unfolds his arms and points at Leo. In a mocking tone, and laughs, "Ha, Ha, Ha, I don't know if you're just an innocent, naive kid or just plain stupid. This kid's got no idea what he's got. And, now he's going to sacrifice himself and with it the future of this planet." He laughs loudly again and sneers. "If you had been smart kid, you would've worked out that we aren't of your world. The truth about you and your past will die with you now. Once you're out of our way, there's nothing to stop us."

Dani cries out," don't listen to them. Run Leo, run!" Leo doesn't run. He moves slowly and deliberately towards the right side of the room. As he does so, he can feel the wooden floor moving under his feet. Thinking I wonder what El-Caro would do? The voice whispers again, "remember, tread lightly and move closer to the window. Remember the prophecy. Remember your thoughts control your destiny."

He moves slowly towards the window on his right, being careful not to pass in front of it. Passively, he stands still making sure that he stays as cool and as calm as he possibly can, under the circumstances. Desperately trying not to be intimidated by the threat they pose. To counter this, Leo pictures both he and Dani running away hand in hand. However, the retro black-suited man has other ideas.

"You obviously have no idea of the extent of our power. So I'm going to give you a little demonstration." The man turns and points at each of the four windows on his left and as he does so, the glass in each window shatters with a large bang. It causes Leo to cringe with each explosion. He can hear the glass breaking up as it lands in the car park below. Leo is stubbornly more determined than ever, to hold the image of them escaping hand in hand. Both mysterious men laugh loudly, as the one closest to Leo reaches into his black overcoat and pulls out a pistol and from the suit coat pocket a silencer. He methodically screws it onto the front of the pistol. Leo's heartbeat grows faster and as he focuses his attention on the dark-suited man, he realises that he needs to breathe deeply to calm down.

Connecting with the man's thoughts Leo is shocked. There's just an angry, hopeless void inside the man as if he has no human soul. Strangely, Leo feels sorry for him. This causes a sudden surge of energy pulsing through Leo's body. His legs shake violently. "Hey look, the kid's shaking in his boots. How does it feel knowing that you're going to die, with your girlfriend watching? How does it feel when you know that we're going to slice her up after we've finished with you?" Leo tries to stay focused and ignores the taunting.

Suddenly, the anger in the man leaves him and Leo legs and arms tremble even more as there is an energy exchange between them. The man's expression changes to one of surprise. Realising that Leo's not a defenceless, cringing kid. He aims the pistol at Leo's chest, but the pistol begins to shake. With the man's anger coursing through Leo, he points back at the man, "how do you feel now that I've taken your anger away? Your purpose is gone. You have no soul. You're a 'thought-form' just like in my Sci-fi books. You have no right to exist here." The man lowers his gun and swears. "You little prick. Shooting is too good for you. I'm going to throw your grubby, stubborn arse out that broken window."

Dani screams as the man lunges forward. Leo loses his concentration and the anger returns to the man with a jolt. At the same time, there's a sickening groan. The floor gives way under the man. Leo is left balancing on the edge of a large jagged hole. A loud crashing sound follows. The wooden floor below gives way too. The man continues to fall right through to the concrete ground floor below. The retro man holding Dani is startled. He moves forward to look down through the gaping hole in the floor. Dani breaks free from his grip. She kicks over the gas lamp as she runs across the room. "Run Leo, Run," she shouts. The gas lamp rolls across the floor and falls down the gaping hole. Sparks fly as it bounces onto the concrete floor and goes out. Dani is the first to the stairs. Leo is right behind her. As they get to the ground floor, Leo can hear Desmond sobbing loudly, who is totally unaware of what has just happened. As it's now pitch-black, the startled retro man cautiously makes his way out of the room.

He makes it to the stairs and pulls out a pistol from his coat as he goes. Leo and Dani negotiate their way around the first man's body and climb through and over the debris of splintered flooring. Leo yanks down the roller door as they leave. "Dani, run towards the Mill," shouts Leo.

They dash across the open space, splashing through small puddles as they go. They run as fast as their legs will go, towards the mill. As they swing around the corner of the building they find they're in an open car park exposed with no cover. Leo grabs Dani's hand and shouts, "come on Dani - across the railway, we can hide in the bush!"

Dashing towards the railway line, they can hear the sound of a train approaching. Their hands slip apart as Dani stops momentarily. Leo grabs her hand again and urges, "don't worry about the train. Keep running!" They scramble up the embankment and over the railway tracks, as a loud crack and a zinging sound startle them. Dani closes her eyes as Leo glances over his shoulder. Sparks fly up as a bullet hits one of the tracks near them. They continue down the embankment towards the safety of the bush. However, the second retro man has reached the railway line. He raises his pistol and has Leo in the sights, Dani screams at Leo, "come on we can make it."

Suddenly, a car comes screeching to a halt in the car park. It is Graham's red Peugeot, with lights on high beam trained directly on the mysterious retro man. Distracted, he turns and shields his eyes just for a moment. Then turning back he can see Leo is silhouetted against the setting moon. Leo stands and stares back at the retro man. Dani shouts, "Leo, don't be stupid, let's run."

Leo ignores Dani and feels the man is full of fear, that he too has no soul. The man mutters to himself, "stupid kid why doesn't he keep running, this is too easy." Leo turns the fear the man harbours into pity. This causes Leo to tremble, again. The man aims and fires. But Dani pulls Leo away. They both fall to the ground as the bullet screams past their heads. As they look up the City Express train hits the retro man. His gun goes off just as Dani stands up. She screams and drops to the ground.

The man's body is thrown down the embankment towards them. Leo can hear the wailing of sirens and the screeching of tyres in the distance. As the City Express passes, Derek and Graham are standing next to the track. Leo looks around and sees Dani lying on the ground motionless.

"Oh my God, Dani! Dani! Are you okay?" Leo goes to squat down as she sits up. "Yeah I'm okay, but no thanks to you. I just stepped in that stupid hole. Now help me up, will you." Dani thrusts out her hand as Leo pulls her to her feet. They embrace. Leo whispers in her ear. "Why didn't you run when I told you?" Dani breaks the hug and responds, "because I wasn't going anywhere without you.

Thank God you're okay, too. I don't understand. What did those horrible men want? They kept going on about you like you're some Bogeyman. And, said some stuff to me about timelines converging and when that happened they said they'd make sure you wouldn't be around."

"It's better that you don't know Dani. If I tell you, I'll have to shoot you." Dani has a horrified look on her face and hits Leo in the chest with her open hand, "HELLO! Get real man! We almost got ourselves killed."
"Sorry, I thought I'd lighten things up a bit."
"After what I've just gone through - that's totally un-funny."
"Okay, okay I got the message. Let's get out of here."

"All this stuff has got something to do with that Sentinel thing, hasn't it?" Leo shrugs his shoulders, "yes and no. I don't understand about that timelines stuff, either."
"Well, I don't want to know. I just want to go home. I told you, you're messing with stuff that was dangerous. I did my bit - so you don't owe me anymore. We're even now."
"I don't know about that. I feel I'm the Derp. I'm the one that got you into this mess in the first place."
"We're both okay. So it doesn't matter, now."

As they walk back up the railway embankment, they can see Arjan arriving in the Combi van. He stops and winds down his window to talk to Derek, Graham and Desmond. Graham is supporting Desmond as they walk across the car park towards them. Derek runs up to Leo and Dani, "thank God you're both safe. The remote viewing stuff works really well, eh Leo? Dani looks at Leo, "remote what?"
Leo rolls his eyes, "tell you later."

Derek dances around the group like a kid at a fun park. "Hey, Leo the Hero. Give us a High Five." Leo jumps up and gives Derek a huge high Five, making a loud smacking sound, as their hands meet. "Man, that hurt's really good. Now give me a low Five." Derek turns around and puts his hand out, but this time pulls his hand away. "Haha, I got you that time." Derek hugs Dani, "so this is your girl, eh. She's a real cutey." Arjan, Graham and a sobbing Desmond join them.

He drops to his knees in front of Leo and embraces Leo's midriff. "Can you ever forgive me? I love those kids so much. I didn't know what else I could do."

"Maybe Des, but words can't describe what you did to me and Dani. Right now I don't know if I can. But I guess, in the same situation I'd do the same. As we don't even know who or what those guys were up to. So, Come on Des, stand up will-ya. You're making me feel like I'm the bad guy here." Both Arjan and Graham reach down and help Desmond to his feet.

Leo anxiously looks around, realising, "where's Ernie?" Arjan gives Leo a hug too and smiles, "Ernie's alright. He's looking after Des's daughter and her two kids, last I saw him. We found them tied up at the old Clayford High School over in Bexley.

"See guys, that's two out of three, not bad eh," boasts Derek. The arrival of a group of police cars, sirens blaring and lights flashing, cause them all to turn around. While someone shouts sarcastically, "here comes the cavalry to save the day!" The cars come to a screeching halt. In unison, the officers jump out of their cars and draw their guns and torches. They point them at the gathering. Leo shields his eyes, then realises something, "Oh no! What are we going to tell these guys?"

Desmond wipes his tears away with this handkerchief and blows his big red nose. "Don't worry Leo. Whatever you're hiding - it's safe with me. I can handle the boys in blue. It's the least I can do after what I've done." As one of the uniformed police approach, he's surprised. "Hey Des, what are you doing here, mate. I thought you'd retired?" While Desmond and the uniformed officer talk, Dani's thoughts are of going home. Knowing that her parents would be frantic she asks, "I need to phone Dida and Mama, can I use your phone Mister?" Arjan responds, "not a problem, go for it." He hands her his mobile phone, "just press that button. Whack in the number and press that and you're away."

"Is that you Mama? It's Danicka – Yes I'm okay, Mama." She bursts into tears, in response to her mother's cry of joy. Breaking into her native Slav tongue, Dani speaks rapidly explaining her ordeal, without taking a breath. Graham elbows Leo. "Here. You'd better use mine. Your folks must be worried sick."

Leo put's the phone to his ear and says, "Hi Mum, I'm okay and so is Dani, the cops are here, but I can't talk now - they want to talk to us. The police will give us a lift when they're finished. Yeah of course everything is okay. I'll explain when I come home. Don't cry Mum, we're fine - honest." The fine rain that had been falling stops and gives way to a chilly wind. The group decides to head back to Graham's car and wait until the police are satisfied that everything is secure. Meanwhile, Desmond is now talking to a detective. Leo recognises him as the one in the brown suit he had seen at Dani's place, earlier.

Leo and Dani are sitting in the back of Graham's car as Desmond and the Detective approach, the Detective squats down next to the open car door with Desmond standing behind him. "Remember me? I'm Detective Maclean. Seems you were right son. It looks like a case of mistaken identity. Desmond here has lots of enemies from his days in the Force and the kidnappers must have picked up Danicka Jerovich by mistake. Because Des's daughter's married name is Jurocich and her first name is Daneka."

Leo is dumbfounded and thinking, that story won't fly. How in the hell do we explain the bodies and the evidence? How's Des going to get around all that? A Police constable approaches the car carrying a black suit, overcoat and gloves. "We only found these. Looks like an old suit - it's got this fine ash all over it. We think we've found the black Cadillac, El Dorado, too. But it's badly damaged, though. It's right under the collapsed flooring inside the factory. But there's no sign of anything else. Oh, except a damaged gas lamp. My guess is this stuff belonged to a squatter.

Desmond winks at Leo, "the kidnappers must have bolted and left before you guys arrived. Looks like they cocked things up when they kidnapped the girl. Must've found out they had the wrong person."

Detective Maclean however, has other ideas. "There are some things I need to get clear in my mind. Danicka, I haven't heard your side of the ordeal?" Dani looks at Leo, knowing that she will have to be careful to protect Leo's secret.

She is about to respond when a car approaches with someone tooting the horn madly. Desmond turns around and the Detective stands up as the car pulls up near them. Desmond is the first to speak, "Oh thank God! It's Daneka and the kids. Oh God I'm so relieved they're safe." He runs over to the car and opens the back door. There are tears as Desmond is reunited with his family and embraces all three of them at once. Ernie slowly gets out of the car. He looks cold as he rubs his hands together and puts them in his pockets. He wanders over to Graham's car. "Leo, there you are. Thank God you're safe. Where's your friend?"

Leo leans back against the seat and replies, "everything's okay Ernie. See, Dani's right here." Ernie bends down and looks through the window. "Hello there. Thank God you're safe, too." Arjan scratches his head as he looks at Ernie, "I left you at the school. How did you get your car?" Ernie turns around and shakes Arjan by the hand, "the police dropped us at home so they could clean up a bit."

Desmond comes back and shakes Ernie's hand and fills Ernie in on the official story for the police. Then Desmond and Detective Maclean move away from the group to chat. "Look Des, despite what you say, there's more to this than what everyone's saying."
Desmond recoils, "Are you calling me a liar?"
"No, definitely not! I'm just trying to get the record straight for my report."
"Look mate, you can get your evidence later. I'm stuffed and I know everyone else is too. So I think it is best you wrap it up for tonight. I got to get those kids home. They're almost out to it."
"I guess you're right." Detective Maclean moves back over to the group and stretches his arms out and yawns.

He puts his notebook into his coat pocket and announces, "Okay I'm sure you folks want to go. There's nothing more we can do tonight. Before you all go, I want you to give your contact details to the constable."

As he leaves, Detective Maclean walks back over to Desmond and they shake hands. He smiles as they share a funny line, before the Detective climbs back into his car and drives off. Desmond comes back to Graham's car. "I'm so glad…bloody hell. I don't know what to say. I'm so ashamed of what's happened. I hope you guys can forgive me someday …I'd, I'd better go." There's complete silence as they watch Desmond walk over to his family and usher them to his car.

Graham is the first to break the silence. "Do you guys want me to drive Leo and Dani home?" Ernie responds, "Thanks Graham, but I'd better do it. I feel kind of responsible for Leo. Seeing how his folks think Leo's supposed to be with me. It wouldn't be right." Leo and Dani scramble out of the Peugeot and into the back of Ernie's car. As they leave and drive across the railway tracks. Leo leans forward in his seat and rests his arm against the front bench seat. "Ernie, I don't understand. They never found any bodies, what's going on?"

"I don't understand it, either. All they found were some old clothes covered in ash. Quite frankly, I don't want to know. It's too spooky for me to get my head around." Leo sits back and holds Dani's hand tightly. They sit quietly, as the events start to sink in. Leo's body begins to shake as he releases all of the tension and emotions that have built up.

Dani responds by squeezing his hand tighter. Ernie pulls up outside of the Jerovich household. There are a number of cars parked in the driveway. The house is lit up like a Christmas tree. Her parents are standing out the front waiting with some of their relatives.

As Dani gets out, Ernie toots the horn. Her parents come rushing down the driveway with arms in the air as they shout excitedly in a mixture of Slav and broken English. They embrace her in a three-way hug. Dani breaks free and asks, "Leo do you want to stay and talk or do you want to go home?"
"Given what's happened I'd better go home asap as my folks must be going mental."

Ernie puts the car into reverse and backs out of the driveway. He toots the horn as he drives off. Both wave. Dani turns and waves back as she and her parents walk arm in arm up the driveway.

Pulling into the Shepherd driveway, Ernie can see the porch light is on. Leo climbs out and walks around to the driver's side. Ernie responds by winding down his window, "Leo you okay now? I'd better go." "Ernie, don't you want to come in and meet the folks?" "Not really Leo, they might give me a big serve for taking you away. Besides, I'm absolutely stuffed. I'm too old for this sort of excitement. I'm supposed to be retired you know. So thanks anyway."

Leo puts out his hand. "I owe you so much. I want to shake your hand because just saying thanks seems nothing for what you and the other guys did. "I don't know what else to say."
"Listen Leo, after what we've been through, whatever it is you've come to do, make sure you bloody well get on and do it, mate. That's all the thanks me and the boys need."

Ernie revs the engine and backs out. As he drives off he toots the horn loudly. As Leo watches the old Holden disappear into the dark, Linda and Bryan come out onto the porch. Both call out in unison, "where have you been?" They both charge down the step and hug Leo. They walk back up the driveway in a three-way hug.

Whether it's a disaster or a celebration Linda's usual response is, "I'll put the kettle on." Bryan however, jumps in and quizzes Leo. "You've got no idea how concerned we were. The police came around after being at the Jerovich place. But they wouldn't tell us what was going on. Except that you were involved in something. We rang the number on the note you left, but there was no answer. We were frantic. So what the hell is been going on?"

Linda interrupts as she prepares the table for tea, "we didn't know what to think. But we're just glad you and Dani are safe, that's all." As Leo sits down at the table he responds with a shrug of the shoulders, "I don't know very much myself.

All I know is that these two weirdos in a Black American Caddy were hanging around. Next thing I know Dani gets snatched. But it turns out she was kidnapped by mistake. These guys were after this retired Detective's family - to get at him. That's all I can say. Right now all I want to do is go to bed. I'm absolutely shattered." Bryan isn't happy with the response, "I don't understand…" however Linda interrupts, "Bryan can't you see the boy's exhausted. Why don't we discuss it in the morning?"

Chapter 10
There's something I want to tell you, but it's our secret, okay.

Drained physically, mentally and emotionally Leo goes straight to his room. He undresses to his underwear and climbs into bed. He drops off to sleep quickly, despite the ordeal he's been through. He sleeps soundly right through the night. While Linda and Bryan have a restless night, including both of them getting up during the night and peak into Leo's room to check that he's okay.

Next morning Leo wakes with a start. He sits up as he hears a noise coming from the kitchen. Realising that he's safe, he lies back down. However, after a few minutes of fidgeting, he finds the bed uncomfortable and gets up. Bryan's in the kitchen having an early breakfast, before going to the garage. He looks up to see Leo standing in the passage. "Leo, how come you're up so early. Normally we have to drag you out."
"Hi Dad, I can't sleep. You know… after yesterday."
"Yes, I want to talk to you about that. But I'll have to do it later as I've got to go shortly."

"Dad I feel all over the place, do I have to go to school today?"
"Well, yesterday was such a shock to us all. I guess it's okay, but only today, right."
"Oh, cool Dad."
"I've got to go, so I'll talk to you later. By the way, Mum's decided to take today off, as she had a bad night too. She's like you - her mind is all over the shop."

Just as Bryan revs up the garage Pickup utility, Linda comes into the kitchen, "Hi Leo my pet, how are you this morning."
"Oh, a bit stuffed today, Mum."
"Likewise. I had a bad night too. I couldn't stop thinking about you both." "Dad said I don't have to go to school today. Will you write me a note?"
"Yes after breakfast."
"Mum is it alright if I go over to Dani's and check to see if she's okay too?"

"You can, Linda responds and waving a finger at Leo as she adds, "But I don't want you to go wandering off, you hear. You come straight home." "Yes, of course, I will." Leo goes off to his room to dress. Then with a quick, "see-you Mum," he strolls purposefully off.

After knocking on the door he finds no one home. This unsettles Leo. Thinking, I hope everything is okay. I have no choice than do as Mum says and he goes straight back home. "You're back so soon," says Linda, adding, "Are they not home?"

"Yeah, so I thought I'd come back and ask if I can go for a walk. "Leo, I told you not to wander off anywhere. Lord knows we've had enough worries to last a couple of lifetimes."
"Come on Mum. I did ask you first. I'm climbing the walls, here."
"Well, I guess I can't watch you every minute of the day. But I want to know where you're going."
"Just across the road and go for a walk in the bush."
"You're not going anywhere near Henderson's quarry?"
"No Mum I promise."

"Off you go then and put on a hat and make sure you take some water with you." Leo races off to his room. He grabs a cap and disappears out of the back door before Linda changes her mind. As Leo makes his way down the driveway, his heart misses a beat as a big black car drives by. He puts his hand on his heart, a little shaken and mutters "Phew! That nearly gave me heart failure." Leo nervously looks up and down the road before he scampers across and into the bush.
"Jeez, I'm still jumpy," he mumbles to himself. "Better take it carefully, in case there are more of them. That's why I got to go and talk to El-Caro.

I have to find out about this converging timeline stuff Dani mentioned. Yeah, I got to find out if those messages in my head were from him." Arriving at the ruin, Leo grabs hold of the large branch covering the hole in the well floor. He yanks at the branch and grunts as if in a tug-of-war, but it's jammed. He tugs and shakes the branch to free it. Suddenly there's a loud shout from the direction of the ruin. "What the hell's going on? Can't a man have some peace and quiet?"

Leo jumps back instinctively. Shocked he stands riveted to the spot. There's movement from behind the wall of the ruin and a rustling sound, as a head pops up from behind the wall. "Well! Aren't you going to answer me?" Leo hesitates, then in a surprised tone replies, "Hey, I know you. You're that old guy at the bus stop ages ago."

"I might be an old fossil, but I remember you. Your Leo Shepherd, am I right?"

"Yep."

"Yes, I remember. You short-changed me when I told your fortune."

"I didn't short-change you, it was all the money I had." "A minor detail my friend, a minor detail. I see you've changed. You're not the self-doubting, down-on-his-luck lad I met months ago." "Yeah, it's amazing. You were spot on with what you said. I thought it was all…ahhh…load of ahhh…you-know. The old man moves from behind the wall and comes up to Leo and eye-balls him, "so you reckon I am in the habit of fleecing young people, do you?" Leo moves back a step, "not any more. I didn't really know what to think, then. Anyway, how come you're here?"

The old man waves one arm around, "Australia's a free country." "Yes. But I wasn't trying to be nosey, just interested." "Well if you must know, I wander where my feet take me. I'm beholden to no one." "You mean you go walkabout, like the Aborigines." "Good choice. I follow my heart and go where nature leads me." "I suppose you don't have a dollar & eighty cents on you to make up my bus fare? You see I can't stay here another night.

The vibes in this place are unbelievable. I can't sleep and I keep getting this buzzing sensation in my head. It's making me dizzy. I think something's brewing." "I've got two dollars, so that makes us square." "Not quite, I have to give you something for your trouble. Perhaps a piece of advice…when I look at you I get this image of someone standing behind you, a guardian angel perhaps?

Anyway, I see the two of you walking side by side along a road until you reach a fork in the road. You go left and whoever they are, goes right. Does that mean something to you?"

"Part of it does."

"Well, it seems to me that you've been given a lot of help. Now it's time for you to figure things out on your own. It's time you found your own path to walk down. That's what I'm going to do right now. Grab my swag and get out of here."

Still in the same crumpled suit, the old man throws his duffle bag over his shoulder. Without saying another word, he marches off down the track towards the main road. Leo keeps his eyes fixed on the old man, thinking, that's weird, fancy bumping into him again. For an old guy, he walks really fast - he's almost out of sight, already. Right got to get back to business. I'm really looking forward to talking to El-Caro. Okay, let's get the rope and then I'll try and move that big branch.

Walking over to the ruin, Leo looks over the wall for the rope ladder and shouts, "Hey! Where's that rope ladder? Bloody hell it's gone." Leo moves around to the other side and mutters, "hey, there are footprints and truck tyre tracks. Someone's been here and cleaned this place up. I wonder who it could be. This is really stupid. How am I going to talk El-Caro, now? I'll have to go home and think of another way to get down the well."

Leo trudges off home observing that for the first time it's very hot and comments out aloud, "clear blue sky, not a cloud in sight - "yep, summer is well and truly here." Arriving home again, Leo goes straight to the kitchen for a much-needed drink. Linda hearing the noise comes into the kitchen carrying a broom, "That was a quick walk, Leo."

"Yeah Mum, I'm dying from thirst. What's in the fridge?"

"I told you to take a drink and you've got eyes. Go and have a look."

"Ahhh, that's better, my mouth was like a desert." Linda has her arms folded as she looks at Leo. "I'm the only one doing the cleaning around here. If you've got nothing better to do, why don't you clean your room?"

"I promise I'll do it later. I want to go over to Dani's place. Their car's in the driveway."

"I'll keep you to that. I hope everything's okay there. Give them my regards, won't you, Leo?"

"No worries, Mum." As Leo walks down the driveway, he can see Dani playing with her netball out the front. He waves madly and shouts, "Dani your home." She waves back as Leo dashes down the road to meet her. "Jeez Dani, I was worried about you. I came over earlier, but nobody was home."

"Yes, I didn't want to go out, but Dida and Mama insisted that we go to church to give thanks for being safe and all that. After that, we had to stop off at the police station to give a description of those weird guys." Leo is still concerned, "Dani are you really okay after what happened?" Dani looks at Leo and shrugs her shoulders." I'm not sure. I didn't sleep much and feel a bit weird today. I keep jumping at noises and thinking they might come back."

Leo re-assures Dani, "I'm positive nothing more will happen." Dani shakes her head no, "But you don't know they won't?" Leo stays silent for a moment trying to think of an answer, eerrr well... because those timelines they were banging on about have passed. So it's too late for them to do anything, right?"

"But Leo how do you know if that's true?"

"Well that's easy I will ask El-Caro."

Dani is about to ask another question as the front door opens and Lena steps out onto the porch, "Mr Leo you come inside I feed you good." She races down the steps and gives Leo a big hug and kisses him on both cheeks. "Mr Leo good boy. He save my Danicka from nasty mans. My English no good to say how this feel for me."

"Mrs J it's okay, I had lots of help too, you know."

"Branco, Branco," shouts Lena, "Branco you must come. Mr Leo here."

"Ahhh, Mr Leo, the hero. Thank you, Thank you, Thank you. I so 'appy I could kiss you."

Branco steps forward, but Leo steps back, "just a handshake will do." He reaches out and grips Leo's hand tightly and vigorously shakes it. "Mr Leo I don't know what me and Lena do, without our Danicka. I pray to God and he answers me."

As he let's go of Leo's hand, Leo grimaces from the vice-like grip and thinks, maybe the kiss would've been safer. "Come Mr Leo, my Lena she mayka special cake justa for you, you come eat with us, yes."

As Branco ushers Leo inside, he grabs Leo and gives him a strong hug. In the kitchen, the table is neatly laid out with coffee cups and a large square dish with a flat looking, light brown cake. Lena cuts a huge square of the cake and places it on a plate, "Come, Mr Leo you sit, eat my special cake." Unsure of what it is, Leo looks at Dani. She responds, "It's Tiramisu, it's really yummy. It's my favourite and it comes from Italy."

Leo tucks in and with his mouth still munching, "ummm, Mrs J this Tim-aroo gear is wicked." Dani laughs, "no, it's called Tira-misu." "I make special for you. You take home later, yes."
"You betcha Mrs J, it's the best cake I've had, ever."

Branco gets up from the table and walks around to Leo and pats him gently on the shoulder, "Mr Leo I must go worka my veges. You stay. Lena, she feed you good, No." When Lena leaves the kitchen Leo comments, "It's embarrassing both your Mum and Dad keep hugging and kissing me every five minutes." Dani laughs, "Us Slavs are emotional people, we can't help it. But you still haven't told me how you and your friends found me?"

"It's really weird Dani. It turns out Ernie the bus driver, you know 'Old grouch face', he came through for me. He's part of some Sci-fi group or something - I'm not sure what they do. His friends seem to have psychic powers and stuff.

They worked out where you were. But you wouldn't believe it, Des, the cop really dropped me in the 'dog's business'. Dani interrupts, "what about the dogs?"
"You know, in the poo - when he locked me up in that cage thing near the stairs." Dani's face lights up, "so that's why Des was crying and all over you. I couldn't work out what was happening. How did you get out?"

"Remember that box with the ball in the Sentinel. Well, I moved the bolt in the wire gate with my mind. Then attracted Des's attention and shoved him in there, instead. You know the rest."

"So, that's what happened. Guess what? After what happened, Dida's going to hold the biggest party, ever. You'll have to invite your friends."
"Yahoo, Dani! Boy, is that going to be 'some' party." In the background, the phone rings and shortly after Lena comes back into the kitchen. "Mr Leo your Mama she ring. She say you come home, Mr Policeman's he wants to talk."
"Dani, I'd better go. Thanks Mrs J, for the really wicked cake. I'll be back for some later. Dani, I'll catch up with you after I talk to the cops."
"Leo, what do you think they want?" Leo shrugs his shoulders, "who knows?"

As Leo arrives home, Detective Maclean is sitting at the kitchen table with a cup of tea Linda has made for him. Playing with the cup handle, he looks up, "hello Leon, come and sit down son. I've got a few questions to round off the kidnapping investigation. There are a couple of things that don't add up.

We ran a check on that American car, particularly the registration plates and engine number. Basically, they don't exist here and no record of the car being imported into Australia. The Manufacturers say that they can't identify the car as ever being built by their factory. Like the clothes we found. They were made in the sixties, yet appear brand new, despite the ash all over them. And there's another thing, the ash is organic in nature with traces of silicon and carbon. But the Pathology guys can't identify any DNA - like its burnt completely. I don't suppose you know anything that can throw some light on these strange anomalies. Because I get the gut feeling that despite what Des says, I reckon there's much more to this story than just a would-be kidnapping."

Leo crosses his fingers under the table, "No, sir I can't. I've told you all I know."
"Okay, I guess that just about wraps it up. That makes things easier for my report to the Superintendent."

Detective Maclean gets up from the table and walks to the front door. He grabs the door handle and turns around, "by the way, we're slapping a 'D' notice on the story. So the news media won't be reporting it, because it may put Des and his family at further risk. So son, it looks like you're in the clear. Thanks, Mrs Shepherd for the nice cuppa. Good day."

*****

As the sun sets on another day, the evening becomes very humid and there seems to be an air of uneasiness around Fielden Beach. For many of the folk living in Fielden Beach, it's a restless night. But not for the Shepherds, they sleep soundly after coming down from the emotional strain of the kidnapping.

Next morning, a loud knocking at the front door wakes Leo. He listens as Linda answers the door. "Oh! Mr Mason, you'll have to excuse me…I was just getting up and I'm not dressed."
"My humble apologies Mrs Shepherd, I'm sorry to wake you like this, but I have a letter that was dropped in my box by mistake." Leo listens intently. Thinking, I wonder what old Mason is up to. He's always nosing around. He could've just dropped it in our letterbox.

Linda adjusts her dressing gown and replies, "Thanks Mr Mason," as she tries to close the door. However, she pauses, sensing that Mr Mason has something else on his mind. "Is there something wrong?"
"Well, I don't know really. I guess it was the bad storm last night. My neighbours were talking about it and I was sort of wondering if you folks are okay?"

"A bad storm last night? No, we didn't hear a thing. Leo jumps out of bed and creeps quietly up the passageway to hear more. "Well, you know how hot and sticky it was last night. Out of nowhere, these dark clouds gathered. Then all hell broke loose with strong winds, strange flashing lights and thunder. It seemed to be worst towards Mt Fielden and over Henderson's quarry. Then it all vanished as quickly as it started." Linda pulls her dressing gown tighter, "that's really weird. We all must have slept right through it."

Mr Mason scratches his head, "But what's got me really puzzled is I could swear that when I got up to have a look out the window, I reckon I saw a huge dark triangular shape like an arrowhead rise up through the driving rain. It parted the clouds then disappeared in a bright flash of light." Leo is now by the front door. "Well, Mr Mason we didn't see or hear anything, did we Leo?"

"No mum I didn't hear a thing." Mr Mason scratches the back of his head again, "it's got me beat. I'm not sure if I saw it or not. Nobody else I've spoken saw anything, either."

Linda looks at Leo and she responds with shrugging shoulders and lifting eyebrows. "I'm sorry Mr Mason we can't help you there. We're fine, so thank you for asking after us. I have to go now and get Leo organised." After breakfast Linda reminds Leo. "Remember what I said to you yesterday about your room. Well, I want you to do it this morning."

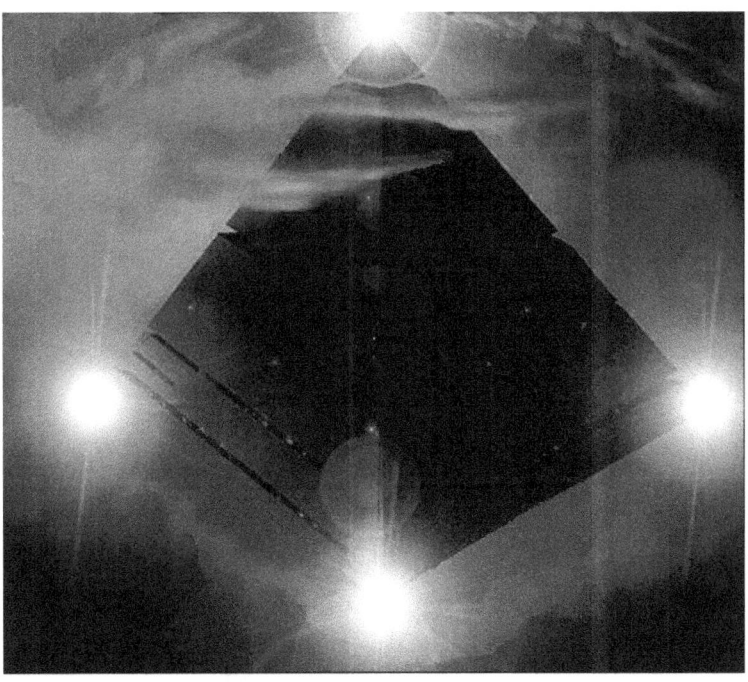

"Aw Mum, do I have to. I was just going for a walk."

"You still can, but the room comes first. Remember you promised" On the way to his bedroom, Leo hears a toot of a car horn and goes into the lounge to see Bryan getting out of the garage utility.

Leo is uneasy. Thinking, Dad's back. Something must be wrong. Hang on, he's carrying a big bunch of Mum's favourite flowers. That's weird, he hardly ever buys flowers. I wonder what's in that little package he's carrying. Leo rushes to the front door and out onto the porch. "Hi Dad, what are you doing home?"

"Leo, with all the hassles over the last two days, I haven't had the chance to do this. Here, this package is for you."

"Cool, what is it?"

"Why don't you open it and find out."

Leo rips at the brown paper parcel. "Wicked Dad! It's the latest Gameboy. Leo does a 360 on the spot and as he looks at Bryan with a questioning look on his face. "But I thought you said we couldn't afford one?"

"Well, let's go for a walk up to Mt Fielden and I'll tell you my news. But first I'd better give these to Mum. Just wait out here and I'll be with you shortly."

Leo admires the new Gameboy console and sits down on the porch to read the manual. Bryan re-appears, "Leo, drop it in the lounge room. You can play with that later. Let's go for that walk." As they make their way across the road to the bush track, Leo is dying to know the news, "come on Dad, what's going on. Let me guess, did we win Lotto?"

"Nope, I wish it was though."

"Ahhh, the Wilson's gave you a bonus?"

"Nope, it's better than that."

"Hmmm, what else could it be? Oh, oh I know. That man from the Bank is going to give you a loan?"

"Leo it's even better than that. You won't believe what's happened. I approached that bloke from the Bank and he said that he knew that we were an honest, hard-working family. And, if the Wilsons came to the party, with a loan and retained a small share of the business, he would give me the loan."

Leo is excited, "go on…what did the Wilsons say?"

"That's the unbelievable part. They didn't want to sell to one of the major oil companies, because they had been harassed by some of them to sell. They thought that if the Bank was willing to lend me the money, they would guarantee the loan and without retaining a share of the business." The chat gives way to puffing as they become breathless on a steep section, just before the top of Mount Fielden. On reaching the summit they both sit quietly on a rocky outcrop for a few minutes to get their breath back.

Bryan is the first to speak. "Phew, no wonder you come up here Leo, it's really a sight for sore eyes. You can see for miles and miles. Look there's a Shell tanker in the sound and I bet it's carrying 'my' petrol. You know son, I got to hand it to you. I never thought that being positive like that would do the trick. At first, I thought I didn't have a chance, but I wanted the garage some much. I know I haven't done the right thing by you or Gramps since Michael died, but I promise I will make it up to you from now on."

Emotionally, Leo feels choked up by this and stares at the ground, without saying a word. But Bryan continues, "There's something I want to tell you, but it's our secret, okay?" Leo tries to clear the lump in his throat, "cough, okay."

"Last night I had this dream. I saw Michael standing in a golden wheat field. He was smiling and holding a portrait of himself and a paintbrush in his left hand and in the other, a pink coloured pointy-looking thing. Leo interrupts, "you mean a pyramid don't you?" "Yes, one of those. It had three sides and they opened up like a flower. Then this white blob with colours around it shot up into the sky. Then Michael faded away."

"Dad I had something similar too. I'm not sure what the symbols mean, but I know it was Michael's way of showing us he loves us and he's happy, wherever he is."

"You know Leo, I told him not to take the tractor out that day, because the brakes needed fixing. But he didn't listen. And I know I'm just as guilty at not listening to you, either. I'm really sorry Leo for that and also for being sore at Gramps too. I wish I could've sorted things out with Gramps. But it's too late for that, now."

263

Leo stands up and gives Bryan a hug. "That's okay Dad, I knew you would come around, someday. You can still fix things with Gramps, just talk to him as if he was here. I still talk to him, when I'm feeling a bit down." They both sit down again. "Yes, it will be good running my own show. I've got lots of ideas to increase business and after a while, maybe Mum can come and look after the office. Well Leo, I think it's going to be a pretty damn good summer. What do you think?"

"You betcha Dad."

"Well Leo, I've got to get back to work. Coming with me?"

"Nah. I reckon I might stay a bit longer."

"Well don't be out here too long will you Leo, it's quite hot. "No worries Dad."

Leo sits in the shade for a while, waiting for his Dad to disappear. He dwells on the sudden and monumental changes in the last few days. Then he remembers the well and the missing rope ladder. He gets up and dusts off his shorts, deciding to take another look. As Leo trudges back along the quarry track he can hear voices. As he nears the old ruin he stops in his tracks.

There are workmen and mechanical equipment right next to the well. It has been cordoned off with yellow and black striped tape with the word 'Danger' repeated along the tape. Leo's mind is racing. Thinking, jeez they found the hole in the well. They must've been here yesterday and cleaned up. No wonder the rope's missing. I wonder who they are. I wonder if they've found the door and the Sentinel. Well, there's only one way to find out. I'll wander over casual like and ask them.

A group of four men dressed in yellow high-viz outfits are standing next to the well, chatting away. As Leo approaches, one man acknowledges Leo, "g'day young fellow, what can we do for you?" Leo stares at the men standing there. One man is wearing a construction helmet, with the word 'Foreman' written in large letters. Another is leaning on a shovel. Leo glances shyly at the Foreman, "I was just curious about what you guys were doing here. Nobody comes here much?"

"Do you live around here, son?" replies the workman with the shovel. Leo points towards the main road, "I live over that way." The Foreman shifts in his stance and replies, "Someone reported that the safety floor of the old well had been breached and was unsafe. So the Council wants the well filled in with rubble from the quarry." Leo is curious and asks, "What's at the bottom of the well?" "Not much. Just some kids have been playing down there, because we found their footprints and a water bottle. We also found an old rope ladder in the ruin they must've used. Don't suppose it was you, was it?"

Leo doesn't answer. His only thought, how am I going to talk to El-Caro now, if they fill in the well? Then the Foreman jumps into his white utility, which Leo notices has the crest of the Fielden Town Council. As the Foreman looks at his watch he remarks, "Jesus, look at the time. It has really flown by. Look chaps, you'll have to figure this out for yourself and finish the job on your own."

He starts up the white Pickup utility and revs it, accelerating away leaving a trail of dust behind him. Leo then realises he has his answer, thinking that storm last night. Old Mr Mason did see something after all, must've been the Sentinel. That old Hobo said something similar about doing stuff on my own and now this guy says the same thing. While Leo chats on with the workmen, the Pickup utility is now on the main quarry track. However, out of sight, the man stops. He takes off the helmet and removes the 'Foreman' sticker. He gets out and tosses the helmet into the back of the utility. He then screws up the sticker and drops it in the dirt. He squats down next to the utility and starts to peel off the crest on the door. He stands up and throws the crest into the bush, then jumps into the utility and drives off.

Meanwhile, Leo has started the walk home. He has mixed feelings about what has happened. Thinking, gee for while there, I thought they'd found the door down the well. It's funny though, I thought I'd be upset about it. But least I don't have to worry about someone else finding it, now. I still would've liked to have talked to El-Caro again. Even just to say goodbye to my galactic friend. I'll miss talking to him. He's so wise and taught me so much and there's heaps more I wanted to know. Because Leo's mind is so pre-occupied, he finds himself back on the track back to Mount Fielden, rather than on the track home.

He mutters, "OMG, I'm all over the place, there's me thinking I'm on my way home and I'm going the wrong way. Never mind. I'll keep going now. At least I can sit and think for a bit, up there." Upon reaching the top, Leo's puffing heavily. He finds a shady concrete bench under the shade sails and sits down. As he gets his breath back he ponders; boy, it's the first time I've had time to think it all through.

It's all happened so fast. I really can't believe this has all happened to 'Moi'. I can't believe how I got through all that stuff after Dani was kidnapped. I still don't understand what all that was about. I wish El-Caro had told me more about what was going on. It's amazing to think. If I'd never gone to the quarry that day maybe none of this would've happened. Maybe it was all just a coincidence. There again, I wonder if they were coincidences at all.

Maybe it was part of something I had to do. Maybe I'm just a pawn in someone else's game. Who knows - the whole thing's completely mad. Leo pauses for a few moments and looks up at the sky as something catches his eye. A giant Wedge-tail eagle is soaring overhead against the backdrop of a clear blue sky. It's riding the summer thermal currents in an effortless manner, circling around in a spiral motion and occasionally flapping its wings lazily.

For Leo, it's one of those special moments when he feels connected to everything. It's an image he will hold in his mind for the rest of his life. It reminds Leo of El-Caro and his messages about the true nature of being.

On returning home, Leo is still in a pensive mood. He goes straight to his room to lie down and flops down onto his bed. His thoughts return to Gramps and how he misses him. Leo gets up and removes the floor mat to reveal his secret hiding place. Leo feels he has fulfilled his promise to Gramps and wants to get out his medals again. As he removes the loose floorboard, he shouts, "how in the hell did that thing get here?" To his surprise, the game console he had returned to the Sentinel, is sitting on top of the box holding the war medals.

As he picks up the console a holographic image of L-CRO appears on the console screen. At the same time, Leo hears L-CRO's voice. "If you have discovered this console, my friend, you will know that it was time for the Sentinel to depart. We are all very proud of you. This is not a goodbye, as we shall meet again. I depart now and with my love leave you with this thought:

What is inspiration without purpose?

Without purpose there is nothingness.

From nothingness comes everything.

Everything has purpose.

How inspiring.

Author's Future Script

Of course, this is not the end of the story, for the summer has only just begun. Five years have passed since Leo Shepherd's 'dive' down the well. Since then Leo achievements have been many:

- He started up a support group at the high school for kids who have lost a family member or friend.
- Was a member of the High School debating team that won the Young Speakers Award at the National Talk-Fest.
- Campaigned successfully at Fielden High for a 20-minute period of sitting in silence, called 'Chilling-out'. Where students learn to clear their mind and be comfortable in a silent space. The Department of Education is currently evaluating this as part of a pilot program.
- Elected the School Captain at Fielden High.
- Elected Chairperson for the State Youth Congress on Youth Affairs.
- Became the Asia Pacific representative at the United Nations Youth Congress.
- Is currently studying Political Science at University.

For the others:

- Bryan and Linda successfully ran the Fielden Beach Shell Garage until Shell made them an offer too good to refuse. They're back farming again on an Angora goat stud near Glendale Valley.
- Dani is still friends with Leo and she still lives with her parents and is studying Graphic Design at University.
- Dani's parents Lena and Branco. Well what can I say; they haven't changed at all. It is good to see some things and some people stay the same.
- Kelvin Slater, alias Fridge left Fielden High and joined a Military College. All I can say is, God help the enemy.
- Ernie the bus driver, aka Old-grouch-face, has remarried. He's currently honeymooning in Florida and is on a visit to NASA.

- The evil Brothers of Anger and Fear lost this battle. However, for Leo the war is yet to be won. But you can help Leo defeat the evil ones, by defeating your own anger and conquering your own fears. He challenges you to see if you can sit in silence and hear what your inner-self tells you.
- L-CRO is still monitoring planet Earth. His purpose yet to be completed.

~The End~

Acknowledgements

Inserted image of a 1954 Cadillac Eldorado, Brougham is an untitled image from a David Temple article in Car Collector Magazine January 2007 edition. Other images are royalty free.
The song: Permission to Shine by Bachelor Girl – writer: Bridget Louise Benenate - lyrics ©Universal Music Publishing Group.
The song: Summer Nights is written by Jim Jacobs and Warren Casey from the musical Grease - lyrics ©MPL Communications.

Author's Biography

I was born and raised on the West Coast of Australia and for a long time have had an interest in all things metaphysical. I have studied sacred geometry and researched harmonics. I've always enjoyed writing and never found it a chore, except editing. As Mr. Miyagi from Karate Kid would say, "Wax on Wax off."
My writing ventures started off with magazine articles of an esoteric nature and are available online from my Website:

New Dawn Magazine
- Sacred Geometry & Secrets of the Great Pyramid.
- Secret Message of Barbury Castle Pi Crop Circle 2008.
- Cracking the Canberra Code – The secret symbolism of Australia's Capital.
- The Matrix Magicians – Who made Who & Who made You.

Uncensored Magazine News
- Blood & Gore of Climate Science.

Email: jameswardpublishing@hotmail.com

Website: https://jameswardpublishing.com

Notes